THE
DEAL

Book Three of the Jordan Saga

Books and Plays by Terence Kelly

THE
DEAL

Terence Kelly

This first world edition published in Great Britain 2000 by
SEVERN HOUSE PUBLISHERS LTD of
9–15 High Street, Sutton, Surrey SM1 1DF.
This first world edition published in the USA 2001 by
SEVERN HOUSE PUBLISHERS INC of
595 Madison Avenue, New York, N.Y. 10022.

British Library Cataloguing in Publication Data

Kelly, Terence, 1920-
   The deal. - (The Jordan saga ; bk. 3)
   1.   Fenwick, Alice (Fictitious character) - Fiction
   I.   Title
   823.9'14 [F]

   ISBN 0-7278-5627-8

Typeset by Palimpsest Book Production Ltd.,
Polmont, Stirlingshire, Scotland.
Printed and bound in Great Britain by
MPG Books Ltd., Bodmin, Cornwall.

One

1929

1

The chauffeur-driven Rolls Royce drew up in Berkeley Square and Solly Kornblath got out and entered his offices through the plate-glass door which Moss, who was in morning dress, held open.

Moss said: "Good morning, Mr Kornblath."

"Morning, Moss." Kornblath paused. "A Mrs Fenwick will be calling. Send her straight up to the flat, will you."

"Yes, Mr Kornblath." Moss's face was without expression.

Kornblath made his way across the foyer into the lift held open for him, up several floors and along the carpeted corridor to the boardroom. Coote, Grey, Hamilton and, less quickly, Cradforth, began to rise but Kornblath waved them down as he sat at the head of the long mahogany table.

"Only one item this morning, sir," said Coote, long, thin and nervous, peering myopically at the agenda. "Burlington House."

"Where's our architect?"

"He's a little delayed," Coote apologised.

"Then we'll wait." He looked at Hamilton, who had hard, pale eyes. "Talking of architects, who d'you think we should have for Plaxton, Hamilton?"

"I thought . . . Chattock and Finn?"

"Grey?"

Grey was one of the new young men. "Leon and de Soutar."

Hamilton pounced gratefully. "After what they did at Walsall!"

1

"Walsall was a tricky situation . . ."

Kornblath waved for silence. "Cradforth?"

Hamilton's eyes were hard but Cradforth was hard all through. "No opinion," he said crisply.

"Why Chattock and Finn?" Kornblath asked of Hamilton.

"I can get them at four per cent."

"You sound," said Cradforth, "as if you were buying apples."

"Could you," enquired Kornblath amiably, "have got Rackham for us on Burlington House at four per cent?"

"I wasn't with you when he was taken on."

Kornblath smiled. His face was round, full, benevolent, and he had nice brown eyes. "Tell you what," he said, "we'll settle on Rackham for Plaxton too and you see what you can get him for." For a moment there was no benevolence. "But see you get him."

Rackham came in just then and Kornblath made the introductions: "Hamilton has taken over as chief surveyor and Grey assists him."

For an hour they discussed the details of the scheme. Then Kornblath said: "Fine. Once we've bought up all the leases, we're in business. How many outstanding, Coote?"

"Three, sir. Sweet and Matheson; Smith, Lane and Melvin; and a man named Desmond Llewellyn . . ."

Meanwhile Alice had arrived and was shown up to Kornblath's flat by the chairman's private lift which opened directly into a small hall. "Mr Kornblath asked me to tell you to make yourself at home," Moss told her, going ahead to hold open for her the door into a sitting-room far larger than Alice had ever imagined a sitting-room could be outside of such places as Crogellan House in Ireland where Sam Jordan, her first husband, had been reared. "He's at a board meeting but shouldn't be long. Would you care for some coffee?"

"No, thank you," Alice said – and at once regretted doing so. Drinking a cup of coffee would have given her an occupation while she waited.

Moss bowed and withdrew.

Alice looked about her. She had hardly known what to

expect. Beatrice Culverwell, who had arranged the meeting, had been reticent on the telephone. "I had hoped to make it easier for you, my dear, by having you meet him over a little dinner but that's not how he wants it. I'm afraid you're going to have to sell your idea without any help from Graeme or me."

"But he *is* interested?"

"Sure. He wouldn't be seeing you otherwise. He's a very busy man."

"In the gown business?"

There had been a chuckle. "Heavens no. He's in property."

Where on earth was the connection between property and women's clothes? She had begun to pose the question, but Beatrice had interrupted: "It'll only confuse you if I start to explain, Mrs Fenwick, and I doubt if I could properly anyway. So I tell you what you do. Telephone Mr Kornblath's office – it's the Mayfair number I gave you – and ask to speak to his secretary. She's expecting to hear from you and she'll offer you a time which you accept whatever else you have to change to be able to do so. OK? Good. Now about what you wear. I haven't told him about your husband having only recently drowned himself and he probably won't have picked it up but he might have, and as it isn't exactly helpful and Fenwick's not *all* that common a name, it would probably be best if you don't turn up in black. Something smart, attractive and up to date and not too dolly or glamorous. Don't be frightened of him. He's disgracefully rich and everyone inside his organisation walks in fear and trembling of him, but in fact he's quite a sweetie and you'll find he'll be very nice to you and he'll make his mind up, yes or no. Remember that. You've got to sell it to him while you're there. If he says no, don't waste your time trying to change his mind – you won't. OK? And there's something else. If you can see you've got him interested, don't hold back. If you can get him hooked, the sky's the limit. Like he'll back me in a major West End production but if I went to him for a hundred or two to try and take something round the sticks he wouldn't put up a dime. Right? So do what I say, Alice. Go and sell yourself and do it big. Don't hold back. Now, I tell you what you do afterwards. You come along to my office, you've got the address, and tell me how it went and we'll have a little lunch . . ."

There was more to it than that, Alice realised, but why Beatrice Culverwell – who was the only American woman she had ever met, and whom she had remembered thinking very soignée and sophisticated – should be going to all this trouble and be sufficiently interested in the result of the meeting she'd set up, quite baffled her. She had taken Beatrice's advice except in one particular; she had dressed with thought and care, investing far more than the meagre funds left to her really allowed, and choosing a classic tailor-made suit slightly longer than calf length with which she wore a chic little hat, a white silk blouse, her pearls and spotless white gloves. But, against Beatrice's advice, she had chosen black for suit and hat. For smartly dressed career women black was *the* colour coming in.

Coote was coming to an end: ". . . and then when Mr Melvin—"
"Never mind. What does this Desmond Llewellyn do?"
"Insurance agent, Mr Kornblath. Just two rooms."
Kornblath nodded. "Right. Until we get those three leases we might as well not have the other thirty-four. I want them all tied up before the week's out. Who's handling Sweet and Matheson?"
Grey explained that Sweet, an engineer, didn't want the bother of upheaval.
"Mr Rackham," Kornblath said, "have you ever worked with Sweet?"
Rackham smiled the attractive smile which crinkled up his eyes. "I thought you'd more or less appointed Gunter."
"Gunter can be disappointed." Kornblath picked up the telephone and asked for Sweet. "What do Smith, Lane and Melvin do?"
"Accountants, sir," said Coote.
"Which means they know we want to get on with demolishing and they've done their arthmetic." Sweet came on the line. "Ah," said Kornblath. "About your lease, Mr Sweet."

He listened good humouredly. "Yes, quite, Mr Sweet. But if we can't buy your lease, we can't start demolishing and I'm sure, as an engineer, you wouldn't want to see such a prestigious scheme abandoned. And of course there are other forms of compensation. For example we are uncommitted to an engineer and if you agreed to sell us your lease . . ."

When he was done, Grey, who had been listening spellbound, said: "Are you going to speak to Smith, Lane and Melvin too, sir?"

"No," said Kornblath. "They're accountants, so all they think about is money which makes it just a matter of negotiation. Mr Cradforth will deal with them. So . . . we're left with Mr Llewellyn and his two rooms. What's the problem?"

"He won't answer letters," said Hamilton, sulking.

"One of yours is he? How many letters has he had?"

"Three. I didn't want to seem too keen. He's in a very small way of business. Doesn't even have a secretary. Anyway, he was the least important of the thirty-seven."

"He's the most important now. What do you think, Rackham?"

"That he sounds suspiciously like a nagging tooth."

"Doesn't he? How much did you offer him, Hamilton?"

"A hundred at first. It's two hundred now."

"Spoken to him?"

"Twice."

"And?"

"He was . . . evasive."

"Yes," said Kornblath. "He would be. The man's obviously heard all about the Solomon Kornblath Investment Trust and knows it's not going to hold up a scheme costing half a million for a few hundred pounds. You'd better get on to him again and fix some sort of deal. And, Hamilton – don't let your enthusiasm for buying apples leave you empty-handed."

2

"I'm so sorry to have kept you waiting, Mrs Fenwick," Kornblath apologised. His voice was soft and gentle, a

5

peaceful voice which went well with his brown spaniel eyes.

Manufacturing a small start of surprise, Alice looked up from the magazine she had hastily picked up and had apparently been engrossed in, as if she had been caught out by her host's arrival. In fact, had it not been that she had heard the lift ascending she might well have been, for Kornblath moved very quietly in the way that some ultra-successful men of considerable girth and weight are somehow able to.

"Not at all, Mr Kornblath," Alice said, resisting a compulsion to get to her feet. "I've been very comfortable."

"Good."

He was standing with his back to the sitting-room door, which he had closed noiselessly, and was frankly weighing her up. For her part, he was totally surprising. She had expected a hatchet-faced man with thin lips and steely eyes – instead, here was a man who reminded her very strongly of a baby; he looked so chubby, so relaxed, so clean, so powdered.

She saw him give a little nod as if she had passed some initial test. He came across to her. "No, please . . ." as in spite of everything she half made to rise. He stood over her. He wore hand-made shoes, and was dressed in a blue suit which looked so superb on him, considering his ample girth, that it had to have been made in Savile Row; his shirt was of South Sea Island cotton and looked as if it was being worn for the first time and his tie, of a quiet pattern, was silk. Apart from his wrist-watch his only jewellery consisted of gold and diamond cufflinks which matched a heavy gold ring he wore on the third finger of his left hand, in which was set a square-cut stone.

"Would you care to join me in a glass of champagne, Mrs Fenwick?" he suggested. "It is rather a weakness of mine to have one at this time of the morning."

"That would be lovely."

"Splendid."

He disappeared into what Alice knew to be a well-equipped kitchen, for while she was waiting, too nervous to sit picking at magazines for long, she had thoroughly cased the flat and found it also contained a luxurious and anything but masculine bedroom with a double bed and a bathroom off it. Opulence was everywhere: in the thick fitted carpets, in the damask-covered settees and chairs, in the drapes, in the prints and paintings, the glassware, china, cutlery; in the order, the spotless cleanliness, the very silence. Here, she realised, was wealth beyond anything that even the richest man she had ever known – her first husband's schoolfriend, Joseph Mott – could have imagined.

Kornblath came back in, pushing an ice bucket on a chromium-plated framework with tiny wheels, out of which projected the end of a bottle of champagne. Alice had never seen such a contraption nor been aware that they existed. Over his arm hung a napkin as if he were a waiter – it was all very remarkable, even confusing. It could not have occurred to Alice that producing iced champagne like a rabbit out of a hat and serving it himself was, Kornblath had long since discovered, a wonderful ice-breaker with pretty strangers.

"There!" he said, and, having removed the cork proficiently into the body of the napkin and poured two glasses, he handed one to Alice who, somewhat bemused by this performance from a man to whom she had come to plead a cause but who was treating her as a most valued guest, smiled brightly, determined to convey the impression of being entirely at ease and not at all unused to such attention.

Kornblath raised his glass: "I hope, Mrs Fenwick, the proposition you have come to put to me will lead us to many occasions when we shall be drinking each other's health."

And with this, having sipped a little of his champagne, he seated himself in the adjacent corner of a second settee set at right angles to hers, putting down his glass on its side table.

"Now, first," he said, "I want you to tell me everything about yourself."

"Everything?"

"Everything."

"Well . . ." Alice began uncertainly. "I'm a widow with two children. At the moment—"

Kornblath stopped her, raising a plump hand on which the diamond twinkled. "Mrs Fenwick," he reproved her, "that isn't

7

telling me everything, that is just telling me what's happened towards the end. Come now, don't be shy."

His tone was quiet and encouraging without being dictatorial but there was within it the compulsion of a man used to having his way and expecting to do so now. Well, thought Alice, if I'm going to get anywhere with him he's going to find out anyway. And, except maybe for trying to get me into that double bed he's got in there, he's not the sort of man who's going to stay interested for long in a woman's who's inarticulate.

"My father was a railway ticket collector in Liverpool and I left school at thirteen and my mother sent me out to work scrubbing other people's doorsteps," she said, almost belligerently. "Then I worked as a shop assistant in a draper's in Warrington. I've been married twice. My first husband was an Irishman by whom I had two children, both boys and now aged nine and eleven. We were short of money and, after I'd worked as a window dresser for Pontings and as dress designer to a man named Culverwell, I set myself up in business on my own, calling myself Paquette, largely on money I borrowed from Mr Culverwell, which I repaid him in full when the business succeeded. I very foolishly gave up Paquette to marry my second husband" – she took a mental breath – "who drowned himself a few weeks ago. You may have read about it in the newspapers. He did it in the Thames near Maidenhead and made sure he wouldn't be able to change his mind by first filling the plus-fours he must have put on specially with snooker balls. I think that brings you up to date."

She said this all at great speed and without once letting her eyes drop from Kornblath's and succeeded in rendering him momentarily without words, which was something few people were able to achieve.

"Is there anything else about my background you want to know?" she went on with the faintest touch of irony, possessed, she knew not why, of a sudden surge of self-confidence.

He chuckled. "No, Mrs Fenwick. I think you have given me your background remarkably succinctly." He made a movement of his hand towards her glass. "Don't you like champagne?"

8

"To be quite frank, Mr Kornblath, not particularly."

"What a pity. It happens to be rather good champagne."

He said this sadly but, realising she had taken him aback sufficiently for him to need a few moments to reassess the interview, Alice wasn't taken in. "You probably read about my husband drowning himself," she said. "It was in all the newspapers."

He nodded. "Yes, I imagine it would have been. But in fact I didn't know."

"And Beatrice Culverwell" – how she had had the gall to refer to her sponsor in such a familiar way was something else Alice quite failed to fathom – "didn't tell you about it?"

"No, of course she didn't. That would have been like delivering a curtain line halfway through a scene. All she told me was that something rather important so far as you were concerned had cropped up, which meant that it would be a week or two before you would be able to find the time to see me. I was naturally . . . intrigued." He removed the smile from his eyes. "May I offer you my sympathies, Mrs Fenwick. It will have been a most distressing experience and the past few weeks must have been very hard to bear. And you have two boys, you say?"

"Yes."

"How terrible for them."

"Yes. It has been. Since my husband's firm was taken over they've been at local day schools and you can imagine what papers the parents of the other boys take, and what a meal they made of it."

"I can indeed."

She was aware that his attitude towards her was quite changed and she sensed danger. She had come here seeking not sympathy but backing for her project.

"Mr Kornblath?" she said.

"Yes?" Her tone had surprised him.

"You're a busy man. And so far as I've been able to find out you've never had anything to do with women's clothes. I'm quite baffled why you've found the time to see me."

"Beatrice didn't explain?"

Alice knitted her brows. "No?"

He nodded understandingly. "No, of course she wouldn't. It's more theatre, you know." And, deciding against explaining what he meant by that: "Your father was a railway ticket collector; mine was an outdoor worker."

"An outdoor worker?"

"A finisher, I think you'd call him these days, wouldn't you?"

"You mean . . . in dressmaking?"

"Yes. He sewed on buttons and did things like that."

Alice couldn't believe it. That any man from such a background could have acquired such power and wealth so swiftly. He couldn't be fifty yet.

"You were brought up in Liverpool," Kornblath was going on, "I was brought up in the East End." And, with an engaging chuckle, "I think you had a better start than I did."

He drank a little champagne, then pushed the glass aside as if he didn't really like champagne either. She could imagine him pouring what was left of the bottle down the sink after she'd left. It was all strangely reminiscent of that last meeting with Joseph Mott, her first husband's business partner, when she'd called on him to try to persuade him to help her start up the new business she had in mind and he'd taken her to the Crébillion and ordered pink champagne, which until then she hadn't known existed, and before they'd half drunk the bottle she'd decided against having lunch with him and had the head waiter call a taxi.

"Well," he said, "now we've got that out of the way and know a little about each other, shall we get down to cases? Tell me what you've got in mind."

"It's very simple," Alice said. "We're in a slump that's going to last a long time yet women will still go on buying clothes. But they're going to be much more cost conscious than they've been up to now. They're going to jib at paying the prices they used to have to pay for the sort of dresses I made in Paquette knowing that's not the end of it. That once they've paid for one, they're going to have to pay some more to have it altered." She explained about sizing. "So," she went on, "there has to be tremendous scope for a firm that makes dresses in a sufficient number of sizes to save them that extra cost."

"Well it seems very logical, Mrs Fenwick," he said. "But surely it's been thought about before."

"You'd think so, wouldn't you? But it hasn't. We've worked on the basis of two or three sizes and adding or taking off an inch or two all round to a pattern we've got when someone came along and asked us to make a dress for them. And of course the result nine times out of ten was unsatisfactory because we all come in different shapes and sizes. That's the reason why ready-made dresses have never really worked for fashion-conscious women without the money to afford to go to a couturier."

"Well it's extraordinary." He didn't sound as if he disbelieved her for a moment.

"It is, isn't it, Mr Kornblath?"

"And this idea . . . of having a multiple of sizes . . . that's entirely *your* idea?"

Alice shook her head. "I thought it was when it first occurred to me. Since then I've had time to do some research and I find that in America they've already started doing it. But" – eagerly – "they haven't over here, Mr Kornblath, and the possibilities are tremendous. They really are."

"Uhm," Solly Kornblath said, looking away from her and across the room at one of the three tall windows which overlooked Berkeley Square. Alice's heart began to pound. In only moments, she realised, he would tell her his decision, and if it was negative that would be the end of it. She had no one else to go to. There would be no hope of Dessy and Thady having the kind of education which both their father and stepfather had enjoyed and encouraged her to expect for them. They would live through till adulthood sharing a double bed in a mice-ridden, semi-basement flat whose kitchen was a converted coal cellar. She would get some sort of job – she still believed enough in herself – but it would be no better than that. There was too much piled up against her.

Kornblath looked back to her. "How would you set this up, Mrs Fenwick?"

She exulted. The self-confidence which for the moment had ebbed was back. She remembered Beatrice Culverwell's advice and spread her plans wider than anything she had imagined before.

"Well the first thing I would want to do, Mr Kornblath," she said, almost disbelieving herself, "is to find an American manager or a . . . oh, I don't know what I'd call him – someone experienced in sizing – and offer him enough to have him come over here and work for us on some sort of contract that wouldn't allow him to set up on his own over here."

"And then?"

"I'd take on all of the girls who used to work for me in Paquette because they know the way I think. I had a wonderful forewoman who knows how to handle girls. She'd come back to me like a shot whatever she's doing now. I'd have to find premises of course, and they'd have to be far larger premises than I had before because this isn't going to be custom making. It's got to be bulk. It's got to be advertised in all the fashion magazines. Did Beatrice tell you the name I've got in mind for the business?"

"No."

"Holly Wood Gowns!" she said, changing by instinct "Dresses" to "Gowns".

He smiled. "And how much do you think you'd need, to establish your Hollywood Gowns?"

"I haven't the faintest idea. A lot of money."

"Say five thousand pounds?"

Alice could have choked. Five thousand pounds! It would have taken fifty years of not spending a penny of Tom's pension to realise five thousand pounds. There wasn't that much money in the world.

"I don't know," she answered, amazed at her own self-control. "It simply depends on how big one wants Holly Wood to get."

"Come and look at this," Kornblath said.

He stood and, taking her hand, led her across the room to a table in a corner of the huge sitting-room on which was displayed a superb, professionally produced model of a development consisting of several eight or ten-storey blocks on some site opposite a river, which in her brief initial survey of the room she had, correctly, taken to be the Thames.

She had been vaguely impressed by the model but, what it represented being totally outside her ken, she had given little thought to it and indeed gave little to it now, being more aware of the touch of his soft body against her side and the scent of his toilet water. What comes now, she asked herself, seeing in her mind's eye the bedroom, which she knew instinctively had been designed for a use that was only transient. Its carpet was soft and deep, the curtains rich and thick, there was a dressing-table and a stool and a velvet sofa and the lights were gentle; but there had been no clue to a woman using it, only a silk dressing-gown thrown casually on the bed and masculine toilet things in the bathroom. If Kornblath had a wife, one thing was certain, she didn't use the flat; and if others did, he obviously took scrupulous precautions to make sure that when they went they left no evidence.

And why show her this model? Was it to overwhelm her with his power and wealth? To indicate the possibilities if she proved amenable to him? And suppose he did proposition her, what was she to answer? If she refused him, then that, presumably, would be the end of it – there wouldn't be any five thousand pounds to establish Holly Wood Gowns. There wouldn't be a future for Dessy and Thady. There'd only be years more of pinching and scraping until they were old enough to go out, half-educated, into a world which held no one who would help them.

Should I agree if I'm asked to, to prostitute myself, if only for them? But if I do, what guarantee do I have that things will turn out any better? I'm still attractive, I know that from the way men look at me; I know it from the way he looked at me when he came in – but I'm thirty-one. Interesting enough perhaps for a turn or two on that bed in there. But it wouldn't last. Not with a man as rich as he is, who can buy all the sex he wants from younger women. So, if what this is all about is sex, then as far as I'm concerned it has to be a heads I don't win and tails I lose situation, so the answer must be no.

She thought of gently but firmly removing his hand, but dismissed the idea – to do so would be to admit the thoughts passing through her mind. And that would be the end of it – she would be either angering a man whose pride wouldn't allow him to accept rebuffs or making a fool of herself by volunteering an unjustified accusation.

She forced herself to concentrate on the model. She could not but be awed by the scale of it and stood looking mutely at the slender tower of some anonymous building, the solid blocks, the open areas, the artificial trees, the shining ellipse of mica indicating water, the curved terrace dotted with minuscule tables and umbrellas, and, outside the bounds of the development, imitation buses, lorries, cars, people. Unimportant people dwarfed to insignificance by this monument to power and money.

"What is it exactly, Mr Kornblath?" she said, feigning total absorption in it.

"A dream."

She couldn't believe that. "Only a dream?"

"We all have to have our dreams, Mrs Fenwick."

"But to go to all this trouble and expense . . ."

"Oh, I shall build it," he said matter of factly. "Before very long, I shall build it."

"What will it be?"

"The largest block of flats in England – if not in Europe."

Of a sudden she understood his motive in showing the model to her. She was to realise that there were to be no limits to the size of the enterprise he had in effect already agreed to back.

She looked up at him, looked into his spaniel eyes, smelt his cleanliness, was very conscious of his flesh.

"I can't compete with this, you know," she said.

"Why not?"

"In comparison to this, anything I've done is tiny."

"In comparison with this, the first thing I did was microscopic."

"What was it? The first thing you did?"

"I bought a dilapidated terrace house in Whitechapel, did it

14

up and sold it at a profit." He released her to free his hand to make a gesture. "There's no real difference you know, Mrs Fenwick, between doing up a dilapidated terrace house in the East End and selling it on to make a profit and buying a piece of land overlooking the Thames and covering it with blocks of flats."

"But the sheer scale of this!"

He shrugged. "The principle is the same. You borrow the money you need and you employ specialists to see the thing through. In this case lawyers, architects and estate agents."

"And builders."

Again he shrugged. "They're unimportant. Just tools. As are the women you'll employ to run up your dresses."

"You make it sound very simple."

"It is very simple. Fortunately most people think it's complicated."

He was right, of course. You could have a workroom in Little Titchfield Street with half a dozen machinists working at treadle sewing machines or, providing you could raise the money, a mechanised factory employing hundreds. But the basic ingredients for success were unchanged – making the right products at the right price.

"I would have thought," she said, nodding towards the model, "to do something like this you needed something you haven't mentioned. Courage."

"Perhaps," he agreed. "But then you have courage, Mrs Fenwick, don't you?"

"You would want it run as a company wouldn't you?"

"Of course."

"I know nothing about companies."

"My lawyers and my accountants will advise you."

"Not you?"

He shook his head. "I shall rely on them as well."

"But you will take some part? Surely? If you are going to invest five thousand pounds."

"I hope I shall be investing more than five thousand pounds. But apart from following your progress with great interest and considering the memoranda our accountants send me, the only part I shall take in . . ." he paused, "Hollywood Gowns, is satisfying myself that it is being efficiently run."

This was genuine and in line with his approach to his own business. Apart from the time he spent arranging the finance for his developments, the memoranda he received on them were the important things with which he concerned himself. They were sent and received every day. They related to the schemes which were in their infancy, the building projects already going up, the buildings finished but not yet let. More than anything his motive was to prevent delay, to see that no one connected with him should fall asleep. He would not accept a single equivocal answer, the sender would receive by telephone or return of post a request to which the only reply could be in specific terms. Prevention of delay was something which he would not delegate entirely; he followed the progress of every job with care, read the minutes of every site meeting, and if the job was running late, cold-bloodedly demanded why, refusing to be fobbed off with generalities. Delay was money and, more than that, delay prevented the turn round of money to extend his operations. It was always a mystery to him why other successful men in the same field of business should bother with what seemed to him irrelevancies if they could not spare the time for this vital facet of their occupation.

And so far as this new venture to which he had decided to commit himself was concerned, he intended to watch its progress in the same sort of way.

"Let us leave this," he said, "and go back to our champagne." And when they were seated: "I think, Mrs Fenwick, you should understand why I am prepared to invest in your new business. There are several reasons. The first, and the most important, is a sentimental one. It was the business in which my father earned the money he needed to support his family when he came to England as a refugee. The second reason is that it will be something new to think about, an interest, if you like."

"Having looked at that model," Alice, now feeling very much at ease, remarked, "I'm surprised you have time for any new interests."

"I have plenty of time," Solly Kornblath said. "My property

16

developments only occupy a small portion of my days and with the slump we're now in, are likely for a while to occupy even less. The third reason is a simple one: I enjoy a gamble. I back horses, I back plays and now and again I back new businesses when they appeal to me and I have confidence in the people who are going to run them. And I have confidence in you, Mrs Fenwick." He picked up his glass: "Is it agreed then? We shall form a little company which we will call Hollywood Gowns, of which I shall be majority shareholder and you will run?"

Alice nodded. A flood of emotion had swamped her. It was going to be all right. She'd be able to take Dessy and Thady out of that ghastly flat with all its awful memories. Perhaps instead of council schools, send them to the kind of school their father had been educated at after all. Surely it wasn't too late? She'd be able to open up the world for them; and put behind herself the tragedies of a broken marriage and a suicide. She looked at him through a sudden mist of tears and hardly trusted herself to speak for fear of breaking down.

"Yes," she managed. "Yes, Mr Kornblath. Yes."

He chuckled. "Then," he said, "I think we might have a little celebration lunch over which we can get to know each other better."

"Oh," Alice said. "I'm afraid I can't manage that!"

"Why not?"

"I promised Mrs Culverwell" – she had forgotten the relative intimacy she had intimated – "I'd have lunch with her."

"That's easily remedied." He took the telephone receiver off its hook. "Get me Mrs Culverwell, will you?" He put the receiver down. "There's a man I want you to meet who I've already arranged to have lunch with. His name's Rackham. Martin Rackham. He's the architect for that." He nodded towards the model. "A remarkable man. Unless I miss my guess, he's going to be one of the few architects who become a legend in their own lifetime."

The telephone rang. "Oh, Beatrice. I thought you'd like to know, I've just agreed with Alice Fenwick to form a company with her . . . Yes . . . And look, I know she's promised to have lunch with you, but if it isn't too inconvenient do you mind changing that to having lunch with me? . . . Well, where have you booked? The Crébillion, I suppose . . . Well, why not? Oh, and we'll be four by the way."

This is absurd, thought Alice: first the champagne; now the Crébillion! And she wondered how Joseph would have reacted if he'd known.

In the boardroom one floor below, the meeting was coming to an end.

"Perhaps you'd care to come to my office, Mr Rackham," Hamilton said. "We have a new scheme we have yet to appoint an architect for."

Rackham looked into the pale, hard eyes. He felt sorry for Hamilton – there was no joy in the man. And he was his own worst enemy: always trying to make himself out as greater and more important than he was.

"I'm afraid it'll have to be another time, Mr Hamilton," he said. "I have a lunch appointment." He neglected to tell him it was with his employer. There was no point in rubbing salt into self-inflicted wounds.

"It's a very important scheme. And the way things are there aren't going to be too many in the future."

Rackham sighed. "How right you are."

"Of course, if you aren't interested . . ."

Cradforth smiled thinly at the hope in Hamilton's tone. And he lacked Rackham's scruples.

"I'm quite sure Mr Rackham will be interested in Plaxton, Hamilton," he said. "But there isn't any hurry is there?"

"I'll come round any time that's convenient, Mr Hamilton," Rackham said, taking pity on the man. "Why not give my secretary a ring and fix a time that works for you." He smiled at the four of them. "Good day, gentlemen."

When he had gone, young Grey, who had been eagerly waiting his opportunity to make the point, said: "Must be marvellous to be able to handle people the way Solly handled Sweet."

Hamilton said sourly: "Anyone can if they happen to be worth what he's worth."

"Precisely," Cradforth said. And, pausing at the door, "How much are you going to offer Llewellyn?"

"I haven't decided. A thousand perhaps."

"Bet you won't get him for under five. Nor any change from Rackham." He closed the door behind him.

"Bloody time server," Hamilton said.

"Aren't we all?" said Coote.

About to leave the building, Rackham was stopped by Moss. "Oh, Mr Rackham," he said, deferentially.

"Yes, Moss?"

"I've just had a message from Mr Kornblath. He says he hopes you don't mind but he'd like to change the lunch from the Dorchester to the Crébillion. There's a lady he'd like you to meet. And could you make it one-fifteen, instead of one?"

"Yes, of course."

"You know the Crébillion, sir? Where it is?"

"Oh, yes."

"Good morning, Mr Rackham."

"Good morning, Moss."

Rackham strode out into Berkeley Square, grey on a raw November day, intrigued – it was rare that Solly Kornblath wanted others to meet his women.

Two

1

N ot by so much as a flicker of an eyelid did Ivor Conti (whose given name was John Greene) betray that he recognised Alice as a lady who had arrived comparatively recently with one of his regular customers, Joseph Mott, and having demanded a taxi be summoned, had walked out on him before their carefully ordered lunch could be served. He made a small obsequious bow. "Good morning, Mr Kornblath. This is a very pleasant surprise."

"Morning, Ivor," Solly said. "Is Mrs Culverwell here?"

"Yes, Mr Kornblath. She asked if you would mind going straight in. She's auditioning this afternoon."

"Right." He paused. "Do you happen to know Mr Martin Rackham?"

"Yes, Mr Kornblath. He dines with us now and then."

"He'll be joining us."

"Yes, Mr Kornblath." He made another little bow and led the way through the panelled ante-room into the restaurant. Outside might be raw with a smell of fog in the air; within, the seasons were banished. The dining-room was windowless and vaguely Moroccan in style, intimate, sensuous, theatrical. The walls were hung with carpets, the tablecloths had embroidered edges, and small shaded lights threw a glow which some of the less young clientele appreciated.

Beatrice was at a table against the wall opposite their entrance. A white-haired man with curious frog-like eyes, his mouth opened in a fixed smile which lifted its corners high and showed rows of teeth far too perfect for his age, was standing by her table, listening to her intently, nodding his head in agreement to something she was saying. Alice, being guided in by Solly Kornblath's soft, plump fingers on her elbow, found his face familiar.

A sudden quick movement of the cigarette holder she was holding high and away from her showed that Beatrice had seen them. She said something to her companion whose disappointment was evident from the sudden death of the eagerness in his eyes. But the smile was back again almost as quickly as it had gone.

"Yes, of course, darling, I quite understand," Alice heard him say. And quickly: "I could have Richard send you the script . . ."

"Why not?" said Beatrice with a brilliant smile.

"Yes, I'll do that." He paused as if hoping to be introduced but when Beatrice made no move to do so, gave them the benefit of his own smile and was gone to rejoin a couple at another table.

"Alice," said Beatrice, making no attempt to rise, "come and sit next to me and tell me all about it. And Solly, you sit there." She patted his place at the table with a kid-gloved hand. She wore an open long-sleeved cream silk jacket with side pockets over a black velvet crossover waistcoat, and in its buttonhole an enormous silk cabbage rose. On her head there was a veritable helmet of matching velvet which quite covered her ears and was extended down almost to her shoulders. It all looked tremendously theatrical and made Alice feel dull in her tailored suit.

"Recognise him, Solly?" Beatrice said, as he sat down. "The man I was talking to?"

"No."

"Well you ought to." She said it quite severely. It was important for Alice that the atmosphere be relaxed and Solly Kornblath's personality shouldn't be swamping. "How about you, Alice?"

Alice nodded gratefully – and was grateful too that at that moment inspiration came. "Yes. Basil Rowe. He was in *The Quiet Stream* wasn't he?"

"That and a lot of other things. It's rather sad. He used to be a good stand-by but he's got the old actor's disease. Can't remember his lines."

"What did he want?" Solly asked.

"Oh, he's got some play he thinks he'd be rather good in that he was trying to sell me. Poor devil." She said it with feeling, then cheered up. "Cocktail, Alice?" And with enthusiasm: "Champagne cocktail! To celebrate." And before Alice could refuse, to the waiter hovering near: "Three champagne cocktails, Eric."

"Four," said Solly.

"Four?"

"I've asked Martin Rackham to join us. He shouldn't be long."

"Martin Rackham? Should I know him?"

"You will before he's done. He's a very talented architect." And, forgetting he'd already made the prophecy to Alice: "Going to be a legend in his own lifetime, which is more than you can say for most of the men who make far too handsome a living masquerading as architects."

"Solly," she reproved him. "This is Alice's day!"

He chuckled. "That's why I've asked Rackham to join us."

"*Touché*," Beatrice said – as if she got the point but didn't mean it. "And we don't have all that much time. I'm auditioning at two thirty."

"So Ivor tells me."

Alice, feeling she had nothing to contribute to the conversation, was embarrassed. It might be her day but the subject of Holly Wood Gowns hardly made for relaxed lunchtime conversation.

"Are you putting a new play on, Mrs Culverwell?" she asked.

"Now look!" said Beatrice. "It is not Mrs Culverwell, Alice – it is Bee or Beatrice as you prefer. And we are not here to talk about theatre or about building blocks of flats. Now let's get the business of ordering lunch over and done with – Mr Rackham when he comes will have to catch up with us – and then I want you to tell me exactly what you've agreed between the two of you and when this new exciting business is going to be got off the ground. Thank you, Ivor!"

The menus were handed out but before they could be opened, Beatrice said: "Ivor, we have a problem. We have another gentleman joining us and once he comes we won't have much time. Do you have any special recommendations that will fill the bill? Something we can order now . . . Any idea when he'll be here, Solly?"

"Quarter past one."

"Will he be prompt?"

"Oh, yes."

"You hear that, Ivor?" And to Solly: "Any idea what sort of thing he likes? That you like too?"

"Steak," said Solly.

"Steak!" said Beatrice with disgust. "You sound like an American!" And, with a shrug, "All right then. If it's all right with *you*, Alice. Good. Passed to you, Ivor." She waited expectantly.

Ivor Conti didn't let her down. *"Entrecôte Mirabeau,"* he decided.

"Explain."

"But of course. It is quite a simple dish. The steak is grilled and decorated with tarragon leaves and anchovy fillets, garnished with blanched olives and served with anchovy butter. And, may I suggest, with it a plain green salad. And for wine, at lunchtime, something not too heavy. A chianti perhaps? A *Montagliari* . . . No!" he corrected himself. "It needs an hour's decanting. A *Castello di Ama!"* It was as if he had found something valuable but long since mislaid.

"Excellent," Solly said.

"And to start with?" Ivor enquired.

"Nothing to start with," Beatrice said firmly.

Ivor bowed and withdrew. Which one of them, Alice wondered, is going to pay the bill? It obviously didn't matter. They wouldn't even know how much it was going to be. And yesterday, she'd been hesitating in the grocer's over whether to buy broken biscuits because they were cheaper!

"Now we've got that out of the way," Beatrice said with satisfaction, "tell me your plans."

As there didn't really seem much to tell, Alice decided that she might as well say so: "Well it's really as I outlined it to you, Beatrice," she said. "It's going to be called Holly Wood Gowns and what I'm . . . what we're going to do is concentrate on sizing." It was extraordinary how the moment she started to be involved in something she understood, her confidence soared. "And on simple, cheaply made dresses without too many frills. This slump we're in is going to last a long time and it's going to change all the attitudes that women have had through the twenties."

"The party's over?" Beatrice suggested.

"Well it is, isn't it? It's all been boyish. But that's finished. Eton crops, waists down to here . . ." She moved her hands. "Women are going to dress in a far more feminine way from now on. And that's going to help because it goes with simplicity."

"What sort of materials will you use?"

"Oh, cotton mainly. American cotton."

"How will you sell them?"

"Well," Alice said, "there are two ways, aren't there, Beatrice? We could market them ourselves, either through advertising them and sending them to customers through the post or perhaps have shops of our own. Or we could sell them to the big department stores."

"Which would you prefer?"

"Well there's advantages and disadvantages either way. On the one hand I already have connections with major stores like Bourne and Hollingsworth and Debenham and Freebody . . ."

She broke off. There was a man by their table. He was standing, waiting to choose his moment, totally at ease; a man of average height casually dressed, compared with Solly Kornblath, in a suit over a Fair Isle pullover. He was well made, crisp and purposeful-looking – but the thing which Alice noticed most about him was his eyes. They were quite the most fascinating eyes in a man she had ever seen: humorous, intelligent, alert and yet half-closed, sheltered by wiry eyebrows of which the left was raised a little, evidently by some skin defect. He looked like a man standing in bright sunlight who was giving his attention to something which both amused and interested him.

Solly Kornblath turned his head. "Ah, Rackham!" he said. And with a wave of a podgy hand: "Mrs Beatrice Culverwell." And with another wave: "And Mrs Alice Fenwick. And this is Martin Rackham."

"Hallo," said Beatrice. "We've ordered you a champagne cocktail."

"How kind." He said this a little automatically – the name "Fenwick" had jarred although he couldn't imagine why.

"And *Entrecôte Mirabeau*."

"How splendid."

He recognised Beatrice as a woman he had seen more than once in the Crébillion (although never in Kornblath's company), who had impressed him by her dress, appearance and, above all, vitality. Knowing that Solly backed plays and remembering seeing her lunching with well-known actors and actresses and others who if not in the limelight were obviously of the theatre, he at once gathered the connection. On the other hand Alice puzzled him. Until she had become aware of his presence she had been positive, spirited and apparently in complete control – but in a twinkling she was uncertain, wary, another person. A pretty woman, he told himself, who when younger must have been enchanting. Who perhaps could be now but for the bruising of tiredness about her eyes and this sudden defensiveness. And what on earth could she be doing in the company of a reprobate like Solly Kornblath and a sophisticate like this Beatrice Culverwell? She just didn't fit.

"Well, sit down then, Rackham," Kornblath said, indicating the empty chair.

Rackham sat between Solly and Alice.

"Mr Kornblath tells me you're an architect, Mr Rackham," Beatrice said.

"Yes."

"I've seen you in here before, haven't I? And always as a host."

"You're very observant, Mrs Culverwell."

"Thank you. I take that as a compliment."

"It was how it was intended."

"And why do you choose the Crébillion which is rather out of the way when there are all the other London restaurants?"

He could have told her that with its walls hung with carpets there was something about the Crébillion which reminded him of a certain restaurant in Paris; instead he said: "It always has an interesting clientele."

"What a charming man your architect is, Solly."

"He could charm the hind legs off a donkey," Kornblath said rather grumpily. "But he's a damned good architect. And a bloody expensive one."

The champagne cocktails had meanwhile arrived.

"Do you know why we're here, Mr Rackham?" Beatrice asked. "No, you don't, do you? Well I'll tell you. We're here to celebrate the founding of wholesale couture." And, at the slight lowering of his eyebrows, which was not so much a frown as encouragement for her to explain: "Alice, with backing from Mr Kornblath, is about to start a new business which is going to revolutionise the English dress trade. And she will, you know. I was never more certain of anything in my life. Before you came, Mr Kornblath – no I can't go on. He's probably Mr Kornblath to you and he certainly is to Alice so far, but he's Solly to me. And from now on you're Martin. Before you came, Martin, *you* were paid a compliment. All right, Solly?"

"I shall never get him to cut his fees from now on if you tell him."

"If you were able to do that, you wouldn't employ him." And to Rackham: "You were described as an architect who would be a legend in his own lifetime. Well, before she is done, Alice is going to be one in hers. And that's why we're here. To—"

She was interrupted. Solly had decided he'd been patient long enough. Like many men who have devoted their lives to becoming rich, outside of his commercial interests he had little conversation – which was one of the reasons why he backed plays and other businesses. It was also a reason for including Rackham in the lunch. But although he had the capacity to play

26

a minor role right through a meeting when doing so would be to his advantage, he could not endure for long the sense of being a small part player in a circle discussing a subject with which he didn't seem to be involved.

He picked up his glass.

"A toast!" he said genially. "To Mrs Alice Fenwick. To Hollywood Gowns!"

Fenwick, thought Rackham fretfully. Why should that name trouble me? While Beatrice, correctly reading the reasons for both Solly's interruption and the shadow of Rackham's frown, added quickly: "Not forgetting Solly's encouragement, without which Holly Wood Gowns would probably never have got off the ground."

They drank to Alice who sat flushed and somewhat embarrassed but, Rackham thought, with the colour rising to her cheeks, she was suddenly quite stunningly attractive. It was, he decided, an intriguing little lunch party: a woman of the theatre, a property magnate and this mercurial young woman who evidently possessed qualities far greater than were evident at a first assessment.

"You're very kind," said Alice in response. "And I'm very grateful to both of you for making this possible."

"Would someone care to put me in the picture?" Rackham said, turning his head to look from one to the other of them in turn.

"Solly," Beatrice said. "Explain."

Kornblath leaned back comfortably enough to make his chair creak audibly.

"Mrs Fenwick, Rackham," he said, "who I had never met until this morning and only did so because" – with a little nod – "Beatrice insisted that I should, is a young woman who has those two qualities which are vital to success in business: imagination and belief in herself. She put a proposition to me. That I should back her in a new business, which we're going to call Hollywood" – in his mind he saw it as one word – "Gowns. Her idea is to mass-produce women's dresses in a wide range of sizes. Apparently up to now it has been almost impossible for a woman to buy a ready-made dress and then

27

not to have to take it back to some dressmaker to have it altered so that it would fit her. You'd agree with that, wouldn't you, Beatrice?"

"Oh, yes," Beatrice said willingly. "Are you married, Martin?"

"Yes."

"Then I'm sure your wife would be the first to confirm what Solly's just said."

He nodded, remembering the early days when commissions had been few and far between and money had been tight. "You're absolutely right, of course."

"So," Kornblath said, "there's apparently a vacuum to be filled and that's what Hollywood Gowns is going to do."

"And you're backing it?"

"To the hilt."

2

Rackham accepted a lift to his office in Mandeville Square and Alice, at Beatrice's insistence, shared a taxi with her to the Mayflower Theatre where she was auditioning.

"Well what did you think of my protégée, Rackham?" Solly asked.

"That she was charming and sound and that you've chosen very well."

It was good to be able to be genuine. Kornblath was his most important client and after the disaster wrought by the Wall Street crash, important clients were going to be few and far between: to be purred to your office in the back of a chauffeur-driven Rolls after a splendid lunch accompanied by a most delightful and probably disgracefully expensive wine, was not going to happen too often in the years ahead. And you had to be very careful when you were with Solly Kornblath. He could make droll remarks and give the impression of being easy-going, but within the man was an iron core and, what was even more dangerous, an obsession not to be thought foolish or in any way incompetent. Raillery, banter and leg-pulling were never to be risked; nor was criticism.

Everything had to revolve around him, everyone had to take second place.

For all that, Rackham liked the man. He made things happen and, so long as you had his respect, you could count on his loyalty. And once he had given his word you could rely on him, if only because his pride would not allow him to back-track on it. Which was where, he reflected, Alice Fenwick, was fortunate. How she had persuaded him to finance her was baffling but he had agreed to do so, and as long as she kept to her part of whatever was their bargain she would be able to trust him.

Even so, there was no doubt, he told himself, that Solly had been out of his element and glad when it was over and he could get back to his chauffeured Rolls and his Berkeley Square empire! Beatrice Culverwell, he reflected, had handled what could so easily have degenerated into an uncomfortable lunch punctuated by embarrassing silences quite masterfully. Whenever she had sensed that Kornblath was on the verge of becoming fractious, she had fed in a question or remark which prompted him to take over the conversation. Looking back on it, he could never remember anyone, man or woman, who had managed Kornblath so easily or dared, as she had, to break a cardinal rule by teasing him. Perhaps it was that the qualities needed to handle such a tricky character as the man sitting beside him, puffing at a cigar, were essential in those who had to cope with self-opinionated or temperamental thespians!

And then the woman who had been the catalyst for such an oddly assorted quartet, Mrs Alice Fenwick, what was he to make of her? She had been on edge all the time. Well that was natural enough. In a dozen little ways she had revealed that lunching in such company, perhaps even in such an expensive and prestigious restaurant, was a new experience. Yet she had never allowed herself to be overwhelmed and had manifested an inner strength which, he suspected, might one day cause Kornblath, engaged in something outside his bailiwick, to ask himself how he had come to involve himself with her. And as for her presence whenever they had been actually discussing anything to do with making or selling dresses, how she had blossomed! All at once there was a new woman come amongst them: a woman utterly at home in her subject; a woman experienced, confident and certain.

But *Mrs* Alice Fenwick. There was the rub. And something of a mystery too. He had expected Beatrice Culverwell, who presumably knew a great deal about her, to fill in her background to him. Instead she had, he was certain, deliberately shifted the conversation the moment it seemed to be heading in such a direction.

"You don't know who she is, Rackham, do you?" Solly said suddenly, as if he had read Rackham's mind. "She's the woman whose husband filled his plus-fours with snooker balls and drowned himself at Maidenhead two weeks ago."

"Good God!" cried Rackham, sickened.

"It seems," said Kornblath (who on a pretext had excused himself from Alice long enough to acquaint himself with the details), "he hired himself a punt at Maidenhead, poled it down past Boulter's Lock, anchored the thing and jumped overboard. They found him in no time. When he didn't bring the punt back, the man who'd hired it to him took out a rowing boat, found it anchored and empty and got on to the Thames Conservancy people, who seem to be efficient."

Yes, thought Rackham, they wouldn't have taken long to find him. As he and Julia had often caught a train from Paddington to Maidenhead and spent the day at Skindles and on the river poling down to Cliveden, he knew the Thames near Boulter's Lock only too well. And at the end of October there wouldn't have been all that fierce a flow.

In fact not too much of what Kornblath was telling him was new because he had discussed it with Julia.

He had come into her bedroom, carrying her breakfast tray.

"Did you see this, Martin? It's macabre."

Her tone had been so anguished that he had paused in the doorway looking at her, her back propped up by pillows, a pretty bedjacket around her shoulders, the contraption like a hospital trolley he had had specially designed so that it could be drawn up in front of her, straddling the bed cleared for his tray. She was looking with horror at the front page of the *Daily Sketch* – which was as large a newspaper as she was able to handle now.

"What's macabre, darling?"

"There's a man drowned himself near Boulter's Lock."

He put the tray on the trolley top. Unless he had to be away on business, he always made her breakfast. Although their maisonette was spacious and their finances these days sufficient to have allowed them to have living-in staff, even a permanent nurse for Julia, she would have none of it, insisting they made do with daily help for the housework and with a Mrs Bolton, who lived close by, who came in after he had gone to work and stayed for most of the day helping Julia generally and doing all the other cooking.

"There's a lot of people get drowned in the Thames," he said. "It can be a very dangerous river."

"There aren't a lot that fill their plus-fours with snooker balls before they do it!" And she held the paper out towards him.

The disease (recently renamed as multiple sclerosis) was ravaging her with unreasonable speed, with the attacks recurring unusually frequently. As Tyrell, their doctor, had warned, while she always recovered somewhat after each attack there was invariably movement lost which could never be regained. But she could still use her hands well enough to make up her face, to eat a breakfast carefully enough prepared, to handle a small newspaper or a magazine if it was not too bulky.

He took the paper. The headline screamed: *"MYSTERY DEATH AT MAIDENHEAD"*. And the opening paragraph read:

Was there a reason why green and brown were missing from the set of snooker balls which anchored Tom Fenwick to the river bed? Was this a straight-forward suicide or could there be more sinister implications? There are many questions which need answering . . . (Detailed report Page 4).

That was all there was room for on the front page, which had to accommodate as well a photograph of the new R101 airship

31

moored at Cardington and a half column reassuring the nation
that the King had finally recovered his health in full and there
would be no more bulletins issued.

"What an extraordinary business," he said. He turned the
pages, found the article. "Shall I read it to you?"

She nodded. "Yes."

Having first dealt with the graphic details which Kornblath
had précised, the article had continued:

> *Mr Fenwick, who was aged twenty-nine, was married
> and had two stepsons. He was a brilliant sports-
> man who played regularly for the Exiles Rugger
> Club in Twickenham and was a leading member
> of the Brownswood Tennis Club near Lordship
> Park, North London. Until rather more than a year
> ago he was employed as a telegraph operator by
> the Eastern Telegraph Company which was taken
> over by Imperial and International Communications
> Limited. The merger necessitated a reduction of staff
> and a number of the operators, including Mr Harry
> Reddington-Quarmby, to whom we are grateful for
> this information, clubbed together to use part of
> their severance payments to establish a lending
> library which, largely because of the economic
> situation ruling, foundered. We understand from Mr
> Reddington-Quarmby that Mr Fenwick was unable
> to find alternative employment and obliged to give
> up all the sporting activities which were so much part
> and parcel of his life.*
>
> *This would therefore appear to be a straight-
> forward case of a man with his balance of mind
> disturbed taking what seemed to him at the time
> an easy way out. However there are a number of
> unusual factors which, we understand, are giving the
> authorities food for thought.*
>
> *Fenwick had himself been married before and
> was divorced on the proven grounds of infidelity
> by his first wife while the widow he has left behind*

divorced her own first husband on similar proven grounds. In the meantime Fenwick's first wife has remarried. Whilst it is a sad fact of life that divorces are becoming only too frequent these days, it is certainly, and fortunately, rare to come across such an interwoven case of marital instability.

Then again, while Fenwick's method of committing suicide is not uncommon, to go to the extreme of filling a set of plus-fours with snooker balls, thus ensuring not only that no second thoughts can be possible but also that the body will be quickly discovered, is surely unique and poses certain questions. Why snooker balls when a couple of bricks, or a bag of stones which could easily have been picked up somewhere along the river bank, would have been equally effective? Clearly the suicide was premeditated. Mr Took, who rented out the punt, has informed us that when he arrived Fenwick was walking normally and had a carrier bag which no doubt held the snooker balls.

Then again, why were two of the colours which make up a set of snooker balls, the green and brown, missing? Fenwick, we have ascertained, was a keen and very effective snooker player who would have known what comprised a set. It is clear that he chose this bizarre form of weighting himself for a purpose and it seems most likely it was to leave behind a message which he felt should not be included in his suicide note. How much of a part do those missing green and brown balls play in this secret message? It is an intriguing question.

"I read about it," Rackham said to Kornblath. "I just didn't connect the name."

"Why should you? It's not all that uncommon."

"What hell she must have been going through the last two weeks. The police, reporters . . . and all the rest. It doesn't bear thinking about."

"It doesn't," said Kornblath softly, leaning forward to knock the ash off his cigar into the ashtray on the back of his chauffeur's seat. He leaned back into the soft leather, regarding Rackham benignly. If he had been less of the usual Solly Kornblath over the lunch, he was quite restored now.

"You knew about this before you agreed to have her come and see you?" Rackham queried.

The spaniel eyes rested on him while Solly decided whether or not to be truthful. He's a little off balance, he told himself, he wouldn't normally ask such a probing question. He's an exceptional man, very self-controlled, the sort of architect you can talk openly to and know he'll keep it to himself until you can tell him he needn't any longer. But she's got below his skin, Alice Fenwick. That's the first weakness I've discovered.

He docketed it away.

"No, I didn't know," he admitted, almost as a question.

Rackham stifled the response which hurried to his lips. Whether or not Kornblath would have granted her an interview had he known this was a woman whose name, if tied up with his own before her brief notoriety had died, would give the reporters a field day, was better not asked.

"And to think she's got two children," he said instead.

"She's a very brave woman," Solly said – and went up a tiny notch in Rackham's estimation.

There was a traffic hold-up at the top of Regent Street where they were about to turn left down Oxford Street so that he could be dropped off. Some coal sacks had fallen off a horse-hauled coal cart and the driver, face black with coal dust, wearing a sort of all in one helmet and leather shoulder apron which put Rackham oddly enough in mind of Beatrice Culverwell's remarkable hat, was heaving them back on again. A few bystanders were catcalling him. Poor devil, Rackham thought, what a job – but his attention was distracted by a rapping on the Rolls' window, Solly's side. Solly turned as well and together they viewed the pinched face of a man staring in at them, mouthing something. To his surprise, Rackham saw Solly put his hand in his pocket, examine some coins he withdrew, pick out two half-crowns, lower the window and give them to the man, who taking them in disbelief stared long at them before crying out, "Oh, thank you, guv! Lord bless you, guv! Lord bless you!" He stood back a pace, still staring at the coins as if he could not believe his eyes. He had a strap around his neck which supported a tray on which there were a few boxes of matches. One arm of his threadbare coat hung limp, unoccupied, and on the lapel he wore the two campaign medals of the war – on his tray was a sign, crudely written: "Wounded at Passchendaele".

One is faced by comparisons all the time, Rackham thought. Five shillings probably just about buys one of those champagne cocktails at the Crébillion, but judging by that poor fellow's reaction it'll feed him for a week. And guilt was inescapable. But Solly Kornblath went up another notch.

3

Julia was in her wheelchair in the sitting-room, a room which seemed, if anything, even larger than it really was because of the lowered ceiling the square's architecture demanded of top floors. But, as became the room of a woman whose life must be largely spent between it and bedroom, it had been furnished for comfort, snugness and convenience rather than to express an imaginative architect's philosophy.

Carpeted from wall to wall, it was scattered with rugs, curtains were floor to ceiling, armchairs and settees invited relaxation. There were bookcases on either side of the fireplace in which a coal fire burned. The mantelshelf bore a brass carriage clock, two bronze and ivory stauettes by Omerth and on the wall above it was a collection of miniatures on ivory and a still life of books, ornaments and fabric by an associate with whom Rackham had trained. Elsewhere there were many other paintings, prints and engravings, mostly collected together in the early days of their marriage and some mementoes of Rackham's wartime days with the Royal Flying Corps.

At considerable financial risk, he had acquired the lease not only of the entire house in Mandeville Square but also of the mews cottage at the rear. The lower two floors and basement served as offices, the upper two as the maisonette in which they lived. He had put in a lift and designed a gently sloping runway to the small patio garden. The long-term plan was that when living in the maisonette became impracticable for Julia, rather than go into a nursing home, she would move into the cottage where he would install a full-time nurse to care for her. There was nothing more that he could do. The hoped for cure had yet to be discovered – and if it were discovered now, it would be far too late for them.

"You've come up early," Julia said. She had insisted that he did not allow himself to be encumbered by her more than was reasonable. "You have a life to live and a career to follow," she had said firmly. "I love you bringing me my breakfast but your days have to be your own. You're only to come up in working hours when there's a special reason."

He kissed her and said, "I have had the most remarkable lunch!"

"I know," she said, her eyes following him as he sat in the corner of the settee near her. "With Solomon Kornblath at the Dorchester."

He chuckled. "He's Solly now and it was at the Crébillion."

"The Crébillion." She said it wryly, rather than sadly. She had been there just the once with him. It had involved quite an effort on both their parts but had been worthwhile for the pleasant memories of *La Taverne du Marais la Chauve-Souris* it had evoked. "I shall never come here without you," he had vowed. But she would have none of it: "I shan't come here again with you, my love," she had responded. "Today? Today's one thing. But tomorrow I know would be another. But for you not to come here when you're invited or you think it's the right place to take a client, would be as absurd as not going to Paris if someone gave you the chance of designing a hotel there."

"What was so special about the lunch?" she went on quickly.

"The company."

"Kornblath?"

"And others. Two ladies. One an American who puts on West End plays and the other a very surprising woman of . . . about your age, I'd say, who's persuaded Kornblath to back her in a gown manufacturing business!"

"What an odd assortment."

"Isn't it? And that's not all!" There was that touch of triumph in his tone which so often presages the delivery of startling news. "Her name's Alice Fenwick and she was married to that man we were talking about the other day who filled his plus-fours with snooker balls and drowned himself near Boulter's Lock!"

"Good heavens!"

There was just that brief spontaneous cry and then quite a silence as Julia absorbed this astonishing information.

Then she said: "What was she like?"

"To look at? Very attractive and smart enough to be noticed even in the Crébillion. As a person?" He thought about it. "It was curious," he said. "It was almost as if she had a split personality. When we weren't talking about her business she was obviously rather overawed at keeping such company and lunching in such style but the moment it was anything to do with Holly Wood Gowns . . ." He broke off, then said with a little chuckle, "Holly Wood in two words by the way."

She realised there was meaning in this – but that could be come back to later.

"Go on."

"Yes. The moment it was to do with her business, she became a totally different woman. Self-assured. Positive. Incisive. And totally convincing."

"What about her husband's suicide?"

He shook his head. "Oh, that was never touched on. I didn't know that she was *the* Mrs Fenwick until Solly let it out on the way back to his office."

"Let it out?"

"Yes. It seems he didn't know about it either until after he'd agreed to back her. She must have volunteered it to him."

Julia moved her head a trifle in an indication of disbelief.

There were so many facets to the situation she hardly knew where to begin.

"And the lunch was a . . . a sort of celebration of his agreeing to back this . . ."

"Holly Wood Gowns." He accented the first two words.

"Oh, you'd better get that over with," she said, a little irritably. "Why two words?"

"Because Mrs Fenwick wants to have her cake and eat it. She thinks the sound of it and the first appearance of it will make good publicity but by distinguishing it with two words the business will keep its individuality." And at her frown: "Yes, it's suspect reasoning, isn't it? But never mind. The point is she was determined to have her way and did."

"Over Kornblath!"

"Remarkable, isn't it? He puts the money up and she has her way over what to call the company! And to answer the question you haven't put, he didn't even sit next to her."

"I'm baffled," Julia said.

"So am I. It's quite out of character."

"I want to get this straight," said Julia, who was far less interested in Kornblath than she was in Alice Fenwick. "He agrees to back her before he realises he's involving himself with a woman whose husband has just committed suicide in a way that's guaranteed to provide maximum publicity and then throws a celebration lunch to which you and this American woman . . . How does she come into it?"

"Oh that's straightforward anyway. Solly backs Beatrice Culverwell's plays and it was Beatrice who introduced Alice Fenwick to him. It seems that Beatrice's husband is in the gown business too and Alice Fenwick once worked for him as a dress designer."

"And what else do you know about *her*, Martin?"

"About Alice Fenwick? Not much. She's got two children. Both boys. Started a previous dress business which apparently did well enough . . ."

"And divorced her first husband. Know anything about him?"

"No."

"Was she very upset? About what her second husband . . . Well, no, obviously she wasn't."

"Well I think she was. That's why she was so . . . well, remarkable. There was suffering in her eyes. You couldn't miss it. And yet she had this capacity of throwing it off. Just as she could throw off being out of her depth in somewhere like the Crébillion and with such exalted people."

Julia made her mind up.

"I'd like to meet her."

He frowned, momentarily surprised. Coping with ill-concealed sympathy was anathema to her and since being confined to bed or a wheelchair, with a few exceptions, she had avoided meeting people. But then it came to him. With Alice Fenwick she would be on a different footing – for once she could be *giving* sympathy.

"You'd like me to arrange it, if I can?" he said.

"Yes, Martin. Soon."

"I'll see what I can do."

"Thank you. Now tell me all you know about this Beatrice Culverwell . . ."

Three

1

The taxi, which had been waiting for a good twenty minutes, took Beatrice and Alice directly to the Mayflower Theatre. As they got into it Beatrice said: "I'm afraid this may be a bit of a bore for you, Alice, but it has to be done. We're due to go into rehearsals on Monday and, after just two weeks on the road, open at the Criterion in six weeks' time and, would you believe it, the girl's got herself pregnant and her husband has point blank refused to let her play, which is just damn silly because it's only for a limited season anyway and she'll have plenty of time to have her baby after it closes."

"Is it a very important part?"

"Every part's important." And then, as if aware that Alice might feel snubbed, "But it's not the lead or anything like that, thank God!"

They entered the theatre by the back street stage door.

"Afternoon, George," Beatrice said to an iron-grey haired man who poked his head out of a room which was not much more than a cubicle. "Has Mr Tarrant arrived?" And, in an aside to Alice: "He's directing the play."

"Aye, Mrs Culverwell," George answered. "He's in there waiting." He nodded his head in the direction of the auditorium. "He's been here a guid half hour and he's been out twice looking for you. He's not a' that pleased."

Beatrice smiled. "No, I don't suppose he is. This way, Alice."

She led her along a narrow passage which *en route* exposed a stage set which Alice had scarcely time to take in as Beatrice hauled open the pass door leading into a corridor whose walls were decorated on both sides with mounted photographs of past productions and whose floor sloped slightly upwards. Where it was joined by another passage from the left, Beatrice came to a halt.

"I have to leave you here while I do this damn audition," she said in a low voice. "Go in as quietly as you can through those doors there." She pointed. "And find yourself a seat right at the back. Try to find one that doesn't squeak. And, whatever you do, don't draw attention to your being there? OK?"

"Yes, of course."

"Sorry it has to be this way, Alice, but if I had you come in and sit with me through the auditioning, I wouldn't put it past Nigel to walk out on us!" She took Alice's hand and pressed it. "Unless we find the right girl straight off this is likely to take up to a couple of hours but at least that'll give you some time to try figuring out the problems you'll have. 'Bye!"

And she was gone, hurrying down the sloping corridor and disappearing through a door on the right hand side of it. Alice hesitated, then, making her way into the auditorium, tested the nearest aisle seat, which to her relief didn't squeak, and sat in it.

She looked about her. She knew the theatre, which was small, Victorian and heavy with plush and gilt. She had been to more than one play in it with the Belmont set: Poppy and Puggy and Dot and Billy Shaw and the rest of them, and once, she recalled, with Greg Vibert to see something which had been called, rather unimaginatively, *Deep Waters* and was about a naval officer coming home on leave and finding his wife didn't love him any more. Greg had chosen it of course, to make a point. She smiled briefly. Poor Greg. But why poor Greg? He'd probably forgotten her years ago and was happily married with a couple of kids and back to living in Wellington where he'd come from in the first place. Thus she dismissed Greg and the Belmont set. Those had been her salad days, her *Bunty* days; she didn't regret them – but she wouldn't have had them back.

What with the overhang of the dress circle and the house lights out, where she sat was comfortably dim and, feeling sufficiently confident she wouldn't be noticed, she settled to put from her mind for the time being the day's events and enjoy her first experience of a theatrical production in the making. She tried to remember what it was that was running at the Mayflower but its title, and therefore its subject, eluded her. It seemed, she supposed as she eyed the stage, to be set in the sitting-room of an hotel for there was a sideboard with newspapers on it, several leather armchairs, a rattan settee and two or three small tables with tumblers on them. In the centre of the room, suspended from an open, raftered ceiling, was a curious and very large piece of canvas on a rectangular frame, at one end of which was attached a rope whose other end passed through a hole in the upstage wall – a contraption which baffled her, as did an ordinary kitchen chair which seemed oddly out of place.

Between her and the stage, seated perhaps half a dozen rows back from the orchestra pit, Beatrice, recognisable by the extra-ordinary helmet of her hat, was taking her place beside, pre-sumably, the formidable Tarrant man. Another man was on his right and on the stage a third man in cream trousers and a coffee-coloured pullover and a girl in a striped sleeveless dress.

Beatrice had evidently come to the end of her apology for Tarrant was saying crossly: "That's all right, Bee, but we've got eight of them this afternoon and I'm due to meet Leslie at the Garrick at six and I've got to climb into a boiled shirt first. So let's get straight on, shall we?"

"Sure," said Beatrice, not in the least put down.

"Right!" Tarrant had a clipped, decisive voice. "Audrey, where are you?"

A woman in a long dark skirt and a high-necked white blouse stepped out from the wings. "Yes, Mr Tarrant?"

"You can start wheeling them out. Who's the first?"

Audrey consulted a list she was holding. "Irene Cross."

"Agent?"

"Nick Driscoll."

"OK."

Audrey vanished into the wings. Beatrice was busy fitting a cigarette into her holder. The man next to Tarrant turned his head to speak to him but their conversation was interrupted by the man in the cream trousers: "Mr Tarrant?"

"Yes, Richard?"

"Would you mind if I move the witness box back a bit? It'll give me more room to move about."

"It isn't you we're auditioning, Richard, it's Irene Cross."

"Well yes, I know, Mr Tarrant but Gilmour—"

"Never mind! Never mind! Have it moved back if you want to. Do it Peggy, would you?"

The girl, who had huge, frightened eyes and centre-parted brown hair which was cut to fall over her ears like a couple of inverted question marks (which reminded Alice forcibly of Lola Peters of Belmont days), hastened to move the kitchen chair, then paused. In her hand she had a playscript and she cast her eyes wildly round for a place to put it.

"Put it on the chair, move the chair, and then pick it up again." Tarrant reproved her as might a schoolmaster to a dimwit pupil.

"Oh. Yes. Good ideah."

She did as suggested and started to move the chair, under precise instructions from Richard, who seemed difficult to please. Alice sensed that nerves were very much on edge. Beatrice lit her cigarette. The man on Tarrant's right was speaking to him earnestly in a low voice but was again shooed away by an imperious hand as a woman, dressed to the nines in a swinging pleated skirt with a slanted hemline, a top with bows all the way down the front of it and a white fur slung round her shoulders, emerged from the wings followed closely by Audrey, list in hand.

"Miss Irene Cross," Audrey announced.

"Good afternoon, Irene," Tarrant called. "My apologies for keeping you waiting."

Irene, who had been killing time in one of the bright-lit dressing-rooms and whose eyes had yet to adjust to the penumbra, peered into the gloom of the auditorium.

"I'm Nigel Tarrant," Tarrant went on briskly, giving her no time to comment," and the gentleman on your left is Mr Richard Hoskins who is company stage manager and will be reading the part of Neville Gilmour. I see you haven't brought your pages with you."

"No, Mr Tarrant. I've learnt the piece Nick tells me you're

43

auditioning on. In fact I've read the whole play right through twice." She smiled brilliantly. "I didn't see how otherwise I could give a convincing performance."

"Well that's splendid," Tarrant said. "And you won't want me to tell you what the play is all about or the sort of woman Moira is supposed to be then, will you?"

"Oh, no, Mr Tarrant."

"Good, then let's get on. Now I'm afraid the set we've got is hardly conducive to the atmosphere of a courtroom . . ."

"What on earth is it?"

"It's meant to be the lounge of the British Club in Rangoon . . ."

"What's that thing?" Irene was pointing to the contraption.

"That's a punkah. A native pulls on the rope, usually with his big toe, to create a draught. They had them in India but I doubt if they ever did in Burma. Or a club room looking like this one. Can we get on?"

"Yes. Of course."

"Good." The irony was unmistakable. "You see that chair. The nasty little wooden one? That's our witness box. You stand behind it looking at Mr Gilmour who is cross-examining you and, it appears, likes to have plenty of room to walk about while he's doing so. I want you to imagine it *is* a witness box and if you feel so inclined use it accordingly. Right?"

"Yes, Mr Tarrant."

"We will start where Mr Gilmour asks you if you love your husband and you reply that you do not."

"But I was told by Nick . . ."

"Yes, darling, I know what you have been told by Nick but I'm afraid that for reasons beyond my control we are running out of time and have to cut the audition shorter than I would have preferred. But I can assure you it will be the same for everyone. Peggy!"

"Oh!" And very nervously: "Yes, Mr Tarrant?"

"Give Miss Cross the marked-up script and show her where she starts and where we finish."

With a flash of white stockings, Peggy, who had unaccountably retreated to the further wings, hurried across script in hand and showed the marked-up part to her.

Irene looked insulted. "It's not very much, is it?" she protested to Tarrant, her eyes having apparently adjusted to the light.

"Darling, I'm afraid the whole part isn't at all as much as both of us might like it to be but it is all the author thinks is required. And it *is* important. So – into the witness box, darling. That's right. Off we go."

Richard, who was a tall and willowy man who had worn well for his fifty odd years and gave the impression he had done so largely by the care he lavished on himself, stepped forward, striking an attitude, viewed Irene for a moment of silence, then shot at her:

"Mrs Brankaster, do you love your husband?"

"No," said Irene, managing to stumble it. And, apologetically, "I'm sorry. Can we start again?"

"Start again, Richard."

Richard eyed the rafters with pain and recommenced: *"Mrs Brankaster, do you love your husband?"*

"No."

"And obviously he does not love you."

"No."

"Well it is very strange. You admit you do not love your husband and that he does not love you and you accuse him in open court of infidelity with a woman you say that you can name but will not name and yet you wish your marriage to continue."

"Yes."

"Why? Because he is a wealthy man who may yet become richer? Because he is an important man who may yet become even more so?" Richard had begun his walkabout. With each question he stopped, then, having fired it, moved to some new part of the stage preparatory to firing the next. *"A Member of Parliament? Even one day a Cabinet Minister? Because one day you may, who knows, become Lady Brankaster?"*

"These are good reasons, Mr Gilmour."

"And there are others?"

At this point Irene grabbed at the back of the kitchen chair,

seeing it evidently as the front rail of a witness box. In her
enthusiasm she rather misjudged what she was doing and
rocked it forward – fortunately not enough for it to fall
and her with it. She recovered. *"Yes. Because a man does
not love a woman, or the woman does not love a man, does
not mean the woman wishes the marriage to end. There are
other considerations. Companionship. A way of life. The fear
of loneliness. And in my case . . . children . . . They are at
an age when divorce can have a terrible and permanent
effect . . ."*

For a while Alice had been taken out of herself by the newness
of everything going on in front of her and the lulling sense of
escape from the brittle world which an empty theatre gives.
But the actress's lines brought back reality. She felt the
pressure of her hands clasping each other. The coincidence
was extraordinary: it might have been her life they were
talking about, not Mrs Brankaster's. Her eyes shifted from
the stage to Beatrice and saw the coil of smoke from her
cigarette rising quite high before some slight breeze in the
theatre broke it and drifted it away, and realised it was *not*
coincidence. Beatrice presumably knew which lines had been
selected and knew how near the bone they would be to her.
She didn't have to be here. They were to go to Beatrice's
office afterwards. Beatrice could as easily have told her to
kill a couple of hours looking round the shops while this was
going on.

Irene Cross had been dismissed. "Thank you, darling. We'll
let you know." Another girl had been brought in. Tarrant
had gone through the same sort of patter as he had with
Irene, tailoring it a little to handle efficiently the change
of personalities. Richard had done his walkabouts. The girl
with the over-educated voice who was a DSM, whatever
that meant, had handed over and collected the script; the
man next to Tarrant, discovered to be the author, had again
tried unsuccessfully to hold the famous director's attention;
Beatrice had lit another cigarette. On and on it went as Audrey

brought girls in and showed them out. On and on and, astonishingly, Tarrant, for all his tetchiness, for all his ironies, had
remained as concentrated and seemingly as untired as he had
been at the start.

But to Alice it had become no more than a background to
her thoughts. She did not so much listen to the lines being
spoken – lines which, had she been required to do so, she
believed she could by now repeat word perfect without a
script – as see herself in the shoes of Mrs Brankaster.

After the day when fleeing from Herbert Clarkson she had been
rescued by Samuel Jordan, this day ranked as perhaps the most
important in her life. A bewildering day, through the course
of which she seemed to have run the gamut of almost all the
emotions she was capable of experiencing: in turn anxiety, hope,
trepidation, disbelief, elation, even pride. A day in which she had
been thrown into the close company of three individuals each with
awesome personalities, each totally different from each other, each
obviously of huge account in their own particular fields, yet all
of whom had treated her with courtesy and respect. It was a day
which marked not only a turning point in her financial affairs but
– and maybe, she decided, this was even more important – one
which had opened up a whole new world and closed the door on
the world she had left behind. And on Sam and Tom especially.
She might bear the name of one of them and her children that
of the other, but from now on they had for all practical purposes
ceased to exist or have existed.

How wrong this play was! She felt like rising to her feet to
tell them so. Mrs Brankaster claimed that her children were of
an age where divorce could have a terrible and lasting effect.
But it wasn't so. Judging by the age the actresses were playing,
Mrs Brankaster's children could hardly be as old as Dessy and
Thady. And how had *they* taken her divorce? In their stride!
They had accepted Tom in Sam's place with ease. And, she told
herself, would accept Tom's ghastly suicide with equal ease. It
would soon be buried in the limbo of the past – an event to be
recounted by them from time to time only as a conversational
exercise. They had lost a father and a stepfather at too young an
age for their influences to count; a father and stepfather neither

of whom had been such as to leave a lasting impression on them anyway. Compared with other children there was in their lives a yawning gap. A gap which, as Joseph Mott had in effect said in his final sally, this far at least, she had failed to fill. They were as good as parentless. And the fault was hers.

2

Brusa Productions' offices were on the fifth floor of a ramshackle building in Great Windmill Street. There was a lift but it didn't always function and when it did it only reached as far as the fourth floor, above which, with the exception of Beatrice's office, the rooms were poorly lit attics with floors which sloped and creaked and into which London dirt drifted continually through ill-fitting windows. No matter; the location was superb: Great Windmill Street crosses Shaftesbury Avenue. This was theatreland. An uneven stream of actors and actresses without parts, playwrights with unoptioned playscripts, would-be directors, set designers, out of work company managers and representatives of advertising agents and the numerous other trades which together make up the complex whole of show business, as often as not had to make their way up all the flights of the steep, winding staircase and pause to get back their breath before hopefully pressing the bell push on the door at which the stairway finally expired. Once inside they were encouraged. Clearly, to judge by the numerous framed box-office cards along the passage and in the reception area, this was a busy and successful management. In fact those in the passage exaggerated: Harry Dobbyn, who had set up on his own as a theatrical management but failed, had bought up a job lot of these posters in a second-hand shop in Wardour Street. Only the half dozen box-office cards in the reception area (where the light was better) bore Brusa Productions' name.

"Never mind," Beatrice had said when she took over Harry's Dobbyn Productions (and Harry himself, because he knew the business even if he couldn't run it successfully on his own), "theatre's only bluff anyway!"

Harry Dobbyn was a jovial-looking Australian of considerable
girth, a man in his forties whose parents had been in vaudeville,
who had never known anything but theatre and couldn't imagine
any other way of life. Aware of the local limitations, he'd
shaken off the dust of Sydney as soon as the war was over and
caught the first possible boat heading towards the West End of
London.

"Settle on anyone?" he asked Beatrice as she passed his
office door.

She paused. "Yes."

"Who?"

"Her name's Margaret Sherlock."

Harry wrote it down on a pad. "Never heard of her."

"That makes two of us. But Nigel was over the moon about
her."

Alice vaguely remembered Margaret Sherlock – tallish,
husky-voiced, intense.

"Agent?"

"Picketts."

Harry wrote that down as well, then said with a grin: "You'll
never guess who's waiting for you?"

"Who?"

"Joanna Mottram."

"Oh, my God! Where have you put her?"

"In with Judy. I told her you'd already got someone waiting
for you in your office."

"Bless you, Harry." She paused. "Alice, meet Harry Dobbyn,
the biggest rogue in show business. Harry, Mrs Alice Fenwick.
Harry, take her into my office will you and look after her
while I get rid of Joanna. Alice, this won't take five minutes
I promise you."

And she was gone.

"How about some tea?" Harry suggested.

They were in Beatrice's office – a room of great style, oval
in shape with a splendid curved window which overlooked
the Apollo Theatre. It was furnished with an elliptical table
which fitted well into the window bay, quite a few comfortable chairs and a chaise-longue. On the walls were framed

photographs of several well-known artistes and a few more playbills.

Although the idea of tea appealed immensely, Alice rejected it. "No, thank you, Mr Dobbyn."

"The name's Harry. You in theatre, Alice?"

"No."

"Didn't think you were. You're a lucky girl. It's a terrible business to be in. Now you take that one." He tapped a playbill. "All set for the West End. The Lyric. And what happens? Jilly gets pharyngitis. Not laryngitis, pharyngitis! Ever heard of it?"

"I'm afraid I haven't."

"Doctor said it was through eating too much spiced food, would you know? Real trouble, between you and me, is she doesn't take enough water with it. Or you take this one now." He tapped another. "Basil Pagett . . ."

And he regaled Alice with the beginnings of a complicated story, only to be interrupted by Beatrice's arrival.

"Sorry about all this, Alice. What's Harry been telling you? Whatever it is, you don't want to believe a word of it. He's the biggest liar in the business."

"Got rid of her?" said Harry, unabashed.

"Yes. And don't you ever do that to me again."

"You tell me how to keep her out then."

"Anything else?" Beatrice was standing by the door, dismissively.

Harry grinned. "Nothing that can't wait. Nice to have met you, Mrs Fenwick."

He closed the door behind him.

"Sit down, Alice," Beatrice said. "Suppose you sit there." She took the chaise-longue herself which was placed opposite the chair she'd suggested Alice occupy. What with her helmet of a hat and the huge cabbage-rose in the buttonhole of her cream silk jacket, she looked, with her legs stretched out, appropriately theatrical.

"Well, what did you think of Mrs Brankaster?" she demanded . . .

"You really want my opinion?"

"I don't know anyone who could give a better one."

"I didn't believe her."

"*What* didn't you believe?"

"Well, she went on and on about her children and how much they'd be affected by a divorce."

"And you don't think they would be?"

"Not at that age. No."

Beatrice nodded, docketing it away. Nigel would be interested. "Anything else?" she said. "I mean, the other reasons she gave for wanting to go on being married to a man who had been unfaithful to her, who didn't love her and whom she didn't love. Would you go along with those?"

Alice thought about it. "I don't know," she said. "My first husband wasn't unfaithful to me."

"Suppose he had been?"

"I don't think I would have wanted to go on living with him."

Beatrice started to remove her gloves. "It's important, you see," she said. "It isn't a big part but the whole play depends on the audience believing in Mrs Brankaster. And you didn't, did you?" She dropped the gloves into the open capacious handbag she had put on the floor beside her.

"I don't think I can give an unbiased opinion."

"You can give a realistic one."

"That's why you asked me to attend the auditioning isn't it, Beatrice?"

"Do you mind?"

"It's a small return for what you've done for me."

"That doesn't answer the question."

After a moment, Alice said: "No, I don't mind. It's all of the past. As for believing in Mrs Brankaster, I didn't really. For the reasons I've given. Especially the one about her children." And, rather sadly: "Mine hardly seemed to notice they'd exchanged one father for another."

"You don't say!"

"And," Alice went on calmly, "I don't think they've lost all that much sleep at having the new one I wished on them do what he did."

"But *you* have, haven't you?"

"Yes," Alice admitted.

"If you don't want to talk about it . . ."

"I don't mind. In fact I'd rather like to talk about it. Apart from the police, I haven't talked about it to anyone."

"The press . . ."

"Were queuing up." And, bitterly: "Even offering me money for my story."

"Which you could have done with."

"Yes."

"Look," Beatrice said, "I don't want to pry and I'm not offering you a shoulder to cry on, but if it'll help you to talk about it, I'm listening. And, frankly, interested. Especially about your second husband and why, if you know or can work it out, he chose such a theatrical way to kill himself."

"You mean the snooker balls?"

"Yes."

"Oh that's simple enough. He had a sense of humour, and he met my first husband, and so me, at a snooker table."

"Good God!"

"I think it was his way of telling me not to spend my life regretting what he'd done."

"He loved you that much?"

"Yes."

"And you loved him?"

Alice shook her head. "No." And prepared herself to reply to the expected follow-up.

It didn't come. Beatrice reasoned that if Alice wanted to explain *why* she had married a man she didn't love, she would do so without prompting. "But if," she said instead, "he loved you enough to kill himself for you, why did he do it?"

"Because he was a coward." Alice smiled wanly. "I don't mean that unkindly. In some ways he was very brave. He once saved a man from drowning, in a situation in which most men I've known wouldn't have risked their lives as he did. But when things were wrong . . . When the chips were down, as he would have said – he was very fond of that sort of saying – when the chips were down and he was thrown back on his own resources, he couldn't cope."

She explained about Tom losing his job, but she said nothing about his drinking.

"He had three brothers who were all successful in law or accountancy or that sort of thing," she went on. "But his father must have realised Tom's limitations, which is why he put him in the Eastern Telegraph Company. Which suited him ideally. He found himself with a job for life, a job he'd been specially trained to do, which paid a reasonable salary and which he shared with men who'd had roughly his level of education. And because of the shift system they worked the job allowed him plenty of time to do the things he loved doing and was so good at doing. Playing tennis, or rugger, or any sort of sport, really. But when the company was taken over and he found himself thrown out on the street . . . well, he hadn't any other qualifications and it wasn't in him to queue up at a Labour Exchange with a million other unemployed trying to get a job on a building site or something. The bottom had been knocked out of his world. There was no future he could see. No future for me and no future for my children. So he decided there was only one answer to it. That there was only one decent thing to do."

Beatrice both disbelieved the faint irony Alice had injected into the last few words and, through her theatrical experience, recognised a speech which had been mentally rehearsed in readiness for today. She had, she knew, heard only a small part of the story. A man in the prime of life needed more than what Alice had chosen to tell her as a motive for killing himself.

She marked time: "He was quite a remarkable man, wasn't he?" she said.

Alice shook her head. "No, Beatrice, he was a very ordinary man who had had it drummed into him that having principles and sticking to them was the most important thing in life." And, with a touch of bitterness: "I think his father could have equipped him better to face the world than he did."

There it was again, Beatrice told herself: a defence of the man who had killed himself. It was intriguing. But to be pursued no further. She had already got very near to the bounds of insensitivity.

"I think, Alice," she said, "you've taken what happened very

53

bravely, and as for what you've achieved today, I'm lost in admiration. I believe in your Holly Wood Gowns – although to lay it on the line I don't think the name's the right one and I hope you'll dream up a better one – and I haven't any doubt you've the ability to make the big time. But . . ."

She emphasised the word and, to give it added weight, swung her legs to the floor and, reaching into her handbag, took out her cigarette case. In the silence as Beatrice extracted a cigarette and fitted it into the amber holder, Alice could hear the muted sound of traffic. A telephone in one of the other rooms of the suite rang insistently, then abruptly ceased. There was, Alice felt, a curious affinity between the place where she had been, a theatre, and the place where she was now, a room in which plays were planned and brought to life, a room in which make-believe was of more importance than reality.

Having lit her cigarette, Beatrice strolled across to the window and glanced down into the street below. I ought to have known better than get myself into this mess, she was thinking, and I have to choose my words carefully or I'm going to have to pay for it.

She turned.

"What did you think of Solly, Alice?" she demanded.

It was so unexpected, Alice was lost for words. "I . . . I thought he was rather . . . rather nice," she answered feebly.

"Oh, come now," Beatrice said somewhat irritably. "You can do better than that."

"Well I did," Alice responded with spirit. "He wasn't at all as I expected he was going to be." And carrying the attack to Beatrice: "You said he was quite a sweetie, and he was."

"He didn't proposition you?" And after a brief pause, "You know what I mean?"

Alice flushed slightly. "Yes, I know what you mean. No, he didn't."

Beatrice hesitated. "Look." She waved the lighted cigarette. "I'm going to level with you, Alice. You've rung a bell with Solly and I'm not sure myself what kind of a bell it is you've rung. I think . . . and I hope it's Holly Wood Gowns. But it might be you. And if it is . . ." She fetched up a theatrical sigh. "If it is, then you've got problems and it's all my fault you have."

Momentarily she looked down into the street again, then went on: "I know Solly's background, what his father did, where he was brought up, that sort of thing. And I thought that because of it, with a bit of luck, if you put it over well enough, he might help you. Write you a cheque for a thousand or two to get you started. I've known him do that before. When he takes to someone he can be very generous. But I never thought he'd go overboard the way he has. Now either way you've got a problem. Because if it's you, you're going to have one helluva job keeping out of that bed he's got in Berkeley Square. And if it isn't you, if it's Holly Wood Gowns, then you'd better be right—"

"I know I'm right—"

"That's not what I mean. I've used the wrong word. If Holly Wood Gowns doesn't work, if it fails because it wasn't a good idea in the first place anyway, that's OK. Solly'll accept that. Nothing to worry about there. But if you try to cross him, or cheat him . . . Or make him think that because he's backing you, you've got nothing more to worry about and can take it easy . . . God help you, Alice. And God forgive me for what I've done."

She came across the room and stood near Alice, looking down at her.

"Now listen to what I've got to say, Alice, and listen good. You're not committed yet. You can still back out. And if you've got the courage to do that in spite of the spot you're in financially – and I believe you do have that courage – maybe it would be the wise thing to do."

"I'm not backing out. I shall never get a chance like this again." Alice said it defiantly enough to be convincing.

"All right. You're not backing out. Then remember this. Remember this all the time. You won't see Solly in your factory any more than I see him here. He doesn't interfere in any productions he puts money into. He doesn't tell me that he wants me to have this actress or that director or in which theatre he thinks I ought to put on the play. But I know he's here, watching me, checking on everything I do – through his accountants and his lawyers. And maybe in other ways I know nothing about. And it'll be the same with you, Alice. And you're going to be worse off than I am because Solly doesn't own any shares in Brusa and I *could* find other backers if I had to. If you were to tell Solly we'd had this conversation and because of it he walked out on me . . . OK. I wouldn't like it. But I could manage. You won't be able to. Because Solly's going to have a controlling interest in Holly Wood Gowns and if he doesn't like the way you're handling it he'll close it down or put someone in your place . . ." She snapped her fingers. "Just like that."

She took the cigarette out of the holder and ground it out in a nearby ashtray, then looked Alice directly in the eyes.

"I want you to go home to your two children and think about it long and hard, my dear. And if you decide you're taking on too much by taking on Solly Kornblath, then let me know and I'll tell you what I'll do. I'll *give* you the thousand pounds you hoped to borrow from my husband and you can use it any way you want. To tide you over or to set yourself up in a little business of some sort – not Holly Wood Gowns, because for what we were talking about over lunch you're going to need all of five thousand pounds, and more, and I just don't have that sort of money spare. I'm not a Solly Kornblath." She paused. "There'll be just one condition – we didn't have this conversation. No one talked about Solly to you. You just thought it over and changed your mind."

3

"Sherry?" Grahame asked.

"No, scotch!"

He smiled and went to the cocktail cabinet.

Beatrice had got back after him, asked him to cancel a dinner engagement, taken two aspirin, run herself a bath and come down in a dressing-gown. Clearly something had gone very wrong with the day.

"Did you cancel the d'Avirros?" she said.

"Yes."

"I'm sorry, Grahame, but . . ."

"Not to worry." He brought the scotch to her. "Do you want to talk about it?"

"I need to. Thanks." She took the scotch, drank some of it, put the glass down and stared into the fire. He made himself comfortable in the adjacent armchair.

"Problems with the play?" he suggested.

She shook her head briefly. "No, the play's fine. It's Alice."

"Solly turned her down?"

"Like hell he did." She told him what had been agreed.

"So?"

"So, I'm scared stiff I've started something we're both going to be sorry about." She explained her concern at what the future could hold for Alice. "I just didn't think it through," she went on guiltily. "I thought maybe he'd give her a helping hand . . . No! That's not true either! I'm just saying that to let myself off the hook. I was just amusing myself, showing off how much influence I had with Solly."

He disagreed. "No, Bee. Not that I'm saying that didn't come into it and that maybe neither of us gave it the thought we should have at the time—"

"Don't you see, Grahame?" she interrupted, as usual pronouncing his name without the aspirate. "That's the whole point. When I first dreamed up the idea of meddling in Alice's life, she meant no more to me than a girl who'd done designing for you, that I'd met a couple of times and rather liked, who'd got a problem because her husband had lost his job like thousands and thousands more. But when we heard that he'd committed suicide, and done it the way he did, surely to God I shouldn't have gone on being so casual. Surely I ought to have tried to get into her mind, tried to imagine what she must be feeling, asked myself if it was right to subject her to all she's had to put up with today."

"Well she seems to have coped with it remarkably well."

Beatrice nodded. "Coped with it? Yes. But what's going on inside? I tell you something, Grahame. There's one hell of a play that could be written about that girl and a helluva part for some actress to play."

He smiled inwardly. They were back to theatre again. And if what Beatrice had organised resulted in the disaster her present fears predicted, that disaster wouldn't have come about because she had wanted to show off to him but because she had been quite unable to resist the theatre of putting Alice and Solly Kornblath together.

But, remembering the girl who couldn't even draw, who had walked the length of Bond Street stealing a collar from here and a cuff from there and put them together and offered the bungled results as her own original designs, he couldn't go along with her apprehensions.

"Maybe," he said, "it's already been written. Maybe what it is, is that we're privileged to be involved in something in which Alice has the starring role and in which, when one day we look back on it, we'll realise we had only walk-on parts."

"I hope you're right," said Beatrice with feeling. "By God, I hope you're right."

Four

1

The Reverend Derek Williams, vicar of St Saviour's church, put a soft hand on Desmond Jordan's shoulder. "Oughtn't you to be getting home, young fellow?"

Desmond, who was in the rearmost pew, swivelled his head. Williams, short and stocky, no more than five feet six inches in height, with a round face made even rounder by the way he dressed his hair to fall either side of a forehead so high it seemed as high as the distance from eyebrows down to chin, looked down on him, an expression of tolerant understanding in his kindly eyes.

"If it's all right, sir," Desmond pleaded, "I'd like to wait until Miss Ritchie comes to the end of this."

Evensong was over and Evelyn Ritchie, buxom, wild grey-haired and carelessly dressed, was playing the organ. Apart from her they had the church to themselves.

"Of course. I'll join you listening if I may. Shift along."

Desmond obediently moved along the pew, doing this with such haste and impatience as effectively to advise Williams that he was quite held by the music and in no mood for chat or lecture. Williams smiled and settled himself to enjoy Evelyn's playing and the company of a youngster he had not merely taken to but towards whom he felt a considerable responsibility.

On the whole his congregation was upper middle class and very much drawn from the houses in Aberdeen Park, which were mostly detached with some, such as number 67, quite grand. The latter's owners, the Stringers, who attended St Saviour's church regularly, were at great pains not to allow themselves to become involved with neighbours and the few

59

who realised they had let their basement assumed it was to accommodate a man and his wife who worked in some way for them.

With Aberdeen Park being a superior enclave hemmed in on all sides by lesser properties, its occupants were not of the type inclined to stand gossiping with each other over a garden fence and thus there had been few who had given as much as a second thought to what sort of lives were being lived by the two little boys who emerged from the gate of number 67A wearing caps which advertised the level of education their parents were affording them. But when it was learnt that their stepfather had put an end to himself by filling his plus-fours with snooker balls and drowning himself in the Thames, all at once the undeniably smart and attractive Mrs Fenwick and her two sons were of absorbing interest and neighbours avidly pooled such knowledge as they possessed, including the fact that Fenwick had had bouts of coming back drunk and proceeding to knock both family and furniture about.

But on the whole it went no deeper: strangers the four Fenwicks had been and strangers the three that were left remained, with Alice when seen shopping being regarded with suspicious awe, and Desmond and Thady heading for school with an at-a-distance sympathy. There were exceptions. Colonel Wharton, who remembered Alice from her days spent in Cranmore Hotel while her divorce was going through, stuck up for her whenever her name cropped up in the lounge and would have been ready to slip a couple of sixpences to her boys if he'd happened to run across them, while the Laceys had got to know Desmond in advance of the suicide when he had ingratiated himself with their twin daughters through the stratagem of fondling the family King Charles spaniel, and, although somewhat uneasy about the situation, they could hardly disassociate themselves from him now.

When Desmond had been brought into his church by Wendy and Angela a few days earlier, Derek Williams had chuckled to himself, accepting that the boy's professed interest in becoming an acolyte would probably last for the exact length of time his interest in the Lacey twins, or theirs in him, endured. And so it probably would have been but for a factor no one had taken into account. Music. Desmond's exposure to music thus far had been more or less limited to such as had drifted up from the dance floors of the local Belmont Hotel in which most of his childhood had been spent or of Seaview Hotel, Shanklin, where he had experienced the holiday spent in the remarkable *ménage à trois* company of father, mother and future stepfather, or been churned out with monotonous regularity on the limited number of records his parents had possessed; but when he found himself exposed within the shadowy confines of the daunting Victorian brick-built church to music of a quality he had never heard before, a love which was never to leave him was born.

Williams was fascinated by this surprising addiction in a boy wearing, a year or so too young, his first long trousers – and those bought over-large for obvious reasons – who when he had entered the church for the first time a week or so before had had no musical knowledge whatsoever. But when, through the unavoidable tittle-tattle poured into his ears after the Fenwick suicide, he realised the pressures under which the boy had lived, he believed he understood. Music, he told himself, was often an anodyne for the insecure and, imagining the seamy life the boy had lived, the threatening shouts of a drunken man, the footsteps, the broken furniture, how could the poor little chap be anything but insecure? Williams was possessed of a burning desire to do anything in his power to help. It was as if God had chosen a mission for him.

In fact Desmond could have told him that he had only partially analysed the situation. It was not so much insecurity which wrought such sudden and fervent interest in music, it was the loneliness born out of insecurity. And his insecurity was as much the result of being so much smaller not only than his peers but even of a brother two years younger; of seeing himself in fact almost as a dwarf. And then again the curious life he had begun to realise he had lived, in hotels rather than in homes and having a name different from his parents and a brace of parents instead of one, seemed to set him apart from other boys. He was aware that most of them had friends who came to their homes to have tea and play with them, but the short-lived idea he himself had had of inviting other boys to visit him – and the possibility of the visit coinciding with his stepfather being in a drunken tantrum – was forever banished. There was even a gulf between him and the brother he had once so dearly loved. He knew that he as much as anyone had created this gulf by the grander airs he had assumed, but all this secret admission did was to give him a sense of guilt which increased the separation. They might still occupy the same bed but, apart from their shared fear of a rampaging stepfather, for a long time now they had had little in common and by being sent to different schools their separation was even further widened. From now on, Desmond knew, they would make different friends and be subjected to different influences: they would never be close again.

While listening to the music being played, Dvořák's "Humoresque", Williams was observing Desmond carefully. With that high forehead, those alert blue eyes, that determined chin, the boy, he decided, had to be intelligent. Even his smallness seemed an asset, for there was a neatness and compactness about him which suggested that, properly harnessed, there could be qualities here which led in the right direction might yield great things. I must, he told himself, discover more about him. I must get him to open up and talk about himself, about his hopes and aspirations. His is a critical age and with his mind filled as it has to be with the awfulness of his stepfather's suicide he is especially vulnerable. In his search for security he could so easily meet with those who could corrupt him. He has only a mother to guide him now, a woman who, rumour had it, has been more interested in amusement and worldliness than her children's upbringing.

And this thought reminded him that there was another young Jordan, more slightly built and taller but astonishingly alike, who quite possibly needed as much help as Desmond. Or perhaps, being two years younger, even more help. It was, he ruminated, a terrible legacy their stepfather had bequeathed on them, and the burden on their mother, however much she may have brought it on herself, must be all but unbearable. I must meet her, he decided, and offer her my services.

When the piece had reached its end, he startled an enrapt Desmond by tapping his arm

"Desmond," he said, "it's time you went home. Your mother must be wondering what on earth you're doing."

"Oh, no, sir."

"Well she must know that evensong finished half an hour ago."

Desmond wondered whether in fact his mother even knew what evensong was. He could not recall ever going to church with her and religion had never been a subject for conversation. Aunt Hetty, of course, would have known all about evensong – but then religion had been as much what she thought about as business had been for Mummy.

"I don't suppose she does," he said. "Anyway, she had to go up to London for something she said was jolly important. She left the key for us under a stone in case she got back late."

"Well I'm going to see you back anyway," Williams said, rising. "Come on."

Desmond couldn't see much purpose in being seen back home; he saw himself back home every day from school. But he didn't object. There wasn't going to be any more music; Miss Ritchie was packing her sheets away.

2

The number nineteen bus passed close by Highbury County School, magnifying the sense of guilt which had gripped Alice since her musings in the Mayflower Theatre. What time was it? It must be nearly six. Dessy and Thady would have left their schools hours ago. If she'd come straight home after the lunch she would have been in time to have a fire lit for them, to have had the kettle on and tea waiting on the table. Thank goodness she'd had the foresight to leave the key under that stone or the poor mites would have had to huddle in their thin overcoats at the bottom of the steps waiting for her, wondering where on earth she'd got to, perhaps even wondering if they'd lost her as well as Tom!

Oh, hurry up, bus! Hurry up!

It was full downstairs. Full of people going home after a day's shopping or work, or visiting friends, or doing the ordinary things which ordinary men and women did. Ordinary men and women with ordinary husbands and wives who led ordinary existences. Like the stout woman next to her balancing a shopping basket on her knee, the couple in front, heads turned towards each other, chatting, sharing a life, the men with their evening newspapers, macintoshes glistening from the drizzle, umbrellas, parcels, coughs and sneezes, the warm damp cosiness compared with the raw night outside, the reliable sameness of it – a number nineteen bus packed with men and women going home, doing most of them today what they had done yesterday and would do tomorrow.

Those three she'd been with. You couldn't imagine any one of them squeezed in against the side of a bus like she was by a bulging woman squashing in beside her, or standing like the permitted five men and women in the centre aisle, swaying at the corners, peering over the heads of those lucky enough to have a seat to try to pick out a familiar landmark that told them the next stop was theirs. Did they ever use a bus? Beatrice and Solly Kornblath and that architect? What was his name? Funny one. One she'd never heard before. What was it? Rackham! Martin Rackham. That's right. No, of course they didn't. It was always taxis and Rolls Royces and liveried chauffeurs . . .

Hurry, bus, hurry! What was it? What was the hold-up? It was impossible to know. It must be at least five minutes they'd been stuck here by that house. How far were they from Aberdeen Park? Perhaps it'd be quicker to get off now. She rose a little in her seat. The woman next to her looked up at her in surprise. A woman with a fat, healthy, cheerful face. "Going to get off, luv?" She made as if to lift her shopping basket off her ample knees.

"No. No, I don't think so."

"How far you goin'?"

"Aberdeen Park."

"Oh!"

She'd impressed the woman. She probably thought she lived in one of the grand houses. No – she wouldn't! Not going home by bus. "How far are *you* going?"

"Highbury Barn."

Highbury Barn! Tom! And all those bottles of terrible scent he used to bring home from the pub as peace offerings for his boozing. Mustn't think about all that! Think of something else. Highbury! How her life had revolved round Highbury since Sam had lost their money trading in jute! If only he'd had a company like Joseph Mott had, how different life would have been. But that was a nice letter he'd sent her about Tom. A kind, thoughtful letter. She'd have to reply to it. Or would she? It hadn't called for a reply. That was intentional of course – the way it was worded. He'd shed the responsibility of Dessy and Thady. He wouldn't want it back. And he'd got his own house and his bridge club now – both financed by Joseph of course. What a strange relationship those two had had since meeting at school. It had been a disaster their meeting, Hetty had always said. On the other hand the one certain thing in Sam's life was that Joseph would never let him starve. What was it Sam's mother used to say about Joseph Mott? "The Jew, he will never let him drown – neither will he let him swim!" Or had that been Hetty?

Hetty! *She* hadn't written. Of course she was back in the wilds of Africa and most likely hadn't heard about Tom . . . But surely there were newspapers even there? It had been in all of them here. Even in the better ones. And in all the evening papers. And on the placards. Hearing the imaginary voice of a newsvendor ringing in her ears, she forgot all about Hetty. "Star! News! Standard! Read all abaht it! Man drahns 'imself weighed dahn wiv snooker balls! Read all abaht it! Star! News! Standard!" It had been everywhere. It had even been two hundred miles away in the *Liverpool Echo*! Ma had cut it out and sent it to her. She saw them in the back sitting-room with the curtains drawn and the table laid and the gas mantle hissing and the kettle singing on the black iron range, and Pa after a

moment speechless, open-mouthed: "Eh, Ma, listen to this!" It
had all been there, even the fact that:

> *The drowned man's widow was a Lancashire girl*
> *whose father used to play rugby league for Widnes*
> *until he lost his arm, and is now the well-known and*
> *much-loved character who's been collecting tickets*
> *at Edge Hill station for more years than I, for one,*
> *would care to remember!*

And on and on. About Sam and the divorce, and what Tom
had done for a living before he lost his job, about Dessy and
Thady, even about Paquette. It wasn't that she or Sam or Tom
had been important – it was those snooker balls. They'd caught
the public's imagination. Especially the two that were missing!
Everywhere, up and down the length and breadth of the country,
they'd been looking up from their newspapers, chuckling,
surmising, coming up with a hundred different explanations.
The reporters had seen in advance how intriguing their readers
would find it, provided they worded it dramatically enough, and
that had made it worthwhile for them to snoop and ferret and
pay bribes to hotel porters. That never occurred to you, Tom,
did it? It was meant to be a romantic message whose meaning
only I would understand. It was meant to take some of the pain
away. And it was meant as an apology. I'd driven you to it and
you'd apologised, tried to remove all blame from me. *This is a
far, far better thing that I go to do, than I have ever done . . .*
   And in a way he had been right. In a way it did ease the pain.
He'd "taken it on the chin" and when he'd slipped overboard it
would have been with "a stiff upper lip". He'd have been loyal
to his principles right to the end and there were worse things to
be loyal to than principles.
   She felt a jolt and was back to earth with an, "Oh, thank
goodness, for that! Beginning to wonder if we was going to
be here all night!" from the woman beside her. "Just as well
you changed your mind, luv."
   "Isn't it?"
   "Still drizzling?"

Peering out through the misted windows. "Yes, I think so."
"Proper November weather. Be getting foggy later I shouldn't
be surprised."

"No, nor would I. Excuse me. This'll be my stop coming."
Lifted shopping basket, squeezing past fat knees swivelled
sideways, catching her brand new skirt on a sprung fibre of
the shopping basket and hoping it wasn't snagged, squeezing
past the file standing in the aisle. "Excuse me. Sorry. Excuse
me. This is my stop. I mustn't miss it." No, I mustn't miss it with
Dessy and Thady huddled in their thin overcoats at the bottom
of the steps wondering what's happened to me. No, that's silly.
I left the key under that stone just in case. And told Dessy I was
going to. "Thank you, conductor. Very kind of you to wait."

"Mind how you go, miss. Could be slippery."

The ting of the bell, the bus drawing away, red outside, lit
inside, top and bottom, warm, ordinary, normal. Oh, come on,
car, come on! I want to get across! They'll be inside waiting,
Dessy and Thady. Why on earth didn't I come straight back
after that lunch? It didn't serve any purpose going to that
auditioning or back to Beatrice's office afterwards. Not as
far as I was concerned, it didn't. Crunch of gravel underfoot.
Aberdeen Park! Cranmore Hotel! Never imagined when I
moved into Cranmore I'd end up in a basement, only a stone's
throw away. Never know what's going to happen in life. Who'd
have thought when I left home this morning . . .

"Hallo, Mummy."

Alice kissed him. "Darling, I'm sorry I'm so late. Where's
Dessy?"

"Out."

"Out?" There was nowhere for him to go. Not at half past
six on a misty, drizzly November evening. "What's he doing?
Where's he gone?"

"Gone to be taught how to be an allo kite."

"A what!" She shook him with alarm and for the first time
noticed he'd still got his overcoat on. "Thady, what are you
talking about? And why have you still got your coat on?"

"I'm cold."

"Haven't you lit the fire? There's plenty of coal. I had a sack delivered yesterday."

"There isn't any wood."

Oh Lord, Lord, Lord! She'd meant to get off the bus and buy a couple of bundles and some milk at the corner shop near Dessy's school on the way home. And she could have done for all the time the bus had wasted – No! They'd have been closed. It had been after six.

"Well you could have lit the gas fire."

"I did but it ran out. So I put my coat on again."

"You haven't had any tea?"

"Desmond bought a swiss roll with the twopence you gave him and we scoffed that."

"All right, darling. I'll get a fire lit. But first, do you know where Dessy is?"

"You can't light a fire without wood."

"Yes, you can, I'll show you how."

They were still standing in the long narrow passage which ran between the bedroom the boys shared and the bedroom in the front where she'd slept with Tom – a passage which opened up into a small internal windowless hall off which were the doors to the rest of the semi-basement flat: next to her bedroom the coal cellar with a gas cooker at one end, and next to that the sitting-room, and next to that the kitchen with its barred windows and linoleum floor, and finally the bathroom with its copper geyser all verdigrised, and off that the lavatory where she'd tried to get rid of the last of Culverwell's letter, which had led to the row, which had led to her flouncing out after saying the terrible things she'd said to Tom – and led to his suicide just a few hours later.

She tried to thrust such reflections from her mind. "First things first, Thady. Where *is* Dessy?"

"In the church I should think. Or in Mr Lacey's house."

Alice was baffled. "What are you talking about? What church? And who's Mr Lacey?"

"He lives in the house opposite the church."

"You mean St Saviour's church?"

"It's the only one in Aberdeen Park, Mummy! Mummy, I'm cold. My teeth are chattering."

She ignored his being cold. There were more important things.

"And Mr Lacey?"

"He's the one with the twins."

Alice's brow cleared with relief. The twins. Twin girls, about Dessy's age. Very pretty with corn-coloured hair and blue eyes and very nicely turned out. Tom had laughed: "Desmond's starting young!" And she'd been so pleased. They were the first girls, so far as she knew, Dessy had ever really talked to.

"And you think he might be in their house? Or in the church? Why should he be in the church, Thady?"

"I already told you. He's being taught to be an allo kite."

"Allo kite? Oh!" In spite of everything she couldn't but smile. "Acolyte! Not allo kite, Thady. Acolyte. They carry candles at the altar."

"Yes, I know they do."

"So what happened, Thady? Did Mr Lacey make a call?"

"No, Wendy and Angela did. And they asked him to go round and have tea with them and then go to the church for Desmond to go on learning to be . . . to be what you called it."

"Acolyte," said Alice automatically. "And they didn't ask you?"

"No. They didn't."

He said it with pique and, looking into his face more carefully, Alice saw he had been crying.

Her heart was rent at the thought of Thady abandoned in a cold and empty flat by his brother and the two pretty girls. "Well that's very unkind of them!" She was of a sudden so angry she could almost have walked down the road and bearded the Lacey twins in their own house.

"They said I was too young to be an . . . acol . . . acolyte. Anyway Desmond didn't want me to go with them. Desmond doesn't like me."

"Well that's nonsense, darling." Why "darling" so often? It was a word she used only sparingly with Dessy and Thady. It was all those "darlings" in the theatre and back in Beatrice's office.

"Now look, Thady," she said, "the first thing I'm going to do is to show you how to light a fire without wood. But before that I'm going to put the kettle on so that when the fire's lit we can sit by it and get warm and have a nice hot cup of tea and you can tell me everything you've been doing today."

"I'd rather have Bovril, Mummy."

"I'll make you Bovril." It was a lie. There wasn't any Bovril. But there were some Oxo cubes; if she put in several he probably wouldn't notice.

She opened her handbag, praying there'd be a shilling in her purse and she wouldn't have to go out into the street accosting srangers to give her one in exchange for other coins. In fact there were three, and with a sense of extravagance she fed them one after the other into the gas meter which was in a small cupboard, also off the hall, which had once been a back staircase to the massive house above.

From the meter she went into the kitchen, filled the kettle and took it through the hall to the cooker in its cubby hole. There was a mouse on the gas stove, its eyes bright and red in the light of the bare bulb. It stared at her for a moment as if disputing her right to occupy its quarters, then swiftly scuttled off down the back somewhere where the cooker wouldn't be blue-mottled enamel and it would be able to get purchase. It scuttled down and apparently disturbed a second mouse for the two of them ran across the cement floor, climbed the dry-rotted frame to the wooden slats which kept the coal from falling out, and disappeared from sight.

Alice lit the gas, went into the bedroom, discarded her hat, bag, gloves and jacket, and going through in blouse and skirt into the kitchen opened a floor-level cupboard and extracted some old newspapers she'd put by for just such an occasion.

Thady, still in the overcoat which was already too short for him, was waiting for her. She noticed that on the table there was a chessboard and men set out in what looked like a fairly new game and beside the board there was a small, slim booklet with a grey cover. She knew what it was because he had asked for it for his birthday: *Pocket Guide to the Chess Openings* by someone with a Russian-sounding name. Sam had taught him the moves of chess and then never played with him. Funny that! Tom had taught him with a tennis ball how to bowl leg breaks to the big blue bread bin in the kitchen of Highbury New Park, yet never played cricket with him. Well it was lucky he found chess so fascinating and could spend hours totally absorbed, silently playing games against himself.

"Learning a new opening?" she suggested.

"It's not an opening, it's a defence," he said with faint scorn. "Alexhine's Defence. He's the world chess champion, you know."

She had heard of Dr Alexhine, who was apparently unbeatable. Sam had talked about him – not as current but as future champion. He had been very prescient. But chess itself quite baffled her and Thady knew it did and scorned asking her to play with him. And it didn't interest Desmond so Thady had no one to play against except himself.

"Yes, I do," she said, resisting bringing Sam into the conversation, which would have interested him. "Now I'm going to show you how to light a fire without wood. You get some old newspapers like these and you start to roll them up . . . Do you see?" She was demonstrating as she spoke. "And then when you've got them rolled you twist them into a knot. Like this. And then you get another sheet and roll it up and make another knot. And when you've got about half a dozen, you've got enough to light a fire. Now the next thing you do is empty the grate of cinders."

They had had a fire the previous evening and before going out that morning she'd cleared the grate, carefully saving the cinders, and then put the cinders back into the grate. Now she removed them and layered the grate with paper, placed the knots on top and carefully spread the cinders on them.

"Get me a bucket of coal, Thady, will you?" she ordered him. "Smallish pieces."

"Yes, Mummy."

He went to the coal cellar, disturbing mice, which didn't

bother him. He was very used to mice and, often by himself, quite enjoyed standing watching them running up and down the pipes. He had names for some of them and hated having to remove the dead ones caught in traps. He gave every one a ceremonious burial in the patch of front garden to number 67, Aberdeen Park, which the landlord, Mr Stringer, had been obliged to leave for the benefit of number 67A, because there wasn't any other way of doing it.

Carrying the bucket in two-handed, Thady put it down with a bang in the hearth.

"We didn't need that much, darling . . . Thady," Alice said. "I don't think the scuttle will take it all."

"It will if we put enough on the fire to start with."

He was fully involved, doing nice calculations of volume. "Can I put it on, Mummy?"

"No, dear, not this time. I want to show you how. You put it on piece by piece. Like this." She demonstrated. "You want to be sure you balance each piece carefully so that it doesn't start falling off and causing an avalanche so that you have to start all over again. And you want to leave enough spaces so that the air can get through."

"That's because it needs oxygen. Nothing will burn without oxygen."

"Won't it?"

"No, Miss Dinsdale was telling us that the other day."

How funny, Alice thought: Miss Dinsdale taught only maths and English.

"I'm sure she's right," said Alice, who had great respect for and great hopes from Miss Dinsdale of Drayton Park Council School. "Well now we're ready to light it. Pass me the matches off the mantelpiece, will you?" She was herself seated beside the fireplace, with her legs tucked sideways and her left hand supporting her on the floor.

"Can I light it, Mummy?

"All right dear, but please be careful. And strike the matches away from you."

Thady struck a match successfully and lit the projecting edges of newspaper and, still in his overcoat, sat down beside his mother to watch events. This was a treat. To have Mummy to himself, to be sitting beside her sharing a new adventure. He glanced away from the curling flames for a moment to look her up and down.

"I've never seen you wear that before," he decided, noticing the frill which concealed the buttons of Alice's blouse.

"No, dear, it's new."

"Was it important where you had to go today?"

"Very important."

"Like when you and Uncle Tom went to St Olive's to see if it was right for us to go to school to?"

It was funny how "Pops" had become "Uncle Tom" again – something decided between the two of them.

"Yes, Thady. Something like that."

"It wasn't to do with us going to another school was it?"

"No."

"You won't take us away to other schools will you, Mummy?"

"You both like it where you are?"

"Desmond says he does. And I've made a friend at mine."

"Have you, dear?" She said it with surprise and genuine enthusiasm.

Thady nodded his head up and down vigorously. His hair was shorn short now – twopenny worth of back and sides at a barber with a fish tank to hold attention while he worked.

"What's his name?"

"Sidney. He's going to get a scholarship as well and we're going to go to the same school together."

"What's his other name?"

"Wilcox."

"And where does he live?"

"Addington Mansions."

Alice knew where Addington Mansions was – it was a large development of council flats she had passed every day when walking up Highbury Grange from Belmont.

She wondered what Sidney Wilcox would be like. If he lived in a council block, it would be improbable he spoke the way that Dessy and Thady did. He might be a bad influence. But she held her tongue. If Thady'd made a real friend it would be his very first.

"It doesn't seem to be doing much good," Thady complained, looking at the mass of twisted paper and coal. The flames had died down and although some of the edges of the knots glowed orange-red, the mass as a whole looked anything but promising.

"Well, now, Thady," Alice decided. "I'm going to show you what you do. And if either you or Dessy have to do it yourself I want you to be very careful and do exactly as I do." She got up on her knees and picking up a spare sheet of newspaper held it across the fireplace opening, leaving a space at the bottom for air to be drawn through. As if by magic, flames at once appeared behind the newspaper accompanied by a great roaring sound. Alice took the paper away. "There, you see," she said. "You hold the paper just long enough to get it going again. Now leave it alone, I'm going to go and make your Bovril and my tea."

"It won't go out will it?"

Alice cast a professional eye on the fire. "No, I don't think so and if it does I'll put the newspaper up to it again."

"Can I do it?"

"No, not yet, Thady, there's something else I want to show you. What to do if the newspaper catches fire. Be a good boy and leave it while I make the tea."

She went into the kitchen, aware of an unusual sense of purpose. Why didn't I buy a cake to celebrate, she chided herself. I could so easily have got one in Oxford Street or somewhere. I didn't really think of *them* at all. I just thought of myself and how bad a mother I've been to them.

She got out the brown teapot which her mother had given her, telling her that it was only brown teapots made good tea, and opened a new packet of Lyons 7d Green Label Tea. Then going to the coal hole she brought the kettle back to the boil, and carrying it into the kitchen religiously warmed the teapot and put in two teaspoons. She got the milk out of the larder and sniffed it to make sure it hadn't gone off and filled the sugar bowl. And then she emptied the sugar back into the jar and refilled the bowl with lumps, because whenever she had tea

Thady liked helping himself to lumps of sugar. Then she peeled four Oxo cubes of their silver paper and put them into the mug with the railway train on it and filled it with boiling water, stirring it round and round till all the lumps had disappeared. She put a tray cloth on the tray and, laying it with the tea things and the fake Bovril, took it into the sitting-room and put the tray down on the Jacobean table, then went back into the kitchen and sorted through the tin of broken biscuits, choosing the largest pieces. The biscuits were Desmond's favourite kind and were called "Playtime", being covered with a smooth glaze on which small figures had been piped; Thady preferred bourbon and she wished she'd bought broken bourbon now . . .

She stopped at the thought, realising what it meant. That she'd had a choice between them and chosen Desmond. And wished she hadn't. And then she thought of something else – that she just could not remember when she had last sat down and chatted about unimportant things to Thady. Or to either of them for that matter. It hadn't seemed to arise. At Belmont it had been all go, or they'd been in Liverpool, or she'd been at work and they'd been at boarding school, or Tom had been with her, or he wasn't and she was worried stiff he'd be coming back drunk any minute. And if she found herself with them on their own, they'd usually been the two of them together. And somehow that was different from how it was now, sitting beside the fireplace with Thady. And of a sudden she was anxious to get back in with him before Dessy came back.

"Can we use the paper again to make a draught?"

Alice looked at the fire. It was a bit choked and disreputable-looking, with blackened remnants of newspaper, but it was going to be all right.

"Yes," she said with sudden eagerness. "Look, I want to show you something."

She took an unused sheet of newspaper and held it as she had before across the fireplace. At once, obediently, the flames began to grow, and grow, and grow, and the fire began to roar, louder and louder, fiercer and fiercer, more and more dramatic. Thady watched entranced. Then he saw the paper beginning to brown and crisp. "Mummy, Mummy!" he shouted in alarm. "It's going to catch fire!"

"I know it is, dear," Alice shouted back with glee. "Watch!"

Thady watched, transfixed, and of a sudden the paper caught, right in its centre where the flames were strongest and the heat was greatest.

"Mummy! Watch out!" Thady shouted.

But Alice laughed, laughed as she hadn't laughed for days, for weeks, for months, and all in a movement brought her hands together then released the burning newspaper, which caught by the draught it had engendered, with a wonderful-sounding *swoosh*, vanished up the chimney! And Thady stared at her in utter delight. Maskelyne Devant himself could not have been more impressive. This was a Mummy he had never known before.

It was at that precise moment that Desmond and Williams arrived. Mr Stringer had provided only a knocker, not a bell, and at first, through her laughter and the roaring of the fire and the swooshing of the blazing paper up the chimney, they didn't hear the knocking. In fact Alice didn't hear it at all and it needed Thady to touch her arm and say, "Mummy, there's someone at the door!"

Oh, no! Alice thought. Oh, no! It did not cross her mind it might be Desmond coming back home, in fact she made no mental conjectures as to who it might be – her soul was too filled with the tragedy of being, at the very moment of drawing so close to Thady, interrupted.

And she knew that Thady shared her feelings.

"It'll probably be Desmond coming back," he said – and in his tone there was resentment, for all the world like that of any young child who is having a wonderfully happy time making sandcastles, or at a party, or fishing, or flying a kite, who is of a sudden ruthlessly informed by an adult it is time to finish and come home.

"Yes, dear," Alice said. "I expect it is." And to his astonishment she put her arms around him and held him so close against her that he could feel the softness of her breasts against his chest and the smell of her hair was in his nostrils. "Oh, Thady," she said, "we must light lots and lots of fires together! And do all sorts of other things. And we will, I promise you!"

And she was gone and Thady knew a sense of joy which was so stunning in its effect that tears started pouring from his eyes.

Alice opened the door. To gain access to the basement there was a flight of steps followed by a sort of alleyway, and with Williams standing a pace or two behind Desmond, she didn't at first see him.

"Oh!" she said, crossly. "It's you! If you hadn't come soon I was going to come out and look for you." And then she saw Williams and his dog-collar. "Oh," she said again in a different tone.

"I hope you don't mind, Mrs Fenwick," Williams said, "but I took the liberty of bringing Desmond back. It's such an unpleasant night."

And indeed it was, with the fog thickening and the trees overhanging the entrance dripping moisture.

"No, it's very thoughtful of you," Alice said over-quickly, without thinking.

"And I did so want to meet you," Williams said as quickly, conscious that otherwise he would probably be dismissed.

"Mr Williams is the vicar of St Saviour's church where I'm training to be an acolyte," Desmond said.

"Yes, I know."

"How do you know, Mummy? I never told you."

"Thady did."

"Well he shouldn't have. It was meant to be a secret."

This couldn't go on. "Please come in out of the wet . . . vicar?" Alice said, stumbling a little.

"If I may. I would very much like to talk to you."

Alice's heart sank into her boots.

"Well it'll have to be fairly brief, Mr Williams," she said. "I have to get the children's supper."

"I won't keep you long, I promise."

"Very well." She turned to show him the way and saw Thady hurrying into the bathroom.

"Go into the kitchen, Desmond," she said firmly. "And when Thady comes out of the lavatory tell him to wait in there with you. I'll be in in a minute to make you your supper." And, rather wearily, as Desmond hesitated, "Oh, do what I say, Dessy, there's a good boy. This way, vicar." And she led him into the sitting-room which, fortunately, had no door from it to the kitchen. "Please get warm by the fire, Mr Williams. I really must get the children's supper. I'll be as quick as I can."

Williams had noted the cooker standing starkly in the coal cellar and the mustiness of a semi-basement assailed his nostrils, but it was the sitting-room which depressed him most. It had the precise emptiness he had found in the sitting-rooms of young newlyweds who had managed to scrape together a sufficient deposit to have delivered on hire purchase dining and sitting-room suites but otherwise had only odd wedding presents with which to furnish their new home; in this case, as it were, a standard lamp, a few brass ornaments and plates, a curious huge brass box, a coal scuttle and fire irons, brass again, and a wind-up gramophone with the usual enormous horn. There were no books, there were no family photographs, and apart from a framed print of *The Laughing Cavalier* there were no pictures. In a word there was, with only one exception, nothing which would have furnished a stranger with the least clue as to the background, history and interests of those who lived here. Taking into account all that rumour had enabled him to piece together of Mrs Fenwick's past and apparently frenetic life, he found this remarkable.

The one exception was the chessboard with the manual of opening moves beside it. A chess player himself (and anyway aware that he was anything but welcome), he refrained from taking one of the armchairs drawn in front of the fire, but passed the not inconsiderable time until Alice (who had been boiling potatoes and cooking sausages) rejoined him, analysing the game in progress, and when she came in, still wearing the expensive blouse and the skirt of her tailor-made suit, asked: "Who's the chess player, Mrs Fenwick?"

Alice did not answer immediately, but studied him in a manner which clearly indicated she wanted to sum him up

78

before she decided how much time she was prepared to allow him. His manifestation had quite put her out of countenance. Quite apart from cruelly destroying an unprecedented sense of intimacy with the son who until now had always had second place in her affections, she had been looking forward, as soon as the children had been put to bed, to relaxing in a bath endlessly topped up with scalding water from the geyser and reflecting on all that had happened in the astonishing day now drawing to its close. About the last thing that appealed to her was to be taken to task by a parson, as guilt suggested she was going to be, for neglecting one son while enjoying the company of the other. And besides – and this not of the least account – she had the typical unease of a non-churchgoer finding herself buttonholed by a cleric.

"Thady is," she said. "It's his favourite occupation." This wasn't quite true; Thady preferred fishing – and stamp-collecting ran chess fairly close. But it seemed a good way of limiting the conversation.

"Not Desmond?" There was a hint of surprise, even of disappointment in the question.

"No, Mr Williams. That sort of thing has never interested him."

That sort of thing. He wondered at the full meaning of the words. "They're very alike to look at," he said.

"They're like their father," Alice said, as she thought unhelpfully, but in fact by her very unhelpfulness providing him with the opening he needed.

"Mrs Fenwick," he said, smiling, "let me get it off my chest. I feel very guilty at not having called on you before. I quite appreciate that my calling might well have been unwelcome to you, but that is something I should have risked."

"Considering that I have never even been in your church I don't see why you should feel guilty," Alice answered shortly.

He resisted responding to this and said, in the manner of a man about to take his leave: "I don't suppose there *is* any way in which you feel I can be of help, but if you think I can be of service to you I hope you will not hesitate to let me know."

Alice was a trifle disarmed. They had been in eye contact

all the time and she could not but absorb the good-natured expression on his face, the kindliness in his eyes and the touch of amusement in upturned lips under the rather bushy moustache he affected. Besides, she had made him wait the best part of half an hour. She could hardly show him the door so abruptly.

"Why don't you sit down, Mr Williams?" she suggested.

"Well, thank you," he responded with alacrity and, seating himself in one of the armchairs, held out his hands to the blaze. "What a splendid fire!"

"Isn't it," Alice said, seating herself in the second armchair.

"Your other son . . . Thady, I think you said; how old is he, Mrs Fenwick?"

"Nine."

"Nine." He cocked his head in the manner of a man impressed – which indeed he was. "That's very young to be studying chess openings."

"He says it isn't an opening he's studying. It's a defence."

"Yes, Alexhine's." His smile broadened. "And the only reason I know that, Mrs Fenwick, is because that's where the manual's open. Does he play at school?" And at the shake of her head. "Where then?"

"He just plays himself. He hasn't anyone to play with."

"I could find him an opponent."

"Could you?"

He nodded. "There's a boy I know who's very keen. He's two or three years older than Thady is but that shouldn't matter. Or, if you wouldn't mind, he could come round and have a game with me occasionally."

"Why should I mind?"

He answered indirectly. "Do you mind Desmond becoming an acolyte?"

Yes, here it comes, she thought. He was bound to drag it round to religion in the end. Well one thing was certain – he wasn't going to do any of his proselytising here.

"Frankly, Mr Williams," she said, "I'm not a regular church-goer and I don't really know what an acolyte is or does."

"He carries a candle at the altar and generally assists." And before she could have spoken. "I don't think you need worry, Mrs Fenwick, that your son has suddenly found a calling in religion. And what I think you might be grateful for, is that he has made a discovery which is going to bring him endless joy and satisfaction until the end of his days." And at her frown: "Music, Mrs Fenwick. Or, to be more precise, although I don't really like the term, classical music."

"Desmond?" She could hardly have sounded more incredulous.

"Desmond," he agreed. And gently: "Mrs Fenwick, if you had been in my church half an hour ago and seen how spellbound he was listening to our organist playing Dvořák's 'Humoresque' you wouldn't be disbelieving me."

"It's not that I disbelieve you, Mr Williams, it's just that . . . well Desmond's never taken the slightest interest in music of any kind."

What an extraordinary ménage this is, Williams thought. Here's a woman who, if half of the rumours I've heard are correct, has had a very eventful life and yet looking around you see nothing, absolutely nothing, which would even hint at it; a woman whose husband committed suicide not a month ago, who lives in a musty, down-at-heel, semi-basement flat but dresses in a style and at an expense that would have half my parishioners green with envy; a woman with two little boys, one of whom the moment he is introduced to music of quality is overwhelmed by it – and his mother finds this almost unimaginable – and the other, aged only nine, who is studying Alexhine's Defence!

"You have two unusual children, Mrs Fenwick," he said.

Excepting only in the general manner in which all mothers are inclined to find their offspring superior, it had never occurred to Alice that either Desmond or Thady were in any way remarkable. Apart from the knack of being able to handle figures brilliantly – which of course they'd inherited from Sam – there'd been nothing momentous in their school reports and, casting her mind back through the years, the only person she could remember who'd ever said anything of the same order had been Joseph Mott, and everything that he said had been suspect anyway. But she would have been less than human if she'd been able to resist cashing in on it.

"Well I gather Desmond's doing very well at school and Thady's apparently been picked out as scholarship material," she said with a touch of pride.

"I'm not surprised. I believe you have two sons of tremendous promise." He paused. A coal shifted in the fire and might have toppled out of the grate had not Alice with, as he thought, marvellously quick reaction, seized the tongs and replaced it safely. Looking at her doing this he sought to find something of her children in her. He found nothing. Here were no large eyes shaded by sweeping eyelashes; their foreheads had a depth hers lacked, only perhaps in the chins was there a similarity. Their remarkable likeness to each other must have been inherited. He wondered what sort of man her first husband was.

Meanwhile, tidying up the fire had given Alice time to decide how best to deal with the situation. The man had come around unbidden, no doubt amongst other reasons to satisfy his curiosity as to what sort of a woman it took to divorce her first husband and have the second commit suicide and how she intended to carry on from here. Well, then, she would tell him.

"It's very nice of you to be so complimentary," she said, sitting back in the second armchair. "And of course I hope you will be proved correct. But they are going to have a problem which most boys of their age don't have. They have to be clothed and fed and all that sort of thing, Mr Williams, and as they don't have a father and I don't have a pot of gold, it means that I am going to have to go out and work. I intend to send them off to school with a good breakfast inside them but after that, until I get back in the evening, they are going to have to manage on their own."

"You have no family who can help?"

"Oh, I've got a family. Quite a large one. But they all live two hundred miles away. In Liverpool mostly." She had begun quite to enjoy herself. She was even tempted to add that, considering the way she'd slighted her brother and sisters because they would never have fitted into the life she had lived while in

Belmont, they probably wouldn't have been willing to help even if they had been near. But she resisted it. "And before you ask," she went on breezily, "I have no friends. Only a large number of acquaintances who would be only too happy to have a game of tennis with me but who would all find themselves frightfully busy doing other things if I suggested they popped in to give my children their tea."

She knew her behaviour towards him to be ungrateful and outrageous, but she had good reason to divine correctly the general attitude of Aberdeen Park towards her and she could not but lump him, their vicar, with it. She saw herself, apart from Dessy and Thady, utterly alone in the world and, however depressing that was bound to be at times, she was at least cleansed of the encumbrances which marriage had always brought. From now on she would be free to make her own decisions; she had no need of advice on what she should or should not do and how she should behave from all and sundry, and especially not from a priest!

Misunderstanding his motives she thus cast herself in a poor light and, in spite of his resolve not to be biased against her by the rumours and tittle-tattle which as the local cleric he could hardly avoid having poured into his ears, Williams found himself making an unjust appraisal. Here was a woman who had obviously divorced one man (he was worldly-wise enough not to take too seriously the grounds on which the locality knew the divorce had been granted, and anyway he had heard from several sources that Mr Jordan was a gentleman who always behaved impeccably with ladies) . . . who had obviously divorced one man in order to marry another – himself a divorcee – and thus put herself ahead of the children to whom she owed first duty. And there were other factors: there was the evidence of an expensive outfit which contrasted so discreditably with the shabbiness of the home her children had to live in; there was the background of a married life spent largely in Belmont Hotel with its local reputation for frivolity at best, and where it was said she had been quite the belle; there was the known fact that even before she'd divorced her first husband she had been in the habit of shipping off her children to Liverpool or boarding schools. No, he told himself, it wasn't really all that surprising that one son had been driven by the emptiness of his home life to seek solace in music or the other to absorb himself in chess at such a tender age.

It was, he decided, time to go. The woman wasn't looking for help, she was enjoying scoring points. But he must be charitable. Losing a husband in such a ghastly way was enough to sour anyone who did not have faith to give her strength and comfort. And however much she had brought this unhappy situation on herself by the way she had chosen to live her life, the future ahead of her looked bleak indeed.

"Mrs Fenwick," he said, "you would not think, I suppose, of attending one or two services at my church, would you?" And he held up a hand to prevent her replying immediately. "If you did, you would I am afraid meet a number of men and women whose behaviour towards you would be embarrassing. On the other hand you would also meet others who are good people and might very well be willing to help you. Not permanently, of course. That would be expecting too much. But who might be able to, shall we say, step into the breach, until you have been able to sort things out."

Alice, who saw this largely as a stratagem to increase his congregation, responded: "Mr Williams, I am a practical woman. I have some idea of the general opinion the locality holds of me and I don't think it is such as to enthuse many of the good people you have in mind to hold the fort, as my late husband would have said, while I am out at work. And the odd ones who might come once or twice would soon get tired of trying to cope with two young boys, who are at different schools and will be coming home at different times, to a basement flat which is cold, damp and overrun with mice."

"In a crisis situation—"

She stopped him. "Yes. It *is* a crisis situation, Mr Williams, but I have been in crisis situations before and found the way to deal with them. And I intend to do so now. And not by some stop-gap solution. That would get neither me nor my children anywhere. I have to find a *permanent* solution and I intend to do so. In the meantime Desmond and Thady will have to manage as best they can. As I've said I shall see they have a good breakfast before they set off for school and I will see they have a decent meal before they go to bed. Over the weekends they will have all my time but in the week they will simply have to manage as best they can. As my husband, my *first* husband, would have said, it's a question of Hobson's choice." She stood. "Thank you again for coming. If you can arrange for someone to play chess with Thady, providing they get on together, and children don't always, that would be very nice; as for Desmond, I have not the least objection to him continuing to be an acolyte and attending your church as often as he likes."

Williams, already on his feet, held out his hand, a wry smile on his face. "I'll say goodnight then, Mrs Fenwick. I take your point of course but all the same I'm sorry that, if only in the short term, you don't feel inclined to let me try to help you in any way—"

Alice had timed it well. "I didn't say that, Mr Williams. It might very well be that in the short term there's a way that you could help."

"Eh?" he said, quite taken aback.

"You know my landlords, don't you?" she said. "Mr and Mrs Stringer. They attend your church regularly, don't they?"

"I hardly think . . ." he began, misunderstanding.

For the first time Alice smiled, and he saw for all the tiredness under her eyes what a pretty woman she was.

"Neither do I," she agreed. "But I wasn't going to suggest you put it to them to have my children up for tea. No." She went across to the sideboard and, opening the tiny door to one of two compartments in its upper half, took out an envelope.

"This came for me by hand this morning," she said. "Just before I went out to keep a rather important appointment. I'd like you to read it, if you would."

As she stood there facing him, purposeful-looking in her expensive blouse and well-cut skirt, holding out the envelope for him to take, of a sudden he saw the strength in her, the same strength which had persuaded Solly Kornblath that this was a woman well worth backing.

He took the envelope and the letter from it. The paper was

of quality, thick, parchment-like; the address was printed: 67,
Aberdeen Park, Islington, N5; the date the previous day's, the
wording typed:

> *Dear Mrs Fenwick,*
>
> *Over the past few weeks I have been put under
> considerable pressure by a number of my neighbours
> to terminate your tenancy. This may seem harsh, but
> Aberdeen Park is a very respectable and prestigious
> area and it is generally felt that the presence of
> yourself and your children is no longer welcome
> in it. I am sure you would not want me to expatiate
> further on their thinking.*
>
> *In view of the burden your late husband's suicide
> placed upon you, I have withheld writing before now
> and by the same token I have decided to ask you to
> terminate your tenancy within twenty-eight days of
> the above date rather than within seven as, with your
> rent being paid weekly, I am entitled to.*
>
> *Furthermore, to assist in some small way with
> the obvious expenses I realise you must incur in
> making a move, I am waiving the payment by you
> of future rent,*
>
> *Yours faithfully . . .*

The letter was signed *Stanley Stringer*.

Williams read the letter in horror and disbelief; when he
raised his eyes from it, Alice's, firm, almost triumphant, were
waiting to meet them.

"Well?" she said. One word which expressed so much: disbelief in his ability to help, scorn for his Christian congregation,
pride in her own ability to handle the situation. A terrible sense,
almost of despair, oppressed him; and as well a burning anger
which so gripped him that for quite some moments he was
beyond replying. And all the while, through them, Alice stood
defiant and contemptuous.

"Mrs Fenwick," he managed, his words thickened by
emotion, "do you want to stay living here?"

"Until I can afford to move, yes, Mr Williams."

"Then stay you will."

"In spite of that letter?" The words rang with irony.

"In spite of it." He handed the letter back to her with a hand that shook. Its envelope, forgotten, was in his other hand.

Alice nodded. He did not understand the meaning of the nod; only of the words following it.

"You have more faith in your churchgoers, than I have, Mr Williams."

3

Williams' call had destroyed Alice's interest in a long hot soak. All she now wanted to do was get the children into their bed as quickly as was decent and then get into her own, so as to be able to have an uninterrupted review of a day crammed with events and formulate some plan for dealing with problems which seemed to be piling themselves one on top of each other with each hour that passed.

As she lay with her door closed to keep out the mice, listening to their nightly scuttlings, hearing the creak of the Stringers moving around in what she had always supposed must be their dining-room above, a terrible sense of loneliness overcame her. It's being in this double bed, she told herself; I've got to get rid of it. Get myself a single bed. It'll give me more room anyway. But then she thought: I've never slept in a single bed, have I? And rack her brain as she might, she could not recall ever doing so. As a child, little Win had shared a double bed with her, then it had been Sam, in Cranmore it had been a double bed – it was what most hotels provided – and then it had been Tom. And at the thought she put her hand out beside her as if to make sure he had really gone, that it hadn't been one of those awful dreams that seem so real that when you wake from them you can't really believe it wasn't a dream at all.

But there was no Tom. She would never know that intimate closeness again: the warmth of him, the smell of him, the sounds he made when sleeping. He would never make love to her again. No man would ever make love to her again; she was sure of that. Not that the physical side of lovemaking had ever been important; she had been nearer with Tom to discovering the secret joy, the magic which some of the girls at Belmont had raved about, nearer by far than she had ever been with Sam, but in the end it had eluded her. Perhaps, she thought, if we'd had long enough together, if he hadn't lost his job, if he'd actually got that promotion, if we'd been able to buy a little house somewhere, a house with a garden, been able to live the sort of life that so many of these people here in Aberdeen Park who so despise me live, I would have found it then, because after all he loved me. Loved me enough to kill himself for my sake. For my sake and Dessy and Thady's.

"Oh, Tom," she said, patting the sheet beside her. But it was cold and she shivered – because the cold touch made her think of the cold waters of the Thames and of Tom, sinking down into them, weighted by the snooker balls, lying on the gravelly bottom and the cold weedy water passing over him. And it had been her fault. If she hadn't thrown his uselessness in his face, he would still be here beside her.

It was no good, she couldn't go on lying here, torturing herself. She couldn't sleep in the bed tonight at all. She knew it with absolute certainty: that all she would do was lie awake creating awful pictures in her mind of Tom lying in the bottom of the river with the weeds and the fish . . . Ugh! She threw off the bedclothes and took her dressing-gown off the hook on the back of the door. Doing so, exposed Tom's dressing-gown which had shared a hook. I must get rid of it, she told herself, I must get rid of all his clothes. It was what I was going to do, but seeing that blazer with the Exiles crest of which he'd been so proud stopped me, made me feel I ought to allow a decent interval to elapse before I rid myself of the last tangible evidence of his being. But it's long enough now. I must get rid of them. I suppose . . . No, that wouldn't be right. Selling them. However much I need the money. I'll give them away. To the Red Cross or something. Anyway, what would I get? A couple of pounds, perhaps? And Mr Kornblath's going to put five thousand pounds into Holly Wood Gowns. Oh, it's so ridiculous!

She had sat on the edge of the bed thinking these things but it was too cold to sit there long. She'd go in the kitchen and light the gas fire. Unless the fire in the sitting-room was still alight. I know, she thought, I'll take the eiderdown and a blanket and get the sitting-room fire going and spend the night there. Or at least stay there until I'm so tired I know I'm going to go to sleep, even in here.

She took the eiderdown and the top blanket of the bed but had to deposit them on the floor to open the bedroom door. It squeaked alarmingly. Oh, dear, she thought, I'm going to wake them. Whatever I do I mustn't wake them. They'll wonder what on earth I'm at creeping around the flat in the middle of the night with a blanket and an eiderdown. Thank heavens their door is closed to keep the mice out. There was after all some benefit in living in a basement flat that was crawling with mice which never seemed to diminish in numbers, no matter how many traps you set!

The light from the bedroom spilled into the inner hall. I'll turn it off, she thought, once I've got myself organised in the sitting-room. I'll come back and turn it off – there's no sense in wasting electricity, it's so expensive.

She made her way across the inner hall into the sitting-room and somehow managed to open its door, again closed against the mice, for all the encumbrance of bedding which she dumped temporarily. She saw with relief the fire was still glowing, reached for the switch by the door and turned on the light, then crept into the kitchen to find a sheet of newspaper to draw it up. There were mice in the kitchen, they'd gnawed a hole in the bottom of the door. It had been something Tom had said he'd get fixed, but hadn't. She saw one scrurrying along beside the skirting and mysteriously disappearing. They probably don't *have* to come in through the hole at the bottom of the kitchen door, she thought; they've probably got all sorts of other entries. She collected a few sheets of newspaper, went out of the kitchen closing the door behind her, crossed the inner hall again and turned out the bedroom light. She heard the rustle of mice in the coal cellar but she was so used to them there they didn't bother her; she went into the sitting-room, closed its door, inspected the fire, put some small coal on it, drew it up the way she'd shown Thady, put more coal on it, drew an armchair near to it, draped herself with bedding and prepared herself to think things out.

She had felt like a thief in the night creeping round the flat but doing so had had a therapeutic effect. She was rid of the hobgoblins of bodies lying on river beds or, even more terrifying, upright, weighed down at the ankles and swaying in the current. Or at least she was rid of them temporarily.

I must think things out, she told herself. I must go through everything that's happened, remember everything that all these people have said to me and decide how I'm going to find a way out of this impossible situation. Oh, but it's so absurd! Here's a man offering me a fortune and I have to buy broken biscuits and daren't even leave a light I'm not using switched on. Suppose . . . suppose I was to ask Mr Kornblath to advance me enough to tide me over. Explain the pickle I'm in. No! She shook her head, every instinct warning her that whatever else she did that was something she mustn't do. Against the background of his opulent apartment and over lunch in one of London's most expensive and exclusive restaurants, he'd respected her; holding out a begging bowl, telling him that within four weeks she was going to be out in the street looking for somewhere else to live, would utterly destroy that respect.

So what do I do? Accept that thousand pounds Beatrice Culverwell has amazingly offered to give me? She shook her head. No. An opportunity like this is never going to come my way again. If I turn it down I'll be regretting it all my life. Somehow I've got to manage until I get Holly Wood Gowns started. But how? In four weeks I've got to find somewhere else to live. That parson's not going to get anywhere with Stringer, that's for sure. And a new landlord's going to want a deposit. And there's the cost of moving. And there's the electricity bill. And Tom's funeral took most of what little I had left. And Thady has got to have new shoes. And there's food and fares and everything. Even the little that Tom had left is held up until those wretched solicitors get probate. And I don't know when Mr Kornblath is going to let me have that five thousand pounds anyway. There's bound to have to be some form of agreement and Lord knows how long that's going to take getting out. Borrow some money? Who from? A bank? She laughed softly and bitterly. Alice Fenwick, can you see a bank lending money to a woman with two children who's just been pitched out of her flat because her landlord can't bear having her living in it?

I need someone to talk to. Someone to advise me. But there isn't anybody. Isn't it extraordinary? I've lived all these years, and done all the things I've done and there's not one single person I know I can go to now. Not even Culverwell any more. And then it struck her. It had always been like that. She had been married to two men and neither of them had ever been of the slightest use in dealing with the sort of problems she had to deal with now. In all these years there had been only one man who could have been of the slightest use. Joseph Mott. And she'd ditched herself with him.

And it wasn't as if it was only money she had to think about. There was Dessy and Thady's ordinary day-to-day existence. It was all very well telling that vicar that she'd send them off to school with a good breakfast and be back in time to give them an evening meal, but business didn't work like that. There were bound to be evenings when she wouldn't be able to get back until very late. And what about the holidays? Christmas would soon be on them. What were they to do with themselves all day? Oh, Tom, she thought, why didn't you think of that before you did what you did? It might have been topsy-turvy, you staying at home and looking after Dessy and Thady while I was the breadwinner, but it would have been an answer. Only of course it wouldn't have been. Because that was what lay behind his doing it. His pride would never have allowed him to be little better than a gigolo.

Oh, dear, she thought, round and round it goes. And I keep looking for the perfect answer and I know there isn't one. So what do I do? Neglect my children? Or turn down the last opportunity I'm ever going to have to give them a decent home and a way of life that at least isn't restricted and plagued by money worries? But she was only asking herself questions to which she knew the answers. She had no choice. Somehow she had to cope with the immediate crisis, and after she'd done that throw everything into making a success of Holly Wood Gowns. It must take priority even over Dessy and Thady because only through its success could they have the opportunities so far denied to them through her own mismanagement of their lives. I have to make myself rich, she resolved, and not just rich, but influential too. I must allow nothing to deflect me. I must be single-minded, self-controlled and use all the skills I have. I must be strong when the circumstances call for ruthlessness and feminine when they call for guile. Nothing must hold me back, nothing must stand in the way, not even Dessy and Thady's immediate comfort. And if they come to believe, as I suppose they must, that they take second place to their mother's business, that will be something I will have to accept and hope that one day when I've been able to give them a decent start in their adult life, they'll understand.

She felt strengthened and ready now to go to bed and sleep. But before she did she tiptoed to the children's bedroom and, very quietly opening their door, stood looking down on them, both sound asleep, heads almost touching.

I'm all they have, she thought and they're all that I have. I must, I will, succeed.

Five

1

The week which followed the arrival of Stringer's letter was one of unremitting anxiety, through which Alice was continually asking herself whether Kornblath was expecting her to get in touch with him and as continually telling herself that to do so would be presumptuous and quite possibly annoy him enough to have him abandon the project. Then another letter dropped on the passage floor and, seeing from the ornate corner printing on the envelope that it was from Hickson, Battersby, Solicitors of Gray's Inn Square, and quite certain it was an official notice to quit the flat, and perhaps even sooner than Stringer had stipulated, she opened it with a shaking hand only to discover that it contained a curt request to attend Hickson, Battersby's offices to meet with Sir Duncan Bebb with a view to furthering the arrangements Mr Solomon Kornblath was proposing to put in hand with her.

Stunned by an amalgam of relief and apprehension, she stared at the note, her eyes riveted to the title which seemed in one short syllable to sum up the world into which she had the temerity to think she could insinuate herself. She had never met, nor ever imagined she would meet, anyone with a title, let alone be required to attend, as she saw it, an interview with someone who had one. Knights and their Ladies, like Lords and Dukes and their Ladies, were people you read about, whose photographs you saw in the newspapers and the better magazines. In the world in which she moved, they simply did not exist.

The children had left for school and for quite some minutes she wandered about the empty flat, letter in hand, her mind a

93

confusion of conflicting thoughts and emotions. But paramount among them was that it was going to happen. *It was going to happen!* The doubts which had plagued her through the past few endless days could be put at rest! Dessy, Thady, you should be here so that I could throw my arms around you and tell you that soon all those things you would so dearly like to have can be yours: that bicycle, Dessy, that special fishing rod, Thady, all the clothes and shoes you need, a wireless, an ice box, a larder crammed with all the things you like to eat and have so seldom! Only one question undermined her rapture: how was she going to manage until the money started coming in? Perhaps, she told herself, I can get an advance from Mr Kornblath? But immediately she rejected the idea, stamping her foot in annoyance at herself for even entertaining such a notion.

"No! No! No!" she called aloud. "You've already been through that! You *mustn't* let on how desperate the situation is." And then she thought: nor must this man I've got to see, *Sir* Duncan Bebb, know either. And at once, new questions assailed her. How do I address him? What do I wear? Oh, she yearned, if only there was someone, someone, someone, I could go to for advice? That vicar of St Saviour's church where Dessy is training to be an acolyte! What's his name? Williams! He'd know. He'd know for sure. Vicars meet all sorts of people. It's part of their business, meeting people, isn't it? And Mr Stringer. If he knew who I was going to see, the things I was going to do, would he let me at least stay here until the money started coming in? Oh money, money, money!

But at once she reproved herself. Stop dwelling on it, Alice! There's a gap to be got over and somehow you're going to have to find the way to do it. Brooding's just a waste of time and energy. What you've got to do is concentrate on what's immediate and important: what you're going to wear when you go to see this Sir Duncan Bebb, how you address him and what he's likely to ask you so that you have your answers ready!

2

After much thought she decided to wear the suit and blouse she had bought to impress Kornblath and catching the number nineteen bus, which seemed to be her inevitable conveyance when anything of importance in her life was about to happen, she alighted at the top of Gray's Inn Road. Trying to suppress a wildly beating heart, she made her way down it until, coming to an opening in the high brick wall to her right, she turned into a narrow courtyard bounded on the other side by a terrace of buildings in the Georgian style and thence by an arch at its end into Gray's Inn Square itself. This, she discovered, was bounded on all four sides by more Georgian terraces, whose repetitive façades were pierced at regular intervals with numbered openings and cream-painted panels on which were lettered the names of the professional firms who occupied the various chambers. After some difficulty she located Hickson, Battersby on the western side of the square and discovered that, unlike the great majority of professional firms who occupied but one set of chambers, they had no less than three.

Mounting to the first floor by a flight of stone steps whose treads had been scolloped out by the feet of occupants and litigants over many generations, she found herself faced by a massive black door with 'Hickson, Battersby', followed by a list of partners' names headed by 'Sir Duncan Bebb', painted on it. She pressed the bell push and after some delay the door was opened by a rigidly erect, bespectacled, ascetic-looking and severely dressed woman.

Alice straightened her shoulders.

"Good morning," she said.

"Good morning, madam."

"I am Mrs Fenwick. I have an appointment. With Sir Duncan." It was all rehearsed. Alice had had a brainwave and picked the brains of the local librarian.

"Ah!" From the change of tone, Alice knew she had scored points. "Will you come this way, madam. I think you are a little early, are you not?"

She was led along a narrow passage and deposited in a waiting-room. There were several chairs and a table with a selection of morning newspapers and copies of upper-class magazines. A military-looking gentleman, immersed in studying a formidable-looking document, rose courteously to his feet and said, "Good morning." And then, as soon as the gorgon had withdrawn, he reseated himself, saying: "If you'll excuse me, I have to do my homework," and reimmersed himself in his document. Apart from the flicking sound as he turned a page it was deathly quiet. Alice reached for a magazine at random and found herself thumbing through a copy of *Punch*, finding nothing in it of the least amusement.

After an eternity the gorgon reappeared. "Sir Duncan will see you now." Alice felt she could easily have been at the dentist's.

Bebb proved to be a tall man with a waxy face, a beaky nose and black hair immaculately laid with a central parting on his dome-shaped head. He was as impeccably dressed as if when he was done with her he was going to go on directly to a wedding. His office was not over-large and its furnishings consisted of nothing more than a massive desk, a sufficiency of chairs and a bookcase as immaculately filled with books to do with law as Sir Duncan's morning dress was filled with Bebb himself. Alice could not but draw a comparison between him and the scruffy Mr Weldon, of Gibson and Weldon, who had handled her divorce, and between the clinical impassivity of an office which was devoid of a single document which hinted at what took place between its walls and the desk and floor of Mr Weldon's office, both of which were always scattered willy-nilly with folders tied with pink ribbon as if the firm could afford neither secretaries nor filing cabinets.

Sir Duncan rose briefly, invited Alice to take the chair across from him and sat down again with his back to the vast green lawns of Gray's Inn gardens.

"Now, Mrs Fenwick," he began. "My letter explained to you the purpose of this meeting. To further the arrangements Mr Kornblath has decided to put in hand between yourself and him."

"Yes," Alice said firmly.

"We have been retained by Mr Kornblath to draw up the

96

agreement. You, Mrs Fenwick, are presumably being advised
by your own solicitors. If you will be good enough to let me
know who they are I will arrange to let them have a draft as
soon as it has been prepared."

Not for a moment had it occurred to Alice to appoint a
lawyer to guard her interests but, looking him in the eye, she
replied without hesitation: "Yes, of course. They're Gibson and
Weldon."

"Gibson and Weldon," Bebb repeated, not allowing a wrin-
kle to crease his waxy face and disclose that they were a firm
of which he had never heard, but in fact giving the game away
by opening a drawer in his desk and taking from it a notepad on
which, with a gold fountain pen withdrawn from his pocket, he
wrote down the name.

"They're in Kingly Street—" Alice began, and would have
gone on to give their address which was etched on her mind,
so often had she had to attend upon them in connection with the
divorce petition.

But Bebb interjected: "Quite."

To her chagrin Alice felt the warmth of a flush on her cheeks.
But Bebb seemed not to notice.

"You will, of course, Mrs Fenwick," he continued, "wish
to confer with your solicitors once they have received and
considered our draft. However, for the avoidance of doubt and
to facilitate the quickest possible completion of these matters,
Mr Kornblath has asked me to outline to you the broad terms
on which he is willing to proceed and seek your agreement
to them."

His eyes, which were very dark brown, held Alice's in
much the way a general might regard a private who was
entitled to respond to some directive but was not expected
to.

"I see," Alice said as firmly as before.

"A company to be known as Holly Wood Gowns is to be
formed which will have a share capital of five thousand pounds
in the form of one hundred shares, each share having the value
of fifty pounds, these shares to be issued as to forty-nine
to yourself and fifty-one to nominees Mr Kornblath will in

due course appoint. You understand the effect of that, Mrs Fenwick?"

Alice, who hadn't the least notion of what a nominee was, decided it would be wise to reply: "Not entirely, Sir Duncan."

"In plain terms, Mrs Fenwick, although it will appear as if Mr Kornblath has no financial interest in the company, he will in fact control it."

Alice had hardly expected anything other than that Kornblath *would* control the business.

"Am I," she asked innocently, "going to be given my forty-nine shares then?"

"No," said Bebb, clearly prepared for some question of this nature and therefore not being called upon to either show or conceal surprise at having it made. "Your forty-nine shares will cost you the sum of two thousand four hundred and fifty pounds" – and holding up a hand both to allay anxiety and avoid an interruption – "but you will be allowed to delay payment for them until the company is making a sufficient profit for you to do so without difficulty. In the meantime Mr Kornblath will make up the shortfall with an interest-free personal loan to the company. Will that be satisfactory to you?"

"Yes," said Alice, amazed. "Yes. Yes, it would."

"Do you have any further questions touching the issue of the company's shares?"

"No."

"Then to continue. The company will have three directors; in the first instance these will be chosen as follows. There will be one from the company's accountants, Messrs Winthrop, Son and Mackeson, and one from my own firm. This is by way of being a temporary arrangement while the company is being established and in due course these directors will resign and be replaced by two others that Mr Kornblath will name. This will be made clear in the company's Articles of Association. You will be third and managing director and Mr Kornblath will not hold office."

"I see," Alice said, quite bemused.

"Now as to your salary as managing director; Mr Kornblath

suggests that in the first instance it will be one thousand pounds a year."

In spite of herself, Alice blinked.

"Is that agreeable, Mrs Fenwick?"

"Oh . . . Yes. Yes, that's agreeable." How did you convey you weren't particularly impressed when your heart was turning somersaults? Tom's redundancy payment! Once every year! It was unimaginable!

"The company will additionally meet such promotional expenses as are necessary for you to incur. I refer of course to travelling expenses, the entertainment of clients, advertising, your dress allowance and so on."

"Dress allowance?" said Alice, unable to control her disbelief.

Bebb nodded, apparently not in the least surprised at her surprise. "Mr Kornblath has made a particular point about it. He feels it is very important that you present the proper image and that you should not feel unduly constrained in doing so. The company's accountants will of course keep a watching brief on how much of the company's money you are spending in this direction, but providing you keep within reasonable limits they will not interfere. To continue: one of Mr Kornblath's companies owns a building in Goswell Road, a building which in fact Mr Kornblath developed a year or two ago. It has yet to be fully let and Mr Kornblath is prepared to make available at a proper market rental one complete floor, subject to your confirming its location and general suitability, and to set aside a second floor to allow for subsequent expansion."

With huge relief, Alice found herself in the position of being able to ask a sensible question: "These premises. They're immediately available?"

Bebb, whose hands were as waxy as his face, put his fingertips together. "They will be available to the company once it has been formed."

"And about how long will that take?"

There was no hesitation. "In, I should say, Mrs Fenwick, two or three months' time."

Two or three months! This was devastating! How was

she to cope meanwhile? "But . . . but why so long?" she demanded.

"Mrs Fenwick," Bebb, who clearly had not expected the least show of opposition, replied with the faintest touch of asperity, "it appears you are not fully appraised of what has to be done before a company can be formed."

"No, I'm not," agreed Alice, determined to stand up to him. "And Mr Kornblath knows that and must have informed you."

"In any case, Mrs Fenwick," Bebb, neatly shifting his ground, went on, "completion will have to wait until Mr Kornblath returns from Cannes."

"Cannes?"

"Which will be mid February."

Mid February was more than two months off.

"Are you telling me, Sir Duncan," Alice said, "that I shall have to wait until mid February before I see Mr Kornblath and have the opportunity of discussing details with him?"

"I have not said that at all, Mrs Fenwick. What I am telling you is that in view of the necessary preliminary steps which have to be taken, the fact that Christmas will soon be upon us and that early in the New Year Mr Kornblath will take his customary winter holiday in Cannes, it simply will not be possible for the company to be formed any earlier than I have indicated. In any case there are surely many preliminary things you will have to see to." The waxy hands parted briefly. "For example the installation of a telephone where you live. That is another matter on which Mr Kornblath was specific."

"Who pays for that?" demanded Alice.

"The company of course." He could have been brushing a fly off his desk. "Then there are surely such matters as the design and printing of the company notepaper, the engagement of staff, the ordering of machinery and so on." He paused, as if to allow Alice time to dispute that such forward planning was necessary. "You will need," he continued, "to have conferences with Winthrop's, will you not? And there must be many matters of which I would not have the slightest knowledge which you will no doubt wish to attend to. Two to three months?" He seemed to leave it hanging in the air before concluding: "I would have imagined you would need all that time and more."

He rose to his feet. The conference – or was it the examination? – was over. Alice felt much like she imagined each of the actresses Nigel Tarrant had auditioned must have felt: unsure if her performance had been adequate.

"I take it, Mrs Fenwick, you agree to the heads of agreement I have outlined?"

"Yes," Alice said. "Yes, Sir Duncan, they seem to be satisfactory. In general terms."

"Good. If there should be any points which on reflection it seems to you we have not covered, please do not hesitate to be in touch with me. By letter, if you please."

He came round his desk and passing behind Alice opened the door for her: "It has been a pleasure meeting you, Mrs Fenwick, on this, which I am quite sure will be the first of many meetings we will have. May I take this opportunity of wishing you every success in this new venture."

"Thank you, Sir Duncan."

"I will see you out."

The fact that he even said this, let alone did it, warmed Alice's heart. Instinct advised her it was something he did not do too often.

3

It was a cold, clear, end of November day and Alice, back in Gray's Inn Square, paused, uncertain what to do. There had been, she admitted, a great deal of sense in what Sir Duncan Bebb had had to say. There *was* so much to be done before Holly Wood Gowns could become operational. There were those things he had suggested: printed notepaper, she hadn't given that a thought; taking on workers, she hadn't even been in touch with her old forewoman Nellie, without whom a successful Holly Wood Gowns was unimaginable; machinery, where did you go to for advice on what she was going to need? And all the rest of it: designs for the dresses she was going to make, the ordering of materials, dummies, cottons, ribbons, chalks, shears, pinking scissors, patterns – the list was endless. And how did you cope with this without a base from which to organise it? From the street? It had been one thing setting up Paquette from Belmont Hotel. At least she hadn't had to think about buying food, preparing meals, making beds, washing dishes, lighting fires and all the rest of it. And there'd been the sense of a background of people with whom to talk things over: Sam and Joseph, Lola and Poppy, Nancy and Ronnie Fielding, Billy Shaw and the rest of them. They mightn't have known anything about setting up a dress business – in fact, except for Joseph, setting up *any* business. But at least they'd been there to *talk* to! Now she'd no one! Unless you counted a priest who obviously despised you as a mother who neglected her children or a landlord who was going to have you out in the gutter in three weeks' time!

The enormity of what she was taking on, of a sudden overwhelmed her. Is this more than I can cope with, she asked herself. Paquette – half a dozen machines in a poky little workroom – that was one thing. But this! With no one who knows the least thing about making and selling dresses to help me. Momentarily her courage seemed to ooze away. I must have been mad, she rebuked herself, to imagine I could organise something like this on my own. And how could I have had the cheek, the audacity, the *brass* to persuade a man like Kornblath that I could? And anyway, how, without money *can* I organise all these things which have to be organised? But common sense at once elbowed aside her fears. Damn! That was something I should have asked about! Presumably, she reasoned, it *is* going to be advanced. They must know I haven't got it or I wouldn't have had to go and see Kornblath in the first place. Maybe these accountants . . . What was their name? What was it? Damn again! I'll go back and ask. No! Bebb had been emphatic – if there were any points not covered, I'm to be in touch with him *by letter*. Perhaps it'll be in the draft agreement they're going to send to Weldon. And if it isn't, then he can raise it . . .

She pulled herself together. "Get hold of yourself, Alice!" she said aloud. And to herself: You've always believed that if there was one thing you didn't lack it was common sense. Well, use it. Don't muddle up everything together. Concentrate on one point at a time. Make a plan. Decide what are the important things which have to be attended to first and what can be put aside and dealt with later. Simmer down. Do something positive. Like going and finding a Lyons and ordering yourself a pot of tea!

She felt more secure if only because she'd made a decision, and set out briskly across Gray's Inn Square, crossed South Square and exited into a Holborn clogged with traffic. And then, as she stood looking up and down seeking a Lyons or an ABC, a horse-drawn brewer's dray which had been partially blocking her view moved on, exposing diagonally opposite to her the end of Chancery Lane running into Holborn. And on its corner, Mott's Typewriters. Just over there, she told herself, crouching amongst his typewriters and office furniture, was the one man she knew who could advise how to solve an insoluble problem. For a split second she was tempted – but then there seemed to ring in her ears the last words he had said to her after she had taunted him that it would never be any good Dessy and Thady looking to him for help. "My dear, Alice, I wouldn't be too sure of that."

He had intentionally left the door open – not for her, but for them. And she saw, and wondered why she had not seen it before, the menace in that brief remark. And it hardened her resolve. Oh, no, Joseph, she thought, not again. You may have taken over their father's life but you're not taking over theirs. I'll see to that – if it's the very last thing I do!

Over her pot of tea she posed mental possibilities. When she got back to Highbury, what about rooting out Williams and reminding him to plead with Stringer to let her stay on – after all the man attended his church, didn't he? And if Williams wouldn't do that – or if Stringer wouldn't agree – then what about going and seeing Stringer herself? What was there to lose? She'd explain what she was about to embark upon and that she'd had instructions to have a telephone installed – that, surely, would impress him. But if it didn't work, if she got nowhere, from tomorrow she'd start looking for somewhere else to live. As Bebb had said, it would soon be Christmas. Well, one thing was certain, Dessy and Thady couldn't spend Christmas in the street, even if she had to herself! They'd have to go up to Liverpool and stay with Mother. They'd like that anyway. Well Thady would – she wasn't so sure about Dessy, he was getting so close and self-contained she hardly knew what he *did* think.

What next? Yes. She'd call in on Mr Weldon, tell him what was happening and ask him to find out how she was supposed to order all the things she was going to need so that there was as little delay as possible once the damn agreement had been signed. Maybe he'd advance her money. Ha! That was a joke. And after she'd seen him, well Debenham's was near, she'd call in on Shea with whom she had been reasonably close in the Paquette days. Yes, call in and open an account ready to stock up her wardrobe. And tell Debenham's to send the bill to those accountants. Weldon could find out who they were. He could telephone Hickson, Battersby while she was with him.

And then? Then she'd take a look at this building in Goswell Road. What number was it? Oh, no! That was *another* thing she should have asked. Never mind. If it was a a new building she ought to be able to pick it out . . . Yes, but it would be dark by then. Yes, dark! And Dessy and Thady would be back from school, back to a cold and empty flat again. Well they'd know where to find the key. And at least she'd got that wood in. There wasn't anything special in for tea, they'd have to put up with bread and jam. There was half a loaf in the bread bin. It'd be a bit stale but they'd have to make do. And then there was supper. She'd have to buy something somewhere. She reached for her bag to check how much money she had and her eyes closed in dismay. It would have to be something very cheap. Herrings? Bloaters? No, she couldn't cart smelly fish into Gibson and Weldon's. And not into Debenham and Freebody's either. Mince? No, even that was difficult. The old stand-by, sausages? Yes. Good idea. We've got potatoes. Sausages and mash. And we've got some rice. They can have rice and jam as a sweet. Anything else? If there is, it'll have to wait until tomorrow. What time is it anyway? She looked about her. No one had come to join her at her table but there weren't any empty ones now. Must be lunchtime, she thought. I must have been sitting here for ages. For a moment she toyed with ordering something for herself. Poached egg on spinach. Fourpence, wasn't it? Or spaghetti on toast? Or beans on toast? Threepence. She shook her head. No, there isn't time. Too much to do. And I need most of what I've got for sausages anyway. She signalled a passing waitress over for the bill.

In fact, apart from buying sausages, none of her decisions counted – Mr Weldon was in court and Miss Shea at a buyer's meeting. There was time to take a number four bus up the Goswell Road in the hope of picking out the building in which Mr Kornblath was offering her a floor, and she rather fancied she had guessed which one it was but couldn't be sure. Fortunately the number four, like the number nineteen, passed by the top of Aberdeen Park and she actually got back in time to make Desmond and Thady their tea – which was important. But not as important as the contents of an envelope delivered by the second post: a printed invitation to Mrs Alice Fenwick from the Directors of the Solomon Kornblath Investment Trust to a pre-Christmas Occasion to be held in their offices in Berkeley Square on the Friday of the following week.

Six

1

No visitor from another planet, thought Rackham, as he stood in the vast foyer of the Solomon Kornblath Investment Trust's Berkeley Square offices, could have imagined that the financial structure of the entire commercial world was currently being shaken to its very foundations, that company after company was going into liquidation, the list of suicides alarmingly increasing, the dole queues, already obscene enough, lengthening daily and despair reaching into the homes of millions of ordinary families. Here, in the aura of unlimited wealth manifested by the easy confidence of the male guests, by the furs and jewellery of their wives or mistresses, by the aroma of cigars and expensive scent, by the waitresses circulating with canapes and the waiters with champagne, by the muted music of a well-known band, by the buzz of conversation and outbreaks of laughter, by the general atmosphere of cheerful bonhomie, one might have been excused for imagining that this was a party being given to celebrate a period of prosperity!

And who better to exemplify such a feeling of wellbeing than Solly himself, stationed with his wife, Magda, both in evening dress, near enough to the entrance doors not to miss greeting a single arriving guest, unhurried, smiling, warm and welcoming. What a formidable pair they were, exuding, both of them, that peculiar sense of certainty which only the possession of unlimited wealth bestows. It was as if they were entirely unaffected by the Wall Street crash and the global reverberations spinning off from it. Was it that by his staggering success in the post-war years Solly had built such a cushion of wealth that he could take a measure of disaster in his stride? Was it that

106

the moment Clarence Hatry – one day one of London's most brilliant financiers and the next exposed as a worthless crook – was arraigned, he had foreseen, or his advisers had foreseen, what lay ahead and had liquefied such assets as were not in land and bricks and mortar?

Or was it something else? He *had* to owe through his various companies incalculable sums of money borrowed from the banks and City institutions to fund his developments, some in the planning stage, some under construction and others completed but not yet fully let – or let perhaps to other companies or individuals who might go under any day. And there was the model for Ivanhoe Gardens, for the first time put on public display, given pride of place ahead of the enormous Christmas tree loaded down with expensive presents from Harrods and Fortnums and even Garrards. It wasn't in hand yet, Ivanhoe Gardens, it probably wouldn't be put in hand for years. There would surely need to be an upsurge in general confidence before Solly gave the go-ahead. But the land had had to be bought or optioned and all manner of other expenses incurred merely to bring it to this state. Here was Europe staggering under the greatest financial slump history had ever known and here was Solly Kornblath proclaiming his confidence in his personal future by putting on display a model of what would be Europe's most ambitious flat development!

Why was he displaying it? Out of an irresistible sense of pride from a man who, starting with nothing, had within a few short years made himself London's leading property developer? As a statement of his invulnerability and a message to the doubters? Or was it deception – bravado, bombast, bluff? Theoretically it was not at all impossible that such was the mountain of his debts, and such the lack of interest in or capacity for renting his parades of shops, his offices, his blocks of flats, that overnight the newspapers would be screaming banner headlines that yet another Hatry had bitten the dust of over-trading. It could be that within a few short months, even weeks, this huge, glittering, marble-floored, high-ceilinged foyer, cleared regardless of cost of everything which connected it with business and refurnished to provide a suitable setting for one solitary night's Christmas junketing, would be echoing with the feet of sequestrators.

Yet somehow, Rackham, glass of champagne in hand, quietly watching Solly personally welcoming each new arrival announced by Moss, doubted it. Not for a moment in their many meetings since the Wall Street crash, had he divined the slightest uneasiness in Kornblath's manner. On the contrary, if anything Solly had *welcomed* the slump as offering him undreamed of opportunities for buying up land and leases cheaply. "You'll see, Rackham," he had prophesied. "One day there's going to be a queue of estate agents offering to give me a handsome profit to buy back property they were falling over themselves to unload on me at knockdown prices. And any number of developers cursing themselves at missing an opportunity that came only once in their business lifetime."

Well, Rackham thought wryly, I hope that's how it is going to be. And, looking at the small press of men and women milling around the model he'd designed: I hope *that* happens, because, even if I have nothing else, as and when it does it will keep my office busy for several years – and it will establish me as a major architect. And the words which Beatrice Culverwell had quoted at the Crébillion lunch as having been said to her by Solly, came to his mind: "an architect who will be a legend in his lifetime". He chuckled: there were worse ambitions.

A waiter with a bottle of champagne materialised. "Thank you," Rackham said, holding out his glass. When the waiter had moved on, he went on eyeing his host and hostess and watching the couple Solly and Magda had just welcomed move on to deposit their coats in the offices which had been requisitioned for the evening as cloakrooms: Hamilton's for the ladies, Coote and Grey's (who shared an office) for the gentlemen. He knew neither of the couple, a woman in all but ankle-length sable with a matching toque, the man in an impeccable camel-hair coat. A rich, successful couple? Or a couple who for all their apparent opulence were these days trembling at every official-looking letter they received? You couldn't tell. At the "pre-Christmas Occasions" – as Solly always dubbed them – you had to project success or be rumbled. And if you were rumbled there'd be no invitation for you next year. There was no room for failure at this level.

Not that there were only people involved in property who attended Kornblath's Christmas shindig. Far from it – many had been invited either because the influence they wielded might one day be of use or else to, as it were, dress the table. Already Rackham had recognised a Labour peer, a couple of Tory Members of Parliament, a Westminster Councillor (Ivanhoe Gardens came under the ægis of the Westminster City Council) and the City Planning Officer, all accompanied by their wives. There was Frederick Scase of *The Times*, the cartoonist, Jason Carrick, and a man with a lion's mane of hair whom Rackham didn't recognise but other guests apparently did, judging by the way they shifted around him like so many bees who had come upon a drifting source of nectar. He had noticed Beatrice Culverwell accompanied by a square-jawed man with wavy hair, firm lips and dramatically perceptive eyes, whom he took to be her husband (but was in fact Nigel Tarrant), Brenda Camroux who had starred in *French Leave* at the Apollo, and the actor who had played Raoul in Noël Coward's *The Marquise* whose name for the moment eluded him. If Coward himself had turned up, Rackham would not have been surprised. The tentacles of wealth reached far and wide, drawing in surprising notables.

"Mr Rackham!"

His thoughts interrupted by a deep unfamiliar voice, Rackham turned courteously to find himself buttonholed by a stranger.

"Yes," he agreed – although there had been nothing of enquiry in the address.

"Marcus Sweet."

"Ah," Rackham said – and unashamedly studied the engineer who was to be his colleague in Kornblath's Burlington House development.

He saw a man of perhaps six feet with a rather triangular face, greying hair curling below the temples yet sparse enough scarcely to cover his scalp, and curiously taut and expressive lips. Even more noteworthy were his eyes, grey-green in colour, challenging, heavily pouched and set off by well-marked arched eyebrows. Well there, he mused, is a face which would certainly have Jason Carrick reaching for his pencil.

"I assumed we would meet this evening," Sweet said. "I take it you are a regular patron of these affairs."

"Patron?" Rackham queried with a slight shift of his head.

"You don't accept the choice of word? But, why not, Mr Rackham. You lend your influence to advance the interests of our mutual client, do you not?"

"Influence?"

"What could be more influential than" – he pointed a finger – "that magnificent model of yours? Even the most cynical sceptic here this evening is bound to go home finally convinced of Kornblath's financial clout." It was said with a touch of mockery, echoed by the compelling eyes.

Rackham decided that Sweet was likely to prove a dangerous, although possibly intriguing man to work with.

"You imagine that's why he's displaying it?" he said. He shook his head. "You're wrong."

Sweet gave a little nod, almost a bow. "I yield of course to your superior knowledge."

"You haven't been to one of these occasions before, I take it?" Rackham said.

"No, Mr Rackham. I've heard of them, of course. It never occurred to me that I would ever be invited."

Rackham understood. Sweet, who was in a modest way of business, was aware he had been appointed as engineer on Burlington House only because by occupying his current offices he had been a nagging tooth. He did not expect any follow-up appointments and was presenting himself as a man with enough irons in the fire to be able to afford a little persiflage. But it was a risky attitude to take with Solly Kornblath even if, as Rackham knew to be the case, Sweet had already got his contract signed.

"I'm sure you will be again," Rackham said. "One of Solly Kornblath's good qualities is loyalty to those he's decided serve him well."

The mephistophelean eyebrows twitched even higher. "Is that a warning, Mr Rackham? Or good advice?"

"I think," Rackham said with a smile to rob the exchange of

offence, "it might be as well to take it as both. Well, I'm glad to meet you, Mr Sweet. I was going to contact you as soon as I knew that last lease was in the bag."

"Isn't it?" The response, just touched with anxiety and too quickly said, told Rackham even more than Sweet's making himself known had done. The man was short of work. Happening to own the lease of a small suite of rooms Kornblath had to possess had been an extraordinary piece of luck. He was terrified there might yet be a hitch.

"There's just one lease outstanding. A man named Llewellyn. An insurance agent with just two rooms who's holding Hamilton up to ransom."

"Hamilton?"

Rackham thought of Hamilton with his hard, pale eyes and his need to make himself out to be a more important person than he was.

"He's taken over as the company's surveyor," he said. "A man with a penchant for buying apples."

With his attention held by Sweet, Rackham missed Alice's arrival but Beatrice, hearing Moss's annoucement, excused herself from Tarrant and Brenda Camroux, and moved near enough to be ready to encourage her when, freed from Solly and Magda's welcome, she found herself uncomfortably alone amongst a throng of well-dressed, in not a few cases over-dressed, strangers.

Watching from a little distance Solly introducing Alice to his wife, Beatrice was relieved and hugely impressed.

"I wonder," she had said to Grahame, "what she's going to wear? I'm surprised she hasn't been on to you to ask your advice."

He had shaken his head. "When it comes to clothes, Alice Jordan" – it was as Alice Jordan he always thought of her – "has an instinct that's seldom wrong."

"It isn't easy," Beatrice had objected, "with maybe half the men in white ties because they're going on somewhere afterwards and half the women trying to prove it's nothing special as far as they're concerned."

"You think it's special, don't you?"

"I wouldn't miss it for the world."

"Why wouldn't you, Bee?"

"It's so droll."

"Droll?" he had said, surprised. He had never attended himself, although he'd been invited two or three years back when Kornblath had first shown interest in backing Brusa Productions. "You're to say you're busy," Beatrice had said, first time round. "Only reason we've been asked is because Solly thinks I'll haul in one or two names the press will latch on to. And I will. And you'll be in my hair while I'm trying to hook him."

"Droll," Beatrice had repeated. "It's like putting on a play with an enormous cast, half of whom speak one language and half another."

He had known what she meant because she always reported back on the occasions. There were the representatives of the building trade and there were the rest. And on the whole the two halves were like oil and water – they didn't mix.

"D'you think Kornblath realises?"

"Oh, sure. I think he's having a great big chuckle."

"Expensive chuckle. Why does he do it?"

"Because it's the thing to do and he's going to do it better than anyone else."

"So why's he asked Alice? She's nothing to do with building anything and no one's going to take *her* photograph."

"That's a good question, Grahame. And one I don't know how to answer although I've given it a lot of thought."

"You're still sorry you started this, aren't you?" he had said, responding to her tone.

"Damn sorry. And damn sorry for Alice. She's going to feel like a fish out of water."

"She doesn't have to go."

"Of course she's got to go."

He had nodded. "Yes, I suppose you're right." And, after a moment. "But one thing you don't have to worry about is what's she's going to turn up in. She'll work it out. And get it right."

And she has, thought Beatrice, observing Alice, who was

wearing a figure-hugging floral-printed crèpe de Chine dress, a little above ankle length, accordion-pleated from calf-length downwards, with long tight sleeves reaching to the wrists, and cut daringly low at the bodice where it was filled in with a triangle of net. Over it she were a loose flesh-coloured silk coat of identical length with huge sleeves to the elbows and a huge fur trimming. On her head was a cap of the same material as the coat, carried down over one ear and finished with a bow, and in her hand she carried an oblong handbag of the dress material pleated like the bottom of the skirt. Her lips, bright red, were very much in fashion, and the stiletto heels of her shoes gave her an added inch or two of height. She looks, thought Beatrice, absolutely stunning – and was baffled. That ensemble must, she told herself, have cost a fortune!

In fact Alice's choice of what to wear had not been so much a matter of instinct as of much thought and long discussion with Bridget Shea, gown buyer for Debenham and Freebody. Out of luck in her attempts to see her before, the very day after receiving the Kornblath invitation, having seen the children off to school, Alice, once again wearing her latest outfit, had gate-crashed the offices of Debenham and Freebody and, having been informed that Miss Shea was altogether far too busy to give time to anyone who hadn't an appointment, sat herself firmly in the nearest chair and announced her intention of staying put until Miss Shea saw her. Within five minutes she was shown into Miss Shea's sanctum and, no sooner was she in it and back into the atmosphere of the one trade she had at her fingertips, than, for all the formidable presence of the woman, a swell of certainty possessed her.

"Morning, Shea," she accosted her – it was the way they had always addressed each other. "Keeping busy, I see." She turned her head from the huge table scarred with cigarette burns that Shea used as a desk, which was littered with fashion magazines, dockets and all manner of other paperwork, to examine some sketch displays of dresses on a mount hung on a wall. "Amanda Bennet's, aren't they? Don't tell me Debenhams are going in for the chorus girls."

"The way business is we might at that," said Shea. "All right,

Jordan, that's not why you've bust your way in and if it's to show me samples you've wasted your taxi fare. There's an embargo this side of Christmas and maybe this side of Easter. We're buying nothing!"

She was a solidly built woman with a prominent nose, no-nonsense eyes and a mass of straight black hair which, entirely covering her forehead, was the antithesis of fashion. Her dress too lacked frippery and she was known to head off implied or stated criticism with: "I'm employed to buy clothes, not wear them."

How many times, I wonder, Alice thought, have I sat here facing her, trying to sell dresses I've brought in on my arm from Little Titchfield Street? How many times has she called some girl in to go and put them on in that little changing room and model them?

"I've come to buy, not sell," she said briskly.

"Plenty down there," said Shea with a wave of a strong, nicotine-stained hand. "Store's full of them." She smoked incessantly. "Even still got some of yours, I wouldn't be surprised."

She reached into an open tin of cigarettes and, not knowing Alice had taken up smoking, took one and lit it. She was the only woman Alice knew at all well who, like herself, smoked without using a holder.

"Well, what is it, Jordan? I haven't got all morning."

"I'm starting a new business."

"You must be mad. You know what's happened to Patrick Nolan?" (Patrick Nolan had bought Paquette.) "Bankrupt."

"Yes, I heard, Shea. It's sad."

"Sad, nothing. You got out at the right time, that's all. Anyway he didn't have your flair." It was rare Shea threw compliments but Alice had always impressed her as a down-to-earth, commonsensical outworker with a nose for what was sellable. She went on: "What you've said doesn't make sense. You're starting a new business and you're here to buy not sell. I don't understand you."

"I'm being backed," said Alice, who had decided to hold nothing back but names, "to open a factory, a large factory, that's going to concentrate on making cheap dresses in a multiple of sizes which will wholesale at fifteen shillings or less and retail at a guinea."

Shea drew on her cigarette, staring at Alice through the smoke.

"I'm talking about mass production, Shea. I'm going to flood the country with them."

"Where's the money coming from?"

"It's unlimited."

Shea pressed a brass bell on the table. A girl came in.

"Tea," Shea said. "And tell Mr Marston he'd better fix another appointment. I can't see him this morning after all." And even before the girl had gone. "Are you talking pipe dreams, Jordan, or reality?"

"Reality."

"Where's the factory going to be?"

"Goswell Road."

"When do you go into production?"

"February. Or maybe March."

"Go on."

"I'm not going to tell you who's backing me or why, Shea, and you won't guess who he is because up to now he's never had anything to do with the rag trade. And you can put any construction you care to on why he's backing me and I won't mind. He's rich as Croesus and we're going to form a company of which I'm to be managing director, in which he has fifty-one per cent of the shares and I have the rest."

"What are you going to call it?"

"Holly Wood Gowns."

"That's a lousy name." She said it without hesitation.

Alice concealed disappointment. "You think so? Why?"

"It's too high-faluting and doesn't go with dresses selling cheap. For what you used to make, Paquette was good. Punchy. Holly Wood Gowns isn't. Think of something else. And a guinea's too dear anyway. We can buy dresses from America at five shillings each."

"You can't!" said Alice, horrified.

"Well, we can. But if they can make them and sell them at the price and if you've got enough money behind you, there's no reason I can see why you can't either. So what's the problem?"

"You're not going to believe this, Shea."

"Try me."

"I'm going to be given a dress allowance."

"Sure you are."

"That doesn't surprise you?"

"I get a dress allowance."

"You do!"

Shea smiled, a wry, self-critical smile. "There are occasions," she said economically.

Occasions! How strange.

"I've got an occasion," Alice said. "Tomorrow week I've got to go to a Christmas Party given by the man who's backing me and I'm told it's about as swanky as can be. I don't know what to wear and I haven't got anything anyway. And I don't get my dress allowance until the company's been formed and that's not going to be until February or March or maybe even April."

"So what do you want me to do, Jordan?"

"Back me, Shea."

The door opened and the girl came in with tea. There was nothing fancy about that either. Just two mugs from the staff canteen and Shea reaching for a bowl of sugar off the shelf behind her. It was like old times.

"What's all this about multiple sizes?" Shea, having helped herself to sugar and watched Alice do so as well, demanded.

Alice hesitated.

"Now look here, Jordan," Shea snapped, hardly allowing Alice's hesitation to be as much as a pause in their conversation, "if I'm to back you, I've got to know what I'm backing."

There was no help for it. In the whole of London, Alice couldn't think of anyone else to whom she could turn.

"I'm talking about manufacturing cheap, ready to wear dresses in so many different sizes that there'll hardly be a woman up and down the length of the country who won't be able to find something to fit her off the peg. That's what I'm going to make."

Shea, cigarette held between two fingers, the smoke filtering through her hair, studied Alice as if she was trying to work out what was going on in her mind.

"You're serious?" she said at length.

"Deadly serious."

"Hm." Her face gave nothing away.

"Do you think I'm mad, Shea?"

"Mad?" She gave the barest shake of her head. "If it could be done it would be one hell of a thing. Especially now with every penny counting. So why *hasn't* it been done?"

"It's being done in America."

"That's a big country. A lot of people in it."

"There's enough here."

"Are there?" And seemingly out of context: "It's not a new idea. We've heard about it." And, after a moment. "You realise what you'll be up against? It won't be like Paquette."

"I know."

"How are you going to sell your dresses, Jordan?" She broke off. "Jordan Dresses? No. Alice Dresses! There you are. Alice Dresses!"

Alice Dresses, Alice thought. Yes, I like that. Oh, how I like that!

"You'll need your own shops," Shea said, answering her own question. "And mail order. That's the way to do it." She waved her arms, dismissing Debenham and Freebody. "We're not of any significance to you, people like us. We couldn't take enough for you to be bothered."

"So you don't think I'm mad?"

"Why should you be? It has to come. Why shouldn't you be the first? This man who's backing you. Can you trust him?"

"I have to . . ." There was no help for it. It might be important to fool Mr Kornblath into believing she could manage until her salary started coming in; it didn't apply to Shea. "All right, Shea. You must have heard what my second husband did."

"Who didn't?"

Alice waited for a comment. None came. "He left me as good as nothing and what's left from selling Paquette's has got to see me through until I've got the business off the ground."

"And you can't start drawing on your expense account till

maybe April." Shea was nothing if not quick-minded and to the point. "You want me to OK you opening an account here."

Alice nodded.

"OK, I'll do that. On two conditions. One: you drop the Hollywood nonsense and call it Alice Dresses. Two: however much of a nuisance you think we are and however small the orders we place with you, we always have an option to buy." She threw the cigarette butt into the dregs of her mug of tea and, as it went out fizzing, got to her feet. "OK. We'd better go and take a walk around and see what we've got."

2

For the purpose of deciding who should be invited to his Christmas party, Kornblath had three lists prepared. Two were prepared by his secretary: the first consisted of those who had attended the previous year; the second from her own knowledge out of those he had been involved with since who might be useful. There was a third list: a short one he prepared himself. From these three lists Kornblath made his own selection.

The Christmas Occasion was important to him not because of the benefits to his operations which might accrue from it – those were merely useful by-products – but because it was a manifestation of his success, as are oars in a rowing man's hall, cups on a golfer's sideboard, a line of books on a novelist's shelf or a playwright's mounted box-office cards. Making money no longer meant anything to him: once he had discovered how easily money could be made, profits became merely hurdles to be cleared on the way to the goal. And the goal? If you had asked him he would have found that difficult to define. It was not a lust for power. Although he dominated all the business enterprises with which he was concerned, he was not, as are many men who devote their lives to commercial success, obsessed with dominating *people*. It was perhaps the other side of the coin of domination which guided him: the fear – or perhaps that is too strong a word – the apprehension, which Martin Rackham exceptionally had divined, of being dominated. For all his wealth, for all the esteem of bankers and the obeisance of minions, Solly Kornblath could not put from his mind a youth of wretched poverty and need, throughout which respect for a down-at-heel Jewish boy with parents with dreadful English, and that marred by heavy mid-European accents, had been at the lowest ebb. He needed regular confirmation that such days were behind him and would never come again and, far more than the possession of Rolls Royces, luxurious homes, cruises and holidays in Cannes and all the rest of it, this evening, in which a throng of hand-picked guests sauntered around his palatial offices, drinking his Bollinger Grande Année and nibbling his smoked salmon and caviare, provided it.

And so the selection as to who should be invited each year was not to be hurried and took on the nature almost of a religious rite. Normally quick and decisive in everything he did, exceptionally he set aside one entire morning for the process. With the effect on his future undertakings of necessity to be taken into account and conscious that if too many were invited it would not be an occasion but a jamboree, he was faced each year with accepting that some who had previously attended would have to be omitted to make room for newcomers. And having completed the easy task of scoring out those who by death, failure, disloyalty or lack of future usefulness presented no problem and replaced them with an approved selection from his secretary's second list, he squared up to the more difficult decision of risking slighting old favourites in favour of successors.

For a long time he considered the wisdom of inviting Alice. So far as his prestige was concerned she was of absolutely no account. He had no intention of making his interest in Holly Wood Gowns public until such time as it had proved successful and, apart from Rackham and Beatrice Culverwell, it was highly unlikely that there would be anyone present who knew her and quite certain that the photographers the glossies always sent wouldn't bother with her.

But there were other considerations. For all his peccadilloes, he and Magda, of whom he was genuinely very fond, had established a good working relationship. Having quite early on faced the reality that he was incapable of staying faithful to her, and seeing no sense in throwing away all the advantages of being married to a man who was obviously going to be rich, successful and important, she had adopted the pragmatic attitude that so long as he did not flaunt his women or embarrass their teenage son and daughter by indulging his affairs indiscreetly, she would look the other way. It followed that there could be no question of him having a liaison with any woman there was the slightest possibility she might meet.

Although thus far, Kornblath had only met Alice once, she had impressed sufficiently for him to know that he would want to see more of her than he would of other partners in a similar enterprise. She appealed to him uniquely through the combination of her attractiveness, her courage and her capacity. He even admitted to himself that under the right circumstances he might, against his principles, be tempted sexually. All in all therefore, it seemed a good idea to invite her to his Christmas party: he would establish her in Magda's mind as a woman about whom she need not be worried and could meet socially from time to time, and by doing so remove the risk of departing from the strong, clear views he had on keeping sex and business separate.

"Mrs Alice Fenwick!" Moss announced.

Magda, by now tired of receiving guests, felt a stir of interest, scrutinised the woman making her way towards them and was impressed.

"Good evening, Mrs Fenwick," Solly said. "I'm so glad you found time to join us." And to Magda: "Darling, this is the splendid young woman I was telling you about who is going to set the world of fashion about its ears. Mrs Fenwick – my wife."

"How do you do, Mrs Kornblath," Alice said unhurriedly, trying to cast from her mind the feeling that a curtsey would not be out of place, for, bedecked with priceless jewellery and wearing an evening dress of layered panels of draped fabric which must have cost the earth, Magda Kornblath presented an almost regal appearance.

She was a handsome woman, dark haired, dark eyed and

unmistakably Jewish, who carried her ample body superbly, and the pair of them in full fig, standing side by side, well built, well matched, well heeled and well drilled for the parts they were playing, were as formidable a couple as Alice had ever met. She had to steel herself to follow Shea's advice: "Convince yourself that you are the person you are going to become when Alice Dresses is a household name and you its founder. You're dressed and groomed for the part. So you don't show surprise, you don't look around as if you're hoping you can spot a friend, you don't look grateful to have been invited and you leave it to other people to start conversations."

"I have been very much looking forward to meeting you, Mrs Fenwick," Magda said. "My husband has told me a great deal about you."

Alice smiled.

"He's very confident," went on Magda, rather driven to it by Alice's apparently easy silence, "that your Holly Wood Gowns is going to be a great success, and even from these first few moments of meeting you, I am sure he's right."

"How very kind," Alice said – a rehearsed remark. "But as a matter of fact I'm having second thoughts about the name." And to Solly, with another winning smile: "But that's something we could talk about another time, isn't it, Mr Kornblath?"

"Not now?" said Solly, rather pleased with her.

"Hardly," Alice responded, relieved beyond measure at hearing Moss announce the arrival of General Sir William and Lady Iving. And she gave the faintest nod and moved off from her host and hostess, as if ahead of her were all manner of people waiting to have her join their circle.

"Uhm," murmured Magda meaningfully – then, raising her head to greet the new arrivals, "Audrey, how delightful to see you . . ."

A flunkey with a tray of champagne glasses was waiting to intercept Alice as, feeling crucifyingly exposed but attempting to manufacture an air of complete composure, she proceeded bravely into the main foyer. She accepted one with relief – at least both hands would now be occupied. She paused, wondering in which direction to make her way and how on earth she was going to be able to get through an hour or more of being an unknown outsider in a mob of chattering strangers who obviously knew each other intimately and whose interests, conventions and ways of looking at things must be vastly different from her own. But then her eyes fell on Rackham's model of Ivanhoe Gardens and, a huge wave of relief sweeping over her, she made her way unhurriedly across to it. Here at least was something familiar, here something on which she must surely have more knowledge than most of the small knot of men and women gawping at it.

And so it proved.

A man of about her age in a dinner jacket, the sudden squaring of his shoulders and sparkling of his eyes suggesting that much as the model might be of interest, the sudden materialisation of such a stylish and attractive unaccompanied lady was of infinitely more account, was quick to engage her in conversation.

"Quite a thing, isn't it?" he suggested.

"Quite a thing," Alice agreed, willingly enough.

"Never seen anything quite like it anywhere."

"You won't have," said Alice with growing confidence.

"Oh?"

"It's going to be the largest block of flats in England – if not in Europe."

"You sound," said another man, a more mature man than the first, "as if this isn't the first time you've seen it."

"It isn't."

"Really?" It was a woman's voice. And by her tone, Alice knew that she had moved into a far higher bracket than she had been according herself. And she knew something else – that she had no need to be concerned that she would have to spend the next hour an embarrassed misfit. But she had taken something of a risk: Mr Kornblath mightn't be pleased if it got around that she had been privy to a development few even of his associates knew about.

"A brilliant architect, Martin Rackham," she said off-handedly, as if she had only recently been talking about him to other guests. And for good measure, "One of the few who's going to be a legend in his own lifetime."

122

"You know him?" said the lady who had expressed surprise before.

"Oh, yes," said Alice, turning her head. "As a matter of fact I was lunching with him at a small party in the Crébillion only the other day."

"How absolutely fascinating!"

"He's here somewhere," a third man said. "I heard his name announced." And to Alice: "I'd very much like to meet him. I'd be most grateful . . . I'm sorry, I didn't catch your name."

"Mrs Alice Fenwick."

"Fenwick . . ." someone said quickly, then fell silent.

But the third man, who was small, bespectacled and eager, was far too enthusiastic for an introduction to relate the name Fenwick with what had been such frequent cocktail-party conversation recently.

"I'd be most grateful, Mrs Fenwick, if you could introduce me to him."

Beatrice rescued. Keeping a little apart she had followed Alice's progress with admiration. The woman, she told herself, was amazing. Unknown, untutored in the society now surrounding her, she was taking Solly's Christmas Occasion by storm! Already other guests, scenting something in the wind, were drifting over towards the group around the model. Only a little more of this and the photographers would arrive! And what the consequence of that might be one couldn't hazard!

"Alice!" she cried, pushing in. "How great to see you! Listen, the most exciting thing has happened! I've just *got* to talk to you about it!" And to the gaggle, with a shake of her head that set her enormous earrings swaying madly: "I'm sorry to drag her away, but it just can't wait!"

And linking her arm through Alice's at great risk of slopping champagne on the model dress, she drew her away and, hopefully, out of danger.

"What is it?" Alice asked, bewilderedly.

"It's you!"

"Me?"

"You! If I'd left you there for another two minutes those guys with the cameras would be moving in and by tomorrow you'd be the talk of the town! And I'm not sure that Solly would appreciate it."

"Oh," said Alice.

Beatrice stood back, inspecting Alice. "Don't tell me it's Paquin," she said.

"No, I think it's Lucille Paray. I'm not sure." It had been a confusing business sifting through Debenham's collection of Paris models.

"And you've had the rest of the treatment." Required to be bang up to date with trends, Beatrice was approving Alice's hair (which, in the very latest of styles, was waved on to the nape of her neck) and the contrast of her bright red lips with an artificially paled complexion. Here, at least prima facie, was a different woman from the one she had been presumptuous enough to advise against taking on Solly Kornblath – perhaps, she thought dryly, it ought to be Solly I should be advising! "Look, Alice," she said. "Get rid of that damn champagne. We'll soon get you another one." She signalled to a nearby waiter and gestured to him to take Alice's glass. When he had done so, she asked, "Have you seen *French Leave* at the Apollo?"

"Yes." Tom had taken her on her birthday. It had been about the last time they'd been to the theatre together.

"Remember the stage name of the leading actress? . . . No. Why should you? It's Suzie Gautier. But the play itself. D'you think you remember it well enough to talk about it, if it crops up?"

"Yes, I think so."

"Great. Come and meet some people."

She led Alice over to Nigel Tarrant and Brenda Camroux.

"I want you to meet a friend of mine, Alice Fenwick," she said to them breezily. "And, Alice, I don't need to introduce Brenda, do I?"

"Suzie Gautier?" Alice suggested, with a faint lift of her plucked eyebrows, smiling.

Brenda Camroux with her own eyebrows plucked to a pencil line, a tiny rosebud mouth, still boyishly coiffeured, wearing a dramatic backless evening dress, waved a cigarette with a scarlet tip which precisely matched the colour of her lipstick and her talons of fingernails.

"Darling, how brilliant!" she said.

"And this is Nigel Tarrant, who's directing *Counsel's Dilemma.*"

"I'm delighted to meet you, Mr Tarrant," Alice said, as if she hadn't just learnt for the first time the title of Beatrice's new play.

She was aware of a resurgence of self-confidence matching her most successful period, financially and socially, at Belmont. And, more than this, aware that whereas the confidence of "Bunty" – her Belmont nickname – had been that of a woman still in her twenties, proud and content with all she had achieved, this was the positiveness of a woman who saw previously undreamed-of heights ahead of her and knew she had the capacity to scale them.

Nigel Tarrant, his interest very much aroused, held out his hand to her and when she took it maintained the clasp – one of London's most prestigious theatrical directors, he had the faculty of being able, almost instantaneously, to get beneath the carefully contrived image most actors and actresses presented to the world. This, he thought excitedly, is a very interesting woman. Not because of how she's dressed (although she does make Brenda a bit old hat and shows Beatrice up for what she is – an American in show business); not because she is quite scintillatingly lovely; and not even because she's refreshingly different. No, what it is, is that inside her there's a bubbling ferment of life. My God, if she were an actress – and she can't be or I would have known all about her long ago – if she were an actress I'd have to have her. I'd simply have to have her.

"Mrs Fenwick," he said, "I'm delighted to meet you." And, still holding Alice's hand, "Beatrice, where have you been hiding her?"

"You're nothing to do with theatre, are you, Mrs Fenwick?" interrupted Brenda Camroux, not a little put out at being upstaged.

"Nothing at all to do with theatre," Alice agreed.

"Well," said Beatrice thoughtfully, "it depends on how you define theatre, I suppose."

"A dramatic performance of a branch of art," said Tarrant glibly, at last releasing Alice's hand. "Do I take it, Mrs Fenwick—"

"Alice, please."

"Alice. Do I take it from Beatrice's enigmatic apophthegm you are connected with the arts?"

"You are talking, Nigel," Beatrice said, "to a young woman who is about to take the world of fashion by its ears and turn it upside down."

"Another apophthegm."

He looked enquiringly at Alice as if hoping for elucidation.

"You're out of luck, Nigel," Beatrice said. "Sealed orders."

"Ah."

"But you can tell us what you do, can't you?" Brenda, unable to stand on the sidelines, insisted.

"She's a dress designer," Beatrice said. "But I'm afraid that's all either of you are going to get."

Adding mystique, this did nothing but enhance the impression Alice was making; furthermore Beatrice, as much it has to be admitted because she was enormously enjoying the theatre of it, had in effect thrown a protective cloak around her. Who is this damn woman, Brenda Camroux was asking herself. She ran names through her mind: Fenwick? It was familiar but struck no chord. She's probably with one of the foreign houses, she supposed. Bertarelli? Lanvin? Vionnet? But she's so English! And then a brilliant idea which would enable her to shift the conversation her way occurred to her.

"You wouldn't be with that new man, Hartnell, darling, would you?" she suggested with a roguish smile. And quickly: "I hear that Gertie is being dressed by him these days. Oh, and by the way, she told me only yesterday she's thinking of doing a new play Noël tells her he's just written."

"Coward's in Japan," said a tall, impeccably groomed man in faultless evening dress who had just joined them and who Alice recognised as Nicholas Benson, an actor and another important theatrical name.

"Hong Kong, darling," Brenda said sweetly.

"Well I heard Japan."

Brenda twitched her shoulders gracefully. "Well maybe you're right, Nicky, but Gertie's wire came from Hong Kong." And having made what she judged to be a telling point: "And talking about Hartnell, you know what I heard the other day? He tried to get a job with C.B.Cochran. Oh, donkey's years ago. And that was *disaster!*"

"Talking of Cochran," Beatrice said, "I hear he's taking a lease on that new theatre they're building at the top of Shaftesbury Avenue."

"The Phoenix," Benson said. "Well you do surprise me, Bee. I mean it's so out of it, isn't it? All that way up there. Why it's nearly in Oxford Street! Would you choose it to put on one of yours?"

"With the right play? Sure. Why not?"

"Well there isn't going to be much passing trade."

Beatrice shrugged. "Maybe not. But when I find I've got to rely on passing trade, I'll start figuring it's maybe time to take the damn thing off. And, Nicholas, I want you to meet a dear friend of mine . . ."

With the theatre always well represented at Solly Kornblath's Occasions, Nicholas Benson was not the last of a comparatively intimate circle of very recognisable artistes Alice was to meet that evening. They talked nothing but theatre. The fact that they were a tiny coterie vastly outnumbered by men and women who made their living in the real world, as distinct from the world of make-believe, meant nothing to them. It was, she decided, time to break away from them and take her chances elsewhere.

"Bee," she said when a lull allowed it, "if you'll excuse me."

"Yes, of course," agreed Beatrice, mentally congratulating Alice on knowing better than to outstay her welcome with a bunch of people with whom she had nothing in common. "Oh, by the way, Grahame sent his love and said I mustn't fail to arrange for you to come and dine with us. I'll give you a ring."

"Do that," said Alice glibly.

Nigel Tarrant touched her arm as she was leaving.

"May I do that as well?" he suggested.

"Do what, Nigel?"

"Give you a ring. I'd very much like to see you again without a mob of people talking theatre."

"How very kind," Alice said. "As Bee knows, just at the moment I really am up to my ears. But maybe a little later on." And she flashed him a smile and left.

"Who have you been hobnobbing with as well as Beatrice Culverwell?" Rackham asked.

"You've been watching me."

"Impatiently."

The half-closed eyes were filled with fun but even so, to her annoyance, Alice felt herself colouring under her heavy powder.

"They're all theatrical people," she said. "You must at least have recognised Brenda Camroux and Nicholas Benson."

"Yes, I did. But who's the fellow with the lantern jaw who let everyone do the talking?"

"You *have* been watching, Mr Rackham!"

"I didn't recognise him."

"It isn't likely that you would. He's a director. Not an actor. His name's Nigel Tarrant and he's directing Bee's new play which is called *Counsel's Dilemma*. She's opening in the Criterion towards the end of January."

"You are well briefed," he chuckled.

"Bee invited me to go along after our lunch to the Mayflower where Nigel was auditioning for some part in it."

"Nigel." But the laughing eyes were kind and she couldn't take offence. How different this was, she thought, from being with strangers who seemed to spend most of their time jockeying for position.

"It's either Christian names or darling!" she said.

"That's better!"

She couldn't help but laugh.

"What," he said, "do theatrical people talk about at a thing like this?"

"Theatre." And, after a moment, "I'm beginning to think that if they didn't have theatre to talk about they wouldn't be able to keep up a conversation."

"You're probably right. Although to be fair, Mrs Culverwell didn't ram it down our throats all the time at our lunch, did she?"

Our lunch. Somehow he gave it intimacy.

"No," Alice said. "She's a very . . . a very charitable person. And one I'm very grateful to."

"How's it coming along? Your Holly Wood Gowns?"

She shrugged. "There's all the spade work to be done. Setting up the company. That sort of thing. Tell me, Mr Rackham . . . Martin, how do you like the sound of it? Holly Wood Gowns?"

"Well, I don't really know, Alice. It's not my bailiwick. Have you gone off it or something?"

"Yes, I have a bit. How about Alice Dresses?"

He nodded approvingly. "Yes. It's to the point. And it's not pretentious."

"Which Holly Wood Gowns was."

"Since you ask, yes. You've made your mind up, Alice, haven't you? To change it, I mean?" And at her nod, "Will his nibs agree?"

"Mr Kornblath? I've already told him."

"What did he say?"

"He didn't have a chance to say anything. I just . . . threw it in – in passing, so to speak. When I was being received. He didn't seem to mind. Mind you he doesn't know the new name yet."

He shook his head in profound disbelief.

"Your model seems to be attracting a great deal of interest," Alice said. "When I was looking at it, there was a man who was desperately anxious to meet you. He asked me if I'd introduce you."

"How did he know you knew me?"

"I've seen it before. The model. Mr Kornblath explained it to me the day he interviewed me."

"He explained it to you. That's astonishing."

She shook her head. "No. He wanted to impress on me that if he decided to back my business there wouldn't be any limits."

Why was she telling him all this? There was no advantage in it; there might even be danger. Significant as Holly Wood Gowns, or Alice Dresses, might become, it would be as nothing compared with the fantastic development Martin's model pre-saged. Martin! She was thinking of him as Martin and she'd only met him once! She looked away from him; looked around at the men and women circulating, chatting, laughing. At the flunkeys and the waitresses. At the display of wealth so out of joint with a country suddenly, like the rest of Europe, in desperate financial straits. This was his scene. These were the kind of people he met and entertained. He designed their houses, their blocks of flats and offices. He was at ease with them. He talked their language – or at least he understood it. And what was she? An interloper. She was as poles apart from his experience, his way of thinking, his attitudes, as she had been from those of Brenda Camroux and Nicholas Benson and the rest of that theatrical gaggle. But there was this difference – that while with them she had been tense, on her guard, attentive, choosing every word she spoke with care, with him there was a sense of repose akin to the relief one felt when an ordeal was over.

"You've been to these parties before, I suppose," she said. "I gather Mr Kornblath gives them every year."

How much it said, he thought, that she can refer to everyone else by their Christian names but Solly has to be hung up on a title.

"Yes," he told her. "He does and I'm on his list."

"Are there lots of parties like this?"

He shook his head. "Not quite like this. Of course there are lots of parties." And the smile, now slightly self-disparaging, was in his eyes. "I'm afraid we're an inward-looking bunch."

"Who are?"

"Those of us who make our living out of property development." He paused, then went on: "Someone once wrote that the building industry is a synthesis of diverse but interwoven interests. And that wasn't far out. Developers, architects, engineers, surveyors, builders. It makes for a vast structure, Alice, and we're all dependent on each other for our existences." He chuckled. "Except that there are rather more of us, we're probably every bit as limited as theatre people are."

She shook her head. "No," she said firmly. "You're not. Because you're part of the real world. As I am." And something occurred to her which had not occurred to her before. That neither Sam nor Tom had been of the real world either.

A waiter came up, topped up their glasses and moved on. They were in the corner to which Rackham, assured and somehow compact in dinner jacket compared with Nicholas Benson willowy in his tails, had guided her.

"Are you enjoying this? Being here, I mean?" she asked.

"Not particularly."

"Do architects give Christmas parties?"

"Some do."

She caught the nuance in his words. "But you don't?"

He could have explained. There were the rules and regulations to consider. Professional men were not allowed to bribe or advertise for work and not supposed to tout for it. But if the invitation made it clear the party was being given for friends – and what better friends for an architect to have than a borough engineer, a planning officer, a few developers – if it did, what better place to give it than in the drawing office where the walls were lined with pictures of the jobs completed, or even of jobs that had never started but looked as if they might have done?

He could have explained that he found the idea sly and distasteful but had he done so she might have judged him smug.

"No," he said. "I don't." He sipped his champagne to make the break. "Alice, I told my wife about you. She'd like to meet you."

"Isn't she here?" she asked with a little surprise.

"She suffers from multiple sclerosis. She's confined to bed or a wheelchair." And as Alice put her hand up to her mouth in genuine dismay. "On the whole she doesn't like meeting new people these days. But she would like to meet you. Would you come and see us?"

"Yes, of course."

"Perhaps I can give you a ring to fix a time."

"I'm not on the telephone." It was out. Just like that. With Nigel Tarrant she'd had to equivocate!

"Well perhaps we could fix a day now. Before Christmas? We always spend Christmas with her family. How about this weekend? Saturday or Sunday? We're free on both."

She read it correctly. He was a busy man. A very successful architect. And he was free for an entire weekend. He had to be devoted to his wife.

"Well?" he pressed her. "How about Sunday, say?"

He reached into his pocket for a wallet and withdrew a visiting card. It gave her ample time to dream up some excuse. But none came to her. Or perhaps she didn't really try to find one.

"There," he said. "Fair exchange?" It puzzled her until she realised that it was exchange of glass for card he was proposing. In the changeover their fingers touched and she felt a strange and quite new frisson of pleasure at the contact. She took the card and put it in her handbag.

"That's settled then?" he said. "Sunday. Half past three, say. And stay long enough for a parting drink."

"All right," she said. And then, recovering poise, "You don't leave me much option, do you, Martin?"

His eyes glinted mischievously. "I didn't have the time to," he chuckled. "Solly's bearing down on us."

3

Alice could ill afford it, but she took a taxi back to Highbury, comforting herself with the thought that it was an option hardly to be avoided with Solly's guests spilling out into Berkeley Square and Moss signalling one by one to a rank of cabs clearly organised to be available for those who were not being collected by chauffeurs or strolling to some nearby restaurant or club. Besides, she could hardly subject her precious finery to a number nineteen bus!

Her head was as seething with ideas as if it was filled with a swarm of bees, and no sooner did she reflect on one facet of the evening before some new reflection, comparison or speculation insisted on precedence.

So far as her own affairs were concerned, nothing had advanced. She had assumed that Kornblath would find the time for a discussion, however brief, on their joint enterprise. He had not even mentioned it. He had merely passed the few moments he had obviously allocated to herself and Rackham with punctilious courtesy, admiring her dress, enquiring after Martin's wife, recounting an amusing incident at a recent dinner party and, with a sly dig at the peer he'd invited, offering to wager the Labour Government wouldn't see 1930 out – then, wishing them both a Happy Christmas, he'd passed on his way.

A Happy Christmas, Alice thought ironically. With Dessy and Thady crammed somehow into Garmoyle Road and herself boarding out wherever Mother had found a place for her. And after Christmas, what were her alternatives? Either she rented that ghastly tenement in Canonbury that she'd recently seen or she took Dessy and Thady away from the new schools they were doing so well at and they stayed in Liverpool.

Oh it was so absurd! So utterly ridiculous! And so frustrating! She stamped her foot in annoyance on the taxicab floor. Here she was on the brink of a venture which promised a way of life in which she would be able to have everything material she had ever wanted for herself or for her children. Alice Dresses – she was quite decided on the title – would not fall; the combination of Kornblath's money and her own experience, imagination, energy, acumen and determination guaranteed that. If ever she needed proof that she had the capacity to cope with business even at the highest level, surely this evening had supplied it. For an hour or two she had held her own, more than held her own, with an assemblage of men and women of sufficient wealth or importance to merit being invited to one of the social functions of the season! And now she was on her way back to a vermin-ridden semi-basement flat from which she was being expelled as an undesirable tenant! Was there ever anything more preposterous?

Seven

1

"You've two boys, Martin tells me, Alice."

"Yes, Julia."

"Why didn't you bring them? It must be very dull for them being on their own on a Sunday afternoon. Or perhaps they've got an aunt or an uncle they like going to?"

"I'm afraid they're all too far away. In Liverpool. And Africa."

"Africa!"

Alice nodded. "My first husband's sister. Hetty. I believe she's in Uganda at the moment. She's a very religious woman and she spends a lot of time in different places with . . . well a sort of missionary society."

"Really! My father would be interested. He's a clergyman."

There was a moment's silence. Alice said: "Do you have brothers and sisters, Julia?"

"No sisters. I had four brothers but two were killed in the war."

"How dreadful."

"War is," with a small smile, "but it has its compensations. If it hadn't been for the war, Martin and I wouldn't have met."

"How did it come about? That you met?"

"She nursed me." He chuckled. "Or at least she would have done if they hadn't discovered what a fraud I was and slung me out before she could get her hands on me."

"Where was this?"

"A place called Poix."

"In France?"

"Yes."

"Tell me about it."

"Julia would do better." He grinned. "You see I was unconscious at the time – or for most of it anyway." And at Julia's hesitation. "Go on, Julia. Tell Alice all about it."

2

Julia Cresswell stands back against the corridor wall to make room for the rubber-wheeled trolley to pass by her. She glances at the face of the man stretched out on it. It is ashy grey as if all the blood has been drawn out of him.

When the trolley has gone by, she goes in, pushing ahead of her her own small trolley with its oil-lit lamps (for there is something amiss with the electricity) and a collection of the items she needs for the early morning round. The room is not of sufficient pretensions to be called a ward – it is just a bedroom in a mansion close by Poix. The beds are ranged along the side walls and at the end of the room there is a huge window which overlooks a garden which has gone to seed through neglect in nearly four years of war. Once the window had fine brocade curtains but they have been removed – whether by looters or for hygienic reasons, no one knows. But it is of no account for this is the early morning round and the night is still black outside.

It isn't too bad a room for a new nurse to be blooded in, for it is what the sister euphemistically calls a light injury ward and unless the most recent arrival, an injured pilot brought in the previous night, doesn't come out of his concussion, there is not too much danger that any of the men in it will die.

As she comes in, rustling in her starched, white apron, those who are not asleep or not in too much pain turn their heads to look at her theatrically illuminated by the lamplight's glow. She is young, just twenty, and very pretty. She is a wonder to them for they have all but forgotten that such a perfection of cleanliness and beautiful decency exists. Below the white

135

headscarf which floats behind her as if caught by a breeze, her curly, auburn hair escapes, hiding her ears and forehead, shadowing her hazel eyes. The tight white belt draws attention to the slimness of her waist, the tight white collar to the slimness of her neck and the billowing of the apron hints at full, young breasts. Their study of her is anything but carnal; she is more angel than temptress, more vision than reality.

She moves slowly and quietly. This is a special time of the day when after a night racked by pain and discomfort some of them will have at last perhaps fallen into a doze in which the pain is muted, even forgotten. The job has to be done but all the same she is unhappy at having to awaken such men one moment earlier than she has to. So she moves quietly, carrying her lamp from bed to bed, her movements failing to spoil the pleasant, competent-sounding rustling of an apron so recently pressed that it hangs almost as a square, the creases of its folds iron sharp.

The eyes of all who are awake follow her and the souls of their owners are warmed, for in a room to do with patching up young men with lives blighted by the sordid reality of war she is as a ray of sunshine on a rain-driven day, as a reminder of times filled with joy and gladness, as a promise in a future bleak with disillusion and despair. She is happiness and hope and above all an assurance that one day, if the luck holds out, there will be a different way of life from mud and lice and pain and fear and hatred – from mutilation, disfigurement, dismemberment and death.

There are eight men in the room – seven who are, hopefully, recovering from operations of various kinds and the eighth is Rackham who is partially hidden from view by a screen. This is not because he is an officer and all the rest are of other ranks but because the doctor has said that as he is concussed he must be shielded as far as possible from light – so there is an L-shaped screen which, as it happens, prevents any of the other inmates from seeing him although Julia is able to do so as she comes into the room. She glances at him and reflects that with his head heavily bandaged and an arm encased in plaster he looks quite as bad as most of her other charges, but she has been told by the sister that providing he comes out of his concussion he should be all right; that in fact he has apparently been extraordinarily fortunate, thrown out of his aircraft before it burst into flames killing his observer, and is no more badly injured than many a man in a minor accident.

She stops by the nearest patient (who has the bed across the room from Rackham), and withdraws a thermometer from a glass charged with them. This one is wide awake and her favourite. He has a snub nose, a freckled face and eyes as bright as a bird's. "Morning, Charlie," she says, leaning forward to pop it in his mouth. Private Charlie Smart who, unlike most of the others, is sitting up and, but for the hump which is a wire cage over the stump of his amputated leg, looks far too well and untroubled to have any business being here at all.

"Mornin', nursey," he responds cheerfully. " 'ad the bedpan and the bottle in the night so that's orl right, eh?"

"That's splendid, Charlie."

She puts the thermometer under his obediently lifted tongue and, taking his wrist gently, begins to read his pulse. She does not see Charlie as a soldier but as a very brave schoolboy who endures his rebandaging without even wincing, never complains and has the effrontery to call the sister "Ducks". She knows that he is nineteen years of age (and having spent more than three years in the trenches must have lied his way into the Army in the first place) and has lived all his life in the East End where his father works as a bargeman. Taking to heart advice given during training, she makes it her business to find out enough about her charges to be able to find something however banal to chat about as an anodyne to the pain which she knows she causes them in her inexperience when rebandaging or even sometimes in the simple remaking of their beds. But she doesn't talk at this moment, knowing (because using less rhetorical words he has told her so) that the touch of her fingers on Charlie's wrist gives him exquisite pleasure.

"We got that new one in last night," Charlie says, nodding in Rackham's direction, the moment the thermometer is removed, clearly having stored this piece of information ready to get it in before any of the others have the chance of doing so and thus detain her.

"Yes, we're a full house again."

"They says 'e's got concussion."

"That's right, Charlie."

"Stops you remembering fings, concussion, don't it?"

"It often does at first. But it comes back later, usually."

"Don't always. Feller my Dad knew 'ad this plank 'it 'im on the side of 'is 'ead. 'E never got 'is memory back."

"Well he was very unlucky."

"'E's an orficer, yer know! The new one we got."

"So sister tells me."

She says it with just enough enthusiasm to respect Charlie's obvious delight at discovering himself sharing a room with such exalted company and just enough indifference not to appear unduly pleased at having someone to nurse with whom she will probably have more in common.

"Never thought they'd do that, you know," Charlie says. "Put an orficer in wiv the likes 'f us."

"It's a question of beds, Charlie," Julia says rather thoughtlessly, reaching for the chart of his temperature and pulse hanging on the end of his bed.

"'E's a flyer yer know." He shakes his head. "Wouldn't catch me in one of those fings. Dunno 'ow it is they stay up anyway."

"Yes, it is rather amazing, isn't it?"

"Wonder what 'appened to 'im. Got shot dahn, I s'pose. Seen it 'appen, y'know. There was this one came right over us one mornin'. Low 'e was. So low yer c'd see 'is wheels spinning rahnd and rahnd. An' right be'ind 'im there was this German, firing 'is machine gun. An' nex fing yer know, 'e's goin' up. Like that!" He raises his hands towards the complicated plaster ceiling, disfigured where, also for supposedly hygienic reasons, a chandelier has been unceremoniously removed. "'E goes up and then 'e seems to topple over and dahn 'e goes. Right into No Man's Land and woomph! 'Orrible it was! Great sheet of flame and yer c'd 'ear the bullets 'e must 'ave been carrying goin' ev'rywhere! An' nuffin we c'd do abaht it, poor bleedin' sod!" And he jams a hand against his mouth as guilty as a child caught at the jampot.

She smiles. "Don't worry, Charlie. I hear much worse. And I must get on."

The room is now stirring with life, wakened by Charlie Smart who never thinks of holding back. There is the sound of men struggling with difficulty to sit upright, a photograph knocked by an elbow falls to the floor and a voice says "Damn!" – but softly. "Don't worry, Sergeant, I'll rescue it for you in a minute," Julia says. The man across the room in the bed next to Rackham is groaning. It is a regular groan, not very loud but expressive, seeming to say: "Oh God, why do I have to suffer so?" repeated endlessly.

The man is named Pinkerton and has abdominal wounds. He believes he is going to die but the doctor insists it isn't so. There is no point in attending to Pinkerton ahead of the others simply because he is groaning and Julia moves to the man next to Charlie who has not only lost a leg on one side but a foot as well on the other. The leg he has lost is the opposite one to Charlie's – and at first Charlie had tried to cheer him up, suggesting they could buy an outsize pair of trousers and make a name for themselves in a circus as Siamese twins. A poor joke perhaps but Private Leslie Mancell had been dismally low in spirit when they moved him in and Charlie hadn't been able to conjure up anything better. It had fallen on the stoniest of ground. Mancell, a good-looking youngster, tall, well made, in the pre-war days very much a ladies' man with thick, jet-black hair and flashing eyes but now yellow and wan after weeks of pain and dismay, is not to be amused by anything, but lies by the hour on his back, staring at the ceiling, ruminating on the cruelty of fate. Julia Cresswell's beauty, far from stirring him merely increases his wretchedness. Whereas had his injuries been no more severe than his neighbour on the other side who has merely lost an eye, he would have been joshing her and pinching her bottom the moment she turned away, perfectly assured that however she protested she would have been secretly pleased that he thought well enough of her to do so – it was, after all, only delectable bottoms Leslie Mancell had ever been moved enough to tweak. Now, with a gloomy acceptance that his Lothario days are over and perplexed as to how even if a girl was prepared to take him on you managed the business anyhow with one leg missing almost to the crutch, the heart has gone out of him.

"Morning, Leslie," Julia says.

He looks at her gloomily, making no attempt to raise himself.

"What's good about it?" He is a Brummager with a heavy Midland accent.

"Come on, Leslie," she says cheerfully. "You can do better than that."

"You try."

"I am trying." She gives him a winning smile. "What sort of night did you have?"

"What sort of night do you think I had?" He hates her because she is lovely and desirable and represents what was once all-important to him in life and from now on will be denied him.

She picks a thermometer out of the glass.

"I'm bleeding," he says cantankerously. "My bandages are wet."

She is sickened. It is all too new and horrible. Not at all how she had seen it when she volunteered to be a VAD nurse. The wounded soldiers of her imagination had all been neatly bandaged round their heads and sitting up in their beds, grateful, brave and uncomplaining.

"Doan't believe me, do you?" Mancell says, profiting by her hesitation and making as if to shift the blanket to prove his point.

"Don't do that!"

"You do it then."

There is grim satisfaction in his tone.

Very carefully, she lifts the blanket with one hand and holding the lamp high in the other discloses the tragedy of what had once been a fine healthy body. To her relief she discovers that the bandage on the shorter stump is stained but not soaked with blood.

She replaces the blanket.

"Raight, aren't I?" His black eyes glitter in the lamplight.

140

"It is bleeding," she agrees. "But not very much." And with decision she is far from feeling: "It can wait until the Major makes his round."

In fact Mancell is relieved. Changing the bandages is an excruciatingly painful business – the worst thing of all.

"Didn't laike lookin' at it, did you, nurse?" he says with a small triumph. "'Aven't got used to it yet, 'ave you? Well you're going to 'ave to, aren't you? I mean this war's going to go on for a bluddy long time, isn't it? Long after I'm back 'ome in Brum, you're still going to be here, aren't you?"

She seizes on the one line of escape. "Brum?" she queries.

He laughs harshly. "Yaice." It is what he always says. Always "yaice" never "yes". "Birmingham." He lays emphasis on the syllables, mocking her. "'Eard 'f it?"

"Oh, yes." He has trapped himself and she is relieved – but guilty at the relief. A man with a beautiful body shattered the way his has been, is entitled to be bitter. "As a matter of fact, I usen't to live all that far away. Now would you open your mouth, please?"

"What's the point?"

"The point," she says in a very deliberate way, "is to make sure you're making progress."

"Not goin' to get me leg or me foot back for me is it? Stuffing a thermometer in my mouth?"

"Put a sock in it, Mancell!" This is from his neighbour, a man in his forties who, with a diagonal bandage over his empty eye socket, looks like a pirate.

"Don't try cooming the sergeant on me!"

The sergeant forces himself even more upright and glares with his remaining eye at Mancell.

"If you don't shut up and do what the nurse says . . ."

"You'll do what?"

"I'll tell what I'll do. Come and change those bandages myself." And he makes as if to remove his own bed-coverings.

"Bah!" says Mancell, but the threat is sufficiently blood-curdling to silence him.

Julia Cresswell shoots a grateful look at Sergeant Smith. "Come on!" she orders Mancell with all the authority she can muster and, while taking his pulse, says conversationally. "I used to live not all that far from Birmingham. Henley."

"That's not near Birmingham!" Bryant, who has a heavy Buckinghamshire brogue you could cut with a knife calls from from the bed beyond Sergeant Smith. "Henley's near Reading, miss! It's where all the rowing used to be done."

She turns her head, relieved. "Yes, I know that, Peter. But there's more than one Henley."

"I know the Henley Corporal Bryant's talking about," calls Private Spink who has been badly wounded in his arm and just above his knee and is across the room from the sergeant. "I used to go fishing there. In the Thames."

"What did you catch, Harry?" Charlie calls.

Julia is now attending to Sergeant Smith.

"Pike!" says Spink eagerly. "My Uncle Will used to take me. He had an old punt and we used to moor it above what's called Temple Island. It was a great place for catching pike."

For a while there is talk about fishing and Julia, who has the capacity to listen to more than one conversation at once, has picked up Sergeant Smith's photograph of his wife and is talking to him about her and how pretty she is. When the fishing talk starts to peter out, she puts the photograph on the bedside locker and deliberately primes the conversation. She likes it so much better when the conversation is generalised and believes it helps ease pain. "That's where the racing starts from," she calls. "The place you were talking about, Harry, called Temple Island. Is that near where you lived then?

"Not me. I lived in Ealing. But my Uncle Will did. Village called Turville. I used to go and stay with him sometimes in school holidays."

"Well I'll go to sea," cries Bryant eagerly. "I lived at Fingest!"

"I know Fingest," Julia says, moving to his bedside in the corner by the window which is streaked with heavy rain. "It's beautiful. That wonderful Norman church."

"It's Saxon," Bryant reproves her.

"Is it? Yes, I suppose it could be."

"Me uncle worked on a farm at Skirmett, y'see," Spink says.

That's 'ow it come about I knew it round there. Lots of farms there was. Did your Dad work on a farm too, Corp?"

"He'll tell you in a minute," Julia says. The thermometer is under Bryant's tongue.

"How did you know Fingest, nurse?" Spink asks. "I mean . . . well it's funny, isn't it? I mean, us all talking about the same part of the world."

"Oh, life's full of coincidences. That's what my father always told me." And she explains: "My parents had friends who lived at Hambleden. We used to stay with them for Henley week. When we went to watch the rowing."

"We used to play cricket against Hambleden!" says Bryant, with the thermometer removed.

"How funny," Julia says. "We used to go and watch it on . . . what was it called?"

"The Dene."

"The Dene! That's right . . ."

"You won't be playing cricket again," puts in Mancell gloomily. "None of us will."

"Shut up, misery," says Sergeant Smith.

"How's the chest feel today?" Julia says.

"'S all right so long as I don't breathe in too deeply," Bryant replies.

Pinkerton's groans continue unabated.

In the corner by the door, in his screened-off bed across the room from Charlie's, Rackham has recovered consciousness. In fact, unknown to any of the staff he had recovered consciousness some hours before and promptly gone off to sleep again. His mind when he first recovered consciousness had been far too confused for him even to query who he was, where he was and how he'd come to be here. In fact at first he had even been unaware that his left arm was in plaster and when he did discover it he imagined it was a support to the bed he was lying on which had somehow come adrift. For a while he lay puzzling over it and then went off to sleep again.

It was only on the second and third and fourth awakenings that he gradually and with increasing coherence began to work things out and even then in a jumbled fashion, with reality and fantasy still somewhat interwoven. He was not disturbed by this confusion in his mind and was in fact only too happy to yield to the temptation of allowing weird transient dreams to retake possession. The dreams were nothing to do with flying, nor on the whole to do with war, although occasionally the faces of some of those he'd met through flying appeared in curious and quite unconnected situations. Nothing was tangible and there was no thread holding any of it together. It was like a book of snapshots of events with which he had had in most cases no experience flicked open here and there.

But gradually he made discoveries – the first of which was that he was in a bed in quite the smallest room he had ever been in in his life. Faced as he was towards the curtain and not disposed to lift his head to discover it didn't reach to ceiling height, he wondered at first if he was in a bunk on a ship. And listening for the expected sounds of water hissing past he heard Pinkerton's steady groaning, which reassured him his judgement was sound, the groans obviously being the sound of ship's timbers under stress. It made sense too of the plastered left arm, which was clearly a bar to the side of the bunk whose purpose was to stop him falling out. But where then was his left arm? He felt along his side for it but there was nothing. Absurd! It must be between his body and the restraining bar. He searched in vain for it and in searching drifted off to sleep again.

When he comes to he remembers his quest and starting again this time at the shoulder discovers he is in plaster from bicep to wrist. To beyond his wrist. He reaches with his right hand for his left, finds it and waggles its fingers. Yes, it is him all right. Extraordinary! He puts his good hand up to his head to scratch it and discovers bandages. Good Lord! He must have had an accident! But how? When? He has absolutely no recollection of the reconnaissance flight. Well he'll have to go and find someone to tell him what has happened. He starts to try to get out of bed and it is only then he discovers that his left leg is in plaster too.

For the first time real consciousness takes over. He lies back to puzzle it out and in doing so discovers it isn't a wall he'd been looking at but a screen. "Well I never!" he breathes. "I'm in a bloody hospital!"

The knowledge gives him a curious sense of satisfaction. I've got away from that damn wind that was cold enough to freeze the balls off a brass monkey, he thinks. But he doesn't know what wind he is thinking about. He struggles for a while, trying to see where such a cold wind fits in, and although he fails to do so draws from it comfort by the comparison of his present warmth and snugness. Now what the hell has happened, he asks himself, his mind becoming clearer and clearer. Where am I? How did I get here? And he concentrates as best he can on remembering the very last thing he'd done before evidently losing consciousness. But he can't pin it down. He remembers flying trips. Remembers men he'd flown with. Remembers his observer, Robin Judd. But nothing comes to mind which gives him the least clue as to how he's ended up in hospital. Well, I suppose someone will explain, he reassures himself and falls to unhurriedly examining himself to discover if there is anywhere else where he is damaged.

It is not quite dark. Somewhere, hidden from direct sight by his screen, a lamp is burning. On the other side of his screen Pinkerton groans steadily, his groans coinciding with his breathing. And listening carefully Rackham becomes aware of other sounds. Someone is snoring softly and worse, far worse, someone is grinding their teeth making the incredible, frightening, crashing sounds that only those who have heard teeth ground can imagine.

Yes, well it's simple enough. I'm in a hospital and I've got a broken arm and a broken leg, a terrible headache and my head's all bandaged up! I must have crashed. But surely I'd remember crashing! He bends his head forward and closes his eyes in a tremendous effort to bring back to memory the incident which has resulted in him being here. But without reward. He tries casting his mind back to the mess, to the people he's flown with, and while he can without difficulty recall all manner of incidents, see faces, hear voices, he finds it impossible to string them together in a logical sequence which leads to an explanation of his present situation. If I'd crashed an aircraft I'd remember that, wouldn't I, he tells himself. Was it in a car? Or did we get bombed? He shakes his head. No good. All right. What was the last thing I remember? Think! Think!

It is while he is engaged in this supreme but ineffective effort at concentration, that Julia Cresswell comes into the room to commence her pre-dawn round. As he is not turned her way he neither sees her nor realises she is a nurse, but although his mind is confused, his senses are acute enough to be able to follow and understand all the conversations which her entry evokes.

Her initial conversation with "Charlie" is especially illuminating. It tells him that the person who has entered so soft-footedly is a nurse – which confirms he is indeed in a hospital – and the man's *"that new one we got in last night"* is presumably himself. And there is more to come: he is suffering from concussion which (and this he hasn't known before), it seems, stops you from remembering things; but apparently in most cases after a while you get your memory back. It is all very reassuring. The things he does remember – such as that he was an officer and a pilot – are confirmed; the assumption he must have had a crash is supported; and the worry that if he had crashed he would surely remember doing so, removed.

He settles himself, content to lie silently doing, as he dubs it to himself, a "Sherlock Holmes" on who and where he is and what has happened to him but, quite soon, realising that he has learnt more or less all that any of the occupants sharing the ward can contribute, he finds his interest switching to the nurse who is clearly doing the morning round and will, presumably, sooner or later be taking a look at him.

She is obviously new to the calling – the man from Birmingham she calls Leslie (an unpleasant fellow, Rackham decides) has made that clear from his snide remark. This indicates that she is probably young, which her voice seems to confirm. But then, he warns himself, that doesn't follow, as it is well known that the one thing which changes little with the passing years is voice and just as, with the war going on so endlessly, Kitchener is scraping the barrel for cannon-fodder so, presumably are hospitals for nurses. Well he will discover in due course. Meanwhile it is an intriguing game. The girl – or woman – is obviously well educated, most likely of gentle birth and has a well-to-do background. Her parents bringing – ah, that surely makes her young! – her parents bringing her down from this other Henley near enough to Birmingham to stay with friends in Hambleden for "Henley week" – one of the year's social occasions – confirms it. As for her character: well she is unselfish, patient and considerate – willing to contribute to conversations which probably in themselves hold little of personal interest and to chip in with promptings when they flag. She is kind and sympathetic yet at the same time capable of firmness – she allowed this Leslie fellow plenty of latitude but knew when to put her foot down. What with carrying a lamp and one thing and another, he tells himself with a mental chuckle, she's quite a Florence Nightingale!

And so, having created in his mind a vague picture of what he imagines the girl might look like, he continues to listen with abiding interest to the subsequent conversations as she continues on her round. And in spite of a splitting headache and an overall sense of haziness, looks forward with pleasurable anticipation to meeting her in the flesh.

She arrives at Pinkerton's bed. His Christian name, it seems, is Eric.

"Morning, Eric," she says in just the same tone as she has used with all her other patients.

"Oh, nurse!" His voice is desperate. "Can you give me something? Please!" It is the cry of an animal in pain. "I can't bear it any more!"

"It will ease, Eric," she says. "I promise you."

She is looking down at him. He is even younger than Charlie and he has a baby face. His skin is pale with shock and pain but quite unblemished. For some reason it seems even more terrible that this boy should have had a bayonet thrust into him than that Charlie should have had his leg blown off by a shell burst. But of course Charlie has been hardened by experience, she tells herself – he's had three years of it. This boy, just a week or two.

147

What was he like a month ago? Did he volunteer? Did he go into the trenches keyed up with excitement and determination, come to avenge a brother like Rupert and Simon did? Or was he a conscript, forced against his will to take his part in this senseless idiocy, hating every moment, terrified for every waking second of his young life, scarcely knowing an unbroken hour of sleep for the horrible nightmares haunting it. Well whatever it was, he's better here. The Major – that was the only way she's ever heard the doctor referred to – the Major says he's going to live. He doesn't believe it. He doesn't believe it's possible to have a bayonet thrust in your belly, twisted and pulled out again and be left in the mud for dead and still survive. And how can you blame him?

Oh, she sighs, how little we know. What is he to me? A boy with a name and the face of innocence who is suffering terribly. And what am I to him? A girl in a spotless uniform who says all the appropriate things that nurses say to comfort patients and denies him the morphia which is all he's thinking of. Who is insulated from pain and suffering. Who lives in a different world from the hell that he and Charlie and all the others have been dragooned into. And if I told him I'd already lost a brother and have three more at risk it wouldn't really get through to him. Because this world of mine is far enough from the front not even to be able to hear, let alone experience, the gunfire and the shelling; is, as he sees it, a different world from everlasting attack and counter-attack, from barbed-wire entanglements, from bomb craters, dug-outs, trenches, from machine-guns and gas and hand grenades, from barrage and bombardment. The results of all this may be here: the mangled flesh, the broken bones, the pain, disfigurement, despair. But we, the doctors and the nurses, are, he thinks, detached from it – he is too young, too immature to realise that agony of the soul can be as crucifying as agony of the body. And perhaps that's just as well – perhaps the very fact he sees us as apart from the horror and madness from which he has been removed will, once his pain has eased, be important in his rehabilitation. It is not only bodies we are here to mend but minds as well.

"I'll speak to the Major, Eric," she says. "I'll see what I can do."

"He won't give me anything. He says I don't need anything." He breaks into sobs.

"No, Eric, he doesn't say that. He says you don't need it as much as others do. It's very difficult for him, Eric. We're so short of medicines . . ."

"He's a bastard. A bloody bastard."

"You mustn't use such words. You're much too nice a boy to use horrible words like that." Her voice is of a sudden strict. She sounds like a schoolmistress reprimanding a pupil. "And it isn't right. How old are you, Eric?" She knows how old he is. Eighteen. When he doesn't answer, she says: "You're eighteen, aren't you, Eric? Only two years younger than me. You should know better than to use swear words to a girl as young as I am. Now I've got to take your temperature."

"What's the point?" It is a cry of despair.

"You're just as bad as Leslie. That's exactly what *he* said." She says this loudly enough for Leslie to hear.

"He's only lost a leg! I'm going to die!"

"Eric, you are not going to die." She is speaking quietly and firmly now. "You've had some damaged intestine removed and the ends joined up again. And it hurts. Of course it does." She has no idea whether or not the remark is justified. She seems to remember learning that the internal organs are devoid of sensation, but whether or not this applies to intestines she doesn't know. But the important thing is to try to get Eric to stop *dwelling* on his pain, to try to put the *degree* of pain he is suffering in perspective and to break the connection he's created between pain and death. "But," she goes on, "it will start getting better soon and before long you'll be wondering what you were making all the fuss about. Now let's have no more nonsense. I'm going to take your temperature and your pulse and then I'm going to take a look at the poor man in the next bed who's crashed in his aeroplane, and then I'll see if I can find the Major and ask him if he can give you something to make you easier."

"Promise!"

"Promise, Eric." They are talking so quietly that although he is only two or three feet away it is all that Rackham can do to follow their conversation. "Let go of me, Eric. I can't take your pulse and temperature while you're holding my hand, can I?"

There is a silence which is transmitted to the entire ward. It is as if the other patients realise what a difficult time she is having with Eric and want to do all they can to assist. A small drama is being played out: a boy and a girl playing parts that only adults should be playing – if anyone should – and sharing a brief unison. They have no common thoughts and know nothing of consequence about each other yet there is a bond between the gentle fingers and the wrist which they are holding, an intimacy which the boy at least may remember all his life.

"Oh," says Julia, startled, "you're awake."

"Been awake for hours. Well, on and off."

She is discomposed. In the few days she has been at Poix she has learnt to steel herself against wounds of awful hideousness but this is her first experience of a man thought sufficiently at risk to merit a precious bed, who has unexpectedly regained consciousness and apart from the bandages round his head looks no worse for wear than brother Nigel, killed at Vimy Ridge, had looked when she visited him in hospital after his skiing accident. What should she do? Find the Major? Or Sister, anyway? Just because the man's recovered consciousness, it doesn't necessarily mean that it's right for him to be sitting up the way he is or, for all his astonishing breeziness, for her to dilly-dally chatting to him.

"Are you all right?" she says absurdly. And hastily: "I mean how do you feel?"

"Well, I've got the mother and father of headaches and I'm a bit muzzy but" – he slaps his plastered arm with his good hand – "apart from this," he leans forward to tap his plastered leg through the coverings, "and this, I seem to be all right. Would you mind telling me what happened to me? I don't remember."

"I don't know what happened to you. No one's told me."

"Well what about this?" He puts his hand more carefully up to his bandaged face.

"Well I haven't seen it, but Sister says it's only a lot of superficial cuts and scratches."

"Well that's good news."

"Yes." She is in a quandary. "Look . . ." She has forgotten his name. "Look, I don't think you should be sitting up. You've had—"

She breaks off.

"Concussion!" There isn't all that much of his face visible for bandages but his eyes aren't covered, half-closed eyes filled with a kind of magnetic amusement as if he not only sees humour in the situation but wants to share it with her.

"I've been eavesdropping," he explains.

She pulls herself together. "Yes," she says severely. "Well you shouldn't have been. And you shouldn't be sitting up either. Now please lie down. I'm going to fetch the doctor if I can find him. And he's very busy so it may be a little time before he comes." She remembers his name. "Captain Rackham, will you please do as I say. Lie down. No, just a minute."

She rearranges his pillows.

"*Now*, lie down." And when he has done so: "Well, as you're awake I may as well take your temperature and pulse."

She goes out of the enclosure to her trolley and brings back a thermometer, and, leaning over him – for he has obeyed – pops it in his mouth.

Close above him, lit by the lamp she is holding, are her full, soft lips, the perfection of young unpowdered skin and her beautiful hazel eyes.

When she has read the thermometer and noted his temperature on the chart hanging on the back of his bed, she takes his pulse. Her fingers are cool and gentle.

"You'll be coming back, won't you?" he urges. "With the doctor?"

"I don't know about that," she reproves him. "I've got another room of patients to look after. But I'll be back later."

"Good," he says with a grin. "Talking about Henley, I rowed there once. Perhaps you watched me."

She resists telling him that her father had rowed at Henley too.

"Captain Rackham, that's quite enough talk for now. You just lie there patiently and wait for the doctor to tell you what you're allowed to do. There'll be plenty of time to talk about Henley and things like that when he's given you permission."

In fact she is wrong. There isn't plenty of time, there is no time. Beds are too precious at Poix for men who have nothing more the matter with them than cuts and abrasions and a couple of reset limbs, and Major Muircroft has Rackham out of his and on his way elsewhere long before Julia Cresswell comes back to change bandages.

3

That morning at Poix which had brought Martin into her life was so incredibly imprinted on Julia's mind that she could almost have recounted it to Alice as it had been and one day, she told herself, if, as I think I'm going to, I get to know this remarkable girl better, I'll tell her all about it. But not now. Today's her day, not mine.

"I was a nurse in this hospital at Poix," she said, "and when I came to do my morning round an extra patient had arrived. Martin. He was the last one I saw on my round and all I did for him was to pop a thermometer in his mouth and take his pulse and tell him to behave himself. Then I left the ward. When I came back to it, he'd gone."

"But . . ."

"I spent three years tracking her down again," Rackham smiled.

There must have been quite a story there, Alice mused. How strange it is how life works out. I met Sam in a Warrington alleyway when he rushed to my rescue when I was being chased by that awful Herbert Clarkson, and within a couple of hours he was telling Ma and Pa he wanted to court me, and Martin meets his Julia for a few moments in a hospital ward and it's three years before he can ask her to marry him.

"Tell me about your first husband's sister," Julia said before Alice could have expressed these thoughts.

"Hetty? . . . Oh, in the war she was in France too. Driving ambulances."

"She sounds quite a girl!"

Alice smiled wryly, visualising Hetty the first time she'd met her waiting for her and Sam, or Sambo as he had been then, at St Patrick's Quay in Cork to meet them off the packet from Liverpool: smart, almost masculine, in uniform – peaked cap, tie, ankle-length skirt and clumpy shoes – bristling with decision. And she thought of her again and of the lunch at the Montpelier in Dean Street, over which, as much as anything because of Hetty's strictures, she'd finally decided to take the plunge and get herself a job. She hadn't been in uniform that day but somehow she'd looked much the same: brown eyed, heavily freckled, thin and angular in ankle-length brown tweeds and heavy shoes. Brown – it was the colour with which she had always associated Hetty. Brown, purposeful and somehow threatening. And even though she was miles and miles away in Africa, the threat remained. One day, Hetty would come back to England, and when she did she'd want to play a part in her nephews' lives – and would have plenty to say about how she had failed them as a mother. Hetty was not a line of conversation which could be comfortably pursued.

"Hardly a girl now," she said dryly. And swiftly: "*I* had a brother in the war. Not for long, thank heavens. It was over before he could come to any harm." But this was not a good escape – there would be embarrassment ahead if *this* line of conversation was pursued. "What were *you* doing in it, Martin?" she asked brightly.

"He was flying aeroplanes until he was shot down. By Baron von Richthofen, naturally!"

Alice looked at Rackham. Not just an architect but a wartime hero to boot. "Tell me about it," she said.

His eyes twinkled with his unique, magnetic smile. "Suppose I save that for your boys when we meet them." He was pleased with the way that it was going. It had been a little stiff perhaps, but they were getting through the preliminaries of strangers meeting comfortably enough. "I'm sorry I didn't think of asking you to bring them along with you," he said.

"Oh, I'm sure that Julia . . . Well, you know, they're nine and eleven. And boys of that age can be very boisterous." It was dreadfully disingenuous. They were never boisterous at home – nor, so far as she knew, elsewhere.

Julia smiled. "You're worried I wouldn't be able to put up with the racket they might kick up, aren't you, Alice? Don't be. I was brought up with four brothers and the two I've still got both have children and I find them very stimulating. And a consolation for the children Martin and I were going to have but couldn't."

With conversation bound to be restrained until both her illness and Tom Fenwick's suicide had been brought out into the open she had said this deliberately.

"Because of your . . ." Alice began. But she couldn't think of an appropriate word. "Illness" seemed too punishing and "disability" demeaning.

"Because of my multiple sclerosis? Yes, that's why we didn't have children. The specialist advised against it. I doubt if he would now."

Alice was shocked. "You mean you could have had children after all?"

"It seems so. But at the time, when the only name they had for it was multiple neuritis, it was believed to be something you could pass on."

"But they don't believe that now?"

"Well let's say, they're not as dogmatic as they used to be."

Julia was wearing a long, comfortable skirt of a caramel colour and a long-sleeved, collared top of the same material checked in black which buttoned at the neck. It went well with her beautifully styled auburn hair and her hazel eyes but it occurred to Alice that it was an outfit she couldn't have got into without assistance. Although she sat well in her wheelchair, her hands, Alice had noticed, seemed to tremble or even move a little wildly from time to time.

"It's something I know nothing about," she said.

"Why should you? Until our doctor told me what was the matter with me, I hadn't heard of it either. And I'd been a nurse!"

"Do you mind talking about it?"

"No. No, I don't mind at all."

4

It had been resolved that when Martin pulled off his first major architectural commission, they would celebrate by making a sentimental journey to Poix and then go on to Paris. It was a full three years before the appointment came for the refurbishing and extension of a major hotel in an East Ridings market town but as soon as the contract was signed they were on their way. Revisiting Poix proved something of a damp squib, with the mansion where they had met unoccupied and shuttered, but Paris was to prove unforgettable

They stayed in an old fashioned Left Bank hotel tucked away in a side street, a hotel typical of its kind, consisting as it did of no more than an entrance lobby, a small exquisitely feminine salon and a limited number of bedrooms of faded charm, and on the first evening they ate in a small restaurant in the oldest of all Paris districts, the Marais.

La Taverne du Marais la Chauve-Souris, a Russian restaurant, had been recommended as likely to offer a curious but rather special evening by a friend of Martin's who had fled to England when the Bolsheviks took over. And so it proved.

It boasted an upper floor and the cellar, which Sergei had insisted they should choose, which was approached by a flight of steps leading down beside a wall of flaking red paint into the stone-floored basement, the flags of which were, like the walls themselves, covered with carpets. The tables had pink tablecloths and each was illuminated by a huge candle stuck into a massive brandy bottle filled with candle stubs and runnelled with runs of candle-grease of a multitude of colours.

Besides themselves, there was only one quartet of diners: a fierce mountain of a man with a massive black beard, a girl with very dark hair and misty eyes, a second man, her lover obviously, who was young and eager, with a long Jewish nose, bushy eyebrows and half horn-rimmed glasses, and a middle-aged woman with strawberry-coloured hair. Apart from them the only other occupants of the cellar were a waiter, a pianist and a violinist.

The violinist, discovered later to be Hungarian, was a heavy man of average height with a fuzz of jet black hair and solemn pouched eyes, who had the mannerism of leaning over his fiddle and pointing it specifically at the customer he had picked out to play to – who as they came down the steps was the dark-haired girl. And scarcely had they taken their seats than she burst into song! They stared at her, amazed and entranced, for she was singing with great power and wonderful purity an aria from *Carmen*! It was a magical introduction to a memorable evening.

The aria concluded, everybody clapped the girl who, in fact, as they were to discover later, was currently performing Carmen at the Paris Opera House, whereupon the violinist turned his attention to the new arrivals.

"What would you like, monsieur?" he enquired in doubtful French.

For all that his own French was respectable, Rackham decided against trying to match him.

"Do you know any English songs?" he asked with a smile.

The Hungarian waved his fiddle like a triumphal flag.

"I know everything," he boasted in a sad sort of way, as if there was nothing new for him to experience. "I know Russian, Hungarian, Yiddish, Irish, American and French."

"No English?"

"Of course."

Rackham decided to test him. "'Parisian Pierrot', perhaps? It would be appropriate."

"'Parisian Pierrot'? Ah." He gave every impression of being caught out, plucked a couple of irrelevant chords and, with a bowed head and the fiddle dangling listlessly from his hand, made his way across to the pianist – a beautiful, polished young man with the bored expression of one who spent his life drifting from one bar to another tinkling tunes out endlessly – and muttered into his ear.

"Martin, how could you?" Julia chided him. "Give the poor man a chance."

"He's spoofing," he responded.

"You think he knows it? I don't believe it."

"You're not supposed to."

He spoke with total confidence and she wavered. He never spoke for effect and it was rare he gave an opinion lacking substance.

"Bet you sixpence!" she said.

"You're on."

And hardly had he said this than the pianist struck up the opening bars which led up to the melody she remembered so well from seeing the revue with Martin. And what was even more surprising was that, as if on cue, not only did the dark-haired girl get to her feet and make her way across to the piano but she was accompanied there by her lover, while the pianist, looking at them without the least change of expression on his bored face, tinkled the opening bars again and the violinist raised his bow. It could all have been rehearsed.

> *"Fantasy in olden days,*
> *In varying and different ways,*
> *Was very much in vogue,*
> *Columbine and Pantaloon,*
> *A wistful Pierrot 'neath the moon,*
> *And Harlequin a rogue.*
> *Nowadays Parisians of leisure*
> *Wake the echo of an old refrain,*
> *Each some ragged effigy will treasure for his pleasure,*
> *Till the shadows of their story live again."*

Terence Kelly

Julia clutched Martin's hand in disbelief. It was Gertrude Lawrence over again – and it was as if the evening had been created especially for the two of them. But there was more to come.

> *"Parisian pierrot,*
> *Society's hero,*
> *The Lord of a day,*
> *The Rue de la Paix*
> *Is under your sway.*
> *The world may shatter*
> *But what does that matter,*
> *They'll never shatter,*
> *Your gloom profound.*
> *Parisian Pierrot,*
> *Your spirit's at zero,*
> *Divinely forlorn,*
> *With exquisite scorn,*
> *From sunset to dawn,*
> *The limbo is calling,*
> *Your star will be falling,*
> *As soon as the clock goes round."*

It was not just the girl singing but her lover as well, making a duet of it. Not just Gertrude Lawrence but Noël Coward too! It was magical! Magical! Magical!

He felt his hand squeezed so hard it almost hurt and heard her whisper.

"Darling! Oh, darling!"

As if he had heard her, the violinist pointed his bow at her, nodded to the couple singing by the piano and while the pianist played on, the three of them came across:

> *"Mournfulness has always been,*
> *The keynote of a Pierrot scene,*
> *When passion plays a part,*
> *Pierrot in a tragic pose,*

158

The Deal

> *Will kiss a faded silver rose,*
> *With sadness in his heart . . ."*

Julia listened bewitched, with not the least embarrassment, and when the song was done mouthed breathlessly: *"Merci! Oh, merci!"*

The girl replied in heavily accented English: "It was a pleasure." And looking from one to other of them. "It is always a pleasure to sing to lovers. Would you be so kind as to join us for the evening? Or would you rather be alone?"

It was all so absurd.

They joined the quartet who all proved to be connected with opera, with the strawberry-haired woman the cantatrice's agent. They ate purely Russian food selected for them by their new-found friends: *Benins aux Oeufs au Saumon*, followed by highly sauced *Chaclik* (as the restaurant chose to call it), which the bald, broken-nosed waiter brought in on great long iron spikes, with at their base a chunk of cotton wool impregnated with something combustible, and lit so that what was offered was not so much a meal as a burning brand, while the pianist thumped out "El Toreador" which the second man, a baritone, belted out with gusto. It was all tremendous theatre. And they drank pink wine with the meal and afterwards innumerable sips of vodka. They talked and talked and talked. And the talk was all about Paris. About its quarters, its restaurants, its café chantants, its theatres – and especially about its theatres. Discovering Rackham to be an architect, the dark-haired singer, who was introduced to them as Colette de Musset, waxed as lyrical as a mixture of French and limited English permitted on the subject of the Opéra, which she unashamedly stated to be considered quite the finest in the world. She had at her fingertips all the relevant facts: its cost – no less than thirty-four million francs, its architect – the great Charles Garnier, its precept – that it must always be distinguished by the talent of its artistes and the taste and artistic merit of its presentations. It was clear that her life was theatre, that without theatre she had no life, that if she was somewhere where there was no atmosphere of theatre, then she would create it. And Rackham, who knew no more of theatre than any averagely enthusiastic theatregoer, suspected that her companions were not very far behind her. It didn't matter. He had no desire to present himself. It was all obviously thrilling to Julia, whose cheeks were pink with animation and whose eyes were sparkling with the joy of such an exciting and totally unexpected evening. And so they drank more coffee and sipped more vodka and no more diners came to spoil their intimacy: six guests, a pianist, a violinist and a waiter. And when finally they parted there was no attempt to suggest they might meet again – it was one of those spontaneous evenings which can never be repeated but live for ever in the memory.

It was fully four before they dragged themselves away, disdaining taxicabs, strolling hand in hand, unhurriedly towards their small hotel. It was not yet light but to think of sleep seemed ludicrous, for sleep would bring to an end a sense of *joie de vivre* it was unimaginable could ever be recaptured. Every sense seemed sharpened, every picture before their eyes had magic in it. The streets were all but empty. Once an open cart drawn by two horses, loaded with milk churns and driven by two sturdy young men in blouses and tall caps, went clattering by; here a street sweeper was wielding his broom and raising a cloud of dust, and there a *clochard* wrapped in a blanket lay sleeping on a bench. But on the whole they seemed to have Paris on a grey and misty dawning to themselves – it was as if, as Julia had heard said, Paris was a city for lovers, and because after three years of marriage they were as much in love as they had ever been, it was offering itself to them alone.

It was the last night of their holiday. Julia, undressed down to a half slip, sat on the end of the bed and, reaching down, began to massage the back of her calves.

Martin, about to hang his jacket away in the mahogany wardrobe, paused: "All right?" he said with a small frown.

"Oh, yes," she reassured him, "it's just that funny numb feeling back." She straightened, tossed her hair. "It must be all that walking." And with a chuckle: "And all these stairs. I hope you're going to put a lift in your hotel."

It was *his* hotel now.

"No, you're all right aren't you?"

"Oh, yes, darling don't worry. It's nothing. Just cobbles and stairs." She looked around the room. "We couldn't be anywhere but in France, could we? I love the wallpaper. You ought to find out who does it and have one of your bedrooms done in it and reserve it for honeymoon couples."

The wallpaper was a mainly pink extravaganza in a pattern much repeated of tall trees and ladies in flowing gowns seated side-saddle with, on the one hand, grooms holding the bridles and, on the other, little black boys holding long-handled parasols, and lovers in brilliant blue gazing adoringly. And in the background, lakes with swans, distant arches and open-air performances of woodland plays. It made the room, which was small enough, seem even smaller and more intimate.

At first they had made a genuine attempt to keep some semblance of order but had finally given in. The bed was too large and the hanging space totally inadequate and the room was now littered with hat boxes, bottles of Vichy water, guide books, paper folders and empty glasses. There were two chairs; one of rich red velvet was strewn with shirts, ties, trousers and socks, the other in a striped Regency pattern with furs and dresses. The floor was a litter of shoes, the dressing-table, its drawers pulled open, a conglomeration of make-up pots, perfume bottles, gloves and crumpled paper money. On the bedside tables there were handouts from restaurants and a week's scrapbook souvenirs. There was nowhere but the floor to put suitcases which, left open, had been impressed as maids of all work and supported a quota of possessions.

There was a bathroom of sorts – a slit, carved from the bedroom – and in it in a long line the commode, the bidet, the basin and the bath. The plumbing was frightening. The equipment in the WC cistern, twisted through subjection to innumerable angry guests, had abandoned the struggle, and left to itself its ball lay limply in the bottom, inextricably mixed with the gadget which kept the water in the cistern, so that all night long could be heard the sound of water escaping through it and careful manual dexterity had to be employed whenever the commode was put in use. The basin was a handsome porcelain affair with massive taps whose dignity was rather sullied by verdigris, and the bath was double-ended, offering a choice of which way to lie in it, and rocked alarmingly when used.

In a word it was quite unlike any bedroom Julia had ever been in before and she would not have changed an iota of it for the world.

"What time's the train tomorrow?" she asked, going to the dressing-table.

"Half past four."

"So what are we going to do?"

"Have a splendid lunch."

"Where?"

"Pré Catalan."

"Can we afford it?"

"No. But it's where we're going."

"I love you."

"That's a non sequitur."

"What's a non sequitur?"

"A conclusion which doesn't follow from a stated premise."

"What was my premise?"

"That we couldn't afford Pré Catalan."

"Well of course it follows that I love you if you're going to take me to Pré Catalan."

"You're just a miser. Look what you're doing."

She had paused in taking off her make-up to begin rubbing the fingers of her right hand against her thumb.

"What?" She was perplexed. "Oh! That? It's those bubbles again. Champagne bubbles." She stared at her fingers. "Funny, isn't it. Sort of pins and needles. Do you ever get pins and needles? No, you don't, do you? You'd have told me if you did."

"Have you always had them?"

She shook her head. "I used to get them as a child if I sat on my hands too long. But . . . No. No, I don't get them. It's funny. Sort of tingling." She chuckled. "D'you think it's because of making love too often? We've made pigs of ourselves in Paris."

He shook his head.

"I don't like it."

"Yes, you do."

"No, I'm being serious." He gazed at her, seated on the dressing-table stool, her head half turned towards him, the mischief in her eyes briefly fading at the gravity of his tone.

"It's nothing, darling. Really it's nothing. I'm just a bit tired from all that walking. All those cobbles." She would have none of such seriousness almost at the end of perhaps the most wonderful week of her life. "And as for the bubbles, it's obviously as I say. An overdose of making love!" She stood, came across quickly and threw herself into his arms, pressing her body hard against him, gazing with sudden passion into his fascinating, half-closed eyes. "But who cares!"

Lunch at Pré Catalan in the Bois de Boulogne was to be of such psychological importance in their lives that Julia was never to forget a facet of it. The dining-room: a great, corniced room with a pale blue ceiling and pink and green drapes drawn back at the windows to reveal the Bois; the buzz and chatter of voices, mainly French but here and there English or American; the fascinating clientèle: a woman draped in green and pink as if to match the curtains with a helmet of a hat, and her escort, a shaky old roué with a raddled face and a nose so long that Julia swore it reached a good half inch below his nostrils; a party of mixed French and English speaking bilingually and loud as if to try to force precedence of one language over the next and one of them, a triumphant woman, with such a face as to have Martin chuckling that she'd obviously had a winner at Chantilly yesterday or at Ascot the week before; a little girl, appearing from nowhere and handing a bunch of daisies to a man with pale blond hair of such profusion that it spilled thick and curling over his shoulders; the head waiter, a tall, sad-looking man with shoulders bowed from perpetual bowing and scraping . . .

Their lunch – costing a king's ransom but to hell with the expense!: *Buisson d'asperges en croustade à la Carème; Saumon aux grains de caviar; Soufflé Ambassadrice.* A bottle

163

of *Chassagne Montrachet*. Afterwards, coffee outside, and so much more to remember: a dazzling white tablecloth glinting in the sun; the shuff-shuff of waiters' feet upon the gravel; a very old woman sporting a daring little hat tilted over one eye, which was a cross between a bowler and Robin Hood; the chestnut trees so laden with pink and white blossom that the sunlight couldn't dapple through and the trees themselves so close that the paths between them soon vanished . . .

And a glass of armagnac!

"We've spent enough," she had said.

"Nonsense! We're not spoiling the ship for a ha'porth of tar!"

And he had signalled a passing waiter.

"*M'sieur?*"

"*Deux cognacs, s'il vous plaît.*"

The waiter frowned and said, "*Cognac?*" thoughtfully.

Martin racked his brain. "*Marquis de Sauval, armagnac?*" he suggested.

"*Marquis de Sauval!*" responded the waiter, suitably impressed. "*Certainement, m'sieur!*"

"That has to cost the earth!" she chided him.

"I expect it does," he agreed with a rueful smile. "Never mind. It's on the hotel."

"You'll need a lot more hotels the way you're going on."

"I'm going to have a lot more hotels!"

There was meaning in the remark. "A lot more?"

He nodded. "I'm going to specialise in hotels. There has to be a tremendous future in hotels."

"I don't see why."

"Travel! Motors. Trains. Ships. Aeroplanes. Particularly aeroplanes!" And in sudden annoyance: "Why the devil didn't we *fly* here!"

"You know perfectly well why we didn't. Because we were going to Poix first. Why particularly aeroplanes?"

"Because it's going to be the way we all travel in the future."

"Oh, don't be so silly," she scoffed. "Those funny little things that take a dozen passengers at most."

He shook his head. "Darling, I don't mean now. Maybe it'll take ten, perhaps even twenty years . . ."

"Just because you used to fly the things!"

"No."

"Anyway what do we live on in the meantime? For the next ten or twenty years."

"Whatever I can lay my hands on and a pencil to—"

The shuff-shuff of the waiter's feet interrupted. It was not just the waiter to whom they had given the order but the head waiter too, the tall sad-looking man with bowed shoulders. The waiter brought two brandy goblets; the head waiter a bottle which he displayed with frightening reverence.

Martin nodded gravely as if to indulge in an armagnac of such great distinction was an everyday occurrence.

The head waiter bowed, instructed his minion to place the glasses and poured two measures. Then, being an experienced head waiter, he nodded the minion away and himself withdrew.

When he had gone, Martin said: "We'd better sniff it properly. It's probably five francs a sniff!" He raised the goblet, sniffed, smiled and said with a chuckle: "Make that ten!"

He raised the glass. "To us!"

Julia raised her glass.

And then a terrible thing happened. Unaccountably, the goblet slipped from her fingers and fell to the table. It didn't break – but the brandy spread across the dazzling white tablecloth like gold.

"Children?"

Norman Tyrrell shook his head. "I don't advise it." And, after a moment, "In fact, I counsel you very strongly against it, Mr Rackham."

Rackham looked hard at him, this mild, stout, rubicund, bespectacled Harley Street specialist seated the other side of the huge mahogany table which served as desk, who had confirmed their fears and delivered the death knell to their hopes of continuity. "And what else?" he demanded.

Tyrell glanced at Julia and back to Rackham, who shook his

head impatiently. "There's no point in holding anything back," he argued harshly. "If you don't tell her everything there is to tell, she'll only go elsewhere to find out."

Tyrrell nodded. "Very well." He paused. "Multiple neuritis, as we call it, is a disease about which we still have a great deal to learn and it may well be we will find ways of dealing with it which escape us now, but I can only advise you on the basis of our present knowledge. It is, we believe, caused by degeneration and breakdown of fibres in small nerves in the body. There are various theories as to why this comes about—"

"Yes. We know. Bayliss listed them – including the ridiculous suggestion my wife drinks too much. A conclusion no doubt influenced by the fact that it was her dropping a brandy glass which finally persuaded me it was time to see a doctor."

Tyrrell smiled faintly. "Don't be too critical of your doctor, Mr Rackham. As I've just said, we still have a great deal to learn." He glanced at Julia seated in the hard chair next to her husband. "Mrs Rackham, after all you have told me about yourself and your way of life I am quite satisfied in my own mind that the cause in your case is a constitutional one, which is the reason why I have to advise you against having children. As I was saying, we believe your complaint is caused by the breakdown of nerve fibres. To a degree these can regenerate themselves. But only to a degree. As you have already discovered, after an attack has taken place you recover much of the use of functions you have lost, but never full use. That is the character of the disease. A continuous series of attacks, sometimes at quite widely spaced intervals, after which only partial recovery occurs. If I were to say it was like a ratchet and pawl in operation, would you understand what I meant?"

"Yes. The pawl allows the ratchet to turn easily one way but stops it turning back again."

"Exactly. Well that's how it is with multiple neuritis. Each attack brings progressive weakness of arms and legs and loss of co-ordination of bodily functions and although you always recover some of the facility you've lost, the recovery's only partial."

"And there's no cure?"

"We have yet to discover one."

"No way of . . . well, slowing it down?" And when he shook his head. "And what happens in the end?" And sensing his reluctance at having to answer her honestly, "Mr Tyrrell, please hold nothing back."

He looked at her with infinite regret. It was not just that she was a pretty woman in the prime of life on whom he had now to deliver a death sentence, which was all the more tragic because of the years ahead of continuing disablement of limbs, speech, sight and mental capacity before death at last released her. As a specialist in the disease, it was always a distressing business but one to which he had inevitably been case-hardened, especially as the vast majority of those he saw came to him as strangers having been sent by doctors he had as often as not never even met. But he sensed in the couple facing him across his table – the woman in her middle twenties, the man three or four years older – rare quality. There was between them a symbiosis so apparent as to have no need of speech. They adored each other – of that he had no doubt – and shared an understanding so profound that a mere movement of a hand was sufficient to express in full. As well, in both of them there were qualities which the world so badly needed in its young: intelligence, enthusiasm, imagination, humanity. The man, he had learnt from questioning in depth, was a brilliant young architect already beginning to make something of a name for himself; his wife restless to involve herself in some worthwhile project yet conscious that if she was going to have children she really shouldn't wait any longer. Now, because she insisted on it, he was obliged to tell her the truth; that to have children would be wrong and any career she embarked on to offset her disappointment must be a limited one. And, and he found this equally painful, in the process he would be telling the husband that he was condemned not merely to having to watch the slow disintegration of the woman he loved but more and more would be called upon to be counsellor, inspirer, nurse, while knowing that in spite of all his efforts at the end he would have to face the hideous decision when her needs were greater than he could cope with of sending her away to die in some nursing home.

But it must be said. The woman insisted and, as her husband had already underlined, had the courage and determination to make it her business to find out if he witheld it from her.

"Very well," he said. "As you require me to be clear on it, I will be. In the end you will be incapable of carrying out even the most simple tasks and will require total nursing care."

Her cheeks were white, but her voice was firm: "And die of it, presumably?"

"And die of it."

"And there is no possible hope of a cure?"

"There is always hope, Mrs Rackham. New discoveries are being made in medicine all the time. But as things are at present . . . No, I am afraid I have nothing encouraging to say."

Julia bit her lip gently. It was manageable because this wasn't new – merely confirmation of what she had been told already.

She looked at him steadfastly, chin raised: "And what, Mr Tyrrell," she said, "is your idea of the time scale?"

"The course of the disease is usually very slow. There are, I have to warn you, exceptions. For reasons we also do not understand, in a few individuals the rapidity of attacks is much more frequent."

"And have been in my case."

He nodded. "Yes. But I have no particular reason to believe they will go on being so. And if you follow the normal pattern, you should be able to lead a more or less normal life for, say, fifteen to twenty years."

"But I don't follow the normal pattern, do I?"

"No."

"So it could be less?"

"Yes."

"After which I shall have to be put into a nursing home?"

"I'm afraid so."

"After which I will live how long?"

168

"I would not care to hazard a guess."

"Perhaps as long again?"

"Possibly."

"Ending up a cabbage."

She said it in such a way as to make it clear it was to be accepted by Tyrell as a statement, not a question. A statement he need not reply to.

And when he did not, she said one thing more.

"If our doctor had diagnosed what's the matter with me earlier – if, say, he had sent us to see you a year or so ago, it wouldn't have made any difference would it? You'd still be saying the same thing today, wouldn't you?"

He understood her perfectly. She had accepted her lot; she must try to destroy her husband's sense of guilt. She was a brave and quite remarkable woman.

"I would," he said. "There is no cure we know nor any way of halting the progress of the disease."

5

Alice had listened in shocked silence to the heart-rending account, from the first symptoms of Julia's disease manifesting themselves in Paris through to the specialist's final diagnosis. When Julia came to the end, she said: "It's so . . . so unfair!"

Julia said gently: "We all have our crosses to bear. And you've certainly had your share lately, haven't you? It must have been ghastly. And all that publicity when all you must have wanted to do was hide yourself away somewhere until you'd come to terms with it. And two children to have to comfort. Has it affected them badly?"

Alice shook her head.

"It doesn't seem to have affected them at all."

The dam of restraint holding her back from speaking about Tom's suicide had been breached. Here, she realised, was someone to whom she could talk – someone whose interest went beyond morbid curiosity.

"I suppose," she said, although not believing this, "it was because Tom wasn't their real father." And, wishing to have Martin part of the conversation. "And that was a funny thing. Do you remember me telling you about Beatrice Culverwell's new play, Martin? The one they were auditioning for at the Mayflower after our lunch?" And, quickly, concerned she might have made a gaffe, that mentioning lunches at such places as the Crébillion might be painful to Julia and avoided by him: "The one that man Nigel Tarrant is going to direct?"

"*Counsel's Dilemma,*" he said, impressively.

"Yes. Well it's a play about divorce. I don't know the whole plot of it but, according to Beatrice, for it to work the audience have to believe that children are desperately affected when their parents part. And mine weren't. We imagined, Tom and I, that it was going to be traumatic for them. And it wasn't. The biggest problem was deciding what to call him. Tom, I mean."

"And what did you hit on?" he asked.

"Pops."

"That's nice," Julia said.

"Yes, but it's funny. Now he's dead they don't refer to him as Pops any more. They're back to Uncle Tom, which is what they used to call him in the old days."

In the old days, Rackham, mused. What a lot that said. How much she was unwittingly giving away. Or was it unwittingly? Did they have with them a girl desperately crying out to disburden herself? In the eyes of the world there was something shaming about divorce, especially when children were involved. And getting a divorce was a long drawn-out and, imaginably, painful and embarrassing business. For a year and more her life had to have been in limbo, however much she loved the man for whom she was prepared to deprive her children of their father. And it had all been for nothing. He brought to mind the little he and Julia had known about the reasons why the man had drowned himself. How strange it was. He had met this woman only twice before: once at a lunch through which she had been impressive and once at a social function where, amongst women of unlimited means, she had stood out as the epitome of fashion. To look at her now, knowing that she had already run her own successful business and was poised for even greater heights while remembering how superbly she could hold her own in quite exalted company, it was difficult to place her as the wife of a man whose principal interest in life was knocking or kicking balls about the place!

"Tell me about your boys," he said. "What are they interested in?"

She was grateful to Derek Williams. "Dessy, that's Desmond, who's the older one, loves music. And he reads a lot." She couldn't think of anything else to allocate to him. "And Thady, which is short for Thaddeus, likes chess and fishing. Oh, yes. And he collects stamps."

"Games," Rackham said casually. "They're not keen on games?"

"No. Not really."

It struck him that if one liked music and one liked chess they sounded far more interesting than any sons Tom Fenwick might have had.

"Are they like you, Alice?" Julia asked.

"No. They're like their father. Very like him. And not just to look at. I mean . . . Well, they're both very good at maths which is something they've inherited. Their father was apparently considered quite brilliant when he was at London University."

"What does he do now?" Rackham asked, interestedly.

"My first husband? Plays bridge."

"Only that?" His smile was teasing.

Alice held her own: "Apart from reading, not much else." And, to underline doing so, she added casually: "He walked out of London University the day before he was to take his Tripos."

"Why on earth did he do that?" said Julia.

"Well," Alice said eagerly, "apparently the day before he was to take these examinations he happened to meet the Provost on the university steps and they passed the time of day. Then Sam, for want of anything else to say, asked what would happen to him when he'd got his Tripos, and the Provost apparently had a warped sense of humour and said something to the effect that he'd go and work in Woolwich Arsenal for seven years at ten shillings a week, at the end of which he'd be able to call himself an engineer."

"What a crass thing for him to say!" Rackham said.

"Yes, Sam thought something like that. He was an impulsive man and d'you know what he did? Said: 'Really? Well, good day to you, sir!' and, clamping his top hat on his head, stalked out of the university."

"What an incredible story!"

"Oh," said Alice, warming to it, "that's only the beginning of it! There was this man Joseph Mott, who's Thady's godfather and has a business in which my first husband's a sort of partner. Well, Mott was at university with him but I don't think he was getting anywhere and d'you know what he persuaded Sam to do? Go off to Paris with him! And that's what they did. And then when they ran out of money, they had a brilliant idea! Sam's father had died and his mother lived in this big house in Ireland and she was very rich. Between them they concocted the idea . . . well, I imagine it was Joseph who really thought of it, he's that kind of man . . . this idea of Sam being very ill with a dangerous complaint and there being only this one doctor in the whole of Paris who could cure him, Professor Gagin – they got the name from the street they could see across from their hotel window, Rue Gagin – and they telegraphed to Sam's mother for permission to hire him and she telegraphed back: *Hire Gagin at all costs. Sam's life must be spared.*" And so they did, and Sam made a slow but sure recovery and his mother sent the money, but she was so pleased that she cabled Gagin to thank him personally and of course it came back that there was no such professor known to be living in Paris. And that was when Sam got cut out of her will and didn't inherit Crogellan House, as it's called."

As she came to the end, almost out of breath, Alice knew the guilt of someone who has allowed enthusiasm to run away with them. But Julia was fascinated, not only with the story but even more with the woman who had told it. The way it had come out, in such a flood, spoke volumes. Here, she realised, was someone who was all bottled up with problems, doubts and uncertainties, nursing a fund of experiences, disasters, triumphs – and no one to share them with! Her own affliction might be unfair but at least she had Martin.

"And your boys have inherited the mathematical ability their father has and doesn't use?" she heard Martin say.

"Yes. When it comes to arithmetic they're quite amazing. Both of them."

"Where are they at school?"

Alice hesitated. With all this talk of Crogellan House and Sam's mother being a rich woman, I've asked for that, she told herself. She shrugged mentally – there was no way out of it.

"Desmond's at Highbury County School and Thady's at Drayton Park Council School," she said bluntly.

She could have said Eton and Winchester for all the effect this seemed to have.

"Can they bring out this ability your sons have?" Rackham asked keenly.

"Probably not," Alice admitted. "You've heard of Baylock?"

"Of course."

"That's where their father went. And it's where I hoped they'd go too. But when Tom, my second husband, had his job taken away from him, it just wasn't possible. We had to do the best we could. And at least as far as Thady's concerned he might still be able to have that sort of education because they're quite sure he's clever enough to win a scholarship." And to Julia, "I imagine your four brothers all had the same sort of education?" And, at her nod: "What do you think I ought to do? Encourage Thady to get his scholarship although I know how much that's going to hurt Dessy, who's just as clever, or try to dissuade him from taking it?"

"You can't do that."

"It's very difficult."

"It must be." Julia thought for a moment and then decided.

"Darling, draw the curtains, will you?" she said. "And then would you mind going and seeing about the tea?" And when he had left the room: "Alice, tell me. Doesn't their father have a view about this scholarship business?"

"He doesn't know."

"Don't your boys ever see him?"

"Not very often." And that was an overstatement.

"But, surely, now that . . . well now that they don't even have a stepfather . . ."

She left it there.

Alice explained. "My first husband wasn't involved with another woman. Nothing like that. I asked him for a divorce so that I could marry Tom Fenwick. And he agreed. And one of the reasons why he agreed, was because it would free him from the responsibility of bringing up two children. Look, all this must be getting very boring for you . . ."

"It isn't in the least bit boring!" Julia said, quite severely. She studied Alice, concealing her puzzlement. Her dress, a jersey suit, the jacket worn open over a sweater and dressed up with several rows of imitation pearls, was an outfit in absolute contradiction to the picture being drawn of a financial state of affairs which required that children whose father had enjoyed such an education be sent to council schools. Yet she failed to give the impression of being a woman as selfish as the contradiction implied. She put it from her mind; there had to be an explanation.

"You've got a hell of a lot of problems, Alice, haven't you?" she said. "And by the sound of it not many people you can share them with. I'd like you to feel free whenever you're feeling low or there's something inside you screaming that you've just got to talk to someone who's prepared to listen to you, to come and see me and cry on my shoulder – if it helps."

And, stifling the beginnings of a protest: "Well you *should* see why! All right. I'm lucky. I've got a wonderful husband who does what he can to make my life as full and interesting . . . yes, and as bearable, as possible. But there is only so much he can do. And he's got his own life to live, his own career to follow. I'm not going to have him held back because he's got a wife who happens to have what I've got. And it's not *just* his career. He's an amusing, intelligent and enormously popular man who's bursting with energy, in tremendous demand, and loves being with people, men and women. And I can't, and I won't, and I don't allow him to fritter his life away mollycoddling me. But the days are long and it's very hard to bear living your life between a bed and a wheelchair with problems which don't bear talking about, knowing it's only going to get worse, never better, passing the time either listening to the wireless or reading a book, because that's about all that's left for you to do. And even reading's starting to get difficult.

"I get lonely. Very lonely. There are times when I could scream with the boredom of it and with the sense of injustice that this should have happened to me. And when I feel like that, I need someone to talk to. Not someone to give me sympathy but someone I can be sympathetic with. Not a nurse to give me pills to ease the pain; I don't *get* much pain. And not a professional do-gooder. No, I need someone alive and vibrant who, because she knows what suffering is, and because she needs help and advice and encouragement as well, will be taking as well as giving."

She paused, her eyes searching Alice's and, reading in them what she hoped to find, that Alice was as hopeful as she was herself that today would not be the end of a relationship, said: "I realise how busy you're going to be, Alice, but if you could find the time, now and then, to call in during the day and spend an hour or so with me, I'd like that very much."

"I'd like it too," Alice said.

"Good. You're on the telephone, I take it?"

"No."

"You're not! How on earth are you going to run this fantastic business you're just starting without being on the telephone? Surely there are bound to be times when people are going to want you in the evening?" And as Martin came in wheeling a laden trolley: "Martin, do you know? Alice isn't on the telephone!"

"Well that's not so remarkable. Only one in fifty of us is."

"But how's she going to run a business efficiently these days without having a telephone at home? Oh, it's absurd. Tell her, Martin."

He nodded agreement: "You must get on it, Alice. And don't worry about what it costs, Solly'll pay."

"Yes, I'm sure he will," Alice said. "But it's not that simple." She took a breath and brought it out. "I've been given notice to leave the flat I'm living in. My landlord's decided that a woman who's divorced one husband and had her second one commit suicide and have his name spread all over the newspapers is hardly a suitable person to be living in such a respectable and prestigious area. His words."

"Good God!" Rackham said incredulously.

"So where are you moving to?" Julia asked.

"I haven't as yet found anywhere suitable that's within my means."

"And when do you have to get out of where you are?"

"In about ten days' time."

"That'll be almost Christmas!"

"Yes."

"What *are* you going to do?"

Alice's chin came up. "Oh, I shall find somewhere. I'll manage. Don't worry. There's plenty of empty flats going very cheaply in our part of the world."

"Which is?"

"Highbury."

This is appalling, Rackham decided. Something has to be done about it.

"Alice," he said with a smile, nodding towards the trolley, "care to be mother?"

"Yes, of course," she answered, surprised.

She got to her feet and went over to the trolley. Inspecting it, she saw that nothing had been forgotten: there was a tea service, spoons and cake knives and forks, side plates and linen serviettes, wafer-thin sandwiches and tiny cakes, and all arranged with a feminine touch which showed that somewhere in the maisonette was help.

Puzzled, she turned her head to find Rackham talking very quietly to Julia who, catching her eye, said brightly: "We both take milk and I like one small spoonful of sugar, Alice, and stir it for me would you?"

176

There was a little conversation, and none of it of the least importance, as they drank tea of a blend quite new to Alice and nibbled cucumber sandwiches.

How cosy this is, Alice thought, how secure it feels. And she could not but compare it with what was facing her and the children in the immediate future – living in shabby, run-down rooms in some area of sordid pubs and grisly eating places, of beggars and drunkards and the hopelessness of unemployment. If this was your usual way of life, to sit with friends in a generous room, enjoying a civilised afternoon tea in front of a blazing fire, you'd never need know there was so much misery only a penny bus ride distant.

"Alice?" The word cut through her thoughts.

She put the teacup on its saucer. Their eyes met and she read compassion. He's going to say kind things, she thought, and we'll talk a little over tea and maybe I'll stay long enough to be given a cocktail to see me on my way – or maybe it would be better to use Dessy and Thady as an excuse to leave before I outstay my welcome.

"Yes, Martin?" she said, falsely brisk.

"How would you like to move in here until such time as you've found somewhere suitable?"

"Move in here!" She could easily have added: "What on earth are you talking about!"

"Well," he said, as if she *had*, and with the chuckle which so often seemed to be part of his speaking, "I don't mean in this flat exactly. But there's a mews house that came with this property when I took a lease on it and it's quite empty and absolutely ready to move into. It's got three bedrooms, not very large ones I'm afraid, and there's a sitting-room and a kitchen. And a bathroom. And it's got a small patio your boys might find useful to play in."

It was quite absurd. It was like one of those inconsequential conversations where people suppose all manner of ridiculous situations and ask you how you would cope with them. Or, even more simply, ask you, if you broke the bank at Monte Carlo, how you would reorganise your life.

"You can't be serious," she said.

"No?" His smile was very broad. "Well let me show you."

The mews house was, as he had told her, ready to move into – she could have bundled clothes and the essentials of living into suitcases, crammed herself and Dessy and Thady into a taxi and be sleeping there that night. For the remarkable thing about it was not just that its decoration was impeccable and that it was carpeted and curtained, but that it was fully furnished and equipped for living in.

She did not need to have this explained: the more doors he opened, the more obvious it became.

She stood in the principal bedroom, absorbing the care with which it had been furnished: the single bed with its pretty counterpane, the mirrored dressing-table, the damask-covered stool, the rich velvet curtains, the soft femininity of it all. This was more than a convenient room into which to shift a woman who could no longer be coped with in a maisonette above an office building; this was a valiant effort at reducing pain. It could have been a bedroom a loving father had prepared for a daughter coming home.

"I couldn't sleep here!" Alice said.

"Why not?"

"Because I'd be intruding. This is something so . . . so very special. Oh, Martin, I just can't put it into words."

"You mean you understand?"

"Of course I understand."

They were very close, just inside the doorway, their bodies almost touching. She could feel the warmth of him. Not just his bodily warmth, but the warmth of a man of great humanity.

"You must do as I say," he told her.

She turned her head sharply, looking up into his fascinating eyes, for once without laughter in them.

"What d'you mean?"

"It's what Julia wants."

"But it's her bedroom, Martin You've created it for her."

"Nil posse creari, de nilo," he murmured

"What does that mean?"

"Nothing can be created out of nothing."

She understood that too. It was love which had created this little bedroom, a love of a depth beyond her imagining. A love beside which Sam's love for her, even Tom's love for her, were shadowy. Of a sudden she felt humbled.

"I have never," she told him, "heard of anything quite so wonderful."

"Then you must accept."

"But why?"

"Because it will have served a purpose." He gestured. "Sit down for a minute."

She sat, on the edge of the bed. It seemed a strange place to have chosen. He went to the window and drew the curtains, shutting out the lights of some building, and stood with his back to the window, a man of no more than average height who yet projected an air of power and certainty, a man of whom she had never met the like before.

"Alice," he said, "there is no likelihood Julia will ever use this room. That's something I've come to realise. It is a very strange illness she has because there is just no way of forecasting its development. She could have an attack tonight which causes such further damage that there will be no alternative but hospital or nursing home. On the other hand the remission she has at the moment could last well into the time when you've got your business off the ground and have been able to organise the right sort of place for you and your boys to live in. Until then it would give her a great deal of pleasure to know that this little house was being used in the way it should be."

And, wryly: "Even illness doesn't stifle conscience, you know, and there is something very wrong in keeping a house empty for a dream which it has been accepted will not come true when there is so much need around us." He made the pace or two which separated them. "Come now, Alice," he said, "don't be proud."

He took her hands in his and helped her to her feet. A sense of being sheltered and protected encompassed her, filling her eyes with tears.

"There now," he said, and, releasing her hands, took a handkerchief from his pocket and held it out to her.

179

"Oh, I'm such a fool," she said, dabbing at her eyes, half laughing, half crying.

"Then you'll take the place," he said with a chuckle, like an estate agent who'd been amused.

"Yes. Yes, thank you. Oh, dear." The tears would not stop flowing.

"I'll get on to the telephone people tomorrow," he said, all businesslike. "And I'll arrange for a bed and furniture to be delivered for the empty bedroom. Now, let's see. You'll have to have your own furniture moved into store. Well there's a man who works for me who's very good at arranging all that sort of thing. I'll have him call on you tomorrow to start getting that organised . . ."

She understood exactly what he was up to – giving her time to be herself again. She was beyond disagreeing. Beyond a proper expression of her gratitude – the joy of having her problems solved for her was inexpressible.

Eight

1

One hundred and seventy-six Highbury New Park although somewhat differently designed was of much the same size and style as the houses Mrs Latta had bought and converted into Belmont Hotel. It was protected from the pavement by a shoulder-high stone wall with the usual pair of columns to form a gateway opening and, although the balls surmounting them had long since gone, the columns themselves were in surprisingly good order, clearly, to Rackham's practised eye, recently refurbished and on each of them was painted in sharp, black figuring the legend 176.

Leaving his Wolseley Hornet parked at a discreet distance along from prying eyes, he crossed the weedy gravel drive in the neglected front garden and, making his way up the entrance steps, selected out of a row of bells one which had beside it a small brass plate bearing the words "Highbury Bridge Club". After an interminable time, during which he had to ring the bell (which he could distinctly hear sounding within) twice more, the door was opened by a heavily built woman of about sixty with a mass of loose, grey hair whose untidiness matched her dress.

"Vell?" she demanded in a heavy foreign accent.

"I would like to see Mr Jordan."

"Mr Jordan is busy. He is playing bridge."

"It's important."

The woman hesitated. "Vell, who shall I say it is?"

"Mr Martin Rackham. He doesn't know me."

The woman stared at him inimically, her lips working as if he had interrupted her while she was in the middle of eating something and she was finding it difficult to swallow whatever was in her mouth.

"Vell you vill have to vait until he has finished off his rubber."

"I'll wait," Rackham said quietly.

The woman exited through a doorway on the left leaving Rackham stranded in a hallway which was devoid of furniture apart from a heavily overloaded hat and coat stand and a curious, crude yet heavily worked oak chair with solid arms and an elliptically shaped back. With nothing better with which to occupy his time he unhurriedly inspected this and discovered that the back pivoted on stout wooden pins let into the shoulders of the arms and could be lowered to form a table.

Never having seen the like before he was sufficiently intrigued to be caught out examining it by a pleasant, cultured voice: "We've always called it a bishop's chair but I doubt if any bishop ever sat in it."

"Oh," Rackham said, carefully restoring the table top to its original position without a clatter, and turning his head he met the eyes of a man who could have been no one but Desmond and Thady's father.

"I am sorry, Mr Rackham, to have kept you waiting," Samuel Jordan said, holding out his hand in greeting, a hand which, as he took it, Rackham found cool, fine-boned and, compared with his own strong hand, delicate. But the grip was firm enough.

"Suppose," Jordan suggested, "we go into the dining-room."

Rackham followed him into a very large, high room with windows overlooking another untended garden. Quite tight up against the windows, whose plain brown curtains were undrawn, was a good dining-room table with six chairs arranged around it, and there were also two armchairs placed either side of an unlit fireplace. The room was divided from the front room by a large opening, which Rackham saw from the hinge marks left behind had once held doors. In their place were rough oatmeal coloured curtains on a wooden rod which, being drawn back, disclosed about half a dozen card tables, located uncomfortably close to each other, at which a varied collection of men and women, mostly of middle age or a trifle more, were busy at their games.

A haze of blue cigarette smoke hung over them and drifted into the dining-room and the calling of bids and the slap of cards were persistent.

"We sometimes have to use this room as well," said Jordan, thus explaining why the dining-table was thrust so hard against the windows that it would have had to be moved out if anyone wanted to sit on the far side of it. "But I limit the number of tables to six on Saturday afternoons. I'll shut them out of sight, if not of hearing."

And going to the opening he reached up, and with a fine flowing gesture pulled the curtains across.

"Now, Mr Rackham," he suggested, "supposing you sit in that armchair and I sit in this one."

"Thank you, Mr Jordan," Rackham said.

Jordan reached out and with an energetic turning of his wrist operated a lever let into the wall. Almost immediately a hunched-up gnome of a fellow entered through a door at the room's far end.

"Tea, Stan!" barked Jordan at him, thrusting out his long legs, which, for all that it was long since gone out of fashion, were gaitered. And scarcely had the man, without responding, withdrawn, before he said, "What news of Alice?" And smiling: "There's no need to be perplexed, Mr Rackham. Yours is not a common name."

Rackham stared at him in disbelief tempered with respect.

"I owe you an explanation," Samuel said. "I know that my wife, that was, is living with my sons in the mews house at the back of the building in Mandeville Square where you practise as an architect. And as she has been living there for what? Why it must be three months now. As she has, she is bound to have mentioned a man called Joseph Mott who owns . . ." he waved a white scrubbed hand, "this house and employs me. A man of insatiable cunning, curiosity and persistence who regales me from time to time with such snippets of information as come his way which he hopes will distress me."

For once Rackham was quite lost for words. This was the man who had stalked out of university on a whim and thrown away the fruits of many years of study; the man who had cast away his rights to an inheritance and settled for the life of a commercial traveller in typewriters; the man who apparently found nothing more with which to occupy his mind than books and contract bridge; this was, above all, the man who had parted from a jewel of a wife and two sons of obvious promise. Julia, briefed by Alice as to his nature, had warned him not to expect to meet a melancholic but he was quite unprepared to find himself facing a man so apparently at peace with life.

"It won't worry you if I smoke?" Jordan was holding up his pipe.

"No. No, of course not."

Rackham watched as, with the practised action of the regular pipe smoker, Jordan filled the bowl from a pouch drawn from a pocket of his formal, dark suit, while in his ears he distinctly heard the murmur of bids, comments and in one case a positive complaint from the adjoining room. But at no time did the fine eyes which seemed to hold a glint of knowing humour leave his own.

"There!" said Jordan suddenly, his pipe well lit and his pouch and vestas put away. "Now we can get on uninterruptedly." And he waited, inviting Rackham to have his turn.

Oh, very well, then, Rackham thought, if this is the way it is to be. He said: "If it weren't for this man Mott, how much would you know about what has happened to the lady who was once your wife?"

"Very little," said Samuel agreeably.

"Or your sons?"

"Again. Very little."

"When did you . . . Do you mind me asking you these questions?"

"Not in the least."

"When did you last see your sons?"

"Oh, it was many months ago."

"Which means you haven't seen them since Fenwick committed suicide?"

"No."

"You know the sort of schooling they are having?"

"In essentials, yes."

"Through this man Mott?" He failed to keep the irony out of the question. But it didn't matter. Samuel was undisturbed.

"Well he *is* Thady's godfather," he replied.

It was such a staggering reply that Rackham wondered if for some reason Jordan saw him as an adversary best dealt with facetiously. But there was no sign of smugness; he could have been explaining to a partner at bridge the reason why he had played a particular card.

"Do you approve of their being educated in state schools?"

"My dear Mr Rackham," Samuel said, "with great respect there is not much point in asking me that question. For me to approve, or to disapprove for that matter, would be for me to express authority and I gave up all authority so far as my sons are concerned when I agreed to allow my wife to divorce me so that she could marry the unfortunate Mr Fenwick." It was spoken entirely without malice.

Another not inconsiderable silence, against the background of occasional coughs, bidding, card shuffling and the like from the adjoining room, followed.

"You haven't asked me why I'm here," Rackham suggested.

Samuel put the pipe stem between his teeth, looked at Rackham and considered the man he already knew a great deal about. How Mott set about assembling his information or who he paid to do his spying for him were of small interest compared with the reasons why the continued existence of a woman he had never been able to get the better of should so obsess him. But one thing was certain: that he would have been unable to keep bias out of judgement and in his mind he would have seen only one outcome of a woman as attractive as Alice moving into a house contiguous to the offices and flat of a man whose wife had been stricken by multiple sclerosis. Well, Samuel mused, in this case he could well be right, and if he were things could be much worse. There were twenty-four men and women, of different ages, different outlooks, even different nationalities battling it out behind his back, but there was not one of them come upon alone in that gloomy hall whose presence would have been as commanding. He sensed flowing out of this man who was neither tall nor, apart from his remarkably fascinating

185

eyes, particularly notable in his looks, a warmth and essence rarely encountered. Here was a man, he told himself, in whom you could place reliance; a man with the deep self-confidence so many strove to acquire and so few achieved. And, and this not least of all, a man of substance.

"I take it," he replied, taking the pipe from his mouth and holding it aloft, "you have called on my sons' behalf."

Rackham nodded. "You no doubt find that presumptuous of me"

"Not at all. I'm quite sure, Mr Rackham, your motives are of the best." He laid the pipe down gently on the ashtray on the side table near him. "But I'm afraid your journey is a wasted one."

"You have no interest in them?"

"I have an exile's interest."

"I have come to know them very well, Mr Jordan, and they are unusual children. Children who with the proper guidance may achieve great things."

"The proper guidance?" Samuel paused, nodding. "Ah, yes. But should their father be their guide? It is a rare father, Mr Rackham, who does not try to re-create himself in his children."

"To re-create himself in his children? Or to create in them the being he would have wished himself to be?" Rackham suggested.

"Well said." Samuel nodded approvingly. But went on: "There are fewer of us who know what we would wish to be than fathers who know what they would wish their sons . . . or daughters . . . to be. My father would have had me in finance – which would have been disastrous. Alice's father would have wanted her to marry a man a trifle above his social level, a clerk perhaps – which would have been a tragedy. Tom Fenwick would have wanted his stepsons to be great games players – which would have been absurd. Tell me, Mr Rackham, what did your father want you to be?"

Rackham could not but laugh. "He wanted me to go into the Civil Service and get a posting somewhere in the Colonies."

"Oh?" said Samuel, a monosyllable which said a very great deal.

The gnome returned just then with a tray of tea which he organised in front of them, drawing up a side table.

"Do you take milk and sugar, Mr Rackham?" Samuel asked.

"Milk but no sugar."

The gnome dispensed, putting three lumps of sugar into Samuel's cup and withdrew.

"He's Polish," Samuel explained. "He had his tongue cut out. A dreadful story." He reached for his cup, stirred it thoroughly and drank half of it. "It seems," he then went on, as if there had been no break in their conversation, "that the only man of importance to us in this context, who did what his father wanted him to do, was Fenwick: which is hardly a recommendation for filial loyalty."

"In other words you don't believe that not having a father is going to have any significant effect on how your sons turn out?"

Samuel shook his head. "I'm quite sure it *is* going to have a significant effect, although what that effect will be I haven't the least idea." He frowned, as a thought occurred to him. "I take it you haven't come round here to suggest I remarry my wife or something like that, have you?"

"Would that be so impossible?" said Rackham, but not seriously.

"What?" said Samuel, pretending shock. "You would have Alice locked up again and deprive me of my little empire? For two boys who would find the ménage stultifying?"

A head poked through the oatmeal curtains. "Mr Jordan, may we have a ruling, please?"

"Excuse me." Samuel stood, drained off his tea and exited through the curtains. Rackham noticed that all sounds of bridge-playing from the adjoining room had ceased. He could clearly hear the ensuing conversation. It appeared that a player had exposed a card out of turn and there was an argument as to what the penalty should be. The matter was soon settled. Jordan gave his verdict, which was accepted without dissent, and after a certain amount of chatter, during which Jordan returned through the curtains like an actor making his entrance, the normal murmur of card-playing resumed.

Yet the incident was not without its effect, underlining as it did Jordan's last remark: 176 Highbury New Park *was* his empire. To the world at large he might appear a failure, a man of outstanding mathematical ability who had thrown away the opportunity of doing great and important things and could do no better than scratch a living as a commercial traveller in typewriters; a lonely middle-aged man whose wife had walked out on him for someone younger and better favoured; a father who, for all his – Rackham suspected – contrived light-minded manner, would spend the rest of his days regretting the loss of the boys he'd sired. But, Rackham saw, the world would be wrong. In contract bridge Samuel Jordan had found a fitting challenge for his intellect and as overlord of the Highbury Bridge Club restored his pride. Here was a happy and contented man. And one who from his sons' point of view was irretrievably lost.

There was no point in staying any longer. Before Samuel could have sat down again he was on his feet. "I won't keep you from your bridge, Mr Jordan," he said. "It was good of you to see me."

"And it was very good of you to come, Mr Rackham," Samuel said unhesitatingly. "You'll remember me to Alice, won't you."

"And not to your sons?"

"Oh, I think," Samuel answered, "it would be better not, you know. They will have enough complications to cope with in the years ahead without my adding to them. Now let me see you out."

"Don't worry. I can find my way."

"As you prefer. Goodbye, Mr Rackham." And with a little nod, Samuel made his way between the oatmeal curtains and was gone to rejoin a group of men and women who in the multiplicity of the possible combinations of just fifty-two playing cards had found a way of life.

2

"So what was he like?" Julia asked him on his return.

"Like a man who has found his Land of Beulah."

"What does that mean?"

"It comes out of *Pilgrim's Progress*. It is a land in which the pilgrims find happiness while they're waiting to be summoned into Heaven."

"And Desmond and Thady?"

"They have no place in it with him." And, after a moment: "You know, he said something very wise. That it was a rare father who did not try to re-create himself in his children."

She remembered something Martin had said in the early days of their marriage: "When we have our children, we're never to forget that they're going to have opinions of their own which are valid from their point of view even if they aren't from ours."

Which wasn't very different from Jordan's view.

"Jordan said something else," he went on. "He said that not having a father was going to have a significant effect on them, although he hadn't the least idea what the effect would be."

He was sitting on the stool which he always placed close by her wheelchair when he wanted to be near her. He took her hand. "It's appalling, isn't it," he said, "what the next ten years hold for those two boys?"

Julia thought about Alice and the pressures Alice Dresses and Kornblath's accountants would exert on her. With the best will in the world there wouldn't be much time for her to be what most mothers were to their children. She said as much.

"No. But I don't think that her not cooking for them or tucking them up in bed," Martin said, repeating her last two examples somewhat dismissively, "is the really important thing. They'll adjust to that. They must be pretty used to it by now anyway. No, what's unimaginable . . ." He released her hand and going to the window stared out into the square below. "What's unimaginable, is how they're going to cope with all the problems of adolescence in isolation. And what the effect's going to be of their being utterly dependent for their standards of behaviour and morality on what they can pick up from other schoolchildren."

She thought about how on the day when Alice had first moved in, courteously, but firmly, Martin had made it clear

189

to her that he wanted no change in their own lifestyle. On the evenings when he was at home and at the weekends he wanted Julia to himself, and neither Alice nor her children would be *persona grata* in the flat. And she remembered how when she had pointed out that with Mrs Bolton, their nurse cum cook, always on hand, it would be perfectly practicable to invite Alice to join him for an occasional meal, and that she would have no objection, he was not to be shifted. He wanted, he had said, things to go on exactly as they had before. When she felt able to cope with being got downstairs and in and out of a car, they could run out to her parents at Beeding or even to some hotel; when she felt up to it they could invite old friends with whom she did not feel embarrassed; otherwise he wanted only to be with her, spending the weekend quietly reading and listening to music or the radio, or chatting to her while he worked at a drawing-board he kept up in the flat.

But the reality of Alice and her boys being near had exerted pressure. It was quicker for them to come through the main buildiing rather than by the mews and it would have been churlish not to allow them to do so. And, inevitably, Desmond and Thady's passing through had become accepted as part of the way of life of number eight Mandeville Square. And in turn this had developed into their having their tea with Julia whenever Alice was out on business – which was most of the time – and she had come to look forward to them doing so. Before, the big moment of her day had been the office closing and the sound of the lift bringing Martin up to join her. And it still was the big moment of the day but as well, now, much earlier, there were Thady and Desmond, singly or together, running up the stairs eager to chatter about the happenings of *their* days. She had not deluded herself that they saw her as a sort of surrogate mother, but, she knew, she filled a bill, giving them something of the sense of homeliness they had known when living with their grandparents and perhaps even a sense of direction they had lacked. And if for her part she did not see them as she would have seen the children she and Martin could, and should, have had, they at least gave her a sense of purpose and helped her to forget her uselessness.

And now here was Martin, after being given short shrift by the boys' father, come back possessed by a feeling that something simply had to be done! How much, she wondered, was this the simple reaction of a decent man faced with the proximity of a couple of youngsters he had taken to and whose unfortunate situation aroused feelings of guilt? Or how much more mightn't it be that their proximity had reawakened the wish – so often expressed before her illness struck, and since so carefully concealed, even perhaps suppressed – to have sons of his own.

There were, it could not be denied, seeds of danger here because a solution to all their problems – hers, Martin's, Alice's, Desmond's and Thady's – was so screamingly obvious: the temporary loan of the mews cottage could be made a permanent one and the exclusion – no, that was too harsh a word – the guidelines for Alice to keep to her part of the building could be relaxed. They could become, as it were, an extended family. Would the general gain offset the risk involved? The risk – the very real risk – that the need in Martin she could no longer meet would be met by Alice. And if it were, would that be so terrible?

Her mind went back to a conversation she had had with Martin before she had even heard of Alice.

"Darling," she had said after the very last time. "Could you bear it? If I said . . . never again?"

He had understood. When the specialist's awful sentence had been passed on her, their life together – with each day doubly precious through knowing it was going to be brutally cut short – had touched transcendent heights of passion and delight. And then, inevitably, the first major attack had come and they had adjusted to it as best they could and continued to do all the things which Julia's physical limitations allowed; and while they sometimes talked of the things which they had once done together and would never do again, they never talked of the things they had hoped to do which would never now be done. Nor did they talk of the time when even the simple fact of making love would become perplexing and problematic and finally impossible.

But as this happened she had talked less and less about the

days when a glint in the eye, the press of a hand, a sudden quickening of the breath cried: "What are we doing with these people? Why are we wasting time with them when we could be making love?" And eventually she didn't talk of them at all.

And when she suggested they gave up making love he worked it out and realised why she had put it to him: that their days and nights of having sex were inscribed on her mind with wonderful clarity and that every tortuous, awkward lovemaking he forced on her from now on risked dulling memories which still kept their love alive and bright; that if those memories were too tarnished, if they were replaced by continual clumsy one-sided sex in which she was mere object, the magic which still remained between them would be lost.

And so he had agreed to her suggestion and they talked it out and a pressure which had been building up between them was removed. Which was good, for this above all had perhaps been the supreme accomplishment of their life together: that it had occurred to neither of them that anything should be withheld whether in word or deed or sex. Their lives had been in those early years so integrated that it was as if they had mutually taken possession of each other, so that when together everything else was of small account and when apart there was an inner yearning to get together as soon as could be.

After it had been agreed, she had said with a smile: "Of course you're going to have to do something about it."

"How?"

"Well, find yourself a woman to have sex with. You're not cut out to be a monk."

He saw the tears behind the smile. A smile can be created simply enough by the mechanical movement of facial muscles but the glands which create tears are independent of the will.

"Tell me what sort of woman," he'd said lightly.

"One worthy of you, of course. One who afterwards you won't regret."

"And what else?"

"You mustn't be in love with her. I couldn't bear that." And although her hands were weak now he could feel their pressure on his own.

"Can she be in love with me?"

"She can't fail to be in love with you." And, suddenly, fiercely: "You're not to pay for it. Not to go with prostitutes."

"You know I already have." He had held nothing back.

"That was different. It was wartime. And it was the thing to do. It was more that than need."

"Yes," he admitted, remembering the embarrassment of several in them in a room and the girls being brought in for them to choose between. "It was the thing to do."

They had never spoken of it again; and he had not had a woman since. But he knew, and she knew, that sooner or later he must.

And if that woman happened to be Alice, what would that do to her? She did not have to think long about it because since Alice had come to live in the cottage she had thought about it many times already – it was so obvious a possibility. And she could not answer herself honestly. But what she did know, and knew without the slightest shadow of doubt, was that if when the time came Martin chose a stranger for his sexual needs and companionship, it would be unbearable. To lie alone in a bed in a nursing home aware that there was a woman whose face, whose voice, whose presence, she could not even imagine, with whom as she thought about him he might be making love, would be crucifying. So much better, she told herself, so much better by far, that the woman who is giving him what he needs to have, what he ought to have, what he must have as a man, is imaginable to me – and acceptable to me. And of all the women I know who Martin knows, Alice is the only one acceptable. And it was in that moment that the decision was made.

She broke the silence. "You're going to miss them, Martin, when they go, aren't you?" she said.

"Yes."

"Then why should they go?"

"Because it's not going to be long before Alice is able to do what she's set her heart on doing."

"Buying them a house somewhere? Oh, Martin! You've always been the first to face up to realities. Do so now. Since they spent Christmas with us at Beeding, the boys, especially

Desmond, have got *their* hearts set on a cottage in the country. Of course they have. But it isn't on, is it? Even if Alice Dresses and Kornblath's accountants allowed it, it's too late for Desmond to change his schooling and it would be criminal to stop Thady getting this scholarship, let alone Alice *paying* for him to go to a better school than his brother instead. They've got to live in London, or somewhere very close to London. So why not here?"

And in his silence.

"I'm never going to use that bedroom. It was a dream. A lovely one, but just a dream: a home in which I was nursed rather than a nursing home. A bedroom next to mine with someone always on call, night and day, wherever you were. But one day, tomorrow, next month, a year from now, I'm going to get an attack that's bad enough for a doctor to insist on my going into hospital. An attack from which perhaps I won't get enough remission to come back here at all. So far I've been lucky – it's only my mobility that's been really affected. My mind, my speech, even my eyes haven't been seriously impaired. But sooner or later they're going to be." And as he began to move towards her: "No, stay where you are! Don't come any nearer. If you were to touch me, I'd burst into tears. And having started this, I want to go through with it. Pour yourself a drink and then sit over there." And at his hesitation: "Oh darling, please, please, do as I say!"

He obeyed her, pouring himself a whisky and sitting with it in an armchair distant from her.

"I don't *want* them to go," Julia said. "They're interesting, all three of them in their different ways. And on the evenings when you aren't here, even when Alice doesn't come up, it's very comforting to know they're there. It wouldn't be the same with some family you let the cottage off to. And I know what's in your mind. That it must depress me having to look at a woman of my own age who can do all the things I used to do myself, who's doing something with her life, achieving things. And it does depress me. Of course it does. But it's a price I'm prepared to pay for what I get in return. It really is. Believe me."

Nine

1

By coincidence, Kornblath's invitation addressed to Goswell Road arrived on the same day as that on which Alice received the first replies to her advertisement for finishers and machinists and, the address on the envelope being typed, she put it aside with other unopened mail, assuming it to be either a bill or a circular.

As distinct from Little Titchfield Street where her office had been merely a rolltop desk behind a movable screen, here she had her own private and very generous room furnished and fitted out by a shopfitting architect whom Martin had recommended. It had cost a small fortune and Alice had been doubtful, but now that the work and furnishing had been completed, she was forced to admit that Mr Mussack had done a tasteful and impressive job.

He had set out to provide a salon rather than an office, a room in which femininity and practicality were nicely melded. There was no desk but there was a working area with a level top along one wall where Alice could sketch designs and lay out fabric samples and the like. There was soft carpeting, rich curtaining to hide the factory-made metal windows, a small settee, comfortable chairs, side tables and a larger table which Mussack had visualised carefully decked with fashion magazines and carrying a vase of flowers. The walls had been panelled out, plainly, so as to provide the proper background for modelling dresses, and the lighting was warm and elegant.

At Alice's insistence access was off the workroom. "I'm sorry, Mr Mussack," she had said, "but if I shut myself off completely from my girls, lock myself away in some secret

195

office they don't even get a glimpse of, they aren't going to see me as one of them and I'm not going to get the same results. In any case I've always spent most of my time at the cutting table and I intend to go on doing so and I don't want to have to walk halfway round the houses to get to it. Just give me a room that works, with enough space in it for dresses to be modelled—"

"But," he had interrupted, horrified, "having your customers walk through a workroom with all those machines making all that noise and the girls gawping at them and giggling and, oh, I don't know—"

She cut him short: "No, you don't, Mr Mussack. But I do. There's nothing like a busy workroom to put buyers in the right frame of mind. So just do what I say and we'll get on fine."

There were two rooms off Alice's office, the first a fitting room with its own separate access and the second a slit of an office for a secretary and a clerk whom Alice had grudgingly been persuaded by Mr Thompson of accountants Winthrop, Son and Mackeson she must sooner than later be employing.

On the first day, as she stood in what she had mentally dubbed her audience chamber, it had struck Alice as over-sumptuous, over-neat and utterly removed from the down-to-earth business of making cheap dresses in huge quantities and multiple sizes; but already, a fortnight or so after Alice Dresses had theoretically got under way (although as yet not so much as a single piece of dress fabric had been cut), as she stood before her worktop sorting the post into two separate piles before starting on opening the glut of replies to her advertisement, her own natural untidiness had given it a character and humanity which would have saddened Mr Mussack. There was no vase of flowers. There were fashion magazines, but far from being arranged in a tidy echelon they were scattered here and there and mixed in with less attractive publications such as the *Draper's Record* and *Buttons and Accessories*. Alice's spring coat and hat were thrown on the settee and a cup of tea she had had in hand when Nellie (who hadn't for a second hesitated to abandon her current employment and accept the old post she'd had at Paquette as Alice's forewoman) triumphantly brought the huge mail in, was cooling somewhere at quite some distance from its saucer, while a cigarette burned in the lid of a tin of pins for all that a perfectly good ashtray awaited use.

Alice opened the envelopes with enthusiastic inefficiency, using a pencil which ripped the flaps of half of them. Slipping out the handwritten letters she scanned the contents rapidly, wrote "yes" on some, drew a pencil question mark on others and dropped the envelopes and the balance in a wastepaper basket she had beside her. There was no question in her mind of acknowledging those she rejected out of hand. These were hard times – an advertisement for daily help brought fifty or more replies; for finishers and machinists there might well be ten times as many before the last stopped trickling in.

After an hour or so, having completed her sieving, Alice called out "Nellie!" There was no one but Nellie in the workroom. The paired lines of sewing machines glistened new and silent, the broad leather belts which drove them were still. A dozen dummies, headless, armless, legless, stood absurdly in a row. Bolts of material poked from a wooden framework like massive bottles reversed in wine racks. On the brand new cutting tables thick layers of fabric lay unrolled waiting. All the required paraphernalia for making dresses was there. Cutting and pinking shears, scissors, chalks, spindles of cotton, measuring rulers, boxes of ribbons, beads, buttons, pins, needles: all tidily laid out awaiting next Monday when Alice Dresses would begin its operations – starting with the tiny band of women and girls who had worked for Alice in Paquette and had, either unemployed and utterly disbelieving their luck at being called, or out of loyalty and faith given up hard-won employment elsewhere, accepted her offer to retake them on.

Nellie came in from the workroom and noted the scattering of envelopes and letters which had missed the wastepaper basket but made no attempt to pick them up.

"Yes, madam?"

"Have a look at those, Nellie." Alice pointed at the query pile and, noticing that her latest cigarette had overbalanced and lay on the worktop burning it, said "Damn!" and fizzed it out in the neglected cup of tea. "I'll make another cup," she said, "while you look through them. Like one?"

"Thank you, madam."

Alice went through into the workroom and, before going to the small kitchen which she had insisted should be provided, paused for a moment to take in again what was as much her personal empire as was his bridge room to Samuel Jordan. Her heartbeats quickened at the sight of it. Vast by her previous standards, silent, empty of people but superbly equipped, it lay waiting as poised as a runner in his block for the switch to be thrown which would send the first lines of machines into action, for the first chomping of shears through the thick layers of material to begin, for the start of the fulfilment of a dream.

It had been a long time of waiting. Kornblath, who seemed to have lost most of his interest in the project, had not hurried to get the company formed, the lawyers and accountants had had their say and there had been the partitioning and preparation of the floor for the equipment. Through frustrating, anxious months, bridling at inactivity, Alice had been filled with doubts. But now all fears had been swept away, all financial worries had been forgotten. Her ample salary, unbelievably backdated, was being paid; she was dressed at someone else's expense; all this equipment, all these supplies were, if not necessarily paid for as yet, underwritten. She had discovered that far from being the ogres painted by Tom, bank managers could be friendly, respectful people; that accountants, even if you didn't happen to like the one you had, were on your side; that even legal knights were manageable. And, above all, Dessy and Thady had a proper home – for which, on her insistence, she was now paying a proper rent. The future was thrilling – and, above all, within her control at last.

She came back in carrying two cups of tea. Nellie was at the worktop reading the applications on which she'd written a question mark.

"Throw any of those you don't like in the wastepaper basket, Nellie," Alice said, putting down both cups of tea.

For another half hour or so they discussed the possibles. It no more occurred to Alice to reject Nellie's negatives than it would have occurred to Nellie even to glance at the letters Alice had approved. They shared total trust and confidence.

When they were done, Nellie said: "Shall I do the answering, Mrs Jordan?"

Alice, when not madam, had always been Mrs Jordan to Nellie and would always remain so.

"Do you think so?" said Alice, surprised. In Paquette she had dealt with all the correspondence, all the bills.

"Yes, madam," Nellie said firmly. "And I think you really must get that secretary and that clerk Mr Thompson is on about. You can't spend all your time opening and answering letters and checking and paying bills."

"I suppose not," Alice said and, reminded, reached for the smaller pile of mail.

It was, as she had presumed it would be, mainly circulars and bills and she was almost through glancing at them when she came upon the invitation.

Mr and Mrs Solomon Kornblath
At Home
Friday, June 20th
Boulters, Fulmer, Bucks

Mrs Alice Fenwick and any Ascot guests
After Ascot or 7.00 p.m
Ascot Dress – Buffet
RSVP Berkeley Square

"Good heavens!" said Alice, in disbelief.

"What is it, madam?" Nellie asked with concern.

Alice handed her the card; but its meaning was above Nellie's head.

"What is it, madam?" she repeated.

"It's an invitation from Mr and Mrs Kornblath to go to their home and bring with me anyone I've invited to spend the day with me at the Ascot races. At least I think that's what it means."

"Well!" said Nellie, much impressed. "*Well!*"

2

Martin was attending a Livery Company dinner that evening and as soon as Desmond and Thady had gone to bed, Alice, invitation in hand, went up to the flat.

Julia's eyebrows raised at the sight of it. "So you've got one too," she said casually and moved an unsteady hand to indicate the invitation.

"You mean Martin has?"

"He always gets one."

"This happens every year?"

"Yes. Kornblath always has a box through the whole of Ascot."

"You've been?"

"Oh, I've been to Ascot. I've never been to one of the parties Kornblath gives after them. By the time Martin got on the list, it was too late for me."

"Does Martin go?"

"He's been to *one*. He didn't enjoy it much. Not going by himself. But he said it was quite a party. Apparently it's a lovely house with beautiful grounds and a lake. There was a band. I think it was Ambrose. And fireworks. You'll go, won't you?"

"Heavens, no!" Alice said.

Mrs Bolton came in without knocking. She was a strong, big-boned widow in her middle fifties who lived close by and had been taken on as a cook when the Mandeville Square property had been leased. As Julia's condition deteriorated she had, with instructions from their doctor, gradually assumed an additional role, and now that the disease had reached such a stage that even with help Julia could manage only a few shuffling, faltering steps and the routine of normal living, eating, drinking, dressing, bathing and so on were beyond her without assistance, she had become a sort of nurse-companion, and especially so on the occasions when Martin was out for the evening.

"Oh, good evening, Mrs Fenwick," she said without enthusiasm. "I didn't know that you were here."

She did not approve of Alice moving in *en famille*. She had come to presume that there would at least be a stage when Martin's original plan would be put into operation and that she would move from her flat into the mews cottage and be allowed to stay on there afterwards. Again, like many who look after ailing people, she had come to have a proprietary regard for her charge, and was aggrieved at having to share any of the precious evenings when otherwise she would have had Julia to herself. And things, she grumbled to herself, had lately gone from bad to worse with Mrs Fenwick being there more and more frequently and sometimes even when the master was at home. If it went on this way much longer, she'd find herself *permanently* banished to the kitchen!

"Mrs Fenwick," Julia said pointedly, "will be staying for a little while." And to Alice: "Would you like some coffee?"

"Well I wouldn't mind a cup," said Alice. And, hastily: "But Mrs Bolton doesn't have to make it for me, I can easily do it myself."

It was, perhaps, not the wisest of suggestions. "Thank you, Mrs Fenwick," Mrs Bolton said primly, "but it isn't any trouble."

And she went out stiffly, closing the door with unnecessary force behind her.

"Never mind that," Julia said. "Sit down and tell me all about how it's going in Goswell Road. What have you been doing today?"

Alice sat where she normally sat: in the corner of the settee, facing Julia. "Answering replies to my advertisement," she told her.

"Have many?"

"Eighty-seven, by the first post. Thirty-seven in the second. And there's bound to be just as many tomorrow."

"Good Lord. How on earth are you going to cope?"

"Wait until they're only trickling in, then have Nellie interview the fifty who sound most promising. There's no great rush. We'll only be making samples to begin with. No, what I've *got* to do is get myself a secretary. I ought to have done it earlier but you know, Julia, it's . . . well I've always done that sort of thing myself. I don't like the idea of not being in *control*."

"You're not frightened Alice, are you? Of what you've taken on?"

Alice shook her head. "No, I'm not frightened. I stood in the workshop this morning, by myself, while Nellie was going through the letters, and imagined what it was going to be like with all that machinery going and a hundred, maybe two hundred, girls at work and I felt proud. Proud of doing something no other woman in this country has ever dreamed of doing before. And do you know what went through my mind? That Solly Kornblath progressed from doing up a dilapidated terraced house in Whitechapel into becoming London's leading property developer and with Paquette I've had a better start than he had and there's far less distance for me to go."

Mrs Bolton came in with a cup of coffee but Alice was so much in full flow as not to see her.

"Of course I'm going to have to take on all sorts of people I never employed before because I did it myself. Or Nellie did. Pattern-makers. Packers. And more cutters. There really ought to be a machine you can get for cutting cloth in quantity. Perhaps there is. . ." She broke off, seeing Mrs Bolton. "Oh, Mrs Bolton, thank you. How kind of you." But she spoke over-quickly, vexed at being interrupted.

"Shall I put it on the table, madam?" Mrs Bolton said, with a stolidity not to be misunderstood.

"Now don't be silly, Mrs Bolton!" Julia reproved her. "Put it down. Fetch that side table." She moved a feeble hand. "Put it beside Mrs Fenwick. Put the coffee on it. And then please leave us."

"Very well, madam."

Mrs Bolton made no attempt to hide her displeasure, exaggerating every action. And when she was done, she said to Julia as if she were the only other person in the room: "If there isn't anything else I can do for the moment, madam, I might as well go home as wait in the kitchen. What time would you like me to come back to help you into bed?"

"I don't know what time," Julia said testily.

"I hope," said Mrs Bolton, now acknowledging Alice's presence, "you won't be keeping Mrs Rackham up too late." And, firmly, to Julia: "We don't want any more exacerbations through getting over-tired, do we, madam?"

"Please leave us, Mrs Bolton."

"Very well, madam."

But as she reached the door, Julia stopped her. "Just a minute." And to Alice: "Alice, I wonder. Would you mind helping me get undressed and into bed to save Mrs Bolton having to come back again?"

Alice saw the sudden scowl on Mrs Bolton's face, and hesitated. But her instinct told her that this treatment of Mrs Bolton, so different from Julia's normal way of handling her, was deliberate.

"No, of course not, Julia," she said.

The effect of this on Mrs Bolton was quite remarkable. The controlled impassivity vanished. Her face reddened, her chest seemed to heave, drawing her heavy shoulders back, her nostrils dilated and her body seemed to tremble. And when she spoke it was clear that only by a supreme effort was she keeping her fury at being so dismissed in check.

"Then I'll go, madam," she bridled. "And I only hope we don't get any more of that blurring or double-vision back!"

And with this Parthian shot she was gone – this time making no pretence of doing anything but slamming the door behind her.

Julia smiled wanly. "Oh, dear," she said.

Alice was baffled. It had been intentional, this sending Mrs Bolton home in dudgeon. And for Julia, normally so tolerant of her nannyishness, quite out of character.

"Don't look so worried, Alice," Julia reassured her. "She'll get over it. If I'm not to be completely dominated by the woman, it has to be done sometimes."

No, Alice thought, that's not it. But she said: "She resents me being here. And I can understand it. She likes having you to herself."

"And being in charge."

"Yes, I suppose so. But . . . It would be dreadful if she left you. Got herself another job."

"Oh, she won't do that." Although Julia spoke quietly, it was with assurance. "For one thing jobs paid as well as Martin pays her are hard to find these days. And even more to the point, she knows that after that last attack I had, it's not likely to be all that long before I get another one that's bad enough to have Bayliss shifting me permanently into a hospital or nursing home. And then she hopes Martin will keep her on as cook and let her move into the cottage."

Alice's forehead wrinkled in surprise. This was the first time since the attack she'd had a couple of months earlier that Julia had allowed talk of her illness into any of their conversations. Nor, studying her, did such a disaster as she threatened seem imminent. She was still an attractive-looking woman, always, as now, stylishly turned out by a dressmaker who came often and a hairdresser who came every week. Apart from the trembling of her hands which made it very difficult, and sometimes impossible, for her even to drink without assistance and a look of tiredness far beyond her years, she could easily have been someone recovering from a minor accident.

"Well I can't believe anything like that's going to happen for ages," Alice said staunchly.

"It could happen tomorrow, which is something I have to live with and take into account. And that's one reason why I'm glad you and your boys are living in the cottage. Because while you're there, Mrs Bolton can't be. Oh, she's a marvellous woman and I know I've been unkind to her this evening but I just can't bear the thought of her becoming a permanent fixture here after I've gone, dancing attendance on *the master,* as she will insist on referring to Martin – as if he were a Scottish laird and she was an old retainer – and doing everything in her power, which she would, to turn him into a grieving widower dependent on her for everything a woman could do for him."

"She wouldn't get far with Martin, trying that."

"Of course she wouldn't. All the same it isn't the set-up I'd like to be imagining when I'm no longer here."

"Now, look, Julia—" Alice began.

"Alice!" The reproof in her tone stopped Alice in her tracks. When she was sure she had made her point, Julia went on. "Now get on with enjoying your coffee before it's cold. And have a cigarette if you want one, it doesn't worry me." With difficulty she shifted a little in her chair and rearranged a fold of her skirt.

This done, her eyes searched Alice's as if trying to read in them the best way to continue.

"You're a very practical person, Alice," she said. "That's one of the reasons I so enjoy your company. And you don't gush sympathy, which is another. So please don't start gushing it now. I know what's going to happen to me and I've come to terms with it. And it wasn't easy, because I'd always hoped to do something positive with my life like you're doing with yours. So when I was told what I'd got, and that I'd got it in a galloping form which is apparently fairly rare, I had to make a decision. Or rather Martin and I had to. And we decided we'd use the years while I was still reasonably mobile doing all the things we could do together – travelling, theatres, dancing, Ascot, Wimbledon, Henley and all the rest – and at least build up a bank of memories, rather than waste the opportunity while I set about some sort of occupation which in the long run was going to lead nowhere. And we were wise, because they were wonderful years and no one can take them away from us."

She paused, hesitating, then decided. If, as she hoped, when she was no longer in the picture the relationship between Martin and Alice and her two boys was to endure, it was very important that Alice should have as deep as possible an understanding of the man she had married. "I've never told you, have I," she said, "how Martin and I met again after that hospital in Poix – in any detail, I mean – and how it took him three years to track me down?"

"No," Alice said. "Mind you, your mother gave me the bones of it when we were with you over Christmas."

"You never told me."

"She asked me not to mention that she had."

Julia understood. Her sudden request to pack out a house, already full enough at Christmas, with a girl of her own age with a couple of children had been agreed to without question. Mother had assumed that Alice was an old friend a bit down on her luck. But when she discovered what lay behind it, and that Alice was an attractive woman of drive and personality, her wary mind, influenced by her years of experience as a Justice of the Peace, had foreseen dire possibilities and she had made it her business to nip in the bud any ambitions Alice might have so far as Martin was concerned. Yes, but then, Julia told herself, for all her perspicacity she had been seeing it from a protective maternal point of view, not from her own as she saw it now.

"Just the bones of it," she said. "That's all she told you?"

"Yes."

"I think," Julia said, "it's a story worth much more than its bones. A story which will tell you so much more of Martin than otherwise you would ever know. And, Alice, I believe it is going to be very important, not just to you but to your boys as well that you really do understand the wonderful man I married. You're not in a hurry are you?" And when Alice shook her head. "I'm going to take you a long time back to the years after the war when, if I've got my facts right, your Desmond was three and Thady still a baby."

3

Canon Owen Cresswell, rector of Beeding, seated at his desk, and hearing the jangling of the front door bell, bent his head further towards his work as if in some magical manner doing so would remove the unwanted visitor and allow him to complete composing the next day's sermon uninterruptedly.

When the tap came on the door and Clara, in her housemaid's afternoon uniform of cap and apron, entered, he said, turning his head, a small wry smile on his face: "And who is it this time, Clara?"

"Gentleman to see you, surr. Name of Rackham." She spoke with the broad accent of a country-bred Cotswold girl.

"Rackham?" he queried.

"That's what he said, surr."

"And it was me he wanted to see?"

"Yes, surr."

He sighed, cast a regretful look at his spidery, unfinished writing and said: "Oh, well, I suppose you'd better ask him to come in."

Clara bobbed and exited smartly. It was no more than

expected – for all his modest protestations her employer never turned anyone away.

As Clara showed Rackham in, Cresswell rose courteously to his feet. Rackham found himself confronted by an exceptionally tall, silvery-haired man aged about sixty, dressed in a rusty black cassock.

"Good afternoon, Mr Rackham," Cresswell said, holding out a delicate hand in welcome.

"Good afternoon, sir," said Rackham, taking the hand and finding it to be of surprising strength for one who at first sight seemed almost frail. "It is very good of you to see me."

Cresswell smiled. "I'm afraid I cannot spare you too much of my time this afternoon, Mr Rackham. But please be seated." A gesture invited Rackham to choose between an old leather armchair, shiny with age, and a shabby settee which was a depository for newspapers, magazines and periodicals – and then Cresswell made the choice by shifting enough of them.

While he was doing this, Rackham took in the room and found it in keeping with the house itself, a massive, uninspiring, comfortable-looking red-brick Victorian structure, totally out of keeping with the locality. The room was high and large, with its embellishments – skirting, cornice, window, door – all to scale. It absorbed with little difficulty a grand piano, whose top was piled high on both wings with tattered music scores, a massive grandfather clock ticking away relentlessly and a huge bookcase stuffed untidily with much-handled volumes. Between the piano and Cresswell's desk there was a large dog basket in which was curled an even larger, old black dog, which had hardly bothered to raise its head at his entry. On the walls and on the mantelshelf above a large, draughty-looking fireplace decorated on this May day with an arrangement of cow-parsley, were many photographs framed variously in silver, wood and passe-partout. Above the fireplace there was a large oil-painting of a forbidding-looking gentleman in black. Cresswell's desk overflowed, each pigeonhole crammed full, the level writing surface scarcely providing room for the sermon to be written for the multitude of paper it supported. The curtains were of heavy stuff to keep out the Cotswold winter chill and the carpeting was tired and threadbare here and there. Apart from the man himself, only an open Bible on an occasional table and a simple wooden cross gave a clue to Cresswell's calling.

"There," said Cresswell. "Plenty of room now." He sat himself down in his armchair. "Do sit down, Mr Rackham, and tell me what I can do for you."

"Actually, sir," said Rackham, hesitating to be lost in the depths of the settee and rather feeling it was hardly the place from which to say what he had come to say. "I've called in the hope of seeing your daughter."

"Julia?" It was as if he had several.

"Yes."

"And your name is Rackham?"

"Yes, sir. Martin Rackham."

Cresswell's high forehead creased in concentration, his silver eyebrows lowering over his penetrating blue-grey eyes.

"I don't seem to recall the name."

"No, sir, you wouldn't. She only met me the once. For a minute or two in a hospital in a place named Poix."

"But that must be getting on for three years ago."

"In fact it was more than three years ago."

"And you say she only met you for a minute or two."

"Yes. I'd just recovered from slight concussion and as soon as the doctor realised I was well enough to be moved they shifted me out to make my bed available for some poor devil who needed it more than I did. By the time your daughter must have come back into the ward, I'd gone."

Cresswell having been silent for a space, absorbing this and working out what most likely followed from it, observed: "Three years is quite a long time to wait, Mr Rackham, before making this call."

Rackham nodded. "It is. Too long. But by the time I was free enough from military duties to try and find your daughter, the hospital, such as it was, had long since been closed down. I had no idea even of your daughter's name and all I knew of the doctor who was in charge was that he was a major."

"Muircroft."

"Yes. So I eventually discovered. But he couldn't help. Or wouldn't. I was never quite sure which."

"So how did you track us down?" The quizzical smile showed Cresswell to be genuinely intrigued.

"There was a man in the room whose Christian name was Leslie, who'd lost a leg and a foot and lived in Birmingham. Not even knowing his surname it wasn't easy and Birmingham's a big place. But there aren't all that many men so uniquely mutilated, and after a lot of false starts I managed to find him and he remembered your daughter's name. Once I'd got that it wasn't too difficult, because I'd overheard her saying she once lived in Henley, which I took to be Henley in Arden."

"That was many years ago."

"Yes. So they said. But they told me there that when you left it was to take over this parish. And if I've put that wrongly, I'm sorry, but I'm not all that well up on what you might call ecclesiastics."

"It mightn't be what I would call it," said Cresswell in a manner strangely reminiscent to Rackham of his daughter, "but it's what you have called it and it isn't far out and I take your point. In fact I'm nothing more than a vicar with the responsibility of serving a local group of country churches. But that is by the way. Well, now." He considered Rackham. "It has taken you three years to find us and you have been to a lot of trouble to do so, Mr Rackham. Surely not merely to thank my daughter for attending you so briefly in hospital?"

"No, sir."

"Then why, may I ask?"

"I've checked that your daughter isn't married. With your permission, I would like to court her."

Owen Cresswell had known many surprises in his career but few quite to match this one.

"After knowing her for . . . What did you say? A minute or two?"

"No. That's all she knew me. But I knew her for rather longer, rector. And far, far better than I knew any girl before or any others I have known since."

209

He paused – a deliberate pause to allow the statement to make its proper weight.

"You have a remarkable daughter," he resumed. "You see, unknown to anyone in the hospital, I'd recovered consciousness before she made her round and I was near enough and *compos mentis* enough to hear and absorb every word she said to the other men in the room. There were seven of them, Mr Cresswell, all badly wounded. One had lost an eye, another a leg, and this man Leslie Mancell who'd also lost a leg and his other foot as well. And there was one who was lying next to me, who'd had his intestines ruptured somehow and the ends sewn together, who was sure he was going to die. They were all of different ages, different attitudes and in different degrees of suffering. But somehow she knew how to deal with each one individually. I lay there listening, marvelling. From what was being said, I knew she was not only quite young but very new to nursing – which I found difficult to credit. Until then I would have assumed that only a woman with years of handling such terrible cases behind her could have found the way to be as sympathetic and yet at the same time as firm – or known instinctively, as she did, when to listen and when to speak. And then, when she came to take a look at me, I saw how beautiful she was and since then I have never been able to put her from my mind."

And it was true – the vision of Julia Cresswell leaning over him, her face near enough for him to feel her breath, the lamp in her hand lighting up her eyes, had been indelibly etched. No other woman had so moved him; no other woman had so completely filled his thoughts; and, when he had decided that no other woman ever would, he had resolved to seek her out and, if she was still single, and would have him, marry her.

"Uhm," said Cresswell, seeing that there were many strands following on from what this surprising man had had to say and wondering which to deal with first.

He inspected Rackham, making no attempt to hide that he was doing so. He saw a clean-shaven man of no more than average height, well made with thick brown hair, a high, open forehead, a determined mouth and an air of quiet self-assurance. But what he had remarked on more, what in fact registered on almost all

210

observant men and women meeting Martin Rackham for the first time, were his eyes – half closed, intelligent brown eyes which while always holding a hint of humour seemed, like the eyes of a man accustomed to looking into distances, to have great depth. And then again, there was a presence to him – you would never, he told himself, be unaware when this man had entered a room.

"Well, Mr Rackham," he said dryly, "now that you've broken the ice, I think you can permit yourself to being seated, can't you?"

"Thank you, sir." Rackham sat.

Cresswell put his scrubbed white hands together, fingertips touching, yet somehow not in the manner of a man about to pray. There was, Rackham saw, an indefinable saintliness about him which made it seem impossible he could have chosen any other vocation. Rackham felt more at ease than he had imagined possible. This was a man of understanding, a man who could, in a few words, make you realise he could step inside your shoes and know the way that you were feeling. It was no longer quite so remarkable that the girl whose voice he had carried in his ears, whose touch had lingered on him, whose eyes had been a wonder he could not forget, had been so incomparable.

"Having been to the lengths you have," Cresswell said, "you will know that my daughter is now twenty-three and that if she was interested in marrying you, you would hardly need my permission."

Rackham nodded.

"And," Cresswell continued, "a man of your ingenuity could easily have organised a chance meeting with her locally rather than beard her father in his den. You have chosen not to do so. Well there are several inferences which could be drawn from that. But you will already have given that thought as well."

"Yes."

"Well! Tell me your reason."

"It would be hole and corner doing it any other way."

"My daughter has never even mentioned you."

"Why should she?"

"Most likely she has completely forgotten your existence."

"I'm quite sure she will have done."

"The three years you have spent in tracking her down may well turn out to be a fruitless exercise."

"Yes."

"Tell me. How did you come to be in that hospital anyway?"

"I was shot down."

"You were a pilot?"

"Yes. I was shot down and apparently thrown out of my aircraft before it went up in flames. I didn't know that at the time."

"How badly were you injured?"

"Not badly. I had a broken arm and knee and superficial facial injuries."

Cresswell looked for scars and found them. They were not severe: a small one on his right cheek and another which bit into his left rather bushy eyebrow, raising it a trifle. "Even so," he said, "you must have been in a state of shock." There was a distant expression on his face as if he was visualising Rackham in his hospital bed, as if he was imagining being there himself. "You lie there listening to conversations and then you see my daughter who is, I agree, a very good-looking girl. You see her for, to use your own words, a minute or two. Don't you think it possible you have built a romantic image which reality may shatter? That, not to make too fine a point of it, if you see my daughter again she may disappoint you?"

"No."

"You've thought of the possibility?"

"Thought of it and dismissed it."

Well, mused Cresswell, he's come out of that pretty decently. "Tell me about yourself," he said.

"Yes, sir. I am twenty-six years of age and by profession an architect although because of the war I have yet to be fully qualified. I have still my final examination to take. I was educated at Radley and although my father, who is currently Colonial Secretary and Deputy Governor in Sierra Leone, would have wanted me to go to his Oxford College, Lincoln, the war prevented it."

Well, Cresswell admitted, that isn't bad and very succinctly

212

put. One could have a much worse son-in-law. I wonder how Julia's going to deal with him – she may be able to scythe through strings of admirers as if they were so much hay but there's too much in this fellow for her to get away with that. He chuckled to himself, and rose to his feet.

"My daughter," he said, "is out at the moment, playing tennis with friends she's going to bring back later. But my wife *is* at home and under the circumstances you ought to meet her first, Mr Rackham, don't you think?" By coincidence the grandfather clock started grumbling and whirring and then striking four. "Anyway it's teatime. Suppose you join us. In the garden, perhaps. It is such a perfect day."

The garden was large and, like the house, a little gone to seed. But it was attractive enough with many trees and large areas of grass, including a tennis court which, Rackham calculated, having no netting to stop balls disappearing into the shrubbery bordering one end of it, was hardly used for serious playing. There was also a rough sort of croquet lawn which, as it sloped rather steeply, like most of the garden, must have presented interesting problems. In all it was a comfortable garden in which he could imagine the local villagers attending such church or parish events as were held in it feeling relaxed, knowing there was little harm they or their children could do to it – a garden which could have been dismissed as a rough-cut grassy unexceptional space except for one delightful feature: the River Evenlode, to which it sloped and which delineated its extensive southern boundary.

Cresswell led the way down to a place on the stream's bank where in the shelter of a quite magnificent oak tree there was a summer house.

"Would you mind giving a hand, Rackham," he ordered him. "There's deckchairs in there. We'd better get out half a dozen of them so that Julia can join us if she comes back in time. And that slatted thing is the table we use. Mind your fingers when you put it up – it has a nasty habit of pinching them."

More than a little surprised that his host should have so taken in his stride the materialisation of a total stranger who had announced his intention of wooing his daughter, and somewhat bemused at the notion of becoming a member of a tea party of at least half a dozen which, most likely, would include male intimates and admirers of the girl he had resolved to marry, Rackham complied, hauling out and erecting deckchairs and the dangerous teak slatted table.

"It was my predecessor, a man named Wilkinson, who had this hut put here," Cresswell said easily, while this was going on. "I'm told he always wrote his sermons here and that that's about all he used it for. The idea was to be able to get down to them undisturbed instead of having to keep breaking off whenever anyone called at the vicarage."

"As I did."

"Yes. And, as it happens, interrupted me writing mine. But you don't have to worry. It goes on all the time. And it's not only sermon-writing that gets interrupted. Most people think that's about all a country parson has to do when he's not conducting services. You've no idea. And I don't intend to bore you to death trying to give you one. But you know . . . No, I think it would be better over there . . . But you know I'd find many more interruptions if I tried to write my sermons here than in my study. There'd be too many distractions. Look at the river there, the way it sparkles where the sun shafts through the branches. Never the same for a moment. Always catching your eye. And listen to the way it chuckles over the shallows as if it's having a conversation with the creatures that live in it. And there's kingfishers here you know. No, Rackham, I defy anyone with the slightest claim to a love of nature and beautiful things to keep his head down writing knowing he's bound to miss one if he does. And it's not only the river." He raised a black-clad arm. "There's that railway line. It's a busy one, you know. Any number of local stations on it. Charlbury. Ascot. Kingham. Adelstrop. Moreton. Trains passing by all the time and people you know waving to you. Besides, there's something riveting about trains, don't you think? All that life shifting past. People to whom the ride is just part of their routine and others to whom the journey's an adventure for some reason or other. Sad people who've just said goodbye to someone they care for perhaps and happy people who are on their way to meeting someone they love."

He turned back to Rackham. "Did you come here by train? Or car?"

"I came by train," Rackham said. "I haven't got a car." And deliberately: "I can't afford to run one yet."

"No," said Cresswell thoughtfully. "I suppose not being qualified you must be a bit strapped. Where did you get off? Charlbury, I suppose."

"Yes. I got a taxi."

He chuckled. "Old Probert's Austin! It's a miracle it still goes. He had it up on chocks right through the war, you know. Locked away in a shed. Never even went in to take a look at it. And then expected it to start first time the moment he could get petrol again! Have you fixed a time for him to pick you up again?"

"No. I'm putting up at the inn."

"The Bell?"

"Yes."

Well, thought Cresswell, with the vicarage a devil of a place to get to except by taxi or pony and trap, and no bus service which comes within miles of us, he's deliberately burnt his boats, hasn't he? Most of Julia's young men, considering the possibility of there being nobody at home – or of getting short shrift – wouldn't have dismissed the only means of getting back to Charlbury short of cadging a lift or a three-mile walk! And booking in at the Bell without the least idea what sort of reception he was going to get from us! Julia, he's going to take some shifting!

"Barbara, this is Mr Martin Rackham. I've invited him to join us for tea because he's called to ask our permission to court Julia."

In fastidiously carrying out her duties as a Justice of the Peace, Barbara Cresswell had learnt many things and one of these was how to control her feelings when presented with unusual situations. To be introduced to a totally strange young man as a prospective son-in-law might be bizarre, but it was by no means as remarkable as many of the situations she had to deal with on the Bench and, masking her feelings perfectly, she regarded Rackham with about the same degree of interest she might have shown had she been told that the purpose of his visit was to inform them he had purchased a neighbouring property.

"Really?" she said. "And what sort of view does Julia take of it?"

"She doesn't know," said Cresswell with a chuckle.

"Doesn't know!" Somewhat shaken out of even *her* calm, she reminded Cresswell forcibly of the time in his thespian days when he had played the part of Jack Worthing faced for the first time with Wilde's formidable Lady Bracknell.

"In fact," he continued, quite enjoying the rarity of putting Barbara off balance, "she probably doesn't even remember meeting him." But then at once, aware he had carried this levity far enough, and that if he continued with it he risked making her look foolish, he went on: "But seriously, Barbara, it seems that Mr Rackham was nursed by Julia at Poix after he'd been shot down – he was a pilot, you see – and was so impressed by her that he hasn't been able to put her out of his mind." And turning to Rackham with an encouraging smile, "Suppose you take it on from there."

Clara arrived with tea (wheeled down in a barrow kept expressly for the purpose) during Rackham's exposition and by the time it had all been set out and before he had time to finish, Julia came into view, accompanied as Cresswell had forecast by friends: two young men and a girl.

"Damn!" said Barbara, feeling much as she might have felt if called upon to make a judgement on the Bench before she had been properly briefed, and viewing her daughter's exuberant approach restively. But there was nothing to be done. It was beyond her to concoct a convincing reason for delaying the quartet. Well, she reflected (having by now learnt the circumstances under which Rackham had met Julia and the considerable trouble he had been put to to track her down, but as yet nothing of the would-be suitor himself), the best thing I can do is start pouring tea!

Rackham, meanwhile, watched Julia's approach with a

quickening heartbeat. The two men were in white flannels and identical gaudy blazers; the second girl wore a broad-brimmed straw hat, but Julia, in an ankle-length white dress nipped in tightly at the waist and with leg-of mutton half sleeves, was hatless, her thick, bobbed auburn hair, low on her forehead, covering her ears, nestling her slender neck, framing her face and giving it an almost elfin look. In her hand she carried a tennis racquet which she was waving as if illustrating some point in a lively conversation the four were having. They were, he saw, complete in themselves, sharing the intimacy of easy friendship. Their laughter underlined his separateness – he was the uninvited guest tolerated out of courtesy: a gatecrasher trespassing on a typical family gathering. Then too, he was, in single-breasted suit, grossly over-dressed for tea beside a sparkling river on a summer's afternoon. It was all right for a canon to be in his robes and it was acceptable for his wife to be dressed as if she had only recently left some women's meeting, but his choice of what to wear was of a sudden far more of their generation than of the happy, animated quartet bearing down on them.

Well there it was. And it probably didn't matter. The like-lihood was that the rector was right – his daughter would prob-ably neither remember him nor be more than vaguely interested in the fact that he had assiduously tracked her down. But he must make a good showing of it.

He rose to his feet and as he did so, Julia, for the first time, turning away from her friends, looked towards him, her eyes closing a trifle in brief puzzlement at discovering a stranger with her parents. And then, amazingly, the smile was gone from her face and her eyes were holding his in the utter disbelief of one who has recognised someone she had never imagined she would ever meet again.

She was near enough for him to hear her cry, "Good heavens!"

Barbara seized on it with relief.

"You know who he is?"

"Well, of course."

4

Alice had listened spellbound, and when Julia had come to the end, she said simply: "I think that's the most wonderfully romantic thing I've ever heard."

Julia nodded. "Yes, it was. I've never thought of telling it in that sort of detail to anyone else, but I've told you because I think it will help you to understand what I'm going on to say. Our love, Martin's and mine, was I think as perfect a love as there ever could be between a man and a woman. We were. . ." She raised both hands a little, palms upwards, as if weighing something in them. "We were like two people . . ." She brought her hands together, cupping them. "Like two people who'd become one person. We knew each other's thoughts, what the other was going to say before it was said. We had friends, lots of friends. Of course we did. Martin's one of those men that people take to, especially other men. Well, you know that. But, Alice, we didn't need friends. It was fun being with people, laughing and joking, and sharing – but we were always glad when the time came to be on our own again."

"He's as much in love with you now as he ever was," Alice said.

Julia looked at her, seated in the settee across from her, the smoke rising lazily from her cigarette, and it struck her how this Alice was, at least superficially, a very changed woman from the one she had met four or five months before. Her cares, her uncertainty, her diffidence of that day were quite gone and in their place were enthusiasm, self-belief and a huge potentiality.

"No, Alice," she said, "he isn't as much in love with me as he ever was, although he tries to convince himself he is. It has to be different now, as you must realise if you think about it." It was said dismissively to enable her to change her tack. "Martin's in the prime of life and at a crucial stage in his career. And I'm a millstone round his neck. Here's a man who's got it all: personality, vigour, determination, courage, drive, imagination.

He mustn't end up being no more than he is at the moment: a good and highly respected architect who in spite of the slump can still keep his staff together – and, let's be honest, that's quite a lot to do with Kornblath appreciating his ability. If he stayed at the same level it would be a tragedy because he has the ability and imagination to become one of the outstanding architects of his age, and that's what he's got to be!" There was a pertinacity in her voice Alice had never heard before. "And what's holding him back, Alice?"

"The slump—"

"No! *I* am. He has no business spending the amount of time he does with me. There are so many things he should be doing and isn't. So many people he should be meeting and isn't. It's not enough him leaving me on an odd evening like this one to go to an all-male affair. If I weren't like this we'd be out *all* the time. At dinners, concerts, first-nights and parties and heaven knows what! And he should be *now*. You know what's going to happen – if he goes on like he's doing now? If he keeps on turning down invitations like that one you've got there? They're going to start crossing him off their lists. You have to go *on* in life. Well I don't have to tell *you* that, do I? If you don't, if you get to a point as you did with your Paquette, and then you don't go on – unless you're so lucky as to be introduced to a Solly Kornblath – you're suddenly yesterday's person. Someone who once showed tremendous promise – and disappointed. And quite soon you're forgotten."

It was impossible for Alice to escape the remarkable similarity between Julia's forecast and what had happened to Sam and she wondered if this was in Julia's mind as well. She knew exactly what was being asked of her. Knew that, from the moment Julia had seen Kornblath's invitation in her hand, the whole of the evening had been directed to that end.

"You want me to ask him to take me to Kornblath's Ascot party, don't you, Julia?" she said.

"And to Ascot first."

"Why me particularly? There have to be plenty of other women you know he could ask who'd be delighted to go with him."

"None that I would trust." She shook her head a little. "Oh, don't make any mistake about it, Alice, I'm suggesting this as much for myself as I am for Martin. Sooner or later that attack's going to happen and I'm going to be carted into a hospital or nursing home and never live with Martin again. Then Martin's going to find himself a mistress. It doesn't matter how much he tries to convince himself he won't, it's as certain as it is that night follows day. And it's right he should. That's unarguable. How I shall feel about it doesn't matter. Maybe I won't feel too bad – when I'm in my hospital bed. I don't know. But I'm not there yet and it's these next months, however many they may be, I'm thinking of. And talking to you about. And asking you to help me through them."

"You must have talked this over with Martin. Surely?"

Julia laughed softly. "Oh, yes. We've talked it over. I once told him that he wasn't cut out to be a monk and he ought to find himself a woman to have sex with and that I wouldn't mind. It was lies of course. I'd hate it. While I was here. Thinking about him working down there below and then going somewhere in the evening to have his sex, or trumping up excuses to be away for the odd night or two. But when I'm in my nursing home and there's physical distance between us, then, I tell myself, I won't mind. And perhaps I won't. Perhaps I'll even feel pleased for him."

"You're not just thinking of this Kornblath party, are you, Julia?" Alice said.

"No. There's all the other important invitations to things he can't go to on his own that he ought to accept."

"You realise people would talk. Put two and two together and make five."

"I don't give a damn."

"And you'd trust me."

"I'd put you on trust."

Alice stubbed out her cigarette and getting to her feet stood for a moment, thinking. Then she picked up the coffee cup, its contents largely undrunk, and took it through into the kitchen. This was another important moment in her life – another time for making a decision which could have a long-term effect.

220

The Deal

She was not thinking about the business of being trusted. She liked Martin, enjoyed his company, respected his ability, was intensely grateful to him and aware that there was something about his physical presence she had never been conscious of in any other man. But, as she told herself, she was not in the least drawn to him sexually. The brief and not overwhelming interest she had had in sex while married to Tom had been all but forgotten and her energies, mental and physical, were devoted entirely to her sons and to making a success of Alice Dresses.

But she had learnt from her years in Belmont that there were very few men who could resist temptation providing they could handle yielding to it safely. She had continually been propositioned, if not in actual words then by the pressure of a hand, the adoring glance, the movement of a body against her own on the dance floor. Greg Vibert had not been the only man to plead with her to give up her husband and make her life with him. She had been attractive to men and now with no limit to what she could spend on her clothes and herself, could go on being so. It was not at all impossible that if she did what Julia was asking her to do, became a companion to Martin on important social occasions, sooner or later it might start getting complicated. And complications were the last thing she wanted. After all the difficult years, of a sudden she had a full, promising and stable life. It wasn't perfect. She was fated to watch her children grow up without the normal background of father at work and mother at home. But they were accustomed to that now and after her previous disastrous attempt to put the matter right by marrying Tom, the very last thing she must contemplate was making the same mistake again and getting herself tied up with another man who liked her children well enough when he had no obligation towards them but who might, as had Tom, find accepting responsibility for them another matter.

When it came to Desmond and Thady, hers alone must be that responsibility. When, excited and proud, she had stood letting her eyes rove over the expensive machinery and equipment Kornblath had subsidised, she had after all faced her own reality – accepted that if it was to succeed, Alice Dresses must inevitably become a monster which would consume practically

221

all her time and energy; that as Julia had come to terms with her disease so she had to come to terms with what life held for her and her two boys. No, it *wasn't* perfect, but it was better, far better, than it had ever been before and the very last thing she wanted was change of any kind in the status quo.

So what do I say, she asked herself? *Yes?* And maybe find myself having to fight for the way I run my life rather than be influenced by what some man wants me to do. Or, *no*, and be judged ungrateful and perhaps destroy not just my own relationship with Julia, but Dessy and Thady's too?

In the end she compromised and, going back into the sitting-room, said: "All right, Julia. I'll ask Martin if he'll take me to Kornblath's Ascot thing. But if anything else crops up after that, I'd want to think very hard about it before I agreed."

Ten

1

Boulters proved to be a large and very fine two-storeyed residence. Its white walls looked from under a slated roof across a vast area of lawn towards a lake bordered by paddocks. The superb balance of the bays on either side of the central hallway with its magnificent staircase, bays repeated on the garden aspect, imparted an air of quiet and dignified assurance, as if to advise that however serious the current financial crisis might be, at least so far as *its* owner's stability was concerned his guests need have no qualms.

The only property with which Alice could begin to compare it was Sam Jordan's home, Crogellan House – but whereas Crogellan House was if anything even bigger, wherever you looked at it, inside or out, your eyes fell on patches of stained and broken plaster, rotting window sills, flaking paint and all manner of other things which needed doing to restore it to its former dignity and stateliness, while Boulters was in perfect order, its approach road and gravel driveway impeccably raked and weedless, its glittering white walls unblemished in the early evening sunlight, its lawns mown to splendid stripes, its borders and rose beds superbly tended, its lake with waterfowl perfectly setting off the whole.

Nor was perfection limited to the property. Equal care had been extended to Solomon and Magda Kornblath's guests, as if to ensure that when they went home and regaled their friends with the day's experience it would not be possible for them to report the smallest fault.

There were servants in plenty to direct vehicles to the front entrance, where a group of drivers stood waiting to help the

223

occupants of unchauffeured cars alight and then to drive away their vehicles and park them with military precision in a distant phalanx of glittering Rolls Royces, Bentleys, Daimlers and lesser marques. Inside the entrance hall their hosts were not awaiting them as at the Berkeley Square Christmas Occasion, instead there was a sufficiency of maids and flunkeys to direct guests to the cloakrooms and hairdressing rooms (there were in all six hairdressers and beauticians in attendance), where further maids and flunkeys stood by to attend to every need. So that by the time they ventured down again – the men spruced up, their faces stinging from eau de cologne lashed on with great abandon, and the ladies with their perfumes reapplied, their make-up reconstructed, their coiffures regenerated and even that accidentally damaged fingernail professionally repaired – they were in a proper frame of mind to enjoy themselves, appreciate the quality of the event to which they had been invited and, above all, as Beatrice pointed out, play their proper part in it.

"Play their part in it?" queried Alice.

"Sure. It's a show, isn't it? One hell of a show. And we're the cast. And Solly's staged it very economically when you come to think of it." She waved a hand as if to encompass the throng of guests, mostly with drinks in hand, strolling the lawn, gathered in small groups on the terrace, continually emerging from or disappearing into the house, the men without exception in morning dress and carrying or wearing toppers, the women in fashionable Ascot dresses. "Just think how much I'd be set back to dress this cast! And all it's cost Solly is a couple of words on a printed invitation: 'Ascot Dress'. If I could get away with it that easily, I might think of putting on a musical myself."

"Is that how you see all this?" said Rackham, smiling.

"Sure. It's got all the ingredients."

"Even the band," Grahame said.

"Even the bandstand," Beatrice (who hadn't the least objection to his coming along to this shindig, which she saw as something totally different from the Christmas Occasions) added. "And *that's* on a turntable!"

"What's a turntable?" Alice asked.

"We use them in the theatre for a quick change of scene. You have one set one side and one the other. Soon as the curtain falls someone presses a button and – hey presto! – round it goes and you've moved from London to Zanzibar!"

They had all turned their heads to look at the band: Jack Hylton's. It was within a huge marquee located at right angles to the terrace, floored for dancing later when the band would be swivelled round. Joining the marquee was a covered walkway to the house, its sides, like the front side to the marquee, rolled up. Nothing had been overlooked. No sudden storm was to set Solly Kornblath's plans awry.

"If we're all members of the cast, Bee," Martin said, "who's the audience?"

"Audience of one."

"Solly?"

"Right."

"And he's enjoying it."

Solly was not far away from them, talking to Jack Hylton, a broad smile on his chubby face, his top hat at a jaunty angle. He wore grey morning dress, which was very unusual, and at his neck was a silk stock held in place by a diamond tiepin.

"With what it's costing him, it'd be a pity if he wasn't," Grahame said.

They watched Solly put out a hand and tap Hylton fraternally on the shoulder, then turn and, having glanced unhurriedly around him, head in their direction.

"How are you hitting it off with the chairman, Alice?" Grahame joked.

"You won't believe it," Alice said, "but since his Christmas party, I haven't seen him or spoken to him."

"I *don't* believe it."

"I do," said Beatrice. "Once he's backed a show that's the last I see of him until first night unless it's at something like this or he's got a particular reason – like when he muscled in at that Crébillion lunch I'd fixed with Alice."

"Doesn't surprise me at all," Martin said. "I must be in his offices once a week at least, but unless I bump into him accidentally the only time I have anything to do with him is when we're involved with something he's not prepared to delegate." He smiled wryly. "And then I discover he's *au fait* with all that's happened in between." He paused. "And in the most amazing detail."

"Check!" said Beatrice.

Kornblath, meanwhile, had been intercepted by other guests and was chatting amiably with them. But from the direction he had been taking it was evident he was going to join them soon.

Alice twitched her skirt a little nervously – a give-away sign from a woman who until that moment, and indeed through the whole day's racing, had looked totally at ease. As indeed she well might in the outfit Shea had selected for her: a long trailing dress of white chiffon fitted to the waist and tied around the hips with a wide sash with an enormous side bow which was repeated on a smaller scale as decoration to a huge floppy hat and which was of a blue exactly to match her eyes.

Beatrice noticed – and some inexplicable instinct warned her that something was about to happen which time would prove to be out of joint with the gay and pleasant spectacle around them.

"Easy, Alice," she said to her quietly. "Easy. You're with friends."

Alice looked at her with gratitude. If her own dress was absolutely the height of fashion, Beatrice's was its equal in impact. It was of the palest oyster pink ringed with rows of black lace. Her hat, which was even larger than Alice's, seemed to be carried on one ear, and was dressed with lace identically, as was the long black-handled parasol she carried. She wore matching oyster pink elbow-length gloves and on the disengaged ear a long black earring.

"I'm all right, Bee," Alice said.

"Sure you are. That ought to be *your* tune."

"Eh?"

"The one the band's playing." She broke off as the thought occurred to her that Solly may have suggested to Jack Hylton that it should be played.

"Amy, beautiful Amy," said Grahame, understanding.

"I don't know it," Alice said.

"Since you've won the praise of ev'ry nation, You have filled

226

my heart with admiration, Amy – wonderful Amy . . ." Grahame
sang, catching up with the melody, such as it was.

"Oh," Alice said, remembering. It was the latest Horatio
Nicholls and Joseph Gilbert song, inspired by Amy Johnson's
solo flight from England to Australia. Her girls had discovered
it last week and sung it endlessly since.

"Why should it be my song?" she asked brightly to cover
up her awareness that Solly had broken away from the couple
who'd detained him and was heading their way again.

"Because," Beatrice said, momentarily catching hold of her
wrist with her free hand and giving it an encouraging squeeze,
"Amy Johnson isn't the only one who deserves a lot of credit
for her daring deeds and you are also just the sort of person
that the country needs. And that's a quote." And as Kornblath
came into earshot: "Swell, party, Solly. But then your parties
always are."

"You're very kind, Beatrice," Solly said – as if he meant
it. And with a little nod: "How nice to see you again, Mr
Culverwell. And you, Rackham." And, having made a point
of leaving Alice to last: "And you, Mrs Fenwick . . ." The
pause was manifest. "How very charming you look." He held
out both soft hands for her to take. And when she had done
so, and stood embarrassed, but making every attempt to look
supremely at ease and not making a bad job of it: "My wife is
full of admiration and says that if that is the sort of dress which
Alice Dresses is going to make it will have her as a customer for
life." He released her hands. "But it wouldn't do for our shops,
would it?"

"Our shops?" A small frown creased Alice's brow.

"No, we mustn't talk business," Solly gently reproved her –
or was it himself? "Not on this sort of occasion. How many
winners did you back today?"

"None."

"None?"

"I backed four horses and all I got was one miserable place,"
said Alice with cheerful ruefulness, relegating her puzzlement
and slight concern at Solly's reference to shops as something to
be made sense of later.

They talked for a while of the day's racing then shifted to other topics. They talked of Sir Henry Seagrave, who only a few days earlier had fatally injured himself on Lake Windermere after having broken the world speedboat record; they talked of Amy Johnson, and quizzed Martin on the sort of problems she would have encountered on such a long and exhausting flight; they talked of the current Test Match series, and whether Don Bradman really was the genius the Australians made him out to be. In a word they talked of uncontroversial subjects. Boulters, swarming with fashionably dressed men and women who had enjoyed a splendid day at the Ascot Races and were looking forward to a perfect midsummer evening with delicious food and wine and dancing to Jack Hylton, was no place for anything which might detract from the sense of companionable bonhomie that Kornblath had been at such pains to create.

And so it came as something of a surprise even to Beatrice, who in some ways knew Solly best of all, when, just as he was leaving them, he paused and said to Martin: "Oh, Rackham, I'd be grateful if you can find the time to come to the boardroom in Berkeley Square next Monday. Eleven o'clock."

"Yes, of course."

"Mrs Fenwick will, of course, be attending." And to a dumbfounded Alice: "I take it eleven o'clock next Monday will be convenient to you, Mrs Fenwick?"

Alice nodded, and stumbled: "Yes, Mr Kornblath. Yes, of course."

"Good," Solly said cheerfully and – just before departing – "I've heard how hard you're working. Why don't you take the morning off and have Martin fetch you? After all you live next door to each other, don't you?"

He raised a parting hand, the diamond set in the thick gold ring blazed momentarily – and he was gone.

Alice stared at his back, transfixed.

"Ai! Ai! Ai!" said Beatrice slowly and meaningfully.

"I didn't know you had any connection with Alice Dresses, Martin," Grahame said.

"The only connection I have with it," Martin responded grimly, "is knowing Alice. What the hell's he up to?"

Beatrice figured she had a rough idea. That Kornblath – who from his box must have noticed Alice and Martin, always together through the day, making their way to place their bets – had registered how delightful she had looked with her cheeks flushed and her eyes sparkling with excitement and *joie de vivre*, in an outfit, superbly chosen, which had taken years off the tense and apprehensive Alice Fenwick who would have presented herself at Berkeley Square six months ago. At best, she fancied, he was piqued at Martin having her exclusively for company. At worst? She hardly wanted to contemplate it with both of them so dependent on his favours. What wouldn't I give, she thought – her theatrical instincts to the fore – to be present at that board meeting.

She inverted her parasol, pointing it like a rifle at the sky. "Permission to speak."

"Go ahead," Martin said quietly.

Lowering her parasol, she studied him for a moment or two, seeing a man who, lacking Grahame's height and bearing, might perhaps fail to catch the casual attention of almost every passer-by as Grahame did but who had the capacity so to project his personality that, the instant you were *involved* with him, he was the one person you wanted to talk or listen to.

"If I were you, Martin," she said. "I'd have an accident."

"Accident?"

She nodded – and, wearing a hat of such huge dimensions, the nod was very effective. "Yes," she said. "Break a leg or something. Don't be at that board meeting!" She tapped the terrace with the tip of her parasol. "Think it over. And now, as we seem to be about the only people here without a glass in our hands, what d'you say we head for the champagne bar?"

2

Driving Alice home, Martin was aware that inevitably their relationship was changed and that the principal reason it had changed was not because they had enjoyed a companionable day together, nor because he had held her in his arms as

229

they danced to the current sentimental melodies and found her light as a feather and so delightful a partner as not to wish to release her to others. No, the cause of their sudden affinity was Solly Kornblath: for in his superficially innocuous words they had both, as had Beatrice, read danger. They had, separately, tried to put it from their minds, not to allow it to spoil a magnificently structured evening. But as they sat with the Culverwells and others at one of the myriad of circular tables to a buffet of salmon served with a fine white burgundy and strawberries and cream with an equally spellbinding sauterne, as they foxtrotted and waltzed to Gershwin and Noël Coward melodies, as they stood side by side enjoying the spectacle of a lavish firework display doubled in effect by its reflection in the waters of the lake, from time to time their eyes met and they shared the knowledge that for all the pleasure of it they were killing time, waiting for the evening to come to its end.

They were one of the earlier couples to leave and, quite soon after doing so, Martin, finding an opening, backed the Hornet into a track in the beechwoods which lined the road on either side.

"We've got to talk this over, Alice, haven't we?" he said. "And we can't do it shouting over slipstream."

"No."

"Can you think of one good reason why Kornblath should want me to attend one of your board meetings?"

"No, I can't. But then I've never been to one anyway."

He could have remarked that she was supposed to be Alice Dresses' managing director, but he forebore.

"Who are your fellow directors?" he asked.

"Well there's Thompson . . ."

"Oh, yes. That's the accountant fellow you don't like very much, isn't it?"

Alice had drawn a picture of him to Julia. "Oh, he's polite enough. But gives you the feeling he's looking down on you and having a good laugh about you behind your back."

"What about the other one? The one from the solicitors?"

"Smitherman. I've never met him."

230

"Never met him! But surely, Alice, he attended your board meetings?"

"We've never had one. Or if we did no one told me about it."

It was amazing. Here was a woman who could successfully run a business yet was obviously utterly ignorant of commercial practice.

"Anyway," Alice went on, "he's gone. He resigned a week or two ago, and we've got a new one I've yet to meet."

"But you can't *do* that!"

"Do what, Martin?"

"Swap company directors as if they were reserve goalkeepers! If you're going to change directors you have to call a proper board meeting. You need a special notice of twenty-one days – or is it twenty-eight? – to replace a company director."

Alice cast her mind back to the meeting with Bebb.

"There was something in the . . . I forget what it's called . . . anyway, the agreement, that allowed Kornblath to change the directors . . . not me, but the others . . . when he felt like it. And that's what he did. We've got the man who's been company secretary up to now. A man named Cradforth."

"Cradforth! You never told us he was involved with Alice Dresses!"

"Didn't I? I suppose it never came up. I mean he wasn't a director, just company secretary – whatever that is. D'you mean you know him?"

"Cradforth? Oh, yes. I know Cradforth." There was a world of meaning in it.

"What's he like?"

He looked at her with sympathy. "What's Cradforth like? He's hard, Alice. Hard as steel." And, with concern: "This is all wrong, Alice. And I'm not even sure that Kornblath can do it legally. Well maybe . . . because of what you've told me he *can* change directors, but you have to give a proper notice when you're going to have a company meeting. You don't just decide to have one tomorrow or the day after because of some bright idea that's occurred to you." He shrugged. They were so close in the coupé their shoulders touched. "But you're having one just the same. Because Solly says you are.

231

It's the old, old story, isn't it? The man who pays the piper calls the tune."

And, after a moment or two, "It *is* going well, isn't it? The business? You're already getting orders, aren't you?"

"A few."

"You're not worried?"

"Not about orders."

"But you've got problems?"

He had turned a little in his seat. Alice had taken off her hat to stop it being blown away, and it was resting on her knees. Her hair was neatly waved and curled into the nape of her neck. She didn't look in the least like a businesswoman. She looked a lot less than her thirty-two years and quite lovely.

"It's not as easy as I thought it was going to be," she answered. "This sizing business. It needs a lot of working out. In fact I think I'm going to have to get someone from America over." She dismissed it. "But it can't be anything to do with sizing. He wouldn't even know I'd got a problem there. Until today I hadn't spoken to him since his Christmas party and he's never been in the factory. As a matter of fact I've even been beginning to wonder if he hasn't lost all interest in the business."

"Suppose he did. Suppose he wasn't prepared to put any more money in?"

"Then I *would* have a problem."

"How many workers have you taken on so far?"

"Thirty odd."

"Can you sell that many dresses?"

She laughed softly, and the confidence in the laugh was good to hear. What a curious combination of femininity and resolve, he thought. And what a fool Jordan had been to let her go.

"Can I sell all the dresses that thirty girls can make? Oh, yes. But it's not going to be only thirty, Martin."

"How many?" he said. And, with a chuckle, trying to fit in with her mood. "Three hundred?"

"Why not?"

"You're joking."

"No, Martin."

"I see." The chuckle had gone. "And when you've got three

hundred, how will you sell all the thousands of dresses they're going to turn out for you?"

There was no hesitation. "Through wholesalers and mail order."

"Not through the shops?"

"Not through those I'm used to dealing with."

He fell silent, absorbing this and trying to relate her business to his own. In one direction they were not dissimilar. In these days of slump and cutback they could both get assistants – or workers – quickly when new commissions or orders came in. But there the similarity ended: he didn't have stock and his machinery was limited to typewriters and telephones. If Kornblath decided to take his work elsewhere it would be pretty devastating, but at least all he'd have round his neck was a building larger than he needed; but if Kornblath blew the whistle on Alice Dresses . . . It didn't bear thinking about.

"Three hundred girls," he mused. "You really believe you could cope with something on that scale?"

"Oh, yes."

She looked so feminine in her white chiffon dress with her hat resting on her knees that he found it difficult to visualise her controlling an organisation of that size. That size and more, because by the time she was employing three hundred workers she'd find she'd also got all sorts of people she hadn't imagined employing: salesmen and saleswomen, clerical staff, typists, cleaners, porters and lord knows who else, besides those that Messrs Cradforth and Thompson had decided she must have. That was where the difference between their businesses really lay: in the final analysis he was in control of his, but it was Kornblath through his tame directors who was in control of hers.

"Perhaps Beatrice was right," he said. "Perhaps I ought to break a leg or something."

"You think it's that serious?"

"I have a hunch it could be."

He saw through the screen of trees the headlights of a car approaching from the direction of Boulters. Probably some other people from the party he thought, cars were rare in the country at this time of night. He wondered who they were – and how beholden *they* were to Solly Kornblath. He listened to the throaty sound of a powerful engine and then as the headlights of the car, a monster, a Bentley perhaps, briefly illuminated them, he saw the concern on Alice's face and instinctively he reached out a hand and put it on her thigh.

"Don't worry," he said.

And then the monster had gone and they were in darkness and he was aware of what he had done unthinkingly, and knew that by doing it he had crossed a barrier. But he waited until the sound of the monster had died sufficiently to hear again the rustling of the beech leaves in the soft night breeze before he took his hand unhurriedly away.

"Have you ever asked yourself if that is what you really want? A business as large as that?" he said.

"What you're saying," she chided him, "is that you don't really believe I *could* cope with it, isn't it?"

"Oh no. You could cope with it all right. But is it really what you want?"

"Well," she replied, "that's a question I've asked myself quite a number of times and especially since we started manufacturing. But it isn't the right question, is it, Martin?"

"What is the right question?"

"What sort of person will I have become by then? That's the right question. You see, I don't have a choice. I have to go on. And not only for Dessy and Thady but for myself as well. I have to have a purpose. I have to do something to fill my life. And you don't have to be sorry for me. It's very exciting and very satisfying."

He tried to visualise her five, ten years on. Or when her sons no longer had need of her; when they had started on their own careers. She would have no family to fall back on. As she'd said to Julia, with every extra worker she took on she removed herself further and further away from the brothers and sisters she'd basically lost all connection with since Samuel Jordan had taken her away from Liverpool into ways of life which to them were unimaginable. *What sort of person will I have become by then?* It was a good question. One inspired perhaps by the knowledge of how different a person she had become from the barely educated daughter of a railway ticket collector who had been sent out to scrub other people's doorsteps at two shillings a week the day after leaving school.

"There's a question you haven't asked me, isn't there, Martin?" Alice said. "The one that lies behind your pulling your car in here instead of driving me straight home. The one you're hesitant to put because you don't want me worrying through the weekend about something which mayn't happen. What am I going to say if on Monday Kornblath wants me to do something I find impossible to agree to and he winds up Alice Dresses?"

She felt free to put her hand on his and found it warm and somehow workmanlike. They faces were very close, their shoulders touching. She was used enough to the light to see the glint of his half-closed eyes holding hers. If he were to lean his head the smallest amount towards me, we would kiss, she thought. And she half expected that they would and made no attempt to prevent it happening. And for quite a few moments they sat like this, looking into each other's eyes, not speaking but with an understanding flowing between them – an understanding broken only by the sound of two or three cars approaching, all with blazing headlights; two or three more carloads of guests leaving Boulters, the leading one perhaps acting as a guide to the two behind it. Instinctively, before the first set of headlights could illuminate them, they moved at least as far apart as the confines of the Hornet coupé allowed. Three times they were illuminated, three times cast into darkness.

"If we've been recognised," Alice said, "they'll think the worst, won't they?" And with a small laugh. "Is this the only road they can take?"

"Heading this way, yes."

"Then I think you'd better take me home, hadn't you, Martin? Before you're compromised."

"I haven't answered your question."

"No, you haven't." She patted his knee. "And I wouldn't bother to now. Come on. Let's be off."

3

Carrington Mews had been built for stabling horses and housing the coachmen employed by the rich owners of the mansions they backed on to. Some, but by no means all, of the stables had been converted into garages, which (with the exception of a narrow entrance leading directly to a flight of stairs) more or less occupied the entire ground floor. Until Alice had moved into the cottage it had been Rackham's practice after he had garaged his car to gain access to 8 Mandeville Square through the link he had had constructed between the two buildings, whereas nowadays he normally entered through a door he had had put in at the back of the garage and thence across the patio.

Drawing the Hornet to a halt well in front of the garage doors, he came quickly round to assist Alice, who was encumbered by her enormous hat.

"Mind you don't slip on the cobbles," he warned her. And when she was out and he had shut the car door. "Give me your key."

She found it in her bag and gave it to him. He opened the door for her.

"Good night, Alice," he said, handing the key back to her. "It has been a very special evening. Thank you." And, with the key still held between them, he leaned forward and kissed her lightly on the cheek.

She felt her heart unaccountably start to thud.

"It's been a wonderful evening, Martin," she said. "A wonderful day. One of the most wonderful days of my whole life."

"Good," he said, releasing the key to her. "Now in you go while I put the car away."

"Why not come through this way? It's easier."

As if he had expected the invitation and had prepared himself to answer it, he replied without a pause: "No, I don't think so. Off you go. And don't worry about Monday. It'll be all right. You'll see."

*   *   *

The patio was always lit at night and, from the window in the room above the garage, Alice watched him as he crossed it to let himself into the back of the house. At the door he paused and turned to look back at the cottage. She shrank back, but as she hadn't switched the light on she doubted if he would have seen her watching him. He had put on his top hat. He looked very smart, very assured and very prepossessing. That was how she had summed him up that morning when he had come round to collect her and drive off to the races. He looked these things now – but there was something more, for which she could not find a word. It was something to do with his individuality and something to do with feelings he had evoked in her.

He could have kissed me, she thought. If those cars hadn't come, I believe he would have. And I didn't want him to go. I wanted him to come into the cottage with me. I was all ready to suggest I made him a cup of coffee. And if I had I don't know what might have happened. She realised her hands were trembling and she put them on the window sill to steady them. She shook her head. "I don't believe this," she whispered. "This isn't me." But she knew it was. That something had happened to her which had never happened before.

It was possible, if unlikely, that Julia was asleep and Rackham decided against using the lift.

The building had a basement but he was able to enter by a short flight of steps at ground-floor level, on which were his own office, his partner's office, his secretary's room, the telephonist and a front room facing the square which was used as a waiting-room.

On the first floor, reached by mounting a wide flight of stairs, were the two main interconnecting drawing offices with another administration office over a back addition. Above were the floors of his maisonette.

On a whim he went into the main drawing office and, switching on the lights, surveyed what was in effect his work-room. The front room which faced Mandeville Square had once been a splendid drawing-room with a fine cornice and tall windows. It interconnected with a rather smaller if equally well-detailed and proportioned room which overlooked the patio and mews cottage at the back. In these two rooms were employed about twenty architects and draughtsmen and, except where one or two of Rackham's more tidy employees had covered up their drawings before leaving for their homes, the projects they were working on were on display.

Idly, an incongruous figure in morning dress and top hat, he wandered from drawing board to drawing board, pausing *en route* to glance briefly at the replanning of a house in Mayfair and some sketches for extra bedrooms at an hotel in Windsor, before halting before some preliminary sketches for Kornblath's Plaxton scheme. Without this and Burlington House, he mused, there would be a lot of empty drawing boards; and without Ivanhoe Gardens on the horizon the future could look very bleak.

He sat down on one of the stools and lighting a cigarette took stock of what his situation would be if, applying Alice's question to himself, next Monday Solly Kornblath asked him to do something he found it impossible to agree to. Well it would not be long before there were quite a few empty stools and unused drawing boards at number 8 Mandeville Square – men like Solly Kornblath did not take kindly to being crossed. What awesome power, he reflected, such men wielded. If Alice's confidence was justified – and he believed it was – at a time when jobs were so hard to come by, three hundred sewers and machinists could be deprived of future employment because one man had lost interest in what had been to him a minor sideline; and if the same man changed his mind, projects such as Ivanhoe Gardens could be abandoned and thousands of men and women would rent flats elsewhere with a total change of direction in their lives.

For himself? Well, he would see it through. Slumps didn't last for ever. He would go on ticking over like other architects he knew who hadn't been as fortunate as himself. One day he would fulfil his ambition of being a leading architect in hotel design. One day. But in the meantime there would be problems, and not the least of these was that this building – which he had seen as one which if it *had* to have its usage changed was so fitting for an architectural practice – could become a white elephant, draining the fund he had set aside for Julia.

Sitting on the stool, smoking his cigarette, in the cold, hard light of an empty drawing office, he considered the immediate future. In his surgery immediately following Julia's last attack, Bayliss had set out to prepare him. It had been unnecessary. He, and Julia, had already faced reality. Within a year at most, most likely less, as well as empty stools and drawing boards – if Kornblath withdrew his work – there would be an empty bed in number 8.

He ground out the cigarette, resolved. There was nothing he could do about an empty bed but there was a great deal he could do about not having empty stools. Through however many years she would be in a nursing home, Julia must have all the care, attention and luxuries money could provide. Unless Kornblath's demands were utterly unacceptable, he would meet them. He had no choice.

And Alice?

Alice Fenwick. A twice-married, widowed mother, purposeful, dedicated – yet still essentially feminine and desirable.

He had known how near to disaster he had been an hour ago under the beeches of Fulmer Rise. But for that trio of cars he would have kissed her – in that moment of nearness she had been all but irresistible. And afterwards? He shrugged. It hadn't happened, so there was no point in thinking about it now when there was something far more pressing than mere afterwards. There was Monday.

He believed, and Alice believed, just as Beatrice had believed, that on Monday they – he and Alice – would be required to make a choice. What exactly the choice they were to be offered would be it was quite impossible to foretell. But when the moment came, he had to be free to make it in Julia's favour. He must not be trammelled by any sense that he owed to Alice Fenwick anything more than that which was due from a man who wished her well, who had helped her in the past and would, if it was in his power to do so, help her in the future, but whose absolute obligation was to his wife. And if, in honouring that obligation, a penalty had to be paid by Alice Fenwick, and by Desmond and Thady Jordan, then so be it, they would have to pay it.

He got off the stool, switched off the lights and went upstairs.

Eleven

1

R ackham drew the Hornet tight to the kerb outside
Kornblath's offices and came round quickly to help Alice
alight, only for Moss to beat him to it.

"Morning, Moss," he said.

"Good morning, Mr Rackham. Good morning, madam."

Watching Alice neatly negotiate getting out of the cramped
quarters of his car, Rackham approved: a well-cut pocketed
suit of a little above ankle length with wide revers exposing
a high-buttoned waistcoat worn with a cravat, rather than the
tie which had recently become something of a vogue for career
women, and on her head, a beret. For dealing with a man like
Solly, it was a good choice: business-like, yet feminine.

"Don't worry about the car, sir," Moss said. "I'll move it along
a little." He glanced at the half-clouded sky. "There could be a
shower. If there is, don't worry, I'll put up the hood."

He opened the door for them, then left them while he went to
report their arrival.

"Ever been in the boardroom?" Rackham said.

"No, Martin. Never."

"Well it's a bit claustrophobic but don't be intimidated by
it."

She looked up at him, grateful beyond words that he was with
her. "I feel like a naughty schoolgirl."

"I have a feeling", he said, with encouragement in his half-
closed eyes, but a touch of grimness in his tone, "that that was
part of the idea."

Alice couldn't but agree with Martin's comment: the boardroom *was* claustrophobic. Panelled from floor to ceiling so cunningly that once the door was closed it wasn't all that easy to find again, without windows, and furnished only with the long mahogany table capable of seating twenty and chairs spaced regularly around it with, in front of every seat occupied or not, a leather folder and propelling pencil and fountain pen, it was quite devoid of softness or humanity. The only things which broke its utter symmetry were three telephones at the top end of the table – a red one which communicated with Kornblath's flat, a white one which was a direct line out and a black one for normal usage through a switchboard. Until she saw these Alice had assumed that, like Henry Ford's motor cars, you could have any colour you liked in telephones so long as it was black.

The two men were waiting for them. Cradforth was in the seat farthest from the door on the right hand side of the table and opposite him was Thompson. At their entry, Cradforth rose to his feet and Thompson, tall and willowy, followed suit, uncoiling himself casually and standing aside from his chair.

"Good morning, Mrs Fenwick," Cradforth said from along the length of the room, in a voice which conveyed quite clearly that he was here for purposes of business and nothing else. And then, with the faintest touch of warmth: "Good morning, Mr Rackham."

Alice, remembering Martin's comment and seeing in Cradforth a powerfully built man with a large well-groomed head of thick black hair, very regular features, a square chin and strong, thick lips clamped determinedly together when not speaking and, above all, eyes which were dark, inflexible and cold, felt a shiver down her spine.

But she held her head up high. "You're Mr Cradforth, I presume."

"Yes." He gestured with a strong, compelling hand towards the empty seat at the head of the table. "Perhaps, Mrs Fenwick, you'll take the chair." And going on without a pause, as if it hadn't crossed his mind that Alice might demur: "Mr Thompson, may I introduce Mr Martin Rackham, who is an architect who handles a great deal of Mr Kornblath's important work."

241

"Heard a great deal about you, Mr Rackham," Thompson said with cheerful brio. "It's a privilege to meet you."

His manner echoed what Alice had had to say about him, for it seemed to Rackham that the man was endeavouring to convey that he, Rackham, had passed a test and henceforth could consider himself free to regard himself as being of equal calibre. Studying him openly, he registered him as a man in his early thirties, dark haired and with a toothbrush moustache, with eyes which were knowing and alert and a jaunty and self-satisfied air underlined by one hand resting lightly on the back of his chair. He concluded that even if Alice hadn't forewarned him, he wouldn't have taken to Mr Thompson.

"Good morning," he responded neutrally.

"Where's Mr Kornblath?" Alice said.

"Mr Kornblath?" Cradforth's cold, hard eyes demanded she explained herself.

"Well, he's coming to the meeting, isn't he?"

"Not so far as I know."

"But when he invited me . . . and Mr Rackham . . . Well, naturally, Mr Cradforth, we assumed that he'd be here as well."

"Then it seems you have misunderstood him, Mrs Fenwick. As I've already said, as far as I know he isn't coming to the meeting."

"And," put in Thompson, as if he could not resist it, "I suppose if we are to go by the rule book, Mr Kornblath doesn't have the right to attend it without being invited."

"If," snapped Alice, having now had time to be better briefed on company procedures, "as I take it from your remark, Mr Thompson, you are regarding this as a board meeting then if we are to go by the rule book this meeting isn't in order and shouldn't be taking place at all. The proper notice hasn't been given – the first I heard about it was at Mr Kornblath's house last week."

"That is quite correct," Cradforth said. "And if it is your wish, Mrs Fenwick, we can abandon it."

"No, of course it's not my wish," said Alice, more angry that ever, realising that Kornblath had humbugged them. "When Mr Kornblath asked Mr Rackham and me to come here this morning he conveyed the impression that he was going to be here too, and here we are and he isn't. And we're both busy people. But if there *is* something about my business which needs to be discussed, then we'd better get on with discussing it, Mr Kornblath or no Mr Kornblath!" And, feeling a great deal better, she turned to Martin: "Mr Rackham, I'd appreciate it if you'll sit next to me. Mr Thompson can shift down to make room for you."

And having quite forgotten an earlier reluctance to take the head of the table, she sailed to the end of it, destroyed the symmetry of the telephones by pushing one aside, plonked her handbag on top of the leather folder, and sat down.

Rackham, smiling openly, followed her.

"Sorry to disturb you, Mr Thompson," he said genially.

His air of self-sufficiency difficult to maintain while playing musical chairs, Thompson's return smile lacked conviction.

"Well, Mr Cradforth," Alice said formally, meanwhile, "as this is the first time we've actually met I'd like to welcome you as a director of Alice Dresses and express the hope we will get on well together."

"As I'm sure we shall," said Cradforth impassively.

"Well, let's make a start, shall we? What's this all about?"

"There are two things of importance," Cradforth said. "The first is that Mr Kornblath has been sufficiently impressed by certain reports he has received to be prepared to increase his investment in the company."

"Reports?" said Alice. "Who from?"

"Mr Cameron and Mr Bowyer."

Alice stared at him, amazed. Cameron and Bowyer were directors of the two wholesalers, Cameron and Middleton, and Pringles, who had shown positive interest in her samples.

"In view of their, I think it is fair to say, enthusiasm," Cradforth went on, "Mr Kornblath is prepared to invest a further fifteen thousand pounds in the company immediately."

Fifteen thousand pounds! The enormity of it robbed Alice of the question she had been about to ask: how Kornblath even *knew* of either Cameron or Bowyer.

But in any case, Cradforth was continuing without a pause. "Mr Kornblath suggests this is done by the issuing of debentures

243

which will carry an interest rate of six per cent." He was reading from notes which had been disclosed by the opening of his folder. He paused briefly to say to Alice with emotionless formality: "Mr Kornblath has asked me, Mrs Fenwick, to advise you that you are of course free to subscribe to as many of these debentures as you care to."

Determined to hide the uncertainty she was feeling, and distracted by the use of a word she had heard spoken before but whose precise meaning she had never understood, Alice was tempted to conceal her embarrassment by laughing aloud at the absurdity of personally subscribing to these *debentures*. She would have given the world to have been able to ask Martin beside her what it all meant and what, if anything, she should say or do.

"Well it's something I would want to think about," she managed.

"Naturally," Cradforth responded, dismissing this reply as clearly superfluous. "In any event this is by way of being an outline of Mr Kornblath's proposals, which will of course be notified to you shortly in a more formal manner after which the proper notice for calling a company meeting will be given, when this suggestion and the one I will be coming to shortly will be put as resolutions." And, with a quick glance at his notes: "To come to the second matter, Mrs Fenwick, subject to your agreement, Mr Kornblath is of the opinion that with the least possible delay Alice Dresses should open at least thirty retail outlets."

If Alice had been astonished at the thought of an injection of a further fifteen thousand pounds of capital, it was as nothing compared to the suggestion of opening thirty shops. She was dumbfounded. She had conceived that the time might come when there *could* be shops bearing the name Alice Dresses in a few selected places, but only after a steady expansion through wholesale outlets establishing the trade name. To, as it were, swallow at a gulp years and stages and accept such a phenomenal explosion of expansion, was quite beyond her. Instinctively she turned to Martin for support.

He read the disbelief and confusion in her eyes and his heart went out to her.

"Shall I continue, Mrs Fenwick?" Cradforth, observing this exchange of looks, said swiftly.

"Yes," said Alice, pulling herself together. "Please do, Mr Cradforth."

"You have no immediate objection to Mr Kornblath's proposal?"

She steeled herself to hold his eyes: "You don't seriously expect me to give you a positive answer to that, Mr Cradforth, do you?"

"Is that the reply I am to minute?"

"I don't exactly know what you mean by that," Alice said. "But what I *would* like to know is where these thirty retail outlets I'm supposed to fill with dresses which haven't yet been made are supposed to be coming from?"

"Mr Thompson will explain."

"But *you* can't?" said Alice, wondering why she said it.

"As Mr Thompson's firm has been directly concerned with the negotiations, it is better that *he* should."

It was quite obvious nothing more was going to be got out of Cradforth for the moment. Alice turned to Thompson. "Negotiations? What is Mr Cradforth talking about?"

Thompson opened his folder.

"You've heard of Perry and Sessions, Mrs Fenwick?" he asked.

"Of course I have!" He might as well have asked her if she'd heard of Lyons Teashops or the ABC. "They sell shoes, not dresses."

"That is not quite correct," Thompson responded with disdain, "they *used* to sell shoes."

Rackham felt the bile rising. Cradforth might be ruthless and apparently devoid of feelings but at least he did not mess about. Cradforth he could take. But Thompson was insufferable. He swivelled in his chair so violently as to have it scrape the floor and rounded on the man: "I suggest you stop trying to score clever little points, Thompson! If you've got something to say, say it!"

Thompson, a little shaken by this fierce attack, moved back a little as if imagining Rackham might actually strike him.

"Really, Mr Rackham," he began to complain, in words stronger than the tone in which they were delivered, "in view of the fact that you are neither a director nor a shareholder—"

Rackham thumped the table so fiercely as to silence him: "I'm here because Mr Kornblath asked me to be here but there are plenty of other things I could be usefully doing. So long as you and Mr Cradforth are concerning yourselves with the affairs of Mrs Fenwick's business, I will possess myself in patience until the time comes when you're ready to explain exactly why I *am* here. But I am not prepared to sit around wasting my morning while you are amusing yourself scoring points over Mrs Fenwick. Is that clear?"

Thompson, aware that he had made yet another enemy for life, said bitterly and with malice: "Yes, Mr Rackham, you have made that very clear." And, turning with relief to Alice, "Mr Kornblath has acquired Perry and Sessions. They will no longer be making shoes."

"You haven't answered my question, Mr Thompson," Alice said.

"I'm not quite sure what your question was, Mrs Fenwick," Thompson said truthfully.

"I think," cut in Cradforth with a humourless smile, which Rackham took to mean that *he* didn't know what Alice's question was either but was enjoying Thompson's discomfiture, "it would be as well if you explained the Perry and Sessions situation, Mr Thompson."

"Very well," said Thompson waspishly. "They're old-fashioned, under-financed and overstretched. They make their own shoes and in the present depressed conditions they own more than twice as many shops as they need for the reduced output from their factory. Mr Kornblath, after several months of negotiation in which Winthrop's have been concerned, has bought them up."

"What on earth for?" said Alice.

Rackham could have told her. This wasn't the first property deal of this kind he'd known Kornblath to be involved in. The probability was that he'd bought the firm up cheaply with the idea of keeping the freeholds or long leases of about thirty of their best outlets, and then, having had someone reorganise the company on efficient lines, selling off the rump for about, or even better than, his original investment. It was a classic asset-stripping operation.

Thompson confirmed: "He's bought them up so as to secure thirty shops in prime locations for your company to sell its dresses in." He now spoke with exaggerated slowness – as do some schoolmasters explaining a mathematical problem to a simpleton.

"I don't want to own thirty shops," Alice said.

"You will not be owning thirty shops, Mrs Fenwick." He was making no attempt to hide personal triumph. "The shops will continue to be owned by the company Mr Kornblath has used to buy up Perry and Sessions and will be let to you."

"And who pays the rent? And what is it going to be?"

"Alice Dresses will pay the rents which will be at going market rates."

"Well, I don't agree to it," Alice said, with commendable finality. "It's quite ridiculous. It's trying to run before you've learnt to walk."

"I'm sorry, Mrs Fenwick," Thompson said with undoubted satisfaction, "but the decision is not for you alone to make."

"But it doesn't make financial sense."

"I assure you that it does."

It was all Alice could do not to lose her temper. "You may be good at adding up figures, Mr Thompson," she snapped, "but one thing is quite certain. You know nothing about the rag trade!" And turning to Cradforth in the hope of doing better there: "How can it make financial sense for me to rent thirty shops before I've even got my production up to the point that I can stock them?"

"You will have the time to increase your production, Mrs Fenwick," Cradforth answered curtly. "The shops will all have to be refurbished to make them suitable for selling dresses rather than shoes."

It had all been, Rackham told himself, worked out to the last detail. The only aspect which had been neglected had been the effect it might have on Alice as a person. Not for the first time, although never before so strongly, he asked himself the inescapable questions: what sort of people were they, these Thompsons and Cradforths, when, if ever, you really got below the surface? What were they like when the office door had closed on them and they went home? Did they suddenly become human beings who had a conscience, cared about other people's feelings and were capable of kindness and affection? Or had too many boardroom meetings, too many years of fighting to hold their positions, killed their capacity to get beyond status, petty personal triumphs and successful balance sheets?

Which brought him to Alice. How on earth had it come about that a warm, decent and, yes, relatively speaking, simple woman like her had got herself mixed up with such people, and what was the best way, without in the process losing her everything she had struggled to create, to extricate her from the hideous situation she seemed headed for?

But at once he saw the falsity of this. Simple, Alice might be, yes. *And* inexperienced. But in these past few minutes – even though in commercial matters clearly technically out of her depth – she had more than held her own. Warm and decent he had called her – as if such very modest laurels summed up her character! What nonsense! How many more qualities she was entitled to have assigned to her. The list was endless. Courage, imagination, fortitude, resolve, tenacity, and the capacity to adjust. Yes, that above all, perhaps. And what a rare quality that was – the ability to modify, rectify, adapt to change. Life was always a flux, a continuous succession of changing circumstances. But for women, perhaps never more so than now. They were moving into a new age in which old ideas to which many clung so loyally and mechanically were going to have to give way; an age which both cried out for women like Alice and gave to such women the chance to fulfil their destinies. And Alice must fulfil hers. Yet the cunning plan – now transparently obvious to himself – which had been hatched almost certainly in this very boardroom could prevent her doing so. He had to get her away before, out of surprise, gratitude, embarrassment or confusion, she agreed to something from which she could not withdraw; before she found herself tied hand and foot in a company she might make hugely successful but which she would never control and from which she could be dismissed the moment Kornblath decided the time was ripe to do so.

He glanced obviously at his watch . . .

"Mr Cradforth," he said, "I am sorry to interrupt these proceedings but I have other appointments to keep. I'd be grateful if you'd tell me why Mr Kornblath asked me to attend this meeting."

"Certainly, Mr Rackham." Cradforth's hard eyes held his own across the table's width. "We were talking about the refurbishment of these thirty shops that Mr Kornblath has acquired. The company, and I am referring to Alice Dresses, would like to invite you to act as its architect in their refurbishment."

This was patently absurd. He was the wrong sort of person to handle that sort of work. What was needed was a man who specialised in shopfitting and interior design – someone like Mussack.

He leaned back and forced a smile: "Oh, come now, Cradforth," he said genially, "you know perfectly well that sort of thing isn't in my line. And in any case, doesn't Mrs Fenwick have a say in who should be the architect for the company she's running?"

"Mr Kornblath has assumed," Cradforth replied – and it was extraordinary how, unlike Thompson, he could give answers devoid of any form of expression – "that Mrs Fenwick would choose you in preference to anyone else, but it goes without saying that if she preferred not to, he would not insist on your appointment."

And that, Rackham told himself, was yet another prepared speech.

"I see," he said quickly. "Well it isn't something which I would want to give an answer to immediately. Do I take it that's the only reason I was asked to come here this morning?" And at Cradforth's nod, "I'll think it over. Good morning, gentlemen."

He got to his feet.

"Before you go, Mr Rackham," Thompson said, "you might

as well have a list of the shops Mr Kornblath has in mind. As you will see quite a number of them are in prime locations." The inference was pitifully transparent: that knowing his name would be displayed in so many important places could be persuasive to an architect. But rarely had Thompson so misread an antagonist.

Taking what was quite a thick clip of sheets, Rackham glanced at the topmost one and saw that full addresses and other details had been included against the outlet. Any lingering idea that Kornblath's remarks at Boulters had been spontaneous could be finally dismissed.

"Mrs Fenwick." Thompson was handing a copy across him to Alice.

"If there is nothing else you have to discuss with Mrs Fenwick," Rackham said to Cradforth, "I can run her back."

"There are quite a number—" Thompson began, but Alice had intercepted Rackham's compelling look.

"I'm sorry but I have an appointment," Alice said, gathering her handbag.

"But . . ."

"If you'll give me a ring at the office we can fix some other time, Mr Thompson." She was on her feet. "Good morning, Mr Cradforth."

He examined her coldly. She felt his look boring deep into her. But she held his gaze – and won. Cradforth rose. "Mrs Fenwick, as I have already said, this morning's proposals will be put to you in a proper formal manner, ahead of a properly constituted meeting at which a vote can be taken on them." And, as Alice turned to leave: "Oh, there is just one other thing. Mr Kornblath asked me to say that so far as the running of Alice Dresses is concerned he relies entirely on your judgement, and that if you consider any of the outlets he has suggested unsuitable, he will give the closest consideration to your views."

2

Outside again in the warm summer sunshine with the fresh

breeze rustling the trees in the square, Alice was conscious of a huge sense of relief.

"Oh, Martin," she said, "I feel as if I've been let out of Pentonville! But what a goose I showed myself to be."

"No. You did magnificently."

"But half the time I didn't know what they were talking about. What's a debenture anyway?"

"Well it's rather like a share but the difference is that it earns a fixed rate of interest which the company has to go on paying until the money lent has been repaid."

"Is it something I have to worry about?"

"It certainly is. For one thing, the rate of interest proposed, six per cent, is exorbitant. The company will have to pay Kornblath nine hundred pounds a year whether or not it's making a profit. And for another thing, if Alice Dresses doesn't work and has to be wound up, the fifteen thousand pounds and any more that Kornblath's going to lend will have to be paid back ahead of anything else. Ahead of anything you owe to your suppliers, any wages you haven't paid your workers and anything you're due out of the business itself."

They had reached Rackham's Hornet, which Moss had parked a little along from Kornblath's offices in the direction of Piccadilly. They stopped beside it and he put his hand on the door to open it for her, then paused.

"No."

She looked up at him in surprise.

"Do you have to go back to your factory?"

"Well, I should. There's . . . Well never mind." She didn't want to bore him with details of dressmaking.

He smiled – and somehow it felt to her as it might have done if a grey day's clouds had been magically swept away.

"You shouldn't be wasting an outfit like that in a dreary workroom," he told her.

"Where should I be wearing it?" she smiled.

"In the sort of restaurant where it will be appreciated, and after we've got the talking over we're going to find one and I'm going to buy you a stupendous lunch. Give me those." He was talking about the clip of papers which were too big to fit into Alice's handbag. Alice handed them to him and he stowed them with his own copy somewhere in the car. He glanced at the sky. "I think Moss is a pessimist. Let's go and grab one of those benches in the square."

Piccadilly was probably jammed solid with buses, taxis, cars, vans and lorries hooting and squeaking and belching their fumes into the air of a glorious late June morning but Berkeley Square was an eye in the storm of London's snarling traffic. No buses circumnavigated it and it was of no interest to lorry drivers; it was a handy cut-through for occasional imaginative car owners and taxi drivers and useful for parking one's car if lunching at the Ritz or Berkeley but on the whole it was a quiet haven, and the garden in the centre of it an ideal place for children to play, for lovers to meet, for affairs to be discussed.

They strolled across and found a bench.

"Now," Rackham said when they were seated, "there's just two things we've got to work out. What Solly's up to and what we're going to do about it."

He was leaning easily against the corner of the bench. He was casually dressed in an open single-breasted suit over a camel-haired waistcoat; unlike the vast majority of Londoners he was hatless and the breeze ruffled without unduly disturbing his thick brown hair.

Even here in this oasis of quiet and serenity, disturbed only by an occasional couple strolling past, by a small boy in the care of a uniformed nanny throwing a ball to an excited terrier or by the sudden honk of a vehicle reminding them that all around them was the busy life of London, the sense of presence which so characterised him seemed to enfold her. She found herself trying to remember if she had ever met a man who remotely resembled him, and could dredge up none. She dwelt, as she had before, on the awareness that he brought back to her something of the sense of childhood and adolescent days through his warmth and down-to-earth reality, like that which the men and women she had known then had possessed and which she had found lacking down here in the more prosperous and sophisticated south. And inevitably the thought made her draw a comparison between him and the Machiavellian wheeler-dealers they had just left, and for all the sunshine she felt the same shiver in her spine she had felt when her eyes had first met Cradforth's.

"*Is* there anything we can do about it, Martin?" she pleaded.

"That depends on whether we're thinking short or long term, Alice, doesn't it?" And, after a moment, "When we were coming back from Kornblath's party you asked yourself a very wise question. What sort of person would you be by the time you'd got yourself a business employing three hundred girls?"

"And now it's thirty shops as well."

"Yes. And we're not talking about some time in the dim distant future. Solly means business."

"You really think so, Martin?"

"No question." He was utterly convincing. "He's had his spies out – and you'll never find out who they are – and between him and them and that awful Thompson fellow, who no doubt knows his job, he's been persuaded that Alice Dresses has tremendous potential. For Cradforth to use the word enthusiasm is little short of astonishing. I'd say he wants to get your sizing business off the ground before anyone else cottons on to it. And that's not all, you know."

"Oh?"

"By no means." There was that wry smile on his face and the twinkle in the eyes that she had discovered she could call to mind at will which were at odds with the purpose in his tone. "Do you really think it's just coincidence you're fitting so neatly with this Perry and Sessions thing?"

She shook her head. "Martin, I just don't know what you mean."

"Because you don't understand the principles of asset-stripping." He explained them and ended: "How can anyone who's put a deal together which leaves him with thirty valuable properties as profit be so lucky as to find himself with a ready-made company which he controls there to take them off his hands at any price he decides to name! That's just too much to ask." He shook his head ruefully. "You've got to hand it to the blighter, Alice. It's bloody clever!"

253

"You mean . . ." Alice would not believe it. "You mean that's why he backed me in the first place?"

He shrugged his broad shoulders.

"Probably not entirely. After all five thousand pounds is chickenfeed to him and he'd be prepared to risk that much on his judgement of your ability."

"But it wasn't just five thousand pounds, Martin. He let me have that factory floor. And all that equipment . . ."

"That floor was unlet, and with the slump we're in likely to remain so for years. Letting you use it costs him nothing. As for that equipment, why d'you think it took so long before he gave you the OK to order it?"

"Because he was on holiday."

"Because he was on holiday nothing! That was just lawyers' talk. It was to give him time to set his spies to work and satisfy himself you were a worthwhile risk before he started spending *real* money." He reached out with his hand and pressed it on hers encouragingly. "So don't underwrite yourself, Alice. He wouldn't have risked that first five thousand unless you'd impressed him. He's not a man who likes backing losers."

He took his hand away and she grudged its going – and chided herself for doing so.

"Suppose," she said rather wildly, "suppose I *am* a loser? Suppose Alice Dresses doesn't work and we've got all these shops and we're employing all these girls and I'm making all these dresses and I can't sell them?"

"You'll sell them."

"But suppose I *can't*. The business is paying all this rent . . ."

"That's one thing you don't have to worry too much about – in effect it's going out of one of Solly's pockets into another. But to answer your question." He paused deliberately. "To answer your question, Alice: Solly will cut his losses and wind up the business."

"And there's nothing I can do about that?"

"Nothing. He's got fifty-one per cent of the company's shares and the man who's got fifty-one per cent is like the man who pays the piper – he calls the tune."

She looked into his eyes and read so much: knowledge,

intelligence, kindness, warmth and humour. And something new – concern.

She put her hand on his arm. "What should I do, Martin? Tell me."

There was no hesitation. "Get out."

The answer shocked her. "Get out? You mean . . ." She couldn't finish the question. She dared not.

He was firm and decisive. "You've got to get out now, Alice. Now. Immediately. Because if you don't you're going to find yourself so enmeshed that later you won't be able to. Even though it's Kornblath who's putting up all the money, you think it's your business, Alice Dresses, don't you? It isn't. It's the old, old story that's been repeated a thousand times. The man, or the woman, who has a good idea and gets someone to back him and is kept sweet just long enough to get the thing off the ground and then finds himself thrown on the ash heap when he's served his purpose. There are two possibilities. The company fails, Kornblath winds it up and you're left with nothing. Or it succeeds. And what does he do then? Floats it as a public company and makes a killing. But you won't share in that killing, Alice. Because long before then you'll have been replaced. And all you'll have is the bitterness of watching others cash in on a brilliant idea that was your own. And as for what it'll have done to you before that happens, attending meetings, being ridden over roughshod by Cradforth and company, knowing the frustration of being powerless to stop them making what was once your child a monster that's going to devour all that was gentle and kind and decent in you . . ." He left the sentence unfinished. "No, Alice, it's unthinkable!"

She had not imagined he could be so passionate. Yet, even so, it could not prevent a small anger rising in her.

"If that's how you feel about it, Martin," she said fiercely, "why didn't you say all this before?"

He nodded. "That's a very good question and one you're entitled to ask. I *ought* to have seen it at the start. But I suppose I didn't really believe that Alice Dresses could be the huge success that Solly's clearly convinced it's going to be. To be honest, I didn't really believe in your three hundred girls. And I never thought of it having shops all over England. Even abroad maybe." He paused.

His tone changed, becoming quieter, more measured, regretful. "And there's something else. I didn't know you then, Alice, as I know you now. You weren't so important to me as you have become. As your children have become. I told you about Desmond coming into the drawing office and saying he'd like to be an architect when he grows up. What I haven't told you is that I've given a lot of thought to that and wondered if maybe, if he keeps on thinking that way, he might work for me – even, if he's got it in him, become a partner one day. If I'd had a son it's what I would have wanted. And then there's Thady. He's bright, he's clever and he's perservering. I can't guess what he'll be, but I think, with a little help on the way, he might do great things."

He took both of her hands in his. "Alice, you and your boys have become a part of Julia's life and mine. We don't want to lose you or the person that you are. To watch as the weeks, the months, perhaps even the years, go by, you being ground . . ." she felt the pressure of his hands increase as he used the word, "being ground down and fundamentally changed as you struggle and fail to hold your own with men like Cradforth."

She withdrew her hands from his, and straightening so that she was just that much farther from him, said in a tone from which the emotion she was feeling was suppressed: "So what do I do, Martin? What do I do to bring up two small boys and give my life some purpose? What do I do when I've quit Alice Dresses and haven't a job to go to? When there isn't any money coming in? When I haven't even enough to pay you the very reasonable rent you charge me, let alone buy food and clothes and have in a doctor when Dessy or Thady needs one?"

"You'll get a job," he said with conviction. "You're too inventive, too resourceful, too visionary not to."

"Even in these hard days?" There was irony in it now.

"Yes, even in these hard days. And if it takes a little time—"

She stopped him. "If it takes a little time, you'll let me go on living in Carrington Mews rent free. Like I did at the beginning. And you'll see me through for the other things – food and clothes and the doctor when I need one." She shook her head. "No, Martin. No."

She began to gather her handbag.

"Look," he said, "you've got to give yourself time to think this through."

She understood exactly what he meant by that and what would follow from it.

Through the long weekend, he had been seldom from her thoughts. She had not dimissed the astounding discovery that she had fallen in love with him as an overcoloured caprice born of a thrilling and curiously intimate day, but, after an initial night of semi-wakefulness and wild imaginings, she had controlled herself to come to terms with the reality of the situation. He was a man who not only loved his wife but was bound to her by the ghastly tragedy of her illness; and she was a woman who bore the responsibility of two sons and had discovered through bitter experience the problems which could arise from asking a man other than their real father to share that responsibility. Some day perhaps, some distant day when both of them had largely shed those responsibilities . . . but she had shrugged those thoughts away. In the challenges which lay ahead of her for years there was no room for such abstractions. She must conceal her feelings and preserve the precious friendship she had with Julia and Martin, the only real friendship she had with anyone.

These had been the decisions she had come to ahead of that morning's meeting, but she knew that there was a limit to her capacity to stifle need and that that limit had been all but reached, that it had needed no more than the touch of his hands on hers for the mastery of her emotions to be under attack. He was about to repeat his invitation for her to lunch with him. But she knew that if she shared that lunch with him, while it would not necessarily follow that when the bill had been paid and they had each gone on their way anything would have been said, or agreed, that would have carried their relationship into deeper waters, would have deepened their relation-ship – just as it had been deepened by Solly's Ascot day.

"You mean like over that stupendous lunch you were going to treat me to?" she said to him, smiling.

And he read that smile, at once quizzical and rueful, correctly. How dangerous that lunch would be, it said. An hour, two hours, of closest intimacy, shared by a man whose body yearned for a woman's and a woman who for the first time in life had discovered love.

"That wouldn't be a very good idea, Martin, would it?" she ended. "Having that lunch with you?"

He smiled back at her, the smile through half-closed eyes she had come to know so well – only this time in the smile was the suspicion of regret which matched her own. "No, Alice," he agreed. "It wouldn't be a good idea at all." And after a moment: "Where would you like me to run you to?"

She constructed a briskness of manner she was far from feeling.

"Thanks, Martin," she said, "but I'm going to walk. I've got a lot of thinking to do."

She pressed his hand and left him. He watched her cross the gardens and Berkeley Square itself, then start to make her way up Berkeley Street in the direction of Piccadilly. He watched her until she had gone out of sight – and she hadn't turned her head. He knew that, were it not for Julia, he would not have hesitated but would have hurried after her, and caught her hand, and as she turned he would have kissed her and held her to him and Kornblath and Cradforth would no longer have been of the least account to either of them.

3

It was one of those days when the lift wasn't working, and by the time she had climbed the four flights of stairs Alice needed a moment or two to recover before pressing the bell push.

A young girl opened the door. Her face was familiar but it was only when she spoke that Alice placed her as the DSM for *Counsel's Dilemma*, which had long since closed.

"Yes?"

"You're Peggy, aren't you?" And, pressing home her advantage, as the enormous eyes opened even wider in surprise. "Is Mrs Culverwell in?" And when, caught off balance, the girl failed to deliver the standard precautionary reply. "Will you tell her, Peggy, that Mrs Fenwick would like to see her urgently."

And with no more ado, Alice stepped past her just as Harry Dobbyn emerged from one of the doors leading off the narrow passage, almost entirely filling it.

"Why, Alice!" he cried with delight – for over the months, Alice had been in the Brusa Productions offices more than once.

"Hallo, Harry." She hoped he wouldn't keep her too long chatting. There was a lot to be done in the rest of the day. "How's it all going?"

Harry had a few good-humoured grumbles about Beatrice's latest production – a comedy which had done well in New York but apparently hadn't travelled well – but sensing he wasn't really getting her full attention, he cut it short.

"You want to see the boss. You're lucky." He led Alice to Beatrice's office and flung the door open unceremoniously. "Someone it'll do your eyes good to see."

He stepped into the room to make it possible for Alice to pass. Beatrice was seated at her elliptical table apparently immersed in doing arithmetic – in fact, she was considering the box office returns of the American comedy and wondering how much longer she should give it before admitting defeat and taking it off.

"Why, Alice!" she said, not getting to her feet but raising her hand in greeting. "What a surprise! What a pleasant surprise!" And, taking in Alice's outfit, "My, don't you just look something. Who's taking *you* to lunch?"

"I am," Harry joked.

"And I wouldn't blame you," Beatrice said. She shook her head in admiration, making today's long earrings sway. "I could tear that off your back, Alice. It's so *smart!*"

"Yes," Alice said, inconsequentially. "Look, Bee, I can see you're very busy and I don't need to keep you long . . ."

Beatrice picked up the urgency. "Say no more!" She was on her feet. "Harry! Scram!"

"It's a poor antipodean who doesn't know when he's not wanted," Harry grinned. And he exited with an exaggerated closing of the door behind him.

"Now," said Beatrice. "What is it?"

"You're sure . . ."

"Forget it." She came from behind the table and, gesturing to a chair, took one herself. "OK," she said. "Spill it!"

For all her mental preparation, Alice found it difficult to know where to start.

Beatrice helped out: "Is it something to do with Solly?"

Alice nodded. "Yes. Last Friday. At Boulters. When he suggested that Martin picked me up for this meeting . . ."

"You've had it?"

"Yes. It finished about an hour ago."

"Did Martin go?"

"Yes."

Beatrice reached for cigarettes. "Go on."

"Well, when he suggested it . . . you were . . . I don't know quite how to put it."

Beatrice paused in lighting her cigarette. "I said 'Ai! Ai! Ai!'"

"Yes."

"Why? Is that what you want to know?"

"No." Alice smiled faintly. "You made that pretty clear when you suggested Martin broke his leg. What I'd like to know is what you think was behind Solly being so . . . so . . ."

"Bitchy?"

"Yes."

"Well, between you and Martin you've put his nose out of joint, haven't you? I mean – as good as moving in with him."

Alice flushed. "Bee, you don't think—"

"That you and Martin are having an affair? No, of course I don't. But I bet Solly does. Christ, Alice, here's a man chock full of go with a wife all but bedridden and . . . well, look at you now! Or what you looked like last week at Ascot! With every male head turning as you passed. You think he's not going to put himself in Martin's place, a man like Solly, and get it wrong?"

"Then why did he ask us?"

"Separately."

"Well, yes . . ."

"Alice don't be so naïve. Look. He's discovered that your number in Carrington Mews backs on to 8 Mandeville Square. That fires him up a bit. So what does he do? Sends you separate invitations to his Fulmer shindig. You come together. That's the first strike against you. But it doesn't have to count too much. But when he sees you from his box, strolling the lawns, placing your bets, chatting, laughing, often arm in arm." She paused. "Answer me something. And answer it honestly. What do you think of Martin?"

In spite of herself Alice flushed.

"Yes," Beatrice said. "You've fallen for him haven't you? Well I didn't need to ask. Anyone who saw you two together at Ascot or Fulmer would have known."

"But I wasn't . . ." She broke off embarrassed.

"But you are now. You're in love with him. And you were then, only maybe you hadn't realised. Well, OK. What's wrong with that? He's one hell of a guy. I could fall in love with him myself so easily. But there's no future in it, is there? Not the way the two of you are fixed. You with two children and Martin with Julia."

"No, Bee, there isn't," Alice answered firmly "But, Bee, even granting Solly thinks I'm having an affair with Martin, why should that upset him?"

Beatrice smoked for a moment or two, working out how to reply. "Difficult to say," she replied, at length. "We're *all* so different. We all react in different ways to different circumstances. Another trouble is we're all inclined to assume that people react as we would ourselves and if they don't we think they're screwy. The *simple* answer is he's jealous."

"No," Alice said. "Since we had that lunch at the Crébillion he's never even been in touch with me."

"He can still be jealous. But I go along with you. It has to be something more. And what I think it is, is that the one thing Solly likes to be, and for everyone else to know he is, is the boss man. And one way of showing he's still boss man was to summon you both to the meeting you just had. So what did he say?"

"He wasn't there."

Beatrice waved her cigarette holder. "That figures."

"Yes, I suppose it does. But I still don't see why . . ."

"Why he's uptight? Honey, look. He's a womaniser. He's got a reputation for it. But the one thing he doesn't do is soil his own doorstep. But that doesn't mean he isn't tempted. Have you met his secretary?" And when Alice shook her head. "She's quite a dish. She'd have to be or he wouldn't have her. But she's as safe with him as she would be with the Archbishop of Canterbury. And I bet that gives him quite a glow. That he can enjoy looking at her and imagining what it would be like to lay her in that bed he's got in Berkeley Square, and still keep his hands to himself. OK. Now, suppose he's discovered his pet architect is sleeping with her. D'you think he's going to keep her as his secretary? And go on giving his architect work? No, sir! He might keep one of them. He might. Depends on the circumstances. But he certainly won't keep both."

"But that's just what he's going to do."

And she told Beatrice about the meeting.

"My," said Beatrice. "You sure have hooked him, haven't you? Thirty shops!" She ground out her cigarette. "And about repuffilating them. Is Martin going to agree to doing it?"

"I don't know."

"He'll be a damn fool if he does. That will be the last commission Solly will ever give him."

"You think so?"

"I know so. I know my Solly."

"But it doesn't seem in line with what you were saying just now."

"Sure it's in line. He'll have shown you who's boss and demoted Martin. Turned him from being the architect he was going to use for the largest block of flats in Europe to one fiddling about with a bunch of dress shops."

"And if Martin refuses to do them?"

"I won't say he'll do it, but he'll have the best excuse in the world for firing him.'"

"I can't believe it, Bee."

Beatrice fitted another cigarette into her holder. "What can't you believe?"

"I remember what he said about Martin at that lunch. Something he'd already said to me. That he was going to be an architect who would be a legend in his own lifetime. Surely, Bee, a man like Solly Kornblath, a man with all that money and all that power, isn't going to risk losing a man he thinks that much of out of spite?"

Beatrice laid down the holder as if after all she had decided there were more important things than smoking. She leaned forward, hands on knees.

"If there's one thing I've learnt in theatre, Alice," she said, "it's that we're all human beings and subject to the defects that come with being that. I've known well-known actors . . . and actresses . . . people who can fill theatres just because it's their name that's up in lights, turn down parts you'd have thought they'd have given their eye teeth to play for the darnedest reasons. Maybe the director once said something snide about them, maybe they've got some stupid superstition, maybe they think the part will dent their image. You can't tell how worked up people can get over things that just seem trivial to us. OK. So Solly's rich, so he's got power, so everyone at a boardroom table trembles when he comes through the door but, like all of us, he's got his weaknesses. And the big one in his case is pride. He just can't bear the thought of being made a fool of." She sat up straight, picked up the holder and lit her cigarette. "What does Martin say about all this?"

"We haven't talked about his side of things," Alice admitted. "So far as mine's concerned, he thinks I should get out of Alice Dresses." She laughed softly at herself. "You said I shouldn't have got into it."

"Water under the bridge. What are you going to do?"

Alice looked at her defiantly. "Mind if I use your phone?"

Beatrice waved her holder. "Help yourself. They'll get your number for you."

Alice crossed the room and picked up the telephone. "Will you get me the Solomon Kornblath Investment Trust in Berkeley Square," she ordered slowly and deliberately. "And when you get them ask to be put through to Mr Kornblath. Tell him that Mrs Fenwick wants to speak to him."

Putting down the instrument she turned to look at Beatrice challengingly.

Beatrice stared at her amazed. "Is that wise?" she said. But the respect in her tone was unmistakable.

The minute or so before the telephone beside her jangled seemed to Alice like a lifetime, while to Beatrice it was as the pause before some intensely dramatic moment which is going to alter the whole tenor of a play. She would no more have thought of breaking the silence than would an audience.

The bell rang. Alice's hand reached out and closed around the receiver. She lifted it off its hook and put it to her ear. Beatrice sat stock still, the smoke from her newly lit cigarette drifting slowly to the ceiling.

"Yes? . . . Yes." There was agreement in Alice's tone.

He's going to be put through, thought Beatrice. I don't believe it.

"Good morning, Mr Kornblath." Was it still morning? "I couldn't wait to phone you! I've got to see you . . . and talk to you . . . about these shops! Oh, and about other things. Ideas I've got. . . As soon as possible!" The tone was that of a woman fired with enthusiasm. Beatrice's head moved in almost disbe-lieving admiration. Who'd have thought she had it in her? "No, I don't think it should wait . . . No, not this afternoon. There's a lot of things I've got to do I just can't put off." Inflexible now! To a man like Solly Kornblath! Wow! ". . . I don't want to leave it long. It's too exciting! I was wondering if you could make it this evening if you happen to be free. Perhaps I could come to your flat, and if we can reach agreement we might have a celebration dinner somewhere afterwards." Jesus, Alice! What *are* you doing, girl? ". . . Six thirty? . . . No, I'm afraid that would be far too early. I could make it by . . . eight? . . . Yes, of course, Mr Kornblath. Eight. 'Bye."

Alice hung up the receiver and confronted Beatrice defiantly, knowing what to expect and finding it.

"Alice, you can't do it!"

264

The Deal

But Alice's eyes had a steel in them Beatrice had never seen before and her words held a grim resolve not to be shifted: "I can't have Martin's career wrecked after all he's done for me. It's Hobson's choice. So let's not argue about it. Will you do one thing more for me?"

"What?" The American's voice was harsh.

"Get hold of a hundred pounds for me? I'll pay you back tomorrow."

Beatrice thought for a long time, then decided: "Yes. I'll get you a hundred pounds. On one condition."

"Which is?"

"You tell me what you want it for."

Alice nodded. "I'll tell you. When we've got our business out of the way, Solly is going to take me to some very special restaurant it seems he likes to use on this sort of occasion. And *I* want to pay for tonight's dinner, Bee. So . . ." She held her eyes relentlessly: "A hundred pounds, Bee. In nice, crisp, brand-new five pound notes."

Twelve

1

"How would you like it if we moved back to Highbury?"
Desmond frowned, impenetrably.

"You'd be able to go back to being an acolyte at St Saviour's,
Dessy," Alice said encouragingly. "And see those Lacey girls
again." And to Thady: "And you'd be able to spend more time
with Sidney, Thady."

She felt incongruous giving them their tea while still dressed
as she had been for the Berkeley Square meeting but there
hadn't been time to change into anything more homely. After
leaving Beatrice she had taken a taxi to a firm of estate agents in
Holloway Road whose board she'd remembered seeing outside
a house in Aberdeen Park. Then, hearing the house was still for
sale, she had gone with one of their surveyors to take a cursory
look at it, dropped the man back at his office and from there gone
on to Debenhams.

"What's it this time, Jordan?"

"An evening dress, Shea."

"What for? Theatre, ball, concert or party?"

"Nothing like that." It was embarrassing but it had to be said.
"I'm having drinks with Kornblath and then he's going to take
me to . . ." She paused. "To an intimate little place he knows for
dinner . . ." And then, as she paused again, feeling the blood
rushing to her cheeks: "And then he'll expect me to go back with
him to his flat."

Shea's eyes were flinty, but not censorious: "You're going to
vamp him?" she enquired succinctly.

"Don't be ridiculous."

"You know what you're doing?"

266

"I know what I've got to do."

Shea shook her mass of straight black hair and said: "Never thought the time would come with Alice Jordan." She actually sighed – and Shea was not a sighing woman.

But it was her sole rebuke. "Well, if that's what you're going to do, let's go and find the best equipment."

"I see Sidney every day," Thady said now.

"I know you do, love," Alice said. "You sit next to him at school."

Thady had explained how it worked at Drayton Park School. Thady was in a class of about fifty boys and girls aged between nine and eleven who were presided over by a Miss Dinsdale, a down-to-earth woman in her fifties who, having been satisfied by the total lack of interest boys, youths and finally men had successively shown towards her that it was most unlikely she would ever marry, had become a schoolmistress out of a burning desire to do something of value with her life. A practical woman who, after a year or so of trying to teach a class of fifty (of which the huge majority regarded lessons as no more than chores to be endured until they were released from them: in the case of the girls to marry, and in the case of the boys to get the sort of jobs their fathers had as labourers, roundsmen, shop assistants, postmen and the like), had come to realise she was achieving little of consequence, stifled her conscience, cast a perspicacious eye over each new intake, selected out of it up to eight who evinced sparks of imagination and intelligence, and set them aside from the rest of the class in a battery of four rows of double-seating desks on her far right-hand side and the other forty or so in five similar batteries to the left of them. To these latter she taught the rudiments of reading, writing and arithmetic but that said, they frankly spent most of their time drawing with crayons or cutting out coloured bits of paper and making patterns out of them which they pinned to the wall. Having got them organised for the day, Miss Dinsdale proceeded to concentrate on the fortunate six or eight who, she had decided, might have enough natural ability to achieve more in life than pulling a lever in a factory or sloshing around in muddy trenches and minds that needed more than yelling themselves hoarse watching Arsenal on Saturdays and easing their throats with copious pints in the local boozers afterwards.

To these fortunate six or eight she gave generously of her time, instructing them in arithmetic and English grammar and composition, streaming them to take the annual scholarships to sundry London day public schools which the London County Council paid to make available. It has to be said of the doughty Miss Dinsdale, who had to suppress her qualms regarding the forty odd she ruthlessly neglected, that so far as the luckier children were concerned (of whom two were Thady Jordan and Sidney Wilcox), their success rate in obtaining scholarships and thus opening up their lives immeasurably was astonishing.

"Yes, I know, you do, dear," Alice said. "But you used to go and have tea with Sidney and his mother and do other things with him out of school and you used to like that very much."

Thady thought it over, balancing the altogether more organised, comfortable and sociable life he was enjoying in Carrington Mews with the cold and mice-infested semi-basement of Aberdeen Park, which he imagined to be the alternative, and the closer relationship he could have with Sidney Wilcox (and his motherly mother who enjoyed nothing more than to spoil Thady – poor little neglected waif – to death) against the possibility of losing touch with Mr Rackham, wartime hero and the one and only person in the whole wide world he felt free to tell his secrets to.

While he was thinking, Desmond said: "I don't want to be an acolyte any more, Mummy – holding a candle and having to follow the vicar around like a pet dog is very undignified. And I'm still seeing the Lacey girls anyway."

"Oh, are you, dear," said Alice. "You never told me."

"There are some things," Desmond said with a very grown-up air, "which are very personal and private. In any case you've always been very busy and mostly not with us and I'm afraid Thady and I have got out of the habit of telling you things in the way that other children tell their parents."

It was not, Alice knew, meant to be hurtful – and in fact it would not have occurred to Desmond that it was – it was the common-sense assessment of a situation by a boy who was more than holding his own at school and whose interests were broadening into directions totally other than her own. How strange it is, she thought, that he was always my favourite and yet now I feel I know so much more about Thady than I do about him.

"In any case," Desmond went on, putting Thady's own thoughts into words, "I can't see any point in leaving here to go back to a vermin-ridden flat where meals have to be cooked in a coal cellar."

"That isn't what I'm suggesting," Alice said, a small anger rising. "That's the last thing I would think of doing."

"Where are you thinking we might go then?"

His eyes were very firm and his lips, unlike Thady's which were full and sensual, were tight from years of introspection. They were still astonishingly alike: the same strong chins, high foreheads, small well-moulded ears, fine straight hair; the same unblemished skins, blue eyes and well-marked eyebrows; the same alertness and sense of pent-up energy. People who counted had said that they could do great things: their teachers, people like Martin and Julia, or Julia's parents, even Joseph. It was up to her to establish the base from which these great things, whatever they were going to be, could be done. That was, after all, what this evening was all about: establishing that base.

"There's a house in Aberdeen Park that's for sale, which I'm thinking of buying," she told them. "One of those on the opposite side to the church and a little farther down." With both of them silenced by this astounding proposition, she went on: "It's got four bedrooms so you could have one each and one as a playroom. And it's got a very nice garden. And it would be very convenient for you going to school and in the holidays you could have Sidney round, Thady, and you could ask the Lacey girls in, Dessy, and any of the friends you have at school I don't know anything about."

"Can you afford it?" Desmond said, breaking a long silence.

"I shall know by tomorrow, Dessy. But I think the answer will be, yes, I can afford it. But first I want to know whether it is something you'd both like me to do."

"Yes, I'd like it, Mummy!" Thady said with sudden enthusiasm. "I'd be very near Sidney and I'd be able to get tickets to go fishing at Woodberry Down reservoir again. You can't get them if you're not living in the district. And having a garden! Would we be allowed to grow things in it?"

Alice smiled. "Anything you liked, dear." And, to his elder brother: "Dessy?" And when he hesitated. "I know you've decided you might like to be an architect. Mr Rackham told me." And as he tensed. "And don't be angry with him for telling me. He's very fond of you and would like to help you if he can. And there's no reason to think you can't keep in touch with him just because we move back to Aberdeen Park."

"Well he shouldn't have told you," Desmond said. "I don't know why it is. People just can't keep secrets." But he was overwhelmed by the idea of having not just a bedroom of his own but a playroom where he could do his Meccano and listen to music – after all, if Mummy had enough money to buy a house she'd have enough money to buy him and Thady a wireless of their own and maybe even a gramophone as well, wouldn't she? And then there were the Lacey girls, Helen especially. And Thady wouldn't be there all the time.

"If you bought this house, Mummy, would you be there all the time? Looking after it like most Mummies do?"

"No, Dessy," Alice said firmly. "I will have to be at work to pay for it and everything. But there'd be someone to come in and do all the cleaning and I'll always be back in time to cook supper for you like I am today, or if now and then I can't, I'll get someone in to do it."

Desmond had made his mind up but he gave the impression of thinking for a little longer before agreeing. He could not have said why he did this, but to do so was compelling.

"All right, Mummy," he said. "If you want to buy that house I suppose it will be all right." And before she could even have reacted: "And if we're going to move back into Aberdeen Park but this time into a proper house, couldn't you go back to being Mrs Jordan again instead of being Mrs Fenwick?"

He said this not as if he was making any remarkable or deep thought-out suggestion but as if he saw an obvious connection between the feelings he had had when his mother's name was the same as his own as compared with those he had now when it was Fenwick.

Alice was taken aback – such a notion had never crossed her mind. When you got married you collected another name and who you'd become was who you remained for life unless you did what she had done, divorced your husband and married another one.

"But . . . but wouldn't it be difficult for you at school if I did, Dessy?" she said uncertainly.

"I don't see why," said Desmond practically. "I mean it's not as if I was at a boarding school any more and you and Uncle Tom were coming over to watch me play cricket or things like that."

Alice got the point. Desmond didn't play cricket for any team at Highbury County School (perhaps Highbury County School didn't even *play* cricket) and the only time they had been to the school had been when Desmond had won the arithmetic prize. They had sat at the back of the assembly hall and, unlike at St Olive's, Tom – and she had understood why – had made no attempt to talk to any of the masters or any of the other boys. Dessy was Desmond Jordan there and nobody thought of him as being anything else. And the same thing, of course, applied to Thady at Drayton Park.

"But it didn't make any difference to you when you were at St Olive's. Or at Findern Lodge, did it?" she suggested hopefully.

"Well actually it did," Desmond said. "It isn't very nice, you know, being the only boy in a school who's got a different name from his parents." And for once seeking support from his younger brother: "It wasn't very nice was it, Thady?"

"No," Thady agreed eagerly, only too willing to go along with almost anything which caused him to be bracketed with Desmond. "Wrigley used to call us half-castes and that always made the other boys laugh."

Alice was doubly horrified. Horrified at the realisation of how much embarrassment and pain she had caused them by her change of name; horrified that such a gulf now existed between herself and them as not to have been told of this before. Unbidden, Joseph's words about most children and their mothers re-echoed in her ears. "While she's carrying

271

out her motherly duties they're asking questions and telling her their hopes, their fears, and the little secrets they'd never think of telling a hotel maid or waiter." What other unhappy secrets, she wondered, had they bottled up inside them which, had they known a normal upbringing, they would have shared with their parents?

Her thoughts went winging back to Nether Street; to when she had been carrying Thady, and Hetty had asked for Dessy to be taken out of his pram so she could watch him playing on the grass. How I loved Dessy then, she thought, and how I loved Thady in those early days. And how I loved them through those first dreadful days in Belmont. I have never stopped loving them. I love them still. She paused, mentally – and then admitted it. But it's become a different sort of love. There's a gulf between us. And there's bound to be: because I'm not to them like their Granny is, or like Sidney Wilcox's mother is to Thady or the Lacey girls' mother is to Dessy. And it's not only through having a different name – it's through living in a hotel, and going out to work and sending them away to boarding schools at such an early age. It's steadily built, this gulf between us, and the final straw was marrying Tom and getting myself a different name from theirs. And now there's a positive barrier between us. How could there not be when there isn't *one* other boy or girl they know whose mother has a different name from theirs. It's made them, in their schoolfriends' eyes, peculiar – set them apart. As Joseph had said: they'd had to find their own design for living.

Although she had had these sort of thoughts before, never before had they been so strongly felt. It was, she told herself, as if with the ordeal which lay ahead of her that evening, fate had used her children as a medium to give her strength of purpose.

"Do you think you could do that, Mummy?" Desmond asked, breaking into her thoughts.

"Do what, dear?" she asked, almost absently.

"Become Mrs Jordan again."

"Well I don't know," she answered. There was something called changing your name by deed-poll, wasn't there? But maybe if once you had a name and changed it, you wouldn't be allowed to go back to the first one again.

"Well can you find out? We'd like that Thady, wouldn't we? For our Mummy to have the same name as we've got."

Thady nodded – and she saw there were tears in his big round eyes.

"I'll find out," she said. "And if I can, I'll get it changed. That's a promise."

And she saw what it would mean if she kept that promise. So long as she was Mrs Fenwick this gulf would through the years imperceptibly widen, while there would remain in their minds the ever-present fear that they would be bracketed with a man with their mother's name who had filled his plus-fours with snooker balls and drowned himself in the River Thames.

But if she went back to being Alice Jordan, perhaps she could at least arrest the gulf from widening even further – perhaps even close it somewhat. And why not change back to Alice Jordan anyway? It's how they know me in business? Mother would like it. Hetty too, maybe. Joseph would chuckle, of course. But so what? Let him chuckle. Sam? Well I'd have to ask him, of course, but I don't think he would mind. And who else is there? Who else in the whole wide world who matters? Martin and Julia? They'd understand – and approve. And Solly Kornblath?

Yes, well that was for another day. There was something far, far more important to be achieved that evening than Kornblath's approval to a change of name!

2

When Kornblath had taken the premises in Berkeley Square he had installed a lift to his flat to which access could also be obtained through a side entrance in Bruton Place. When Alice came up in it, he was waiting to open the gate for her. He was wearing a burgundy velvet dinner jacket.

"Good evening, Mrs Fenwick," he welcomed her. "Do come in." And, as she went by him into the huge sitting-room, "I thought we might have a little drink before we get down to discussing business." He indicated the usual bottle of champagne awaiting them in its ice bucket. "Suppose you sit there."

He waved a hand to the corner of a settee. "May I take your wrap?"

The wrap was a magnificent feather boa which framed Alice's face and which, Shea had insisted, was exactly appropriate for such an evening.

Alice slipped it off her shoulders and taking it and looping it over one arm, Kornblath ran his free hand lightly over it and said, "It must feel delightful against your face." He put it down over the back of a convenient chair and turned to study her.

"How very charming you look," he said.

Alice, who was wearing a backless evening dress held up by bootlace shoulder straps, which was as daring as anything she had worn in the heady days of Belmont, did a little pirouette which made the skirt flare up showing her pretty ankles. "I'm glad you like it," she said.

"Charming," Solly repeated. "Now do make yourself comfortable, please." And as Alice sat, he set about opening the champagne, chatting easily while he did so.

"I hope you enjoyed my little party, Mrs Fenwick. We were very lucky with the weather, weren't we? Especially when you consider that on Royal Hunt Cup Day there was that terrible storm and that poor fellow was killed sheltering under a bookmaker's umbrella."

"Yes, we were lucky, weren't we?" Alice said.

"You didn't back Brown Jack in the Queen Alexandra Stakes?"

"No, Mr Kornblath. I backed something but it wasn't that one and I can't remember what it was called."

"Oh, you should have backed Brown Jack. It was bound to win. It's Sir Harold Wernher's horse, you know, and that's the third time it's won in succession."

"Did you back it, Mr Kornblath?"

"Yes, of course." He came across with two glasses of champagne, and sat so that a small table was between them. "What shall we drink to?" he said, raising his glass. "To Alice Dresses?"

"Why not?"

"To Alice Dresses then."

"To Alice Dresses."

Solly put his glass down. "Now I think the time has come," he said, "when we should get on to Christian name terms, don't you?"

"Yes, I think we should," Alice smiled. And, constructing a chuckle: "Especially now we're going to be owning thirty shops between us."

"Alice then?"

"Yes. And you're . . ." She broke off. "No, I can't possibly call you Solly."

"Why not?"

"It seems discourteous somehow. Do you have any other names."

"Bernard."

"Bernard? Yes, I like that. Can I call you Bernard?"

"If you like."

"I did so enjoy your party, Bernard," Alice said. "It was so kind of you to invite me. And what a lovely house you have."

"My dear," he answered gallantly, "it scarcely did you justice."

He was attempting to give the impression of being entirely relaxed, while watching her very carefully. In the comfort of a soft and slightly scented bath he had given a great deal of thought to the evening which lay ahead. He hadn't for a moment believed that she had been too busy to see him in the afternoon and now the dress she was wearing spoke volumes. The thought that she was hoping to enchant, perhaps even seduce him, both intrigued and amused him and this, combining with his recollection of the impression she had made at his Christmas party and how dazzling she had looked at Ascot, persuaded him to go along with things.

"You are a very beautiful woman, you know, Alice," he said testingly.

I have to answer that, Alice thought, and I mustn't be coy because he's too experienced; and I mustn't be indifferent because hard-bitten women almost certainly wouldn't appeal to him. And I have to be very careful because he isn't a fool and he knows perfectly well that I've come here with a purpose.

"That's always nice for a woman to be told," she said smiling.

275

He reached for the bottle and, topping up their glasses, said: "So, my dear, I can take it you've no objection to the company leasing all these shops."

"Objection! Why should I have an objection? I'm absolutely delighted. But it does raise quite a few points."

He reseated himself. "Such as?"

"Well to start with, this idea of having Martin Rackham as architect for converting them."

"I thought you'd like to have him."

"Well, no. I'd much rather have the man who did my office for me. Mussack. It's going to be very important we present . . . well, the right image I suppose you'd say, and I can't think that Martin would be the best man when it comes down to detail, or even be very interested. I mean it's *big* things he handles, isn't it? Things like that scheme you showed me when I was here last time . . . the one whose model you displayed at your Christmas party."

"Ivanhoe Gardens," Kornblath said briefly and dismissively, not wishing to be sidetracked. "I imagined," he insisted, "that as you're living in a property Rackham owns and must be seeing a great deal of him, you wouldn't want anybody else."

"Well," Alice said, "it's very important we use the right person and I don't feel that his helping me out at a difficult time is a good enough reason for asking him to do something he probably doesn't want to do anyway. In any case I'm paying him rent for the use of the cottage now and I'm only staying there until I can find something more suitable and within my means. And Mr Cradforth said that if I didn't want to use him you wouldn't insist I did."

He nodded thoughtfully. "And the next point?" he suggested.

"Well if we're going to have thirty shops as well as my idea of mail order, which Mr Thompson must have told you about, it means stepping up production enormously, and apart from taking on a lot more girls, which is easy enough, we're going to have a sizing problem. And if you're agreeable, I think the best way of solving that is to get someone over from America with the right experience."

"You've someone in mind?"

276

Alice shook her head. "No. I think the best and the quickest thing would be for me to go over to New York for a week or so to do some research and interviewing." And at his nod of approval. "Have you ever been there? New York?"

"I go there occasionally."

"Ah. Well perhaps you could suggest the best hotel for me to stay in. And if you have connections over there and could give me one or two introductions." She smiled. "Of course if it so happened you were going over at the same time that would . . ." She broke off. "No, of course you wouldn't be . . ."

It was, she knew, a tremendous risk she was taking. But in the limited time she had had for planning how she was going to handle her side of the evening she had not been able to come up with anything better. To look into his soft brown eyes and hold them while she said it took every atom of self-control.

It did not occur to her that he saw right through this double-think and that he was amused and more than happy to enter into the spirit of the thing.

"It's not impossible," he said.

"Isn't it, Bernard? Well, that could be fun, couldn't it?"

He reached across from his chair and was able to lay his hand on her bare arm resting on the settee's armrest.

"My dear," he said, his spaniel eyes devouring her, "it could be more than fun. It could be an experience we would not forget." And his hand stroked her arm in much the way it had stroked her boa, lightly, appreciatively.

Alice was quite taken in. How extraordinary it is, she told herself: here's a man who's a multimillionaire; who, to use Beatrice's words this morning, has everyone at a boardroom table trembling when he comes through the door. Yet when it comes to sex he's just no different from the rest of them. Put him with a woman who attracts him and have him think she's available and he becomes just another Tom, Dick or Harry.

"It's extraordinary, isn't it, Bernard," she said, making no attempt to have him cease his stroking. "It's six months since I was in here last and you've done so much to help me and yet until last week, apart from when I went to your Christmas party, we haven't seen or spoken to each other. I've often thought of phoning you but I just didn't have the courage."

"And I didn't have the opportunity?" His hand had ceased its stroking but was lightly gripping her arm instead.

"I don't understand that," Alice said.

"Well you seemed to be . . . fully occupied. Moving in to that mews house Rackham owns."

"Oh, that!" She laughed – and seized the opportunity. "Surely you haven't been drawing the wrong conclusions, Bernard? I've only been living there because it was Hobson's choice. As I was saying just now, I'll be leaving Carrington Mews just as soon as I find somewhere more suitable and within my means. Well, as a matter of fact, I've found a house in Highbury which would do very well, and because of the current slump we're in it's a wonderful buy. The only trouble is I don't have the money to buy it." She constructed a brilliant notion. "I suppose you wouldn't be willing to lend me what I'd need, would you? You could pay yourself back out of the company when it starts making a profit."

"How much is it?"

"Eight hundred pounds."

"I think that could be arranged."

"You do!" She did not have to pretend excitement. "Oh, Bernard, you're a dear. An absolute dear!"

"I can do better," he said. "Do you know who's handling it?"

"They're called Pilch and Hetherington. They're in Holloway."

"Just a minute." He got to his feet, and going across to a pad beside the telephone took a gold pencil from the inside pocket of his velvet jacket. "Pilch and Hetherington?" She nodded. "And the address? Of the property, I mean."

"Well, I'm not sure of the number. But it's in Aberdeen Park and I think it's the only house that Pilch and Hetherington are handling. The man who showed me over it, a Mr Hoskins, will know."

He wrote it down. "I'll get someone on to it tomorrow. It will be handled as a normal business transaction with a charge on the property. That mayn't seem a very friendly way of doing it, Alice, but I've long since learnt that business and friendship don't mix."

He put the pencil back in his pocket. If he had been secretly amused at her tantalising notion of their sharing a few days together in New York, he had been sufficiently fired by it to imagine how it could be. And looking at her now with her bare shoulders and her firm if modest breasts, he treated himself to the fantasy of imagining them in some luxurious hotel bedroom and her slipping down the cobweb shoulder straps, and the dress slithering to the floor leaving her, hopefully, all but naked. A small pulse beat in his head – and his resolution wavered.

"I think that's enough business for one evening, don't you?" he suggested.

He came across, pausing *en route* to collect her boa, and was, as before, unable to resist passing his hand over its softness. The action said much to Alice and looking at him, clean and soft, she imagined him naked, white and flaccid and asked herself the question she had already asked a dozen times. If I *have* to, am I prepared to go through with it? And then she asked herself another question. Do I have to decide that now? And yet another question. Even if I have to, is it better to say what I've come to say when we come back here, or better to say it before we go to dinner? And she thought of the hour or two which inevitably lay ahead before he brought her back, of the ogling and the touching and the rest of it she would have to tolerate and it decided her.

"Bernard," she said, "there are a couple more things and I'd rather get them dealt with now than spoil our dinner together still talking business."

He put the boa down impatiently. But he came and sat in the other corner of her settee. "Well?" he said good-humouredly enough.

"The first is that man Thompson. I can't stand him and I don't trust him. I can't bear the thought of having to put up with him at all the board meetings we're going to have while we're building up the company. And anyway he knows nothing about the dress business."

"You want me to get rid of him?" He was not particularly disturbed; Thompson was only a stop-gap anyway.

"Yes."

"And I suppose," he said with a touch of irony, "you've got someone else in mind to replace him."

"Yes."

"Who?"

"Well you could consider Beatrice's husband. Grahame Culverwell. He's sound, reliable and he knows the dress trade inside out."

"Uh huh?" he said unenthusiastically and went on with even heavier irony: "And after I've got rid of Thompson, is Cradforth the next to go?"

"Cradforth!" said Alice with quite unexpected passion. "Good heavens, no! We *have* to have a man like him. It can be very tough, the rag trade, and there has to be someone who can handle some of the people we're going to meet. A man with . . ." She raised two small clenched fists and jiggled them. "An iron man!"

He was mollified.

"I'll think about it. What was the second point?"

"I want you to sell me two of your shares. I will give you a hundred pounds for them."

She had finally succeeded in surprising him. He stared at her in utter disbelief.

"In fact," said Alice, steeling herself, "it has to be a condition of my going on, that you do."

He was too amazed to be angry. "And do you mind," he said, "telling me why I am to sell you two of my shares?"

"Yes," said Alice. And now that the worst was over it was easier. "Because one day when Alice Dresses is the success it can be, you're going to want to float it off as a public company and make a killing. And I want to be sure to be there at the time, not on the sidelines seeing other people cashing in on all my work and my ideas." It was all pure Martin and she blessed him for it. "It's a risk I'm not prepared to take, Bernard. Either you sell me those two shares or I'm not going on with Alice Dresses."

He felt outraged. The woman had bamboozled him! Got herself an invitation to drinks in his flat and dinner under the guise of being a simpleton, turned up in a dress that left her half naked, buttered him up with the possibility that if he was nice to her and lent her the money to buy a house she'd let him have sex with her! What sort of dimwit did she think he was? Anger rose in him. But he controlled it. He had long since learnt that losing one's temper was the best way of losing control of a situation. If there was one facet of his character he would have given to explain the reason for his success, it was that under even the greatest pressure he could stay calm. Calm he would stay now. But the woman would have to be taught a lesson she would not forget.

"You *have* to go on," he said. "You have no choice."

"I don't have to go on. There is no way you or anyone can make me."

"Isn't there? Well, my dear, I will give you three good reasons." He raised a finger. "One. You have a service contract. That's why you get a salary. If you break that contract the company can sue you for breach and the cost to you will be appalling. Two." Again he raised the finger. "The company is capitalised at five thousand pounds, of which so far only one hundred pounds has been paid up, fifty-one by me, forty-nine by you. You can be required to pay up the difference for the shares you own. Two thousand four hundred and fifty one pounds, my dear! And three . . ." This time he didn't raise a finger, but getting to his feet went across to the telephone with a quicker stride than anyone in his boardroom had ever seen, and, picking up the slip of paper on which he had made notes of the house in Aberdeen Park, brandished it. "This, Mrs Fenwick! Unless you agree to going on, I shall tear this up."

"Then tear it up!" It was all or nothing now. Everything. Her children's future, her own future, perhaps even to some degree Martin's future hung on what took place in the next few minutes.

"If," she said, her head held high, "I decide to pull out of Alice Dresses there is nothing you can do about it. I *have* no money. All you can do is bankrupt me. I know what that's like: to be bankrupted. It's happened to me before. And it's a terrible thing to have happen. But it isn't the end of the world. I recovered from it before and I can recover from it again. And what are you left with? Thirty shops, most of which you aren't going to be able to let until the country turns the corner. A lot of expensive material and equipment. And a factory which nobody wants, which is why it was available for me. But sell me those two shares and you'll have a business and I'll work every hour God sends to make Alice Dresses a company which will be so successful that when it's floated you can stay in or out as you choose but either way you'll make a killing."

He was amazed, indignant. What had happened to this woman? "Who have you been talking to?" he demanded. "Not those useless Gibson and Weldon people, I'll warrant."

There was nothing that he didn't know.

"I've talked to nobody," she said. "I've just used my common sense. What's it going to be? A share in a company that'll pay back your investment in it a hundred times over? Or the pleasure of putting me and my children on the street?" She reached for the handbag on the settee beside her, a bag that was really too commodious to suit the flimsy dress she wore, and unsnapping the catch took out the money Beatrice had got for her. One hundred pounds in crisp five-pound notes. She held them up. "You said just now I didn't have a choice. Well I've chosen. It's your turn now. Do you take these, or don't you?"

Unhurriedly she put them down on the table beside her champagne glass. In the silence of the room they rustled as she did so. Mentally she held her breath. Which was going to make the decision for him: his pride or his common sense?

In fact it was not quite either. It was something which both Beatrice and Martin would have prophesied: the fear of being shown up as foolish and ineffective before those who counted. In front of men like Cradforth. It was quite unimaginable for him to face them with a useless company on his hands, into which he had sunk many thousands of pounds already, and no one to run it for him. He could hear Cradforth's words burning in his ears: "The woman got him over a barrel!"

And there was one other thing – there was Alice herself.

He looked at her from across the room and saw her not as she was now – a clever, imaginative, yet still relatively inexperienced woman who had momentarily stirred his lust –

but as she was going to be: the dominant member of a successful and prestigious, possibly even international, company. You did not, he thought wryly, lust for that kind of woman. He writhed at the thought of what she had done to him but he was filled with admiration. And he thought of Cradforth. And what she'd said of him. That he was an iron man. He smiled.

Alice watched him as he went across to his desk. Watched him opening it and, taking out a sheet of notepaper, begin to write.

It crossed her mind that there was still time to take Martin's advice – to get out before she had reached some point of no return. But it was no more than a passing thought, instantly dismissed by the others she had already been through time and time again: Dessy and Thady had absolute priority. They had no father to advise and protect them. Hetty, who must soon be coming to the end of her African stint, might try to step into the breach. With all her overseas commitments up to now she hadn't been as big a problem as she'd once threatened to be, but even so she had had her effect – after all, if it hadn't been for her Alice wouldn't have gone after that job with Pontings which started her on the road to this. But no, she told herself, I could handle her even if I was on my uppers. But Joseph Mott was another matter, and his final threat was not to be ignored. He wielded power, the power of money. But not the sort of money Kornblath wielded. No, Martin, she thought, this is not a time for taking your advice. Only by staying in with *this* man can I provide the background Dessy and Thady ought to have. Theirs is my responsibility and I must have the strength, and the capacity, to handle it.

The sheet of notepaper in his hand, Kornblath recrossed the room and held it out to her. "Will that suffice?" he said with irony.

She read it carefully, a single paragraph, a signature.

"Yes," she said.

He reached out and taking the money, folded it and, with some difficulty, stowed it in his pocket. She noticed as he did so the two champagne glasses which the notes had lain between. She glanced at the ice bucket with the bottle protruding from it. It occurred to her that it was becoming commonplace to leave half-emptied bottles of champagne.

She folded the sheet of paper more carefully than he had folded the notes and put it in her handbag.

When she stood he was holding the boa out for her to take.

"I'll get you a taxi," he told her.

She looked into his spaniel eyes and saw respect in them.

"I thought," she said, "we were going to have a celebration dinner."

"I don't think," he replied, "you would find the place I had in mind entirely suitable now."

"Perhaps not, Bernard," she smiled, "but there's always the Savoy."

Even as she said it, she knew it for a flip remark which it would embarrass her to reflect on in the years ahead. But it served a purpose. It eased the tension and so let Kornblath off the hook, while sealing a compact which would ensure her own and Desmond and Thady's future.